Node Riders:
A Tale of Possibilities

A Science Fiction Novel

by

Richard Formato & **Philip Nigro**

Published by CEM Company
P.O. Box 1714
Harwich, MA 02645 U.S.A.
+1.508.896.0060

ISBN 979-8-218-19540-3
U.S. Copyright Office Reg. No. TX 9-173-450

Cover Photos © 2019, 2011 R.A. Formato

Text © 2021, 2023 Richard A. Formato & Philip M. Nigro

All Rights Reserved Worldwide.

No part of this work may be reproduced, stored, transmitted, or otherwise distributed by any means whatsoever without the copyright owners' written permission.

Please address inquiries to:

Richard A. Formato, Esq.
PO Box 1714
Harwich, MA 02645 USA
+1.508.246.2876
rf2@ieee.org

Dedication

This novel is dedicated to Vicki and Janice who have been encouraging and supportive throughout the process of writing the book, and who provided helpful editorial comments and contributions to the plot. Without them this project would not have come to fruition for which the authors are truly grateful.

Table of Contents

Ch. 1, p.   1 - *OOPS!*
Ch. 2, p. 30 - The Wave Makes its Appearance
Ch. 3, p. 43 - *The Birds*
Ch. 4, p. 55 - Node Tracking
Ch. 5, p. 70 - *Professor* Ravelli
Ch. 6, p. 91 - What's in a Node?
Ch. 7, p.110 - The 25th Day of July, 1972
Ch. 8, p.127 - The 26th Day of July, 1972
Ch. 9, p.146 - Emilio and Isabella,
                 Isabella and Emilio
Ch. 10, p.163 - Kepler Books a Ride
Ch. 11, p.186 - Kepler Takes a Ride
Ch. 12, p.199 - Kepler Returns
Ch. 13, p.209 - Buckle Up!
Ch. 14, p.221 - Where No Cat Has Gone Before!
Ch. 15, p.234 - How Fast Can That Node Go?
Ch. 16, p.254 - Isabella's Twenty-Ninth
Ch. 17, p.276 - The Maiden Voyage
Ch. 18, p.312 - The New & Improved *NR-1701*
Ch. 19, p.321 - GC Goes for a Ride
Ch. 20, p.328 - *When* is the *Present*?
Ch. 21, p.337 - The Mechanics of Time Travel

Epilogue, p. 343

Node Riders

Chapter 1 - OOPS!

Emilio Ravelli fumbles with his briefcase, stuffing all his papers in it while finishing breakfast. He's on his way to a meeting at the University and, as usual, running late.

One page in particular catches his eye. He studies it carefully, very carefully, mumbling to himself "this actually *could* work! It really *could*! It *should*!" His excitement palpable, but he's late.

Emilio, "M" to his friends, scrambles out the door to his old, beat-up, mustard yellow Datsun, tosses the briefcase in the back and sets that page of interest on the passenger seat. He heads down the road as he has a million times before, but this time constantly glancing at that page that he can't help but look at.

But the next thing M sees is the ceiling, and some very bright lights. And the voices - he hears voices.

"He's conscious, I'll get the doctor."

"Where am I? *Where?*", his panic quite evident.

"You're at St. Martins Medical Center. You were in a car accident. Luckily, in front of someone's house who called it in. You hit a parked car!"

The doc paused, shining his penlight into M's eyes from below, first one, then the other, then back again.

"So what was it? Drugs, booze,...both?

"No, no,... I'm not using, never have, never will, and I only drink in moderation. I was distracted today. And I'm late for a meeting – I have to go."

"Not today, Mr. Ravelli, not today. Your head injury is a pretty bad concussion, and it might be serious - we have to observe you at least overnight. You also have abrasions on the left leg, forearm, and the right knee, not to mention some badly bruised ribs from using them to break the steering wheel! And your head shattered the windshield! Fact is, you're a very lucky fellow, my friend - I'm told your car didn't make out nearly as well..."

M settled into his hospital bed, realizing he had no choice, and, yes, he thought, it probably was the best thing to do because his head did hurt, a lot, but it was his ribs that hurt a lot more. Whenever he moved or took a deep breath it was excruciating.

"Nurse!" M said in a hoarse voice as he positioned to get more comfortable. "First of all, what's your name? Will you be looking after me?"

"Yes, Mr. Ravelli. I'm Kathy. It's 11am, and I'm just starting my shift, a double, so you're stuck with me, all night. You're on the 7th floor where we treat head injuries, and I have four other patients to take care of. You're the best of my bunch, MRI came back ok, good vitals, pupils now responding normally. There's not much we can do about the rib bruises, which are pretty bad, except give you the pain meds you're on, a more potent combo of Ibuprofen and Acetaminophen than what you get over-the-counter. That's it. A good night's rest, and I think you'll be good to go tomorrow if nothing else shows up. Please.. try to get some rest. Makes all the difference. Press the call button if you need anything."

"I do, need something. Don't leave."

"Yes, what can I do for you."

"My briefcase. Is it here?"

"No, your clothes are, over there in that closet," as Nurse Kathy motioned to a tall, thin closet near the room's entrance.

"Couldn't say where your briefcase is. I would guess still in your car?"

"Where's the car, do you know?"

"I'll find out for you, as long as you promise to get some rest, and actually do, get some rest, ok?"

"Yes, thanks. Thank you *very* much."

A short time later, Nurse Kathy came back, having learned that M's car, what's left of it, was towed to the Charlestown Garage across the city. She tells M and asks if she can contact anyone for him.

"Yes, please give my girlfriend's brother a call, Brian, his name is Brian, his number (777) 832-9588. Ask him if he'd mind stopping by the garage and retrieving my briefcase and, more importantly, the sheet of paper that is - was maybe - on the passenger seat. Could you, would you do that, please? It's very important, really..."

"Sure, Mr. Ravelli, I can make that call. And, what should Brian do? Bring the briefcase and paper here, right?"

"Yes. And thanks, I can't tell you how much I appreciate this. I'd call myself, but this damn phone, oooh, pardon my language, well, the phone doesn't work for outside calls."

"Did you press nine first, for an outside line? Bet you didn't. A definite tell that you haven't been in hospital much" as Nurse Kathy grinned.

"Ahh, that's what I missed. Scrub making the call. I'll ring Brian myself, now that I know how..."

"No problem, and if you still have trouble, press the call button, and I'll make the call for you. Sometimes the phones actually don't work...," snickered Nurse Kathy as she turned to leave, but quickly pivoted, "And we still have our deal right? Rest. You're going to rest."

M sheepishly agreed. Now he was obligated, not to mention embarrassed."

- - - - -

"My good man, how they ha...", said Brian, cut off mid word.

"Shhh, Brian, watch what you say. There are nurses all over, and..."

"I'm sure they've heard worse, M, but I give in, no levity, even though I thought I'd try to cheer you up."

"Problem is, Brian, your levity isn't funny, not levitous, whatever the word is, at least most of the time. But I do appreciate your being here for me and getting my stuff. It's important, thanks," as Brian hands M his briefcase and *the page*.

"How's Isabella. Does she know the details?"

"No, not yet. Haven't filled her in yet, and I must say when she finds out, I'm thinking my sis will be (a) very concerned and (b) pretty pissed off."

"Why? Why do you say that."

"Well, for part (a) she loves you. For part (b), how many people drive full steam ahead, square amidships straight into a behemoth of a Buick station wagon without even braking? Without trying to avoid the collision? And all this while driving a flyweight Datsun that crumples like paper when it hits a frozen snow bank, huh? That's why she'll be pissed."

"So, what happened, M, really? How *did* you hit a parked station wagon?"

"Okay, Brian, I'll tell you, but you may find it hard to believe. On the other hand, you might find it as amazing as I have. Why? Because you're the smartest mechanical guy I know, and this is all about mechanics, gravitational mechanics, to be more precise, *gravitational kinematics*."

"Whoa! That's a mouthful! But I do get the drift, hee-hee... The kinematics part is the motion of objects, and the gravity part is just that, what's causing the motion, right?"

"As I said, Brian, a mechanical genius are you! And you're right about what this is about. It's all on that page, *the page*, the sheet of paper that actually caused the accident."

"Oh, I see. You mean the picture of the tennis ball you drew surrounded by all those equations? *That* page, right?"

"Yes, that drawing, plus the math. I hit the parked car because I was staring at that page thinking more about what I had discovered, how it would work, what it would mean."

"Got it," as Brian rolled his eyes. "You were daydreaming! So you hit a parked car and, I'm pretty sure, totaled yours!"

"Guess I was completely distracted, yes. Fact is, I don't even remember seeing the big Buick. What I do remember is being scraped off the road by two beefy guys in uniforms. The EMTs who brought me here."

"Okay, okay. Got it, you drove into a parked car because your mind was elsewhere. Got that part. So where, pray tell, *was* your mind? On Earth? Or your home planet? A distant galaxy? By the way, on my way in the nurse, Kathy, I think was her name, told me they did an MRI. She said you weren't eligible for a brain transplant, yet, but the stuff between the ears does need a tune up... I'm thinking an implant of some sort, like the android brains I saw at the Star Trek Convention back in January? How cool would that be, if it were real!"

"Funny, Brian, funny. Hilarious. Here I am in excruciating pain, and you're into 'levity' again! Do you want to know or not?"

"Is there money in it? Will this brainstorm that I'm pretty sure totaled the Datsun pay off? Should have happened sooner," under his breath, "As in, make enough dough to cover that Ferrari my beautiful, gorgeous, fabulous sister has always wanted? The girl of your dreams? The car of hers!"

"Nope. Hmmm... maybe not. I don't know. Actually, it might. So, if it can, if it does, as of this very minute I appoint you CFO of CFO. You accept, right?"

Brian was having fun with M, but the jocular look suddenly changed. "Good grief, you *are* serious? Good deal, a buck to be made, maybe. I'm good at that, M, you know that. But I'm wondering if you're still on your rocker, so you have to convince me. I hope the MRI didn't miss something important, really. What *are* you talking about? *CFO* of *CFO*? What nonsense is this? I know you're not pulling my leg because of the look on your face, plus you're the least humorous person I know, on this planet anyway, so maybe it's the head injury, worse than they thought!"

"Nah, I'm serious, Brian, very. If there's money to be made, you make it. You are good at that! I have other things to think about, with what's left of my brain, that is."

"First funny thing you said!" snickered Brian.

"Okay, the first CFO is *Chief Financial Officer*, and the second one *Central Force Optimization*. Now that I ponder this, Brian, maybe you're right, some money to be made if this pans out as I expect it will, maybe even a lot. Does that wet your beak, my friend?"

"Sure does, M, now I'm actually curious, and now that I run CFO Enterprises, good name, huh, what the hell, oops.., what exactly am I running? What does the second CFO do? Who would care about it, can you tell me that?"

"Alright, Brian, from the ground up. First of all, you know that my PhD dissertation research, the stuff I do at the Observatory, is about the effect of atmospheric internal gravitational waves on the ionosphere's electron distribution, which, in turn affects different communication systems, right?"

"A mouthful, but, yep, and I do get the drift because we've talked about this so much before. What's CFO got to do with this, the second CFO, that is?"

"Well, I got deeper into gravitational physics generally, more than what I needed for the thesis because the physics is fascinating. It connects to all sorts of things on the cosmological scale especially, and Relativity - Einstein's theories - figure in a big way. Anyway, long story short, I got into it, gravity, that is."

"Still adrift, M. So what is CFO? *Central Force Optimization*? A military thing of some sort? How to deploy the troops? I ask yet again - what is CFO? Because I still don't know."

"Okay, here's a simple not-so-simple problem for you to ponder. Beside running a business as you do, and that you're very good at, let's say you branch out and become a mutual fund manager. Your job is to maximize your clients' return on investment, by allocating their money across a bunch of stocks, a portfolio of stocks. How do you do it? Let's say there are ten stocks. How much in each one to max ROI? If you think about this it's a hard problem, right? In fact it's *very* hard!"

"This *is* heady stuff, M. Never thought about something like that, but, wow, I'm guessing you're going to tell me that CFO, the second one, solves it? Wow!"

"Not quite, Brian, not quite, but it's a step, and I think a big step. Nothing to do with the military. The name comes from gravity because the force between two gravitating masses is called a *central force*. The page, the one with your tennis ball, is a mathematical way of solving the ROI problem that's based on gravity. And as far as I can tell there's no reason why it won't work. Cool, huh?"

"Yes, sure is, if you really can figure out how to get people a maximum return on their investment! Using gravity of all things! That's a golden goose for sure, M. So how sure are you? And why are you doing this? What's it got to do with your thesis?"

"Nothing, nothing at all to do with my research at the Observatory. Strictly a matter of my getting more and more interested in gravity, and one day it just hit me, that you could solve some very hard math problems, maybe, using gravity as a model. It just hit me! Then I thought about what kind of problems, and the financial one came to mind along with all sorts of engineering problems. So I fiddled with the gravitational math, and lo and behold, it works! Or I should say it should work..." M was fading fast. His head was worked up over the CFO discovery, but his ribs weren't. "I have to take a break, Brian," as he rolled into a more comfortable position.

"So what you're telling me, M, is that the second CFO solves my portfolio problem as the Financial Manager, right?" M winced and nodded yes.

"Okay! I'm not going to ask Nurse Kathy, she's very cute, by the way, available do you think? Anyway I'm not gonna ask her to get the Doc in here so he can really juice you up! Unless you want me to."

"No, I'll use the call button if I need more juicing as you put it. Levity? Actually that is pretty funny." M groaned slightly as he wiggled into a less painful position.

"I have to get back to the Shop, and I'm glad I could help get your stuff from the wreck, and I know Isabella will be coming by soon, so you'll have her to lay this silliness on her, how you hit the Buick. I suppose you could explain the *page* to her, too, your call. Maybe she loves you enough to get into it, especially as a business major, but maybe not under the circumstances. Anyway, gotta go. Hope you get better, soon. I'm outta here, bye!"

Brian glanced at his watch. He did have to get back to the 'Shop,' as he called it, actually NovaTek Engineering, Inc., Brian's company. And the 'Shop' was more a laboratory and development center, but Brian worked there alone most of the time. He designed and built new products and prototypes, did some contract work, and often was brought in as a consultant on the hard problems other companies had. The 'Shop' was Brian's engineering sandbox, and he loved it! He was very successful in bringing in work, very lucrative work, but he wasn't good with records. He turned to Isabella for that. Right now Brian's focus was putting on the finishing touches for special springs he had just finished for the novelty bird product. It wasn't time-critical, but he was anxious to see how the improvements worked out. *The Birds*, as he fondly called them, were very profitable, although another outfit, *Feathered Friends*, did the packaging, advertising and sales. It was their product, and NovaTek was paid a percentage of each sale. *The Birds* were wildly popular with children and, of course, with bird lovers generally, so there was a big market, one that always had new potential buyers entering it. But Brian's focus always was on technology, in particular unique ways of handling difficult mechanical processes, and he was very good at it. Occasionally his work strays into related areas, like electronics, but only as required, and he tried to stay away from anything involving water, in effect plumbing, because it seemed there always was a leak, somewhere..."

"Thanks again, Brian. You're a good guy."

Whereupon Nurse Kathy coincidentally walked in to let M know that he has a visitor. Isabella's right behind carrying a box of what M guesses are goodies. He knows that she knows that St. Martins grub isn't the best, in fact, it's pretty bad, so he's expecting something really good. But no, what a disappointment! Hmmm... Books? Magazines? But not even ones he'd read? Cooking magazines? Really?

"Thanks, Izz, very thoughtful," as she plants a big kiss on his forehead and M fakes delight at her gift. On thinking a little more, M shouldn't have expected more because he knew Izzy probably was elsewhere worrying about him and she didn't have time enough to prepare anything elaborate. "I knew you'd be stopping by, Izz, and, oh, boy, I was hoping for something like eggplant parm, or maybe your fabulous ravioli." But he had to let her off the hook. "Good thing I can't eat, my ribs hurt too much. So let's see here, the current issue of Painter's Quarterly, fascinating, although with enough of the right seasoning..." Izzy's look was enough. "Just kidding, just kidding."

"Stop it! Right now! You know I'd bring a whole restaurant, if I could. So, stop it! I called before coming and was told you were on a strict diet because of the head injury, and that your ribs were very painful, making eating a real chore. I wasn't about to break the rules, especially if it might keep you in here longer! Please,

M, don't make me worry even more! Do whatever you have to get out of here! Like put up with the crummy hospital food. That way you can get out and recover at home where you'll feel better just by being there. And... then I'll cook whatever you want, gladly."

"God, Izzy, this is why I love you so. You're thoughtful, smart, talented, a wonderful cook, and, hmmm..., did I mention gorgeous? You win, you're right. Hospital grub 'til I'm let loose."

"And when will that be?"

"They say tomorrow, maybe, as long as my head seems to be okay because there's nothing much to do about the bruising. And I can live with that, as long as I don't move around too much. Then it hurts, and the more I wiggle, the more it hurts. So when I'm out, at my place, I'll stay still, curl up with a good book on gravitational physics, and, oh I can taste it now, a nice plate of your eggplant parm! That'll get me better lickety-split, my love."

M and Izzy had been a thing for some time now, a couple of years anyway. He always wanted to ask Izz out, but her being Brian's sister made it difficult, until one day he just blurted it out, "How about a movie? You interested?" Isabella, much to his surprise and delight, said yes, and their romance took off. It didn't have far to go. Longish term plans including getting married, but not until Emilio finished his PhD at Polytechnic University. He was ABD status, all but dissertation, having completed all the coursework and exams. So all that was left was a good thesis, one that he could defend and get published. His research was being done at Polytech's Ionosonde Observatory, and was almost finished. M expects to graduate in May next year, and there's a lot to do in the next year or so. After that? Who knows, maybe a post doc, maybe a teaching position at a smaller college, maybe, maybe, maybe...

- - - - -

The next day was just as bright and clear as the one before that took the Datsun, but M wasn't fumbling or running late. In fact he enjoyed the slow wheelchair ride to St. Martins' front entrance. He wanted to get back to the University to meet with his thesis advisor, Dr. Michael Hanlon, as he was supposed to do yesterday.

He loved Poly, especially in the early fall when classes started, when the air was crisper, and the shadows longer, unlike these days of mid-summer heat - for M, they couldn't pass soon enough. In the fall when classes resumed, M often got to the University early in the morning to sit on a bench with work, usually something related to his thesis, or, when he was still taking courses, a textbook or problem notebook. Many days he was there for a couple of hours before class, or before heading off to the lab. But now those days were memories. Now his only time on campus was mostly to meet with Professor Hanlon, his mentor, to discuss his research and the latest scuttlebutt in ionospheric physics community. They usually got together every week or so depending on each other's schedule. M would head up to his "office," a room about the size of a large broom closet that he kept from his days as a Teaching Assistant. But it had a window with a nice view and a big-enough book case, besides a desk. All that M needed, and all that M wanted.

As the wheelchair brakes were applied M saw Brian pulling up. Thank you Nurse, very much, you've all been great, but to be honest I can't say I'll miss being here!"

"Have a good day, Mr. Ravelli. Watch the driving!" The nurse chuckled and smiled as she helped M to Brian's car.

"Hey, Brian, good to see you and Izz. Thanks for picking me up you guys. What's the plan?"

"Back to your apartment where you'll be more comfortable and can take all the time you need to heal, to get better," was Izzy's reply.

"Oh, no, no, not right now. I really have to go to Poly first because I missed an important meeting. Let's compromise. I won't be long at the University, you can wait for me, Izz. Just let me get this out of the way, and then I'll gladly go back to my place... where you can pamper me as much as you want, Izz,...hint, hint... How's that?"

"I'm not so sure, M. The last thing you need, or we want, is for you to get all worked up with those almost broken ribs. You heard the nurse, plenty of rest, plenty, just take it easy until they feel good enough for you to get back into the swing of things, however long it takes... I'm not so sure. Maybe this isn't such a good idea? Can't it wait?"

"Look, Izzy, I know how concerned you are, but I think we can give into M on this one thing, let him go, and then we can deposit him at home. I really don't think that's too much of a stretch."

"Alright, alright, I guess, just this one stop," and off went the three to the Polytechnic.

While they were driving, M piped up "By the way, Brian, thanks so much for loaning me a car. Can't get around without one! So which one? The GTO, right, I hope?"

"Funny, very funny. And if wishes were fishes... Not a chance, none whatsoever! I'll let you use my old '67 Camaro SS 396."

"Wow! Really? That car may be a little long-in-the-tooth in this fabulous year of 1972, but, wow, what can I say? Really? As you would put it, Brian, that's a 'cool ride'!"

"That *is* the way I put it!" Brian interrupted.

"A real step up from my '69 mustard yellow Datsun, I must say," M continued. "I don't know how to thank you, Brian, really, this is so nice of you. Thanks!"

"Aww, shucks, ... cut it out, you're getting too mushy... But you are right, the SS sure is a step up, actually a staircase up from that crappy '69 Datsun of yours. That thing had to go, M, and its was a fitting demise, except for what happened to you. So you can use the SS for as long as you need, but if you so much as scratch the paint, well there will be... rhymes with 'well'... if you get my drift, my friend."

"Thanks again, Brian, so much,.. and I will be very careful, promise. Okay, drop me off right around that corner," motioning to the curb." Dr. Hanlon's office is on the second floor, and, to put you at ease, yes, there's an elevator," as the car rounded the turn in the Quad. "Great! Right here. I'll be about half an hour, maybe a little more. If the campus police stop by, just explain the situation, give them my name, and there won't be any problem - they all know me after my six years here, and they're all nice guys, er, and one girl."

"Okay, M. We'll keep busy and be right here when you're done. Izz and I will talk, or listen to the radio, or play cards, or watch the students go by and guess their majors, or whatever. Don't give us a second thought, M, we're okay. Go take care of your business," as Izzy chimes in, "And say hi to Dr. Hanlon from me."

"Will do, Izz, will do."

It was uncomfortable to walk, all the more depending on where he shifted his weight, but M was smart enough to be careful because he knew what would happen otherwise. Needless to say, the best laid plans... "Oh, crap," M thought as he considered a quick about-face, but, no, that would be too obvious, plus he simply couldn't pull it off without really, really hurting. Instead he picked up the pace, which was painful, but forged ahead thinking "Maybe I can get by the jerk before he snags me?"

Nope, too late. He had been seen. M winced as Greg Mandrake pounced, "M, my dear boy, how *are* you today?" M cringed. It was a visceral reaction because he disliked Mandrake so much, and he knew what was coming.

"You know, M, I know the M's short for, what is it, Emilio, right, but I didn't know it was your driver's handle as well, 'M' as in Mario, Mario Andretti the race car driver. Oh, sorry, no, that's a *different* M. That Mario crashes, too, but not into parked cars! My dear boy, it's all over the department, ahem, Emilio.

Everyone's chuckling over it, some people laughing hysterically. After all, who drives into a parked car at nine in the morning on a bright, cloudless day? Who? *You*!"

"You're really a jerk, Greg," thinks M, "no, make that a double jerk, you jerk!" M and Mandrake's feud was longstanding and deep. They collided over just about everything, who got which course to teach, who represented the department at the next ionospheric research conference, who set up the in-department lab, and so on, and so on, and so on. While they started grad school together, they came from different undergraduate schools, Greg from the snooty one. Mandrake has an inflated opinion of himself, and he likes to tell people that, and what to do, too. It showed immediately after they first met, and it grated on M ever since. The solution? M stays away from Mandrake, except when he has no choice, for example, at meetings of the grad student advisory council where they're both members.

"Thanks, Greg," M's sarcasm evident in his voice and visage. "You've always been supportive, and I don't appreciate it. That's right, I said *don't*. Not your kind of support." Mandrake had scored points. "Maybe you could ask how I'm doing, Greg? After all, I *was* in an accident, a pretty serious one. Wait, let me see, oh, no, ...no, you won't do *that* because you don't care how I'm doing!" More points, as M stomped off holding his side, enduring the pain, all the way down the corridor to his office. M slammed the door.

The knock was soft at first. "Busy now, come back later, please" was M's response, suspecting it was Mandrake again. Then it was louder, "Emilio, it's Michael. Please, open the door."

"I'm so sorry, Dr. Hanlon, so sorry. Just had, shall I say, an 'encounter' with Greg, and I thought he was back with more salt. Sorry."

"No apology necessary, M. I know well how you and Greg get along, and I know why. Of course, I can't get in the middle in any tangible way, but between us, you, me, no fly on the wall, you're right. Greg is too much an egomaniac and control freak. I'd guess most of the faculty see it, and I would suspect, disapprove. But we don't discuss those sorts of issues for obvious reasons, and Greg's faults notwithstanding, he works hard and he is a good scientist as measured by his record. Don't get me wrong, M. This isn't a pep talk for you two to kiss and make up, not at all. But do be practical. You're both graduating next May, and when you do you're out of each other's lives, at least I would hope so..."

"Thanks, Michael. I do feel better, now that I've calmed down, and I do appreciate your words of wisdom. I'll do my best to get Mandrake out of my head so we can talk about important things."

"Yes, important things, M, first on the list being, How are you? Physically? Mentally? After yesterday's misadventure? Sure, I know about it like everyone else in the building, and we're all sorry to hear what happened. So what's the answer?"

"Good, Michael, good. I banged my head pretty hard. Broke the windshield on my car with it, bruised some ribs and got some scrapes. I'm not going to minimize any of this, but all-in-all I'm doing well. The head's back to normal even now, and the other stuff, well, that will heal with time, no biggy."

"You sure? How about some time off? A few days vacay with your lovely girlfriend,... Izzy, right?"

"Nope. Thanks. Got a lot on my mind, a very lot. Some of it unrelated to the ionospheric research. In fact I'd like to bounce some ideas around with you, but not now. I have to digest my own thoughts more before we do that. By the way, Izzy says hello. She's waiting for me with her brother Brian. They gave me a lift here from St. Martins, and Brian is loaning me a car."

"Whenever you're ready, M. Whenever you're ready. In the meantime, what's up at the Observatory? Fill me in, please."

Dr. Hanlon and M went over all of what happened since their last meeting, the new data that were acquired, what M thought it signified. But there wasn't anything earthshaking, more more-or-less routine data that fit well with M's theory of how the ionosphere's electron density profiles changed over time and altitude and why. That would be the core of his dissertation.

While they were 'waiting' Isabella and Brian decided tour the campus. Neither had spent much time there, and Polytechnic University had expanded considerably in the past several years, especially since the start of the Apollo program. The Apollo 11 moon landing in 1969, just three years ago, was burned in most people's memory, truly a 'giant leap for mankind' that never would be forgotten, but even at that the interest in space exploration has diminished somewhat because, to a degree, it has become 'routine.'

"That's the new mechanical engineering building, Sis, pretty impressive, huh?" as Brian pointed out the four-story modernistic structure."

"Yes, my dear brother..." Brian could sense it coming. "I have a bone to pick, the car business."

"What about it? I'm helping your boyfriend, my friend going back to high school, what's the big deal? What bone?"

"You're lending him the Camaro SS, that's what you said."

"What about it? I'm not using it."

"That's a 'muscle car,' am I right, a 'street rod' in the lingo, right? You think I haven't heard all this stuff?"

"Oh, I see. You think M's so far in the clouds that he's likely to hit another parked car, or worse, and because the Super Sport sports 395 horsepower from a beautifully engineered GM L8 V-eight engine you think M can really get hurt, right? After all, hitting a parked car at 25 miles an hour is one thing, hitting it at seventy, well, quite another."

"Yes, yes. You're giving my soon-to-be-fiancé a *weapon*! He's not a good driver to begin with, and you're just making him seriously dangerous. I don't think M can handle the speed, and I don't think you even thought about any of this when you made a bad commitment. You know, he could get around by hitching rides, and when he has to get to the Observatory I'm more than happy to ferry him back and forth. But, no, my smart ass brother just blurts out 'I'll loan you a muscle car for as long as you want'! I'm really upset, Brian, really upset!"

"Don't be, Isabella. You think I don't know all this? You think I don't agree with you completely? You're wrong, Sis, very wrong. Just for M, I turned the Camaro into a four-cylinder buggy by deactivating four of the eight cylinders, the four in the middle. That car now runs on only the two front and the two rear cylinders, which lowers its horsepower to less than half because the inactive cylinders still move and suck up power when they do. Okay? Feel a little stupid for crawling up one side of me and down the other? It's all under control, believe me, all good. In that 3300 pound car M will be lucky to break 60 miles an hour downhill, and he'll have very little acceleration, so the SS will behave a lot like the Datsun, but with a lot more metal protecting the sometimes ditzy driver. You okay with this?"

No words, just a look of amazement and a big kiss from Isabella. "Brian, you're a genius, really, when it comes to mechanical things. And I can't tell you how much better I feel, and how much I appreciate what you're doing for us! Thank you, thank you!"

"Welcome, Izz. Glad to help. And now that I think of it, maybe I can turn my cylinder deactivation scheme into a business. It is a good idea, a *very* good idea, and I'm pretty sure I'm the first to do it. There's one more thing to do," Brian mused, obviously lost in a cloud of V8 engines, "I have to modify the engine controls to allow the driver to de/re-activate. What I did to the SS is permanent until I undo it. Could be big, Izzy. Could be big! Who knows, if gas prices were to skyrocket, or, worse, yet, if gas were less available because we get most of ours from OPEC, then, wow, how useful would cylinder deactivation be? Could change everything!" as Isabella's smile dissipated and Brian glided to a stop in the very spot they left to begin their tour.

"How'd it go, M?" asked Izzy as he approached.

"Great, Isabella, great. Dr. Hanlon says 'hello' back. He's very happy with how my research is going, and he wants me to start writing, very soon. I've got about ten months to write the dissertation, submit it for publication, and then a few weeks to prepare my defense seminar. Lots to do, lots to do. So off to my apartment. Tally ho! Off we go!" as Brian pulled away from the curb.

- - - - -

"Good morning, Brian. Beautiful day. I'm here...," as Brian interrupted, "You're here to do the monthly books, right?" which *was* why Izzy was there. She had started college, but before finishing took a couple of years off to work at a financial services firm. Then she went back and was now completing her B.S. in Business Administration with a concentration in accounting. Doing Brian's books gave her a chance to practice her profession, and, besides the experience she already had, it would look good on her CV when she graduated.

"Very astute, my dear brother, very astute, that like a trained dog you know I do the books once a month always around the same time. What does that mean? That you're trainable? Kidding, just kidding, Brian. Sorry if I come across as a bit edgy, but what happened to Emilio yesterday really has me spooked, the more I think about. I worry. He drove into a *parked* car. Who does *that*? That's the part of what happened that scares me. He says he got a clean bill of health on head issues, and I know that's true, but I don't know that it's correct. What if he has some underlying brain problem, one that doesn't show up on an MRI or neurological test. Ever hear of glioblastoma, Brian?"

"No. What is it?"

"A form of very aggressive brain cancer that's undetectable until it forms tumors that can be detected. But even then, if the tumors are removed, this type of cancer usually remains throughout the brain at a cellular level. It's distributed, so it's usually is fatal in the end because there's no way to excise it completely. Oh, Brian, what if he has *that*?" Izzy sobbed as tears welled up.

"Isabella, calm down, please, calm down. M bumped his head, yes, badly, yes, but that's all that happened, not some sort of sneak, what is it, gliblast... whatever it is, attack. And I know why he got into the crash, and under the same circumstance I would have hit the parked car, too. It had nothing, nothing at all to do with some underlying brain dysfunction. Quite to the contrary, your boyfriend's brain is working all too well. He's on the verge of something, Izzy, something that's possibly really big, I mean *really* big, something that might have an impact on the financial world, your world of figures and accounting and investing, and all that stuff that you're so good at and I could care less about."

"Really!? You sure? That makes me feel so much better, if you're sure, if you're right. Really sure? So..."

Brian interrupted, "Yes, Sis, calm down, no doubt whatsoever. Emilio is fine, and what I said about something big is true. We didn't spend a lot of time talking about it because of how he was feeling, but mostly because he has to digest his own work more, to be sure he's right and that it works. He's *very* excited about this, Izz, more than his thesis work, and it doesn't even involve that. It has something to do with using gravity to solve complex problems in engineering, finance, anywhere the problem is too hard for even our biggest, fastest computers. Emilio thinks he's on the verge of discovering something *very* important."

"Gravity?!" Izz exclaims. "Yes," Brian replies, "yep, the stuff that sticks us to the ground. Cool huh?"

"Tell me, tell me, Brian, I want to know everything."

"Nope, not my place, number one, and, number two, M didn't explain it in any detail, only the broadest outline, and, number three, I need the books because the quarterly taxes are due the end of the month. So get crackin', my sister the accountant, and let me get back to work, okay?"

"Before I do, the books, bird springs? What gives? What's that all about? Doesn't sound like you, Brian, so what's up?"

"What's up, you want to know, what's up? Birds, that's what's up, and... what's down... and everywhere in between! Here, let me show you. A custom project to manufacture the springs that these bird novelties hang from," as Brian whisks Izzy into the back room and shows her a wooden bird hanging on a six foot long spring. Go ahead, Izzy, pull the bird down to see what happens."

She does, and very much to her surprise the bird executes the most beautiful motion, almost like really flying, and the spring is essentially gone, almost invisible, which lends to the flying image.

"Wow! That's neat, Brian. Not what I expected."

"And, guess what, no two birds behave the same way. They're all different! It's all in the spring."

"Very nice. You said these were selling like hotcakes. I can see why. How do you do that? I can't really see the spring, it's almost invisible. Is this some of your mechanical magic, my brother?"

"Thanks, Izz. Yep, magic-like it is," as Brian puffs his chest to emphasize the point. "What I did ain't easy, Sis, not at all. In fact the bird manufacturer went to half a dozen outfits before coming to NovaTek, and none could solve the problem. But we did, er.., I did, and I don't mind tooting my own horn about it!"

"Doesn't surprise me at all, Brian. I do know how good you are at this stuff, and I'm proud of you!"

"Well, what I did was design and manufacture the spring, which actually is quite hard to do because it has a variable spring constant. That's what creates the flying illusion. And it's made of a special variable diameter spring wire, which is an extruding nightmare, and it has to be wound on a lathe with a proprietary spindle profile and pitch. And no two springs are identical because the extruder randomly adds or subtracts metal as the spring is made. Not easy to pull off, so I'm pretty proud of this work, and you see the end result and you like it. That's my satisfaction, thanks again, Izz. Well, not *only* that. NovaTek is paid a percentage of the bird's sale price, that's the deal I struck, and it's starting to mount up to a 'handsome sum' as you financial wizards would say! I could have done this as a fee-for-service contract, which is what I usually do, but I had an intuition that this could be big and get bigger over time, so I opted to negotiate the current deal. And, boy, am I glad I did! They can't keep *The*

Birds on the shelves, and those used an older version of my spring!"

"Well, I *am* impressed. Between you and Emilio I know two of the smartest people on the planet! Okay, off to the books... By the way, can I have one? A spring bird? Please..."

"Get to work, Sis. I'll wrap one up for you. Unfortunately I have only one kind, so that's what you get," Brian says as Isabella heads to the Shop's office. "By the way, M called a while ago and said he's up for lunch today if we are, and I should let him know. I'm good with this. You?" Izzy nods as she closes the office door.

- - - - -

Antonio's probably was their favorite restaurant, M's, Izzy's and Brian's. They often got together there for lunch or for dinner, today for lunch, because the food was great, the service impeccable, and, most importantly, they could linger, stay as long as they wanted over coffee or an aperitif or occasionally another bottle of wine. Through the years they got to know Antonio because they were such frequent customers, and he valued their patronage and was more than happy to invoke 'old country' hospitality, which meant staying as long as you wished. Of course, the trio had sung Antonio's praises whenever and wherever they could, and that, they were sure, brought Antonio some additional business, maybe even a lot.

"Great to get together like this, you guys," M says. "Glad you could make it. I know you're busy with the 'bird project,' Brian, and I know it's approaching tax time for you and NovaTek's books, Izz. So just chilling over a good meal, especially after yesterday, well, it just makes me feel good, and I hope you, too. So what else is new and exciting with you two? By the way, you both know *all* the details of my car (mis)encounter, so that's off the table. Izzy, love of my life, you first."

"Before I get into what's been happening, M, I have to yell at you!"

"What, Iz, what are you talking about. Yell at me? For what?"

"You know, or you should know, and if you don't know, well, there's something wrong. It's what happened, the car accident. I was terrified when I heard you were in the hospital with a serious head injury, terrified! I'm just saying that as long as we're together, hopefully a long, long time, ... ahem...." Izzy held back some tears, "I hope you'll *never* do that to me again, never! I don't want you doing dumb things, like reading a page of scribbles while you're driving, or worse yet, something dangerous. You know, I remember that only a few years ago you and my equally spacey brother had to run from the police and fire department when you set the field on fire testing your 'rocket engine,' yeah, the one made from the flashlight tube! How dumb, how dangerous was that?! That's what I'm talking about, M, please, don't *ever* put me in a position like yesterday..."

"Okay, okay, Iz, I promise, never again" as Emilio consoled her by putting his arm around her, tightly and kissing her cheek. Isabella now was visibly calmer as she squeezed M's hand back. "Sorry, " she said. "I had to get that out. I'm better now."

"So, let's see, my turn to say what's been happening. Hmmm... well, okay, on the work side, you know I'm in the NovaTek salt mine for a couple of days trying to unsnarl that tangled web of what my brother euphemistically calls 'accounting ledgers.' I tell you, back in Ebenezer Scrooge's day, I swear, Brian would be in the pokey for accounting malfeasance and losing someone's money, not stealing it, mind you, just not being able to find it. Lord knows, Brian knows how to make money hand over fist, but he's terrible at managing it! The problem with you two is, you're both dreamers with your heads in the clouds, different kinds of dreams and different kinds of clouds, but you get the idea,... you're up there, not so much down here with us mere mortals. Now aren't you so happy to have *me* in your lives? So I can tell you things like this? The even keel, the steady hand, the..." as Brian interrupts, "Got it, sis. What wound you up today?"

"I don't know, I'm just so happy. I love you both, and I'm happy. I'm happy M's in one piece - I hear his car isn't - and I'm happy my mechanical genius brother's doing so well, and I'm just happy to be happy, that's it, nothing complicated like what you guys do."

"Wow! That was some speech, Izzy. I love it! That's why I love you, Izz, you're such a good person. And thanks for being so concerned about my driving - won't let that happen again, scout's honor. Whew, okay, Brian, your turn."

"No, isn't it yours, M. Aren't you going to tell Isabella about the tennis ball?"

"Nope, not now, not until I pin this down to where I know it works." Turning to Izzy, "Look, Izz, I know Brian told you about our conversation yesterday about using gravity to solve some tough mathematical problems, and I explained some of it to you yesterday, too, but I really don't want to get into this anymore right now because I have to be sure I know what I'm talking about, and that it works, and right now I'm not. Please put up with me, both of you, and give me some time to dig a little deeper, agreed?"

"Okay by me," Izzy responds.

"Me, too," adds Brian. "So I guess I'm on the hot seat. A couple of things. You know about my birds, Izzy. You saw them this afternoon, but M doesn't know the details." Brian goes on to describe the bouncing birds, much as he did with Izzy. "By the way, I still have a lot to do to finish up *My Birds*,...ooh, I like the ring of it, *My Birds*, like that Hitchcock film from a few years ago, what a great movie!" Brian gets the same look from Iz and M at the same time and continues, "Okay, okay, I digress. An in-between thing, I'll be working late all next week, mostly on *My Birds*, probably 'til around eight anyway, maybe later, just so you'll know where to find me. Alright, on to the second thing. Good, you're both sitting. Smile... This is a biggie. Remember that VW Minivan I was looking at? Well, now it's mine. Yep, I bought it, and, boy, do I have plans! You're gonna love it! It is tiny(ish), and it's a fixer upper, up to a point, but the 'bones are good,' you know what I mean. So what I'm doing is converting it into, get this, a *super camper*. Cool, huh, I mean full accommodations, just like a hotel room. Bed, bath with shower, running hot/cold water, TV, generator, and, maybe... just maybe if I can work it out... flotation!"

"What? Flotation? Why?" Izzy looks perplexed as M speaks and her face reflects his confusion. "Whatchyamakin? A submarine? With torpedoes I expect?"

"Nah, not a sub... but now that you mention it... nah, no underwater craft... yet...just a small houseboat that I can bring down to the lake for those lazy summer afternoons, that's all. Yes, in thinking about it more, I suppose I'll call it an 'apartmentboat' because it's too small to be called a 'house'boat...'"

M picks up, "Speaking of where we'll be next week, Izz, I'm probably going to be working late at the Observatory most nights. There's a lot of seasonal variability showing up in the ionograms, and I want to be sure to catch anything interesting, just so you'll know. And we're having a bit of a problem with seeing some LEO satellites that might be skewing the data, but I think I know how to fix it."

Izz replies. "Fine, M. I don't have any specific plans. Thanks for telling me, and remember your promise - I'm holding you to it - no reading while driving!!" M deserved Izzy's reprimand and he knew that, so he responded accordingly, "Yes, Izz, I won't, no reading while driving, promise."

And with that they spent most of the rest of the afternoon kibitzing about all sorts of things, laughing a lot, and just about emptying the 30cl bottle of *Liquore Strega* that Antonio brought over compliments of the house.

- - - - -

"What a beautiful day, GianCarlo, what a beautiful day!" exclaims M as he and his grandson GianCarlo, GC for short, walk to the dock.

"Papa, it is a beautiful day. Look how the lake looks, it's like a mirror."

"Yes, GC, just like a mirror, and if you look across to the other side, see how the trees are reflected in it? You're right! Just like a real mirror. And see how beautiful they are now, but just wait until fall. That's one of my favorite times of the year because the trees are so colorful, and the air gets crisp and the shadows get long. What do you think?"

"Well, yes, Papa. I like the cool air, I think, but I never thought about shadows, and when fall comes summer vacation ends. I always have a lot of fun in the summer, so it's sad to see it go. I especially loved summer camp at the Museum, and I hope I can go again next year."

"OK, GC, enough chit-chat. Now I need your help, because I am an old man."

"No you're not, Papa. You're not old, you're not *that* old! You just turned seventy-six on your birthday, and I'm twelve. Well, I guess you are pretty old after all..."

"If only you knew, GianCarlo, if only you knew."

"Knew what? What are you talking about? I'm confused."

"We'll get to that later. Right now I need for you to untie the ropes after I get in the boat, then you jump in and start rowing. We have to get to the middle of the lake, and I want to be there before 9:45, a little earlier is okay, but we cannot be late."

"Late? Late for what" Papa, what's going to happen if we're late? Something bad?" M tousles his grandson's hair as they set off. "No, no, GC, nothing bad. Don't worry about that, nothing's going to happen."

"What's in the backpack, Papa? Something good for lunch? Maybe a picnic on the other side of the lake?"

"Nope, not lunch, although there are some protein bars and soft drinks. Want one?"

"Sure, I'll have a bar, and a drink," as M fishes out GC's snack.

"Oh, Papa, what's that big thing in the backpack? It looks like a basketball?"

"No, GC. You'll see. It's why we're going to the middle of the lake. You'll see."

"Okay, Papa," as GianCarlo put a little more effort into his rowing, protein bar and soft drink by his side.

The whole world was split in two. The lake was so calm, so smooth this day that looking up or looking down made no difference, it was so perfect a reflection. You could almost be on either side. But this tranquility was disturbed by M's opening the backpack and retrieving a cloth bag containing something spherical, somewhat smaller than a basketball. He dawned a pair of latex gloves and removed a shiny sphere placing it on the boat's deck on top of the bag.

"What's that, Papa? It's beautiful, too. Another kind of mirror? But there's something different about it. The reflections are different, aren't they? They're funny."

"Yes, GianCarlo. You have a good eye. What your noticing is that the images you see have a three dimensional sort of quality. They're different than what you see in a normal mirror."

"Why, Papa? Why are they different? Can I touch the ball?"

"No, please don't do that GC, look but don't touch."

"What are we doing with it? It doesn't look like it would be a good anchor, plus the lake's very deep here in the middle."

"You'll see, GianCarlo. You'll see," as M glanced at his watch, 9:42am, a couple of minutes to go. He picked up the sphere and gently placed it on the water next to the boat."

"Papa, Papa, don't do that! What *are* you doing? The ball is going to sink, and we'll never get it back! Don't do that!" yelled GC just as M took his hands off the sphere. But it didn't sink. Instead it floated a few feet from the boat on the lake's quiet surface. It didn't go below the water's surface at all. M could see GC's eyes open to the size of golf balls staring at the shiny sphere that barely touched the water's surface.

"Papa, do you see that? How did you do that? Why isn't the ball sinking? Why isn't it in the water at all? How *did* you do that? Is this a magic trick? Is the ball so light that it just floats? Is it filled with air, like a balloon? What is..." GC was cut off mid sentence by what he saw next. The ball became translucent, and then in an instant, it vanished. Right before GianCarlo's and M's eyes, it disappeared. Into thin air, it was gone.

Papa, Papa, did you see that? It's gone! The ball is gone, but it didn't sink!"

"GianCarlo, that's why we're here, to bring the sphere to this place so what you just saw could happen. If it didn't happen I would be very disappointed! Don't be frightened, GC. It's not magic, it's not a trick, but it is something the time has come for us to discuss. Let's head back. Grandma Isabella is waiting for us."

GianCarlo rowed slowly, craning his neck to look back to the middle of the lake as if expecting the ball to reappear. But, of course, it didn't. After tying up, Emilio and GianCarlo headed back to the Lake House to relax, and to fall into a long, long conversation about what happened this eventful day, and about what he and Izzy have done, and where and when they have been, and the amazing sights they have seen and the things they have learned.

Chapter 2 - The Wave Makes its Appearance

Brian picks up the phone and dials his cousin Tom. "Hey, Tom. Still on for tonight? Great! How about George and Mike? Have you talked to them? Are they coming? OK, sounds good. I'm going to be a little late. Swamped with an order I have to get out, so maybe half an hour or so. You guys go ahead and get started on the pizza and beer. I should be there, oh, around 8:30. Save me some. See you then," as he hung up and headed back to the lab from his office.

The "Adams Street Gang," as they called themselves, got together about once a month for beer and pizza at a little dive, *Stella's* its name, that made the best crunchy, thin crust, wood-fired pizza and served brew by the pitcher, the gang's usually being a lager from a local micro brewery. It was a long-standing tradition. The gang members grew up together, all now in their late 20's, and plotting a collective super-bash for their thirtieths, but tonight was just the monthly meeting, Wednesday, June 28th, a time to catch up, reminisce, and laugh a lot.

Brian mused, "Okay, one last slinky spring, then I'm done, just about. These have been tough, one of my better projects because it's been hard." To confirm performance he hung the last of several test birds, small wooden ones that the manufacturer supplied, all the same. There was a plastic version as well, about the same weight, so testing these samples would be sufficient to see if all the springs actually worked as they should. The preliminary ones, like the one he had given Izzy, all were fine, but a final quality check had to be done. If this test worked okay, then he was done, which is what Brian fully expected. While most people would think of a spring as nothing much, a coil of springy wire, that's it, these springs weren't that at all. They were quite special because of their dynamics, how they moved when stretched, nothing at all like any 'ordinary' spring, all a result of Brian's careful engineering and design, and his use of techniques that never before had been used, like the variable diameter extrusion process he invented.

"Okay," under his breath, "here we go, one at a time," as he set *The Birds* in motion. And, sure enough, each one performed beautifully, with no two flight patterns being the same! They really looked like real birds flying, another remarkable achievement accomplished by Brian's skill. He breathed a sigh of relief. Final test, <Passed>. He could write it up, pack up the test springs, and deliver it all to *Feathered Friends*, the bird manufacturer. "Ahhh, I can smell the pizza now! And a frosty one to wash it down!" Brian thought as he began collecting packing material. All the birds lay motionless with their springs fully extended, each one about six feet long leaving about two feet of clearance at the floor. There were twelve birds in the row about a foot apart, all hanging from a wooden beam, a collar tie, in the cathedral ceilinged test lab.

"Ooohh, better get a move on," ran through his head as Brian glanced at his watch, 8:13 on the nose, and just as he did he was startled, frightened actually, as each bird in the row suddenly flew up to the rafter and then immediately back to its resting position, motionless, not all at once, but one bird after another right down the line. As one bird flew up, its preceding neighbor was on its way down, and thus the birds danced from one end of the line to the other.

Brian was aghast. He rubbed his eyes and looked again, carefully, at the twelve motionless birds, all hanging there as they were before... "What?" he thought, then aloud, "What the hell just happened? Did I really see that?" Brian knew that what he had seen actually did happen. He just couldn't understand what it was, or why. He went back to his office, sank back into his desk chair, and reached into the desk's tall bottom drawer, slowly extracting a glass, and the bottle of *Glenfiddich* Grand Cru Scotch Whisky aged 23 years, which he carefully coddled before pouring two fingers, neat. The *Glenfiddich* was reserved for special occasions, *very* special occasions. Was this one of them? Not the usual kind, he thought, but he needed some help processing this particular occasion. Brian held the glass to the light, then to his nose, and although tempted to down it, took long, slow sips. "Ahhh, that *is* good," he sighed. "What the hell just happened? I did see it, I know I did, no question there, not imagined. So what the hell was it?"

Brian waited, keeping a constant eye on *The Birds* wondering if perhaps the phenomenon he had witnessed might return. *What was that?* circled in his head, over and over. But it didn't happen again, the birds remained motionless. So, after calming down, the scotch certainly helped, Brian inspected each of the twelve birds, carefully, one at a time, looking for the slightest imperfection that might somehow explain these strange happenings. Nothing to be seen, nothing obvious, so he looked for some kind of magnetic effect using an industrial grade Neodymium magnet. Maybe a ferromagnetic inclusion embedded in the bird when it was manufactured, he thought. But nothing there either, no magnetic effect at all, and likewise with the springs because if anything their metal was very weakly diamagnetic, nothing ferromagnetic. Brian was flummoxed. Try as he might, he couldn't come up with an explanation, but his gut told him the event was not only unusual, it was important as well. As any good engineer would, he documented everything in his lab notebook, what happened, his testing to uncover an explanation, and the time of onset ad duration, everything a trained observer would do, at which point he figured closing up Shop was the best thing to do. He felt he waited long enough to see whether or not the disturbance would come back, plus he now would be much later than expected hooking up with the 'gang.'

"Tom, George, Mike, my good men, how they ha... whoops, can't say that anymore. Got excoriated by Emilio when he was in the hospital a couple of weeks back, and believe it or not I haven't forgotten, like there's some 'M presence' following me around. Weird, huh? And that's not the weirdest thing, but, first, how are y'all? Been about a month, so fill me in while I order another pizza since you guys didn't save me any, thanks..."

The gang, one by one, brought Brian up to speed. They had already gone through this once with each other, but tradition required the update for each member. Tom was a teacher, high school science and math, so he was a good sounding board for Brian, and he often played that role. But Tom's 'problem', if you could call it that, was his very linear thinking. 'Outside the box' invariably demanded non-linear thinking, maybe right angle departures or even back-tracking, but Tom simply wasn't there. He always was in the box, going from A to B to C, never skipping A and going right to B then C, maybe even jumping to E from B or try going back from D to A, never. So how did this help, Brian? When Brian's thought process became so scattered, as sometimes it did because he had too many ideas crammed into a larger one that he lost sight of the larger one, well, then Tom could bring him back into the mainstream, sometimes. In any event, he and Brian both enjoyed the technobabble, but tried not to get into it too much in front of the other guys.

Mike was a banker, vice president in fact of a good sized community bank, big enough to handle some very large deals, yet small enough that the local branch manager knew most of its customers. Mike had worked his way up after a stint in the Marines and completing his degree in economics on Uncle Sam's nickel, a good chunk of it while he was still in the Corps. He was a people person who immediately got noticed by the bank's higher-ups who then put him on a rocket to the top. Now Mike was only three notches away from the bank president, but he no longer ran a local branch where he would greet customer Mary Simpson with "Hi, Mary, how are the kids? What can we do for you today?" That was Mike, and genuinely so, he loved the person-to-person interaction, and he loved helping people with their financial needs. Now his was more of a corporate role, and while he missed the customer connection, he certainly didn't miss his old compensation.

George, ahhh, Georgie, Georgie, Georgie, the quintessential pol. What started out as a genuine desire to serve soon became a career. Someone who championed term limits once upon a time, he swore only two, wouldn't hear of them now! Those two terms provided experience that couldn't be 'lost'! "Hi, I'm George Harper, and I'm running for a third term in Congress. Are you a resident of the District? Registered voter?... Great! I really can use your support. Please consider my candidacy because I'll keep working hard for *you*. Would you be willing to sign this Petition that I introduced to *lower* the gas tax, *your* gas tax? It's way too high, and the money's often wasted. Yes? Great. Thank you. And, here, if I may, let me give you some campaign materials? Thanks again! And, remember, please VOTE!" as George handed out the usual folding yard sign, two lapel pins, a bio, and two bumper stickers: "We need a winner! That's George!" followed by "Harper for Congress" in smaller letters, but not too small.

Pol though he was, George always was good for a laugh. He regaled the gang with his tales of how government *really* worked. "Well, you know I'm chairman of the Taxation Committee, right? That makes me the Big Kahuna. I set the Committee's schedule, when members can speak and most importantly whether or not a bill, a new law, can go to the floor. If I kill it, then it's dead, no floor vote, no further consideration, done, *kaput*. Tell ya, you can't beat being the Grand Poobah! So how does it work? How do we dip into your pockets, take your money, then squander it? How? It's like this, the Committee meets, closed session mind you, shuts the door with a Capitol cop outside, and gets down to the serious business of creating new tax laws. First thing is to figure out how much dinero we need. So we talk about that, usually a lot. Next thing, and this is the biggie, we figure out which is the most pluckable goose with the least political clout. Can't have the law lose us votes! Then we write it, a new law, simple!" Tom and Mike are mortified.

"You can't be serious, George? That can't be how it *really* works!?" George smirks, not going to tell. "Pass the beer, Tom, my pizza needs attention. Thanks."

What the Founding Fathers envisioned as a part-time job, the 'citizen legislator' who contributed his or her time and insight to running the government, in many of today's venues had become a career, a way of life unto itself driven by an insatiable drive to win the next election, and the next, and the next,... until retirement. George started out really thinking he could, and wanting to make a difference in politics, a difference for the greater good. The reasoning that brought him to politics was spot on. He could become a doctor and help many people over a career. Or he could teach as Tom does and influence the lives of thousands of students. Or he could become an engineer and provide the products or infrastructure that influences the lives of tens or hundreds of thousands of people. Or... he could become a politician who would craft laws that benefited *millions* of people, maybe the entire population of a state, or maybe, eventually, as indeed was his plan, the entire United States! When he started, George aspired to that, to become a U.S. Senator or Representative or, the Fates willing, maybe even President! He still sought that goal. Very ambitious was he, and equally susceptible to the siren's song to compromise whatever it took to get there. George was a nice guy, but first and foremost he had become the consummate politician, with all that that required. But, George's peccadilloes notwithstanding, the 'gang' just wouldn't be the 'gang' without him. George was a cherished member, and his tales always livened their get-togethers. Ahhh... what *can* be said about George?

"I can smell it! Mmmm... All mine, too, because you lunks already gobbled up what should have been my share! Yumm-o, crispy, thin crust, slightly charred bottom, not too much sauce, topped with 'shrooms, green pepper and onion, dee-lightful!" as Brian lifted his first slice, folded it and bit off the bottom third. "Delicious, my friends, delicious. So it wasn't so bad that I was late after all, later than I thought, because now this puppy's all mine, ha!" Brian was enjoying himself needling his buddies, but they all took it in stride, this wasn't the first time, and it wasn't always Brian who was the needler.

"Who here knows the temp to bake the pizza? Anyone?" Nothing but blank stares followed Brian's query.

"No one, I guess," said Mike, "But I bet you're gonna tell us, Brian. So, enlighten us lunks... or is that *we* lunks?"

"Around 800 degrees! Isn't that amazing? You're lucky to get your home oven to 500, and a lot of ovens may say it's there, but it's really not. In a wood-fired stove it's a real 800 degrees, *eight hundred*, and the pizza bakes in only a couple of minutes. It's that fast cooking that yields the crunchy crust and charred bottom, but it has to be done right, else the pizza comes out a briquette."

"Well, thank you so much, Oracle of NovaTek," Tom replies. "Just what we all wanted to know, you know."

And the three spent the rest of the evening laughing, reminiscing, and having the good time they always had.

"Whew! Almost 11:30, guys. I have to go. Got an early class tomorrow, so off I am."

"Hey, Tom, before you go, I have a technical question, and I hope you can help with it."

Mike and George chimed in, "Yeah. It's late. We're going, too. You guys stay and chat technobabble-ish stuff unless there's a reason for us to stay, too? No? Okay, see you next time."

"Brian, it's late, I'm tired, and I think you've already had your way with us tonight. If it's for real, why don't we get together sometime next week?"

"No, really, Tom, ten minutes if that much, okay?"

Tom mulled Brian's request. It sounded serious. "Sure, what is it?" Brian describes exactly what happened earlier in the evening, and how it caused him to arrive later than he expected, and how he was beside himself searching for an answer but all the while drawing blanks.

"Holy cow! Really, Brian, you're *not* pulling my leg, are you? This isn't a joke?"

"No, Tom, no joke. This actually happened, and I cannot explain it, try as I might. It's really driving me batty!"

"Maybe your imagination? Working too hard? Could that be it, do you think?"

"Again, no, Tom, I did not imagine this. But in thinking back, there is one other thing, I'll have to get this in my notebook. The lab window was open, the way I usually keep it to get in some fresh air, and right around when this happened the crickets and tree frogs became noticeably louder, actually very noisy, very obvious. They're usually a background noise, always there but much less noisy than when this happened. And when the birds sank back to their normal positions, the crickets and frogs quieted to their usual background level. It's like something passed by, or, good grief, *through* the lab, like a *wave* almost, and the bugs, and the frogs, and... *The Birds*, they all knew it! Any ideas, anything at all?"

"Look, Brian, I believe every word you've told me, of course, but, no, off the top of my head I've never heard of anything like this, nothing, and I can't explain it either. It is very strange, no doubt about that! Maybe a gust of wind? You said the window was open. Besides something like that I'm plumb out of any ideas that could explain what happened. From what you describe, it's like gravity suddenly stopped, which is impossible. Did you feel anything, or sense anything? Anything else in the lab start moving? Anything at all, even the slightest thing? Try hard to remember."

"No, nothing else moved, Tom, nothing that I saw anyway. And nothing else happened that I saw or sensed. I was carefully observing the birds for their final inspection, so I was sitting down holding a notebook, staring at the birds. Even if something else moved, I doubt I would have noticed it. These are all good questions, Tom, thanks for bringing them up. But they actually deepen the mystery, I think. Okay, thanks for your counsel, my friend. If you think of anything else, let me know, and I'll let you know if I ever figure this out. Hi to Alice, safe ride home. Goodnight." And with that Brian and Tom left, Mike and George having already waved goodbye as they departed earlier.

- - - - - - - - - - - -

M's head was full of 'gravity' thoughts, that is, until the Super Sport forced its way in. "Geez, I'm really surprised the Camaro is having trouble making this hill! It's not *that* steep," M thought as he drove the twisty road to the Observatory and was forced to abandon his thoughts of gravity, at least for a while. "Oops, another possum! They're out in force tonight!" he thought. "Be careful my little friend, or you might get smushed." M was glad to be driving slowly, no smushed possums, but he was quite surprised at the Camaro's lack of pep. "Hmm... maybe I should tell Brian. Maybe it needs a tune-up or something? Or maybe he'll think I broke it and take it away? Hmm... I have to think about this," as M coasted to a stop in front of the main building, an unimpressive one-story grey cinder block structure nestled beneath the 50 meter diameter USIR, the acronym for Ultrawideband Satellite Imaging Radar.

The contrast was stark, the beautiful, at least to the scientists, glistening white radome housing USIR and the drab, grey Science Center and control building below. As expected, practical for the science, but not attractive for the architecture. Off to the left, at some distance, were M's 'toys' as he called them, two ionospheric radars: the steerable ISR, the Incoherent Scatter Radar that measures parameters of the atmospheric plasma; and TBSR, an earth-fixed vertically pointing Thompson backscatter radar. There were several other instruments at the Observatory, and, smartly, all were controlled from the Science Center unless an on-site operator was required. The facility ran 24/7 doing various kinds of research ranging from ionospheric studies, to deep space radar imaging, to VLBI, Very Long Baseline Interferometry. The facility was operated by a consortium of eleven universities, Polytech being one of them.

"Hello, Emilio," said the entrance guard. "Here for the night, I take it."

"Yes, Fred, for the night. Got a lot of work to do setting up runs, but after that I can do some reading that I'm really anxious to get into."

"Anything I'd like, or understand, maybe a good technical article in magazine with 'boy' in its name, huh?"

"Nope, no can do, Fred. Not my cup of tea, but, and I'm serious about this, the concepts in the stuff I'm reading, well, you can understand them, really, and they might actually be more interesting than your magazine!... or, then again, maybe not... If anything comes up, Fred, I'll be in my usual spot," which was sitting at the ISR's control panel. Tonight M was setting up a series of automated ionospheric sweeps to gather data at different 'look angles.' Once programmed, the ISR computers would do all the work, and M could kick back and get to the reading he so wanted to do. Sometime around dawn the data collection would finish, and he could take home the printouts for analysis.

"Here we go, my friend," M said aloud, talking to the radar as if it were alive, as he was about to push ISR's start button, a big, bright red momentary pushbutton switch protected by a flippable safety guard. Of course, at any time the ISR program could be interrupted and the antenna's motion would stop. But otherwise, once engaged, ISR was on autopilot. M then could turn to other things, and he did.

"I love this book! Just love it!" M muttered as he settled in to a not-so-comfortable-but-adequate chair in front of the ISR console while spreading out his notes, not notes on his ionospheric research, his dissertation, but instead notes on gravity, on what Brian called the 'tennis ball.' The book was a pre-publication copy of *Gravitation* by Misner, Thorne and Wheeler scheduled for release early next year. It was oversized, and 1279 pages long! Not a tome to drop on your foot! M was able to get an early release copy through the W. H. Freeman Company sales rep with whom he had dealt through the years on course textbooks. M knew the book was coming. In fact, there was an earlier not publicly distributed version from the early '70's, but this, this was the very top of the mountain. "I'm holding a classic," thought M, "This book will set the standard and become required reading for every PhD physicist, I just know it!" M had made it through the first two hundred pages or so covering the physics of Flat Spacetime, and he was anxious, very anxious, to move on..

Tonight he was starting *Part III: THE MATHEMATICS OF CURVED SPACETIME*. Sooo excited was he! But he couldn't tell anyone about his new scientific infatuation, not yet, not in its true depth, at least not until his gravity discovery, the 'tennis ball,' panned out, or imploded like a black hole, whichever. And on the personal side he was smart enough to know he couldn't ignore his dissertation research for too long because that might delay his writing it up and graduating next May. He couldn't abide that, and Izzy's reaction, well, he didn't even want to contemplate what that might be, what she would say if he said to her "Izz, my dear, I'm not graduating in May... because I've been diddling with ways of using gravity to solve hard math problems, my dearest." Divorce, probably, even before getting hitched? M decided that only a balanced approach could work, thesis first, CFO second, and in the event of a real conflict, thesis first. As he resolved to handle the situation this way, he cracked MTW, opening to page 195, which begins "*Gravitation is a manifestation of spacetime curvature, and that curvature shows up....*" Mesmerized, the only word that could describe Emilio's enchantment with gravity, and what it could,... would,... might... do for solving hard math problems. M had been sucked in, completely.

But M's gravitational reverie was not to last. Whenever something unexpected happened, or whenever a fault was detected, ISR automatically sounded an alarm at the console, a pretty loud one at that. Fred bolted around the corner as M pushed the silence button, "Everything OK here, Emilio?" "I think so, Fred, I think so. I don't see a mechanical or electrical fault showing up, so it must be either a software glitch, or...", "Just my luck!" thought M, "... or a data error, which is what I hope it isn't. Go back and relax, Fred, no reason to call the cavalry just yet, because whatever's going on, ISR isn't having an electrical or mechanical problem, and those are the serious ones. I'll track it down and let you know. Let's follow protocol, please enter the event in your logbook, and I'll do the same in mine." "Good enough, Emilio," Fred replied with the remnants of a drawl, "As long as you say ISR is okay. If anything else comes up, holler, so I don't wet my pants because that cotton-pickin' alarm goes off again. It's really loud, you know, and I think the way this building is shaped makes it worse, maybe concentrating the sound, something like that," remarked Fred as he left.

M was perplexed. He had worked with ISR for years now, and only once before had the alarm sounded, when a pigeon managed to get into the radome and decided to nest inside the waveguide horn of the L-band monopulse tracker. Energy intended to be transmitted into space was reflected nearly completely, causing the transmitter's voltage standing wave ratio to go sky high, a condition that can result in serious equipment damage. Two things happen if this occurs, 1) the transmitter automatically shuts down, and 2) the blaring cotton-pickin' alarm is triggered. But that wasn't it tonight. M checked all the readouts, and at this time everything was nominal, no problems anywhere. And, he mused, "That was one lucky pigeon! Probably an urban legend, but rumor has it that some of the White Alice radar beams are so intense birds flying through too close fall from the sky, literally having been microwaved in flight. I wonder... but, whatever, true or not, that still was one lucky pigeon, and it's not an urban legend!"

"Damn," thought M," as he pored over the last diagnostic dump, no software problem anywhere, everything checks perfectly, damn!" M sat back, collecting himself, coming to the realization "So it has to be a data error, just what I didn't want!" and after a pause, "What a pain! Only one way to find out, pore over all the data, too, around when it happened. Such a pain in the ass!" But, to M's surprise, and confusion, it was right there, immediately evident in the data, right at the time the alarm sounded, precisely 8:02pm and some change. The radar had been tracking any satellite that passed through its beam so that spurious reflections from the satellite could be removed from the ionospheric reflections, a data manipulation procedure that was followed all the time, that *had* to be followed to preserve the ionospheric data's integrity. But tonight the radar caught a small but significant deviation in the satellite's trajectory, and that signaled that there might be a problem with ISR which in turn tripped the alarm. But within seconds of when the blip appeared, it disappeared, and the satellite track returned exactly to where it should be.

"What's happening here? M said to himself. This is *bizarre*! What the hell...?" M could think of no explanation, he never had seen anything like it before. Satellites don't just make course changes on their own, but that's what this looked like, a slight deviation to one side of its smooth path followed by a quick return to the path, all in a matter of seconds, like it had been shoved by something that ISR didn't see. M was perplexed, and because tracking satellites or, for that matter, having anything at all to do with them, wasn't his concern, he logged the event and jumped back into MTW, which is where his head really wanted to be anyway. Someone else, sometime later could ponder the spooky satellite path.

Chapter 3 - *The Birds*

July Fourth dawned bright and cloudless, although it was a bit sticky with predicted temps in the high 80', low 90's, definitely a beach day, or for Izz and Brian, a lake day. Of course, M would be with them, too. The Lake House was owned by Brian and Isabella's folks, and they visited fairly regularly from their new digs in Florida, but not this year, too much to do in the Sunshine State. They had sold their main residence, bought a condo in Ponte Vedra Beach, but kept the Lake House for sentimental reasons and for the kids' use. Brian and Izz just loved the place, right on the water, a long dock nearly forty feet into the lake, which technically was a 'kettle pond' carved by retreating glaciers some fifteen to twenty thousand years ago. The lake was quite large, about 600 acres, crystal clear right to the sandy bottom, quite deep, approaching one hundred feet in places, and fed by groundwater and underwater springs. It was the perfect place to be on a day like this, hot and humid, because nothing beat a dip in the oh so cool water!

Today's festivities were typical of the Fourth, a big cookout with lots of guests, family and friends, today about thirty in all, and lots of good food, dogs, burgers, all the fixin's, and what was a real treat for many, Italian sausage and peppers Cucinato da Ravelli, the snooty term for prepared by Emilio, one of his specialties. When it came to that most difficult of choices on the Fourth, dog, burger, or sausage and peppers in a soft submarine roll, SPR for short, the kind you get outside the ball park, well, hands down SPR wins. Emilio planned on spending much of the afternoon feeding the hungry masses, so high was the SPR demand, plus he thoroughly enjoyed his role as chef and everyone's company as they stopped by the kitchen while he cooked.

Isabella rounded the corner from the living room heading straight for M when he said to her "Nope, Izzy. I love you, but no cutting the line, no special treatment!" as he motioned her away. Of course, there was no 'line,' just several people milling around making small talk amongst themselves and with M. Izz knew that M was putting her on, but she could play the game better than he, and she did by pursing her lips, donning her best pout, and slightly but noticeably stomping her left foot, turning away as she did, waving to M saying "Too bad you won't hear Brian's story about the strange thing that happened to his birds!"

Needless to say, Izz won. "No, wait, Izz, wait. I was lost thinking about, of all things,... sausage,... sorry. Please come back," was M's pitiful response. "Extra sautéed onions, my dear? Just the way you like your SPR, right?"

Of course, Isabella did come back because, among other things she thought M should know about Brian's bird tale, which for some reason, an intuition, she thought was important, while the 'other thing' was an SPR with extra caramelized onions, just the way she liked it!

"Yes, make that to go, please. And when you can take a break you probably should hear what happened."

"You mean, with the birds, right?"

"Yes. Brian said that the other night a while after eight there were twelve birds in a row that he was testing, and all of a sudden one-by-one they jumped from the floor to the ceiling and then back down with nothing causing it, like the birds were 'dancing' he said. He was very upset because he couldn't figure out what happened, then or now, so it's still a mystery to him. He said it was like a wave or something passed though the lab, but he doesn't know what. I know he wants to talk to you, he told me so, but I think he thinks this probably isn't the right time, right in the middle of our annual Fourth of July bash. Go see him, and tell him what I told you. He's still in the living room."

"On my way, Izz. Thanks!" as he planted a big kiss on her cheek and remarked, jokingly, "You smell good,... like sausage and peppers with extra onions. New shampoo? Perfume? Can I have a nibble...?" Isabella pushed him away, "My brother's in there", pointing, and with the slightest gleam, "Be a good boy - Scram!"

"Hey, Brian. Izzy filled me in on your dancing bird mystery. Fascinating! We should talk about this, but I know now isn't so great. I had a weird thing happen with a satellite a few days ago, no explanation either, then or now. Maybe we're in the same boat, huh? Maybe these events are somehow connected? How about I stop by the Shop tomorrow, and we can go through this, what happened to you and when, what happened to me and when, and look for some commonality that might explain what was going on, or at least give us a clue. What do you think?"

"Absolutely! Absolutely! I've racked my brains trying to figure this out, M, but no luck. Your scientific take may help crack the nut, so show up tomorrow whenever it's good for you. I'm there all day."

"I'll be there, Brian. Thanks for the kind words, by the way. Hope I can measure up" as M turned to return to his cooking task, thinking as he did, "Should I mention the SS? Maybe tomorrow."

- - - - - - - - - - - -

The fifth of July was a carbon copy of the fourth, hot and sticky but cloudless and bright. Emilio was so excited about seeing Brian to discuss the bird episode that he showed up early, before even Brian got there.

"Wow! How long have you been here, M?" as Brian looked at his watch. "Geez, it's only 7:30! I'm usually in around 8, sometimes 9, but today I knew you were coming and I have some cleanup to do on another project, my engine project, so I'm here early. And yet you beat me! Good memory, thanks," as M handed Brian a large black coffee from Dee's Donuts, the best donut and fast breakfast Shop for miles. So where's the jelly filled? No jelly-filled? Mmm... that would've made my morning! Just kidding, M, I actually prefer glazed... Let's get settled so we can solve this bird problem, maybe, and yours too, which I'll call the funky satellite."

"Brian, would you nuke, er... microwave, my coffee, too. It got cold while I was waiting reading this book on satellite orbital calculations. Oh, and what new engine project? A car engine? What kind?" M asked as the Camaro question displaced all his other thoughts. "Should I tell him? Now? Later? It is his car, so I should," as M paused to consider his next step on the SS. "No, I will tell him, but not now, maybe later today after we discuss the birds and the satellite."

"Shit...," thought Brian, "Now the camel's nose *is* under the tent! How stupid of me to mention a 'new engine project.' If I explain it he'll know in a second that I sabotaged the Camaro, and how do I explain *that*? Ahhh...maybe lay it on Isabella?" as this sinister train of thought was interrupted by M.

"Ok, Brian, I've been thinking a lot about this whole business, the birds, the satellite, and I have some ideas, mostly from this little book," which actually wasn't so little, 455 pages worth, as he held up a copy of Bate, Mueller & White's 1971 tome *Fundamental of Astrodynamics*. Got this from our library, and it's the bible on orbital mechanics, a good place to start for what I saw in the satellite track. Whether or not it sheds any light on the birds, well, maybe that's something we can figure out today." M sipped his coffee as he handed Brian the book.

"Alright, where to begin?"

"Go over everything that happened with the birds that night, everything, even the littlest thing that you might think as inconsequential, anything and everything. But, the facts, please, and only the facts. Go!" Brian went through what happened in minute detail, start to finish, and he did confine himself to only the facts, no interpretation, no guesses.

"In a nutshell, M, the twelve hanging birds, just like the one over there," as he motioned to one of the birds he kept for further work if necessary, "were all in a line and suddenly cascaded up like they were weightless, one after another, and then came back down after a second or two. It was like a wave of some kind passed through. Never before did any one of them do this, unless someone yanked on them, which, of course, is how they're supposed to work. Oh, and another thing that I noticed, the crickets and frogs. They were noticeably noisier, just for a short time before this happened, and then they went back to normal a short time after it happened. I'm guessing, but I'd say maybe fifteen to thirty seconds before and about the same time after, but as I said, I'm guessing. What I'm not guessing about is that they got louder, which I couldn't miss because the lab window was open."

"As I said yesterday, Brian, 'fascinating,' really fascinating. Why? Because none of this makes any sense, none at all, yet there *has* to be *some* explanation! And it has to be consistent with the laws of physics."

With a smile on his face Brian begins flipping pages in the satellite book, "Geez, nothing like the mechanics *I* studied in college!" and then he looks up at M expectantly, "Ok, your turn. What happened to you that night? And what night was that?" M blurted out the date, Wednesday, June 28th. Brian's demeanor and countenance immediately changed. "*When?* Say that again."

"That's the night the 'bird dance' happened, that's what I've been calling it, *the same damn night!* Can this be coincidence? Seems unlikely. When did funky satellite show up, what time?"

"Let me look, around eight as I recall, but let me pin it down. It's here in the ISR printout," as M rummaged through the pile of computer output that was the ionospheric data from that night that included the satellite episode. "Here, here it is - funky satellite, as you put it, it showed up at 20:02:39 EDT, that's 8pm and two minutes thirty-nine seconds, around ten minutes before the dancing birds according to your timing, and it lasted, let's see, 5.4 seconds, the time from initial path distortion to recovery. That's what the ISR recorded that night."

"Holy Moley!! So these two events occurred on the same night separated in time by around ten minutes. So if something were moving through the Observatory and then through the Shop, well maybe they are manifestations of the *same* thing, no? Almost like a *wave* of some kind?" queried Brian. "But *what*? That's the sixty-four thousand dollar question! *What* was it?", as M smiled, slightly, as if he knew something Brian didn't.

"It hangs together, Brian, this harebrained idea I have. So sit down and I'll tell ya." Brian grabbed his desk chair as M pulled up a folding chair and leaned forward, as if about to reveal some important secret.

"*Gravity stopped!* That's it in a nutshell, I think, gravity stopped! Sounds crazy, but I do believe that's what happened." Brian interrupted, "You sound just like Tom. That's what he said because it was the only explanation for the birds' behavior. But he also said it was impossible, so he tossed it. And, let me add, Tom's no slouch when it comes to this stuff. Teaching high school as he does, Tom's not working at a PhD level, but he does have a Master's degree in general science, which you probably didn't know."

"Well, I think he's half right. *Gravity stopped*, literally. Tom and I agree on that. And, if I'm right, he's half wrong, that stopping gravity is impossible. Quite to the contrary, not only is it possible, believe it or not it happens all the time. We just don't see it!"

"Holey Moley times two!! Okay, that explains *The Birds*, but what gives with funky satellite? And how does the light reading help?" holding up the *Astrodynamics* book.

"Actually, Brian, that book is the key. It's what explains the perturbation of the satellite orbit, which was a brief suspension of gravity. *Gravity stopped!* And, what's really remarkable, as I mentioned, is that it happens all the time. But... unless the satellite is in exactly the right place at exactly the right time, there is no orbital deviation. Now most satellites, and there are tens, maybe hundreds of thousands orbiting Earth, they aren't tracked *continuously* in *real time*, so when one of these very unlikely encounters does occur it simply is missed. Even though the zero-gravity points are common throughout space, remember, to be seen on the Earth a satellite has to 'bump' into one and at that very instant its trajectory has to be looked at by radar. See why this phenomenon isn't above-the-fold headlines? Satellite orbits are disturbed for a very short time, which is rare, and when it does happen no one is looking. Ergo, none found. Make sense?"

"Sure does. And boy am I happy it does! You know, for a while, M, I really was beginning to doubt what I saw, and I saw it *before* breaking into the *Glenfiddich*! If you're right, and I'm sure you are, a gravity anomaly explains both my birds and your funky satellite, and it makes perfectly good common and scientific sense! We just had to know about it, that's all!" as Brian looked over at the Shop's very accurate quartz movement punch clock that told him the time the night the birds danced.

"It's approaching 10 o'clock our time, which means well after Noon across the pond, so to acknowledge and celebrate your superb sleuthing, M,..." he extracted the *Glenfiddich* and two glasses, pouring two fingers in each, neat, handing one to M, and nosing his as tradition demanded after holding it to the light, then he continued, "... let's raise our glasses and enjoy the spiritus frumenti, my good, very smart, friend!"

M was on the verge of declining. After all, it wasn't even ten in the morning! But he knew what Brian's reaction would be, so he played the game, nosed the whisky, held it to the light, took a sip, and pretended to love it. "Great stuff, Brian, great stuff. I'll have to pick up a bottle, *GlyndaWitchIt*, what was it? Thanks for sharing!" as he thought, "Maybe now's the time to bring up the SS..."

"Now, to the serious stuff, M. I want you to explain to me the science behind this, how does it work? I really want to know, and we have the rest of the day to do it. Where do we start? Hope it's not that orbital mechanics book!"

"Nope, not even close. No hairy math, probably none at all. The idea is really simple, very easy." M leaned back, placing his hardly drunk glass on the floor and picking up his pad and pen. He drew two circles one large, one small, with a line connecting their centers. Scoot over here in your wheel chair, oops, I mean wheeled chair, Brian." It didn't take much eighty proof whisky at 10am to muddle M a whisker! Plus, and probably more importantly, he was very tired, dog-tired, from staying awake almost the entire the night before, of all things, and reading *Astrodynamics*, researching possible explanations for the funky satellite.

He held the drawing between them and started, "Let's say this is Earth" pointing to the larger circle, "and this is the Moon," pointing to the smaller one. Gravity attracts each to the other as well as anything that's in-between them along this line," pointing to the line joining their centers. "With me so far?"

"Sure, my ten year old nephew would understand this. Keep going..."

"Imagine an object on the line. It's attracted to the Earth by the Earth's gravity, and to the Moon by the Moon's gravity. Those gravitational forces act in opposite directions. Now if the object is close to the Earth, the Earth's attraction is much stronger than the Moon's, and the net gravitational force will pull the object onto the Earth." M looks up at Brian to be sure they're on the same page. "With me so far?"

"Yeeessss. Easy-peasy. How 'bout something complicated? I thought this was going to be complicated?" was Brian's derisive reply.

"Nope. I said it was simple, and it is. One more step. If the object is close to the Moon, then at some point the Moon's gravitational pull exceeds the Earth's, and the object will be pulled onto the Moon. But... at *some point* along the line the Earth's and the Moon's gravitational pulls are equal and opposite, that is, they *cancel out*, net gravity of *ZERO!* That's what happened to *The Birds*, and that's also what happened to funky satellite, pure and simple. The birds and the satellite experienced *zero* gravity because a 'Node' passed by, and inside the Node there is no gravity! The gravitational forces from other larger objects combined so as to cancel out and create the Node. Voila! No gravity, ergo dancing birds, and funky satellite! Cool, huh?"

"Geez, M, my head's going to explode. Really! This *is* simple, high school stuff, if that, and it *does* explain what happened. But, knowing you, there's got to be more to it, right?"

"Yes, Brian, and I'll get to it in a minute. First I want to straighten out some terminology in case you do spend any time in the orbital mechanics book. The 'official' names for a zero gravity point is 'neutral' or 'null' point. 'Nodes' refers to specific points in celestial coordinates, but I think it's a better descriptor for what we've seen, so that's what I'd like to use. You good with that?"

Brian winced, "What? You're serious, aren't you? So you're making a big deal out of what we *call* these things? That's gotta be the scientist in you, M. As far as I'm concerned we can call these zero gravity points 'pigs' because then the pigs will fly." Brian gently shook his head with a quizzical look. "I can hear it now, you telling Isabella, 'Wait, wait, Izzy, look that way, the pig will fly by in just a few minutes, and when the pig arrives the birds will dance!' She'll be impressed - with *something*, I'm sure, hmmm! M, feel free, any word you like I like, it's fine by me. Let's stick with 'Node,' which I like, too. Node it is," and the terminology issue was settled.

"Alright, good. Let's get on to what happens next. I have some ideas."

"Is one of them, 'Will this happen again?' I sure would like to know. You thinking along those lines, M? Has this entered your cranium, or maybe somewhere else between your ears?"

"Yep, it certainly has, Brian, it certainly has. In fact, based on what I've found so far, I think we actually can calculate Node trajectories so we'll know when and where they occur. How's that? The only problem is, I'm not one hundred percent sure. I have to dig deeper, but I think I can have a definite answer, say, in a few days. Let me go work on this, and I'll give you a call."

"Do that, M, and, by the way, don't forget your thesis work. That comes first, really, and I know how Izz would react if you started spending too much time chasing this down. She'd start out with, 'The windshield did a lot more damage to the old bean than the docs thought!'"

"Will do, Brian, will do. And, oh, by the way, at some point we should talk about the Camaro. It's not as peppy as I expected. I'm sure it's fine, but we should talk about it. Later,"as M grabbed his pad and the orbital mechanics book. "Oh, I need this book. You can have it when I'm done, but for now I do need it - great material!" On his way out M thought, "Whew. I broke the ice, the Camaro, now all I have to do is fill Brian in... as he would say 'easy-peasy'!"

M walked away as Brian yelled, "No problem, M. I figured you were going to dive into the hairy math to learn about our 'Nodes,' so you're welcome to it. Maybe at some point I'll get ambitious enough to try to understand it, but right now it's better that you use it," all the while knowing full well that he never would crack the binding of Bate's tome again because his head wasn't there. "Drive carefully, M, don't go too fast!" Brian snickered, his back to M as M drove off, thinking "Sure, great material? Good thing M's wading through it and I'm not!"

After the meeting with Brian, M headed straight back to his apartment, a one bedroom walk-up about quarter mile from Poly, a very convenient spot for a grad student and one he was lucky to get, demand for off-campus housing being what it was. M started out in a grad student dorm, but after a year he just had to get away. He found it depressing, a small room, painted cinder block walls, no cooking or toilet facilities except down the hall, all-in-all rather stark and uninviting. Most grad students didn't have the wherewithal to afford better, so they stayed, but those that could bolted as soon as they could, M no exception. He cobbled up enough cash to rent the walk-up, and after all these years it really did feel like 'home.'

He brewed a cup of tea, sweetened it with honey, pulled up to his desk and picked up where he left off, Chapter 9, *Perturbations.* " It begins *A perturbation is a deviation from some normal or expected motion. Macroscopically, one tends to view the universe as a highly regular and predictable scheme of motion.*

"There it is," he thought, "right before my eyes," Yes, there was no doubt, a satellite's passage through a Node would cause *exactly* what ISR recorded, a perturbed orbit, but the Node wasn't stationary in space, just sitting there. It moved, though space from where the satellite was in low earth orbit, LEO, onto the Earth's surface and then along the surface passing through the Shop. "So what are Node dynamics?" mulled M, "What determines that motion? How can I calculate where a node is and where it's going to go, if that can be done at all? This is tough!" But, was there a way? M's tiredness began to catch up. It was only about noon, but his meeting with Brian was draining, and the *GlyndaWitchIt*, or whatever it was, didn't help. M needed some rest, so he plopped on the couch and quickly dozed off.

"How long... was I out?" M thought upon waking. 3pm read the wall clock, so around three hours, a good nap, a good break that did clear his head. A splash of cool water, then back to Bate, Mueller & White, this time straight to Chapter 4, *Position and Velocity as a Function of Time*. But it wasn't a satellite's ground track that concerned him, it was a Node's. Why not use the use the equations of motion for a satellite? "Nope, no can do, because a Node," M thought, "well, a Node isn't anything...it's *nothing*... not a physical object with mass, it's more like a hole in space where there's simply no gravity. Not physical, no mass!" M was stumped, frustrated, "The equations of satellite motion just don't apply. I can't use them. So what *can* I do?" and then it struck him.

"A Node is *created* by two or more real objects, the planets, their moons, the Sun, some combination of real masses! And it's the vector sum of their gravitational fields that produces zero gravity at some point, a Node...hmmm...," M interrupts his own thought process. "...hmmm... maybe more than one Node?" And just as quickly snaps back, "Work on just one! Can't handle more than one right now!" as Emilio, forever the romanticist, recalls a headnote in *Astrodynamics*, *". . . the determination of the true movement of the planets, including the earth. . . . This was Kepler's first great problem. The second problem lay in the question: What are the mathematical laws controlling these movements? Clearly, the solution of the second problem, if it were possible for the human spirit to accomplish it, presupposed the solution of the first. For one must know an event before one can test a theory related to this event."* A. Einstein, 1951.

M's head spins. His problem now was Kepler's second problem almost three centuries ago, yet he senses he's close, like a lion closing on its prey. "How can I determine where a node is and where it's going? What *are* the mathematical laws?" He thinks hard, very hard, bringing to bear all his training in physics, and problem-solving. And then he sees it - the lion pounces! "Whoa, not that hard after all, but I bet the calculations will be hairy as hell." M's solution, "If I know the motions of the objects that created the Node, then I can combine their gravitational fields as *they* move to determine where the Node is now and where it's going! Forever! Conceptually easy, calculationally, hmmm, if that's a word..., calculationally a bear!" But I think I can do it, with the right computer!"

"QED," thought M, and he loved it, just the idea, '*quod erat demonstrandum.*' Problem is solv-ed, as Hercule Poirot would say,... in principle at least. Now he had to figure out how to do the calculations, not a simple task, to compute a Node's actual trajectory through space! It required a massive amount of data if it was to be exact. "Put on your thinking cap, M," thought M, "How can we do those calculations? Not only does it need a big machine, a really big machine, gobs of memory, but also some sophisticated data processing, not at all run of the mill stuff. This needs more work!" But computational complexity notwithstanding M felt good, really good, about having already gotten so far on the Nodes. Now he had to tell Brian.

Chapter 4 - Node Tracking

Brian's Shop was a good place to meet, but *Stella's* was better. There you could get beer,... and pizza,... and a steaming hot cup of homemade Pasta Fazool, that very tasty white bean soup from Venice, Italy, more precisely 'Pasta e Fagioli.' M loved it, and he often ordered his with a little sausage in it for another layer of flavor. So, a few days after M's discoveries on Node tracking, he and Brian got together at the hangout. M had worked the details and was able to run the case of the Node that made the birds dance and that shoved funky satellite off course. A major accomplishment, it was, and he was anxious to fill Brian in.

"What'll it be, M? My treat, I'm looking forward to a good lunch, *and*, mostly, for you to tell me what you've discovered!" The waiter approached, "Good day, gentlemen, welcome to *Stella's*." The waiter recognized Brian. "Start off with a pitcher? The Pilsner Urquell, right?" "Please, replied Brian, and you may as well take our order while you're here. You go, M, pizza and beer and your soup, I'm guessing. You order. My palate's not discriminating like yours." "Let's see," M says, "yes a large pizza, half with mushrooms, green peppers, and onion, the other half with pepperoni, and five other toppings that you and/or the chef picks out. Surprise us! ahem, him," and after a couple of seconds, "Oh, and two cups of Pasta Fazool with a little sausage added." The waiter jots down the order, asking "Are you sure about having us pick the toppings? That's the first time I've heard this." "Yep," says M, "definitely, thank you, and mix them up!" at which point Brian jumps in, "Having fun, M. Ordering *me* a garbage pizza?" "Yup, and I'm sure you'll love it!" "You're probably right. Fact is, I don't have your refined, discriminating palate. For me, if it's on a plate and not moving I'll eat it, and I feel blessed that I don't have your refined tongue!" whereupon they settle in to their tasty lunch. And, yes, Brian wolfed down his garbage pizza!

M could tell from Brian's look that he should start explaining his findings. "Well, Brian, much like Tom was half right, and half wrong, Node tracking is half easy, and half hard."

"Eh, what? What does that gobbledygook mean? How about straight up, my friend? What have you found out?"

"Okay, first, I managed to calculate the track for the Node that bounced your birds around and knocked funky satellite off course. We got lucky, because our Node apparently was created by a convergence between the Sun, Jupiter, Earth, and the Moon, and I know its trajectory because I know theirs. That's the first big thing, that we can compute a Node's motion from the motions of the objects that created it! The usual orbital equations don't apply because the Node is not a physical object, it's like a 'hole is space,' no mass."

"This *is* impressive, M, that you figured this out. Bravo! And, you're right, this part *is* easy, makes complete sense, and, dare I say, 'obvious'..."

"No, don't dare say. Not 'obvious,' Brian, until you know it, and before then it's obtuse. I spent hours combing through the orbital mechanics book thinking that the equations of motion would work for the Node. It was an 'aha' moment when I realized they didn't," M countered. "But all that work still paid off because now I know how to calculate the trajectory of just about every object in the Solar System, and now we know that's the key to calculating a Node's path. As long as you know the motions of the masses that *created* the Node, you know where it's going to go! Forever!!"

"You're a genius, M! Bravo again! So what's the deal with our Node - maybe we should give it a name? - will we ever see Gertrude again?"

"Yes, we will, but 'Gertrude,' that's a terrible name for a Node! First of all, how do you know it's a girl? And, second, who's Gertrude, maybe a distant relative you don't like, an old girlfriend who found someone better?" M pulled Brian's leg while letting him know 'Gert' would be back. "The Node will return five times in the next few weeks, and then head off to deep space for about two hundred years before retuning. What a trip! And I can calculate exactly when and where it will be all that time,... and when it, er, she will be back here back here! What do you think?"

"Holy sh...", Brian cut short his exclamation because of the public place, "I mean 'cow', M, my mind's already wrapped around our Node's return and maybe what we can do with it."

"*Our* Node? It's Mother Nature's Node, not ours, point one, and, point two, 'do with it'? What are you talking about? Stuffing it into a jar? Knowing you, probably yes, and then set up a business selling 'bottled Nodes,' kind of like the one a few years back selling 'canned air', something like that?

"Well, it's our Node. *We* found it, kind of like finding gold nuggets. Mother Nature made those, too, but if we find them, then they're ours, not hers anymore, *capische*? And don't insult me, please. I don't do scams, and I resent any implication that I might. 'Bottled Nodes,' no, that is a scam, and as I said, I don't do scams. A solid business, yes, I'm good at that, so that's what I do when it's a good opportunity. And once the business is developed and doing well, I sell the business, and they've all been technical products, good, no make that very good products! Several are medical devices. I'm particularly fond of my needles, hypodermics, and someday I'll tell you about them."

"Whoa, Brian, please calm down. By the way, minor point, we didn't find Gert, she, no, it found us... I was trying to inject some levity, that's all, not accuse you of being shady, and you should know that. Look, I'm on the verge of marrying your sister, so we'll be brothers-in-law. I couldn't think more of you, Brian, and I want to keep our great relationship. You're a great guy! Please, accept my apology if I struck a chord. It wasn't intentional, really. I'm sorry."

"Apology accepted, M. Maybe I was a little twitchy because, I am thinking of what we can do with Nodes, not just Gert, but any other Nodes that may be out there! And it's shredding my head, brother-in-law-to-be. There are some things about this that we have to discuss, but I'm wound a little tight right now. Got change? Let's dump some coins in the jukebox and chill to some tunes for a while, ten, fifteen minutes or so. What do you say? Take a break?"

"Sure, good idea," replied M. Each booth in *Stella's* was equipped with an individual jukebox so diners could play some music while enjoying their meals, plus it gave them some sound privacy as well. M scans the available songs. "How about 'Here Comes the Sun' and 'It Don't Come Easy,' both songs I really like,... and maybe oddly relevant to this discussion, huh?" Brian jumps right in, "Great, two great tunes, and any other Beatles songs, all of them are great. Just ten, maybe twenty minutes. I have to collect my thoughts. Thanks, M." And they listened to the music without saying much, sometimes humming along, Brian obviously lost in deep thought, M drawing diagrams and scribbling on his pad. The minutes passed like seconds, then their conversation resumed.

"Ok, first thing," as M drew a rough map, "here's the Observatory and here's the Shop, about five miles apart as the crow flies. Taking the time that the Node was first caught by the radar, when it was directly overhead ISR, and when it showed up in your lab, these two events were about ten minutes apart, one sixth of an hour. My rough calculations show that the Node descended more or less radially to the Earth's surface, straight line, very quickly, then it moved along the Earth's surface to your lab, but much more slowly, not at all like it dropped from the sky. Combining it all, the bottom line is that the Node moved along the Earth's surface at about twenty miles per hour, roughly, very roughly."

"Why do you say 'roughly'? Why isn't this accurate? Seems to me like it should be accurate," interrupts Brian.

"Well, yes, if funky satellite were on the ground we could get very precise even now. But most NASA LEO birds are up there," as M pointed to the ceiling, "somewhere up there, in low earth orbit. If they're on the ground, well, a pretty bad sign," M chuckled. "So 'Gert,' as you insist on calling this non-thing thing, moved along a path for which my back-of-the-envelope calculations are only approximate. Now I can pin this down to five decimal places, and I will, but I need a pretty good computer to do that, and I know just where to get one!"

"Oh yeah? Where?" Brian asked.

"At the Observatory, silly. Now *that* should be obvious? We have the world's best machines to process the terabytes of data that the radars acquire every day. They're state-of-the-art and kept up to date, very fast, lots of memory, everything we need to accurately calculate Node trajectories."

Brian has already planned the next step, verification that M is right, that he really can predict Gert's behavior. "Okay, M, today is, let's see, July 7th. Can you find out when, I suppose that should be 'if,' Gert is coming back like she did before and when, exactly?"

"Sure, Brian, can do. I start tonight. Because I know the Earth's and Jupiter's motion relative to the Sun, in fact they're already in the Observatory's data base, I can gin up a program to do the Node calculations pretty quickly. In fact, I'm off to the Observatory tonight, so I'll do it then."

"Right, great! But don't forget the thesis. We don't want to incur the Wrath of Isabella, not that she wouldn't be one hundred percent right given that hers and your futures depend on it..."

"Don't worry, Brian. Tonight's stint is just like the one when funky satellite showed up. I set up ISR runs, and the radar takes care of itself. Next day I look at the data. The last time while I was killing time I got really far into *Gravitation*, the new book that's coming out soon, the one I told you about, having to do with CFO, remember? But instead of that tonight, tonight is Node night. I will have Gert's trajectory, exact to five decimal places, with me on my way home tomorrow morning. I'll get a couple of hours shut-eye and then give you a call."

"Good deal, M, good deal! As one of my young nieces used to say, 'sounds like a planet to me.' I'll wait to hear from you," and with that they quaffed the last of the Pilsner Urquell and departed *Stella's*.

- - - - - - - - - - - -

Brian's phone rang just as he hung the last of twelve 'spring birds' on the same rafter and in the same locations as were the first twelve when the Node passed through. He had something specific in mind, and the first thing was to replicate as nearly as possible the events on the night of July Third. It rang, and rang, but he couldn't interrupt what he was doing for fear of damaging the bird. "Hello, hello," out of breath was Brian's greeting when he was able to get to the phone."

"Hi, Brian, it's M, and I was just about to hang up because you didn't answer. You sound winded?"

"No, I'm good, just couldn't get to the phone fast enough. Good news, I hope. Could you do it, get Gert's trajectory?"

"Yep, got it! And it's beautiful! Not quite what I expected. You'll be impressed, I'm sure, so I'm heading over. That OK?"

"Sure is," as Brian smiled and sat back in his Captain's Chair, as he called it, relaxing in anticipation of M's revelation."

M pulled the Camaro up to the Shop's front door, thinking "Maybe now's the time to tell him? He'll be so happy with the Node results that slipping in the SS's bizarre behavior might not be such a big deal. Yeah, I think now's the time," as M grabbed a pile of computer printout and walked in. "Hey, Brian, you're gonna love this, as he dropped the printout on Brian's desk."

As they pore over the data, and Brian's mind begins to wander. The numbers are boooring, and he wants to get to the heart of the matter, the way he sees its nitty-gritty anyway. "Great stuff, M, great stuff, but, frankly, I'm not so much interested in the details of your calculations as I am in the details of the Node's trajectory. Can we talk about that? Can you distill these hundreds of pages of numbers to that? What I want to know, specifically, is whether or not the Node comes back here and when. And if not here, does it come back somewhere else? And where, and when? Like a bus schedule, all the stops and their times Can we do that, please, just that?" Brian was growing exasperated, and M could see it. He realized that as technically inclined as Brian was, he simply couldn't get into the minutiae of any problem that wasn't *his* problem. At those, of course, he excelled, but even then, not if the minutiae were mathematical. That wasn't his cup of tea. Brian was the quintessential experimentalist. M had known this for a long time, many years, but until this very moment he had no appreciation of its depth. "Well, I'm not surprised, " he thought, "should have known better. Yep, that's what Brian needs, a bus schedule for 'Gert'! M responded as he should have started, skipping how the calculations were done and getting to the nitty-gritty of 'Gert's' future path.

"Our friend will be back July 9th at precisely 7:10pm on the Earth's surface basically at the Observatory, travel along the same path as before arriving here at the Shop at precisely 7:28:42, then skipping like a stone on a pond more or less straight up, into space, then following an elliptical trajectory until it comes back here again a couple of weeks later. Is that what you want, Brian?"

"Hell, yeah, M, exactly what I want. Thanks! And the next time? You implied it's coming back here again after the ninth, right."

"Yes, July 25th, and again on the 26th, but earlier on the 25th, 6:33:15am, first thing in the morning, but not here, not through the Shop. That time it's in the middle of the lake!" Brian looks puzzled. "Yep, the lake house lake, *your* lake. And the very next day, on the lake again at 2:32:54pm. How's that for precision?"

"OK, ok," acknowledges Brian, his mind racing at lightspeed, already planning what he'd like to do at each Node encounter. "I want to do some experiments, M, and although you're a theoretician through and through, you have spent some time in a lab, and while you may not like it as much as the orbital mechanics book, you are pretty good at it, setting up and using lab gear and all. What I'd like you to do, is help me, essentially be my lab assistant. What I have in mind can't really be done by one person, I don't think. Will you give it a go?"

"Absolutely. You're the experimentalist, and a damn good one, and even though I'm the equations guy, this sounds like fun, very exciting. Cool. So might I ask, lab boss, what are we trying to do?"

"Tell you what, M, before we get into that too much, let me fiddle with my ideas to see if this whole thing hangs together, and then I'll bore you with the details, deal? And, even though I wrote it down, I have to be doubly sure, the next Node arrival will be here, right here at the Shop, at 7:28:42 two days from now, the ninth, correct?"

"Yes, no question."

"So what gives with the weird times of arrival and even weirder places? At night, in the morning. Weeks apart, then days apart. Here at the Shop, then down at the lake. This is enough to make one batty, no? And... and it raises the question, is it correct? Seems like there should be less, what can I call it, 'randomness; in where the Node is and when. What's the answer, M? These are *your* numbers!"

"Good question, Brian, actually an excellent question, and right on point. Why the variability? It doesn't seem right." Brian bent over with anticipation, and so did M in response. "Remember how this works. The Node's location, trajectory, path, whatever you want to call it, is determined entirely by the motion of the masses that created the Node, in this case the Earth, planet Jupiter and the Sun. Well, their trajectories are smooth, and we know what they are, so why is the Node's so seemingly erratic? A great question!"

"Yes, yes, I'm with you, M, and the answer is...???" Brian couldn't be more alert or attentive.

"The moons, ours and Jupiter's. Jupiter has seventy-nine! That's a *lot* of variability! It goes like this, the Node is created by the large masses, Earth/Jupiter/Sun, and its nominal path is derived from theirs, the 'smooth' trajectory. But each mass with a much smaller mass in orbit around it, or in Jupiter's case, seventy-nine small orbiting masses, has its gravitational field perturbed ever so slightly. That perturbation shows up in the Node's motion, because, remember, it is a region of exactly zero gravity, not a little bit of gravity, not a smidge, but literally none, nada! So you might not think a miniscule disruption of Jupiter's gravitational field could affect our Node so dramatically, but it can. The computer says so, because all of these objects and their orbits are in the Observatory's database and they're all taken into account, each and every one. And the computer says so! Got it?"

"Sure, I get it. So this whacky behavior is due to Jup's having a huge number of really tiny orbiting moons, huh?" M interrupts, "No, no, Brian, don't forget our moon, it's in there, too."

Whereupon Brian continues, "I'm shaken, M, really. I thought this was simple, like add two and two, get four, be done. But no, the difference between the Node's setting down here or fifteen miles away on the lake is because of where Jup's thirty-third moon went that day compared to where it was a week before, something like that!"

"Something. It's really more complicated, but something like that."

"And what if your computer is wrong, to five decimal places? What then?"

"Then I made a mistake. I'll have to fix it."

"And I'm sure you will, but not before two days from now because we won't know if you made a mistake until then! This sucks, M, really sucks! I thought you had this figured out!"

"Chill, Brian, I do, I know I do. Have a little more confidence in me. I know what I'm doing, and, God knows, I don't want to mess it up."

"You know, you're sounding more and more like the pointy-eared Vulcan character on Star Trek. Remember that TV show? Cancelled a few years ago, but entertaining, and the pointy-eared guy - *Spock* was his name, I think -well you're sounding more and more like him. 'Then I made a mistake, Captain. I'll have to fix it," Brian's voice mimicking as best he could *Mr. Spock*'s inflection, "Fix it? Fix it? You never make mistakes, Spock, and we cannot afford one now, do you understand? That enemy ship is almost on us!!"

M nodded sheepishly. He got the message. He had to get the calculations exactly right, or not bother at all.

"Okay, the experiment the day after tomorrow is all the more important, and now you *have* to be here! Will you, M? Get here, say, an hour before? I'm counting on you."

"Let's see," as M thought about what he had to do on Sunday. "I was scheduled for the Observatory Sunday night, but I'm sure I can switch with another grad student. That's easier to switch over a weekend on Sunday, especially a Sunday night. Don't worry, I'll work it out. If I have to, all of a sudden I took ill Sunday afternoon..."

"Good, next thing. Can you be here some time before the 25th, say, for an entire day, or maybe half a day on two days? Not too close to the 25th, say before the 18th? I need someone to work on some electronics. A remote control device. See that bench over there?" as Brian points to a large, well organized electronics work bench replete with electronic test and fabrication equipment. Marty's my electronics tech, but he's on vacation this entire month, somewhere in Central America, Costa Rica, I think. Can't get him back, so I need someone to do some fab while I work on some other stuff. Are you game?" as Brian interrogates M with his look. "Sure, what is it again? What am I doing?" Brian replies, "I'd like you to build that Heathkit GRA-227-6 remote control system - see it there on the bench, in the corner, in the white box? I was going to use it for some other development work, but Gert has re-purposed it. She's, and I'm convinced it's a girl,... she's more important, way more important if I'm right."

"Yep, I'm game."

"I need to have it built, tested, transmitter and receiver both, and then modified for the experiment?"

"What experiment is that, may I ask?"

"The one we're going to do on the 25th, the one I'm going to tell you about when I tell you about it."

"Ah, a mystery. Fine, I like mysteries, and, yes, I'll do your bidding, lab boss. So what kind of mod?"

"That's a television remote over there. I need it to control some mechanical devices, so the interface between the TV remote receiver and the TV has to be reworked to interface with what I hope will be our experiment using some control relays and magnetic releases, that sort of thing. We can discuss the details when I have them worked out. I figure you need a solid day to do this, and if you could pry loose even a little more time, that would be better still. Thanks, M."

- - - - - - - - - - - -

It is interesting how quickly the weather can change, especially in a continental climate compared to a maritime climate. July 9th dawned crisp and clear due to a passing cold front, although 'crisp' is an admittedly relative term in July. Brian didn't notice the temperature, really, nor did M. But what Brian did notice was that as twilight progressed the usually noisy frogs and crickets were quieter than usual, not by much, but enough to be noticed by someone who listened at lot, usually a few days every week. "I wonder what they'll do this time, that is, if the Node shows up? That is, if M is right?" he thought.

"M, dear boy, right on time," it was 5:30. So here's what we're going to do." Brian settled in his Captain's Chair and motioned M to pull another to the desk, as M remarks, "I see the birds are back," noticing twelve of them hanging from a rafter. "Geez, Brian, what's going on here. I left my sunglasses in the Camaro. What is it with the floodlights? You could blind someone. That's *awfully* bright!"

"Part of the experiment, M, part of tonight's experiment. And, yes, the birds are back, twelve identical ones to what was hanging on the 28th, and in exactly the same places. Now, you predict that the Node will be here at 7:28:42, about two hours from now..." M. interrupts, "Ooo, before I forget, which I wouldn't, but before I do because we're getting too much into your weeds, here's Gert's bus schedule," as M fishes in his briefcase for a handwritten page labeled 'NODE ARRIVAL TIMES.' He plops it on the desk. I culled the times from the printouts, you wanted them, so here they are," M said with a certain smugness.

"This is great, M, really great," as he scanned the page in neatly printed block letters:

NODE ARRIVAL TIMES

Date/Time	Comment
June 28th, Wed, ~8pm	Node's 1 appearance, dancing birds/funky satellite
July 5th, Wed	Learn that we both experienced the Node on the same night!
July 9th, Sun 7:28:42pm	Node's second appearance, Observatory then NovaTek.
July 25th, Tue, 6:33:13am	On the Lake
July 26th, Wed, 2:32:54pm	On the Lake
Aug 12th, Sat, 11:17:17pm	At NovaTek
Aug 13th, Sun, 1:08:19pm	On the Lake
Sep 12th, Tue, 5:05:07am	On the Lake

"We know - I mean *I* know - what we have to do for the 25th. After that, depending on what happens, it's up for grabs. By the way, maybe we should call this the 'GertHound Bus Schedule', hee-hee?'", Brian's retort with a silly look, "What'dya think? "

"Sure, whatever you want to call it. After all, you named the,... oops, I mean *our* Node! You're sounding mysterious again, Brian, and silly, so let's concentrate on tonight for now. Tell me about tonight, please."

"Basically what I want to do tonight is two things: One, confirm that you're right, to five decimal places, as you keep saying, about the Node showing up, the exact time. And, two, measure its properties, if we can, how big it is, how fast it's moving, what the wave looks like. The equipment you see here, including the bright lights, is to do that, and you're here in case I need any help, probably not, but definitely as an observer to confirm what happens, *capische*?"

"I do, indeed I do. So what's the setup?"

"Okay, you see those two cameras, and the birds?" as he points to a couple of cameras on the same side of the rafter, each about three feet from the end of the bird line and about six feet away from it, and pointing to the bird line itself, twelve of them in a row about a foot apart, exactly where they were the night the Node passed by. "About every two feet there's a vertical ruler that I cobbled up, marked in inches. They run to the floor from the rafter. Finally, see the horizontal rulers? There are three of them, one near each end of the bird line, and one near the middle, and they're perpendicular to the bird line starting at the line and protruding about ten feet to one side about half way up the extended springs."

M surveys the setup, and he's duly impressed. It's clear from the arrangement that Brian plans to make measurements as the Node moves through, and for a hastily crafted 'experimental rig,' as it would be called at Poly, this one was pretty good. "Props, Brian. Nice job. What about timing, got a handle on that?"

"Yes, I'm using the cameras as my 'clocks.' They're Nikon F2 Photomic FTn's with the mirror locked up shooting high speed, four frames per second. This is similar to the hardware that flew on Apollo 15. The lights, by the way, are to give us a good exposure, and, yes, I have checked it! That's a Nikkor 55mm f/1.2 lens, very fast, shooting wide open, and the cameras have 250 frame F250 motorized cassettes loaded with Fujifilm Neopan 1600 sixteen hundred speed black and white film. We can push process it to 3200 if necessary, so we're going to get some very nice, and I hope very interesting pictures! With the high frame rate we have a time resolution of 1/3 of a second, which based on how fast the Node moved through before, should be more than enough to measure what it's doing. On the other side you'll see a quartz wall clock, very accurate, and I'll set it to agree with the National Bureau of Standards time broadcast just before the Node should arrive. That will check the accuracy of your predicted arrival time. What do you think, M?"

"Fabulous, Brian, really good, the kind of experiment we *would* design at Poly, and so fast, you did it so fast! This Node thing really has you 'juiced,' to borrow a term I heard not that long ago. Must say, I *am* impressed. And I think we will learn a lot about the Node... One question, though, the little bright orange pieces of twine all along your rulers... what for?"

"Oh, should have explained that, sorry. They're to measure the Node's size, I hope. Streamers that are in the Node will become weightless, no gravity, and should begin to float I would think. The demarcation between the ones that do and the ones that don't will be the approximate Node boundary, where it starts and where it stops. The reason the streamers are only on one side and only below the rafter is that I would expect the Node to be symmetrical, am I right?"

"Well, off the top of my head, beats me Brian, beats me! Maybe. I think that's a reasonable assumption, at least to first order. But, asymmetry, hmmm... I can think of reasons why the Node may not be symmetrical, but I don't know that we can compute that with what we do know... not even to a couple of decimal places, let alone five..." was M's sort-of-wiseguy reply. "On the symmetry business, remind me later to tell you the tale of the physicist hired by some Midwest milk producers, but that's for another day. Let's see what tonight brings. Good experiment, Brian, good experiment, well planned and well executed. Now I'm *really* anxious."

Brian pushed back in his Captain's Chair while M relaxed in his. 7:02 read the punch clock. "Less than half an hour. This is nerve-wracking, M, pretty stressful. I don't often get into stuff like this, actually I *never* get into stuff like this."

"Chill, Brian, relax. There's nothing we can do but wait, only a few minutes to go. Calm down, And don't break out your *GlyndaWitchIt*,...or whatever it is, at least not just yet. I do believe you'll have reason to, but not now," as they both stared at the punch clock and took deep breaths slowly exhaling to calm their nerves.

Chapter 5 - *Professor* Ravelli?

"Hello, Jean? This is Emilio. I was wondering if you, and maybe Leigh, and I could get together to talk about..." Jean interrupts," Bet I can guess. Someone's birthday party?" "Yep, you guessed. Could you call Leigh and ask if she can make it, I'm thinking some late afternoon next week, pretty much any day? What do you say?" As Jean feigns pondering Emilio's request, "Sometimes, M, you're sooo... serious! Of course we'll be there. We're Izzy's two best friends. Think we'd miss helping you plan her 29th birthday party? It is the birthday, right? And it's going to be a surprise, right? That's why you want to talk to us, right?" M replies with noticeable excitement, "Correct again, Counselor, all that, correct on all counts,... oh, and one more thing we can discuss next week. A plan?" "Sure is, M, I know Leigh will be excited, so we'll let you know which day is best, thanks. And, hmm, I'm guessing the 'one more thing,' you're not going to tell me now, are you?" "Nope." "Bet I can guess that, too...but I won't..." Jean trails off with the auditory equivalent of a smirk. "She knows," thinks M, "She knows!" "You're great friends, Jeannie. Izz loves ya! And so do I. See you next week," as M ended the call.

M was relieved that Jean and Leigh could make it. He knew that not including them in planning Isabella's surprise party would hurt their feelings deeply, not to mention Izzy's. They were the female equivalent of the Three Musketeers, without being swashbucklers, M hoped anyway, spending a lot of time together, often girls' weekends away, inseparable as best of friends ever since high school. Each went her own way, Jean becoming a successful, much sought-after criminal defense attorney, Leigh turning to teaching and coincidentally working in the same high school as Izz and Brian's cousin Tom, and, of course, Izzy just finishing up her B.A. degree in Business Administration. Jean went to law school and Leigh to graduate school straight from college, but Izzy didn't graduate when they did. She decided to take some time off half way through college, after completing her sophomore year, a couple of years she figured, because she felt that she wouldn't really be able to use her degree without some 'real world' experience, and she didn't want to pursue an MBA right away, if at all. Those 'couple of years' became nearly seven while Izzy rose through positions of progressively greater responsibility, finally as head of accounting in a mid-sized financial services firm. In a sense, she had arrived professionally, but not having completed her bachelor's degree was an impediment, the sort of thing not mentioned but clearly sensed. So, Isabella Healy, as she was wont to do, went back to complete her degree and now held a 3.98 GPA with graduation coming in May, 1973, the same month Emilio would graduate with his PhD if all went as planned with his dissertation.

Like the watched pot, the punch clock in NovaTek's lab ticked at a rate much slower than one second per second, at least that's how it seemed to both M and Brian. "It's only a matter of minutes, Brian, but it seems like forever. If this doesn't work, if the Node doesn't show up in,...let's see, it's 7:05:10 in five seconds,... so in 13 minutes 32 seconds, then I would have to wonder if I deserve a doctorate after all. This is a real test, Brian, a real test, and, hate to admit it, but I'm nervous," M's distress being apparent. "You know, in all the work I've ever done, nothing has been as precise as this, as I've been saying, 'to five decimal places.' The ionosphere is an altogether different beast, especially when you're trying to understand how things work on a scale of meters in length, not millimeters. Very different, and certainly not to 'five decimal places,' very different."

"You done, M? I know you're uptight, so am I, but you have to calm down, chill a little. What's the big deal if you're not right, and we're going to know in just a couple of minutes? What's the big deal? Sure I'll be disappointed, but that's all I'll be. I won't be devastated, they way you're sounding. '...deserve a doctorate,' good grief, how can you even ask such a dumb question? Don't suck up any more of the air in here! Please, don't, you don't want to scare Greta off, do you! Look," as Brian points to the very accurate punch clock, "we're on final countdown, thirty seconds to go," as Brian rests his cheek on the back of his hands that form a teepee with their fingertips touching, and his elbows on the desk. "Ten, nine, eight, seven, six, five, four, three, two, one..." and... nothing happens. "What the hell? Geez, nothing! It's time, 7:28:42pm, so where's the damn Node? Well, M, maybe you should talk to Professor Hanlon about this PhD business after all?" Brian says sarcastically with a look almost bordering on contempt. "Sorry, M, sorry. I didn't mean that, I'm sorry. It's just that there was such a build-up to this very moment, and now such a letdown. I was emotionally crashing, didn't mean what I said. Sorry."

"You're right, Brian. A real roller coaster. I was as high as you, believe me, and I think I crashed even further. But at the very instant Gert didn't show, I realized why, and we're back in business!"

"Cut the bullshit, M. You said it yourself, high and low, and now we're low, and now you're on your way up again!? So what exactly did you 'realize,' what gets this sorry episode back on track? You who accused me of maybe selling 'Nodes in a Bottle,' or something like that? So what flavor of snake oil are you peddling now? You did something wrong, M, pure and simple. Now you shouldn't drop out of graduate school because of it, but c'mon admit the obvious, you screwed up somehow, big time!"

"Right again, Brian. I did screw up. Look at the clock right now, what time is it?"

"7:35, M, and you're not blind, you can see that just as well as I can."

"Yes, indeed, it's 7:35pm *Eastern Daylight Time*. But what is the *Eastern Standard Time*?"

"Shit! Oh, yes, I think I see it! Right now it's 6:36 EST, not 7:36 as the clock shows! That's it, right? Your calculations are based on Coordinated Universal Time, the international standard, not on our Daylight Savings Time, right? That's it, isn't it?"

"Yes, Brian. What I did wrong was I failed to consider that one hour time difference. Gert will be back in a little less than an hour, at 8:28:42 EDT. We just have to wait!"

And so they did. And Gert showed up precisely when predicted, to the second. Brian and Emilio were so thoroughly relieved that the *Glenfiddich* was uncorked and poured glass after another. M's calculations were accurate after all, to five decimal places... "It's been a day, Brian, and after this *GlyndaWitchIt,* or whatever it is..." M said with a bit of slur, "I think we should to the debrief in a couple of days, plus you have to develop the camera film. What d'ya think." "Agreed, M, I'm spent, too, and yep, I have to develop the film. Today's Sunday, so how about Tuesday afternoon, say, four o'clock at *Stella's*?" "I'll be there , Brian, 4pm straight up, E.. D.. T," M replied with a snicker and smirk of great satisfaction.

- - - - - - - - - - - -

You wouldn't think traffic would be a bear a little before four in the afternoon in a mid-sized city, but it was, and besides that, as usual, M was running late. "Four PM straight up, E D T, isn't that what you said Sunday night?" Brian remarked as M shuffled up the booth. "Would you believe 'The dog ate my computer printout, and that's why I'm late?" "Nope, pretty hackneyed, I'd say, plus Kepler is a cat, and cat's aren't known for eating homework, or printout... But that's OK, you're rarely on time, I know that, and I'm here sipping on that pitcher of beer thinking all kinds of thoughts about Gert, and what this might mean. So your being late is no big deal," said Brian as he poured M a tall glass of the frothy, pale lager.

"This is the official 'debrief,' M. Let's start. I've gone through all the data we got Sunday night, Gert's approximate spatial extent, shape, and ground speed. Here are my calculations and the measured data," as Brian opened a lab notebook replete with diagrams and measurements, and a pile of photographs. "Very impressive, Brian, very impressive. I see you remember well how to write a lab report, and this is a doozy! Hats off," whereupon M and Brian went through the notebook, page by page, photo by photo, checking and rechecking the measurements taken from the photos, things like the streamer distortions, their duration and angle to the vertical, and so on. It was a veritable gold mine of data, sufficient information to accurately characterize its essential features.

"Geez, nearly 6:30. That took a while, but well worth it," was M's conclusion. "To summarize, (1) Gert was more than twenty feet wide, and as far as we can tell, at least eight feet high above ground, that is, the floor, with no conclusion for extent below. (2) Gravity suspension was maximum at the geometric center and tapered more or less linearly away from there. This is consistent with the notion that the interior spacetime isn't *perfectly* flat but very close, that, in turn, because of some inevitable 'ripple' in how the vector fields add up. (3) The Node moved at about 25 mph along the Earth's surface. (4) And, of course, the Node's arrival time and course can be predicted...yes, to five decimal places!" and M closed the notebook, picked up his beer, and motioned to Brian that a toast was in order. "Well, may not seem like much, M, but the fact is we learned a *lot*, certainly the Node's key parameters, and I'm very satisfied," as his glass met M's, "Cheers!"

"But there is one thing that puzzles me, quite a bit,..." M starts almost as if talking to himself, "the streamer distortions. They're not much, very hard to see, but they're there and all in the direction of the Node's motion. And if you look very carefully at the birds, ditto, a barely perceptible, a miniscule but visible offset the Node's direction of travel. This puzzles me because I would expect the just opposite, a random distribution because there is effectively zero gravity within the Node. Oh, well, something to ponder, which I will." M's soliloquy was cut short by their order arriving. "Pizza's here, M, we can get to the fine points later, the pinpoints I'd say. Let's eat!" Brian was obviously excited.

The talk over a hot pizza, half 'shroom/green pepper/onion, half pepperoni with five other toppings chosen by the waiter, who happened to be the same fellow that waited on them last time, was mostly small talk, about how things were going in each other's lives, generally, that sort of thing. But just as Brian picked up the last slice of his 'garbage pizza' his tone and look changed. "M, there is something I think we should discuss, now, and it's serious business - what to do with what we know. I'm guessing no one else knows about this, that it just fell on us, my dancing birds, your funky satellite, and just by luck two people with the right backgrounds to pull off Sunday night's experiment because you can calculate where Nodes go and when. I'm thinking there's no one else on this planet who knows about this! What do you say?"

"I think you're probably right, Brian, and in between relishing this pizza and beer, I've been thinking about what we do with it, knowledge I agree is probably ours alone, remarkable, truly remarkable, out of almost four *billion* people, only us, kind of scary!! This really does require serious thought. And that streamer business, that puzzles me."

"Yes, M, I agree completely, *very* serious thought, it's what should we do next. But I don't think this is the time to get into it. I have some ideas already, and I'm sure you do, too, but at least for me, I want to digest this and, as you would say, *ponder* it. How 'bout we both do that and get together again, say, at your place, Thursday night? Is that good?"

"Deal, Brian, that's good, around seven o'clock. There's something else I want to talk to you about, though, nothing to do with Nodes. It's Izzy's birthday, a little more than a month off, and I want to give her a great surprise party, a real bash, something special for her 29th. I'd like to do it at the Lake House, and I need your OK for that?"

"Of course, M, no problem. The Lake House is yours... am I invited?" was Brian's wiseguy reply.

"Keep his up, and it'll be 'no'... maybe I'll put you in charge of decorations?" was M's.

"Well, now that I think about it, 'modern industrial' as a theme, you know, pipes, and gears, and light bulbs with curly filaments. How about that?"

"Done kidding around? The serious thing I want to talk to you about is I'm thinking of making this a joint birthday and 'ringing' party, if that's the right word, as in an engagement ring. God knows, it's been long enough, Izzy and I as a couple, and we've talked about making it official when I'm done in school, so this actually would be a kind of short engagement if we do the wedding, say, shortly after I graduate next May. And she'll be done with her degree, too. Think she'd like that, maybe a June wedding, maybe on the 22nd, the longest day of the year? I want to know what you think? I know Izz will be asking your opinion, too."

"I just wonder why it took you so long, brother-in-law-to-be! Of course Izzy's talked to me about this, usually asking if you said anything to me about it. And of course I told her 'no,' because that's the truth, at least as far as timing goes. You've made your intentions crystal clear to her and to me, M, so none of this is a surprise, except possibly that you didn't do it sooner..."

"Great! So I have your blessing, not that I need it... How do you think your parents will react? They love Izzy more than you, M, but they love you, too, and they'll be delighted, nothing short of thrilled that their only daughter is marrying a fine fellow, smart, hard working, completely committed, what more would they, could they want? Of course, there's the Italian-Irish issue, but I think they can look past that..."

"Huh? Really? You mean Dublin versus Rome, which wins?"

"Nah, it's Dublin versus the Vatican, and the Vatican wins... and I'm only joking. The only other thing better than marrying you is maybe Isabella's becoming a nun. Fat chance, that! Good talk, M. I'm off. See you Thursday around seven, your place," with which Brian dropped cash on the table, grabbed the notebook and photos, and headed out waving to M as he left.

- - - - - - - - - - - -

"Hello," M picked up the phone as he put down a dog-eared, beat up copy of NASA Technical Note D-1539, *A Satellite Orbit Computation Program for Izsak's Second-Order Solution of Vinti's Dynamical Problem*, February 1963. "Oh, hi, Jean. I was hoping to hear from you. Have you talked to Leigh?" while still fingering the Note. "Great, that's great. This coming Wednesday, works for me. In fact, it works well because at two o'clock I'm meeting with my thesis advisor, Professor Hanlon, so getting together late that afternoon is perfect." "I'll let Leigh know, M. She's really excited about this, being in on planning the party, and she has some great ideas."

"On the calendar, Jean, let's say 4:30. That good for you guys? How about a spot where we can get some munchies and drinks, appetizers, that sort of thing, take our time and not feel rushed? Do you have any place in mind?"

"Hmm... let me think," as Jean mulls the question. "Yes, I do, how about *Fortune Cookie*? Ever been there?"

"Nope, I haven't, and I haven't heard of it. Is this a place you think is good?"

"Yes, Emilio. A very good spot, you'll see. Maybe a bit pricey, but believe me, well worth it."

"That's a ringing endorsement, Jeannie, all that I needed. We're on, and, no argument, my treat, right?" while all along M's thinking, "Well, this may not be cheap, but Jeannie and Leigh are such super people, not to mention Izzy's best friends." "Okay, M, your treat, we're looking forward to this! See you there, four thirty. Bye." And Jean's call ended.

- - - - - - - - - - - -

Emilio and Dr. Hanlon often met in M's cubbyhole of an office, but today Michael wanted to get together in his office. M walked up the two flights of stairs rather than take the elevator because the ribs were feeling much, much better, and he knew that moderate exercise would hasten the healing process. Hanlon's office was fairly large, well lit with large windows overlooking the quad, a good sized desk, a couple of free chairs, plenty of bookshelf and file cabinet space, and a six-foot table covered high with papers. In that office were thirty years of books, reference papers, project reports, as well as piles of Hanlon's published work, mostly but not all in the field of ionospheric physics. The frosted glass window in the entrance door read simply, in plain gold foil letters on two lines, Michael J. Hanlon, Ph.D., Professor of Physics. He had been at Polytechnic University for some three decades, having started his career there as a post doc in atomic physics. That research catapulted his work in ionospheric phenomena in part because of Polytech's participation in atmospheric research at the Observatory.

Hanlon was a key figure in the Observatory's expansion into serious ionospheric work using radio and radar techniques, and he was the Principal Investigator for all of the University's work in that area. Dr. Hanlon had so far supervised twenty-two doctoral candidates and easily twice that many master's level students. He loved figuring out how the ionosphere worked, but he loved teaching more. His students gave him a satisfaction that an ionized gas never could. Emilio Ravelli was one of Professor Hanlon's prize PhD students who met and exceeded every expectation that Hanlon and the University had of him. Their personal relationship grew and deepened over the years, and Hanlon would help M in any way he could, fully expecting M to embark on a spectacular scientific career.

"Hello, Emilio. Please, come in and sit," as he motioned M into the office with a sweeping gesture towards the two chairs opposite his desk. As M took up a chair, Hanlon sat in his, taking a relaxed posture, smiling. "Good to see you, M. You seem to have recovered nicely from the accident. How are you feeling?"

"Very well, Dr. Hanlon, very well. The ribs and bruising are pretty much healed, and my head trauma never was an issue, a bad knock, but beyond that nothing much. So, bottom line, I'd say I'm back to normal."

"I can't tell you how happy I am to hear that, M. The entire faculty was quite concerned because of the, how shall I say it,... because of the 'odd' nature of your crash. Fact is, we're still puzzled by it. Do you want to talk about it, or no? I don't want to pry."

"Well, Michael, not now if you don't mind. I do want to talk to you about it because it involves some work I've done on an application of gravitational theory, but, really, at this point I have more pressing concerns regarding my thesis, things like that."

"Of course, M, when and if you're ready. I'm more than a thesis adviser, you know that. I'm a friend, and I happily will help you in any way I can. Just keep that in mind, okay?"

"And you've become a good friend, I do know and appreciate that, thank you! One thing makes me curious, though. Why meet here instead of my palatial grad student digs in the old building?" M sensed that something was going on besides a routine thesis checkup, and he hoped Hanlon would explain.

"You're smart in more ways than just science, Emilio. You're quite right, there is a reason for meeting here, and it has to do with that," as Hanlon pointed to a several inch thick pile of papers at one corner of the long table. "Those are proposals for the extension of funding for ongoing projects, most from various agencies of the federal government, as you well know, some from state agencies, and a small number from private businesses, corporations. The project that funds your work has an extension proposal in that pile."

M's eyes narrowed, ever so slightly, and his forehead furrowed, ever so slightly, reflecting a sense of foreboding as he moved his chair over to the table. "This pile?" as M patted the corner pile to which Hanlon clearly had pointed. "Yes, M, that pile."

M hoped that he wasn't about to be hit by the proverbial brick. "Okay, is there a problem, Michael?"

"No, not at all. Not at all. Good news all around, which is why I wanted to meet here. You'll see. Here we are at the end of July, and, again as you well know, the federal fiscal year begins October 1st. Proposals for that year are usually evaluated and they're funded, or not, sometime in late August or early September."

"And?" M interrupts, not liking where the conversation seems to be headed. "God," he thinks, "What if my work isn't going to be funded? What a disaster that would be!" as M's thoughts immediately fun to Izzy. "And what does this have to do with me? Anything?"

"I learned a couple of days ago from your project's COTR that extended funding would be forthcoming through the *entire* fiscal year! That's the good news, for both of us. The cuts in federal spending that you probably have read about are across-the-board, but your work has been singled out as "critical" to the national interest, which means it goes right to the top of the list of projects that must continue, no if's, and's or but's! Your support as a Research Assistant next year is guaranteed...", but M interrupted.

"Okay, okay, Michael. Sounds like great news, fabulous news, and I must say I really am grateful. Thank you. This couldn't come at a better time! Izzy and I are on the verge, and I'll tell you about that. But before we get to that, I am confused, about how all this works. What's a 'COTR'? Sounds like some sort of nasty bug..." was M's honest but awkward interruption.

"Oh, I should have known, you're a neophyte in this professor-eat-professor world of living contract-to-contract. COTR is the acronym for 'Contracting Officer's Technical Representative,' the fed's go-between between the government officer who actually awards a contract and the person actually doing the work. Over time most COTR's develop good and often close working relationships with the contractor, in this case, me. Bill Gayle and I have worked together for years on all manner of ionospheric research, and he's a good guy, always straight-up with me. In this case he's doing me, make that us, a favor by giving me a heads up on the continued funding. And I'm delighted, now that I know, to let you know. I thought here would be a better place for this conversation than your 'palatial digs' as I've heard you call them, " Hanlon chuckled while rolling his eyes.

M's apprehension dissipated far more quickly than it came. "Whew, and I was thinking you had bad news. Boy, am I relieved. Such a relief to know I will continue to be paid my outlandishly high stipend," M's obviously unsuccessful attempt at levity.

"That's right, no RA, no stipend, so let us both thank Bill for letting us know that that won't happen. We also should thank Bill for letting us know that something else is in the works."

"Really, Michael, what?"

"A no-bid add-on to the existing project." Hanlon sat back in his chair and slowly rubbed his chin as he evaluated M's response, confusion evident in his slightly squinted eyes and gaze off to the side, slightly, a quizzical look, and keen interest evident from his leaning forward, slightly, with his hands on his knees. "Okay, Michael, I'm perplexed, but curious. What is this, exactly, and what does it have to do with me?"

"What the add-on does is pay a PhD student who's nearly finished, someone like you, a partial TA stipend. Whoever gets the award has to teach one undergraduate course to encourage an interest in ionospheric physics because that's an area of growing importance to national security. Hence, its 'critical' nature. In short, what over government wants is more people like you, scientists studying the ionosphere. Cool, huh?" M knew that the outwardly calm and composed Dr. Michael J. Hanlon, PhD, Professor of Physics, was on the inside at this very moment like the five year old who just got a puppy for her birthday. How? Hanlon's look and language.

"Want the job, Emilio? It's yours, if you want the job," said Hanlon with a Cheshire Cat grin.

"May I ask, Michael, who else is in the running?" although M was quite sure he knew.

"Greg, Mandrake, he's the runner up so to speak, next in line in the pecking order because both you and he are in essentially the same position in terms of finishing up."

"That alone, Michael, is enough for me to jump at this! Mandrake! Pity the undergrads who would be stuck with Mandrake! If the purpose is to encourage students to get into ionospheric research, believe, me he's the wrong guy, make that times two, wrong, wrong!" as M became visibly agitated just thinking about his nemesis. His disdain for Mandrake was extreme, to say the least.

"I figured as much, M. I know how you feel about him, as we've discussed before. So this a 'yes,' I take it, you'll be the department's new part-time Teaching Assistant?"

"Sign me up! In thinking about it, this will be fun, back to the days when all I was a TA, and I thoroughly enjoyed it. Thank you, Michael, thank you!" as M nodded his head while smiling to acknowledge his new job.

"You start with the fall semester, one course, and your RA stipend will be increased by twenty percent. I'll let Dean Scott know you've accepted so the Curriculum Committee can plan accordingly. Everyone will be pleased with this, M. I'm very happy you said 'yes.'"

Thank you, Michael," as M smiled, his tone reflecting true appreciation for Professor Hanlon's concern and support. "Alright, on to the next topic," continued M, "Let's talk about my research."

"Before that, M, you mentioned Izzy, your being 'on the verge.' Of what, as if I can't guess?" Hanlon asked with a broad grin.

"I'm proposing to her on the thirty-first. I hope she says 'yes.' I think she will. We've been together a long time and talked marriage many times, so I think she will. Wish me luck!"

Dr. Hanlon obliged, wishing M the best with Izzy, and then he and M spent the next hour or so going through M's most recent data. They showed convincingly that the high altitude electron density profiles fit well with M's theory of a strong latitudinal dependence resulting from different atmospheric thicknesses and densities, data that were acquired by ISR's 'look angle' runs the night Gert showed up. M's theory allowed accurate calculation of the profiles, which, in turn, were critical in accurate long-range radiowave propagation estimates. M's theoretical work now had extensive experimental verification, and Professor Hanlon reiterated that M did not have much more to do before starting to write.

"Thanks again, Michael, for all your help and support. I and Izzy, too, I know, really appreciate it," as M glanced at the time. "Speaking of which, I should run. I'm meeting two of Izzy's friends to help plan her 29th surprise birthday party on August 12th. You're on the list, hope you'll attend."

"My pleasure, M. Good meeting, now go, make some good plans. And, please say hello to Izzy from me." M picked up his packed briefcase, and turned with a slight wave of the hand as he walked through the door, self-satisfied knowing that Izzy would approve of his new role as TA and that it would help his finances considerably.

- - - - - - - -

M parked his car, just as Jean and Leigh happened to pull up beside him. He was out of the Camaro first, walked over to Jean's door, and greeted the two best friends, "Well, hello, ladies. What perfect timing! Allow me," as he opened Jean's door and motioned for her to exit with a bit of a flourish. "Please, stay there, Leigh, and I'll be right over to get your door." But Leigh had already opened hers and was on her way out as M rounded their car. "My goodness, M, chivalry lives on! I can't remember the last time I was treated so courteously, thank you so much!" as Leigh giggled slightly with a somewhat fawning look. "I think I'm jealous of Izzy..." "Don't be, Leigh, I'm only nice on Wednesdays," M jokingly remarked.

Pleasantries aside, M led the way up a short but twisty walkway to the restaurant's front door, a large, ornate, double panel wooden affair sporting two carved dragons, one on each side. The door looked hand-carved, but maybe not. Immediately inside was a hostess's lectern staffed by a very attractive young lady in a flowing black Chinese print sheath dress adorned with dark maroon dragons.. "Greetings. Welcome to *Fortune Cookie*. A party of three?" as she surveyed the new arrivals. M replied "Yes, but we're not here for an early dinner, a 'business' meeting of sorts, so just a few appetizers and drinks, and if possible a quiet table where we can linger," at which point Jean chimed in, "Is Linda here today?" "Yes, ma'am she is. Shall I tell her you asked after her?" "Yes, please, my name is Jean Simmons." "Happy to do that," as the hostess took the hint, "and I think I have the perfect table, by a window overlooking the garden, in a corner that's usually quiet. Will that do?" she asked in a most obsequious tone. "Yes, indeed," replied M. "Please follow me," as dragon girl led the triumvirate off to that quiet corner table overlooking the garden.

"Jean, good to see you. Back so soon? I'm delighted, of course! And welcome to your associates," said Linda Lee, chef/owner of *Fortune Cookie*. Over quite some time she and Jean had developed a friendly personal relationship because Jean often brought clients or associates, other attorneys, to a working lunch or dinner. Jean had become a 'regular,' and was acknowledged as such by being invited to celebratory private dinners at *The Cookie*, as many called it, usually around a holiday, Christmas or Thanksgiving or in the summer on Memorial Day or the Fourth. It was Linda's way of expressing her appreciation, saying 'thanks,' for the repeat patronage that contributed so much to *Cookie*'s success.

"Thank you, Linda, good to be back. Let me introduce my friends, Leigh Jackson, and Emilio Ravelli, soon to be Doctor Ravelli," as she gently pointed to each with an open hand. "Pleased to meet you, Leigh, and you, Doctor Ravelli. I assume you're completing a degree soon?" "Yes, ma'am, my PhD in Physics at Polytechnic University, next May." "My, how impressive, Emilio. Congratulations! And I hope you and Leigh become regulars at *Fortune Cookie* as Jean has. If you're here, please let me know." "Thank you for those kind words, Linda, and for the kind invitation. I already know I'll be back," replied M, as Leigh piped up, "Me, too, Linda, with some other friends, I'll be back son, I already know that."

Whereupon M said, "Linda, we're here to plan my, I hope, soon-to-be-fiancé's 29th birthday party, so we'd like to order several appetizers, not a big meal..." but before M could continue Linda interrupted. "Let me see what's cooking in the kitchen..." and Linda departed leaving Jean, Leigh and M to get to the business that brought them there that day, Izzy's 29th. She returned about twenty minutes later accompanied by her headwaiter. "Jean, Michael, Leigh, please allow me to introduce Hai Rong. Hai is *Fortune Cookie's* Major-domo and Sommelier. He will be waiting your table today," as Linda turned and left.

Hai began, "May I recommend the Chateau Latour 1965 Pauillac, a truly excellent wine, as well as a selection of dim sum. These all will be prepared by hand by Linda using only the freshest ingredients. Perhaps you might start with two dim sum, and I can bring others as your stay progresses?" M was hungry and his response immediate, "Yes, indeed, Hai. What's on the dim sum menu?" "Right now, handmade dumplings, Pork or Shrimp, Vegetable Spring rolls, Miso Butter dumplings, House-Made Pork and Egg rolls, and Hand-Folded Crab Wontons. And if any of you enjoys sushi, Shrimp Tempura roll, and two spicy sushi rolls, Kung Pao Dragon and Spicy Tuna, all quite good."

"No doubt, Hai, no doubt. Sounds delicious! How about we start with the first three you mentioned, enough for the three of us, please. And because I think we'll be here for a while, we can work our way through the rest of the list as the afternoon progresses! And that wine sounds fabulous, let's do that, too." M *was* hungry! Then, turning to the women, "Is this OK with you, Leigh, Jean? I suppose I should have been more polite and asked, but I figure if you like Chinese, well, there has to be *something* agreeable on Hai's list." Both answered at the same time "Yes", "Sure", with Jean saying "Really sounds great, and... your treat, right?" M remembered his remark when he and Jean spoke, replying "Yes, indeed, my treat, and I'm celebrating in a way. Just got a raise for my work at Polytech. So today I'm a big spender! I'll tell you about it later," and the three began in earnest the work they were there to do.

But, first, M had a question. "Jean, before we get into the party planning, wasn't this place the snooty old French restaurant, *Acquitaine*, I think it was? Not a place Izz and I could afford..." "Yes, M, they closed Shop, oh, maybe five years ago, and Linda picked up the lease shortly after that. *Fortune Cookie* is her pet project. She's the chef/owner. She worked at some very high end Chinese restaurants all across the country, and finally decided to open her own, name notwithstanding. Linda's degree is from the Culinary Institute of America, and that's a big deal, a real feather. She engaged our firm for legal services, and although I do only criminal defense, I met and got to know Linda. She's a good egg, and she prepares the best, I mean 'best,' Chinese cuisine I've ever had." M was impressed, and it showed on his face. "Wow, impressive. I'm adding the *Cookie*... - still don't get that name, by the way, maybe before we go? - I'll take Izzy here, and from your ringing endorsement, I know she'll like it. Thanks for the introduction! Now to work."

M had been carrying a lab notebook with him, which he laid open on the table, and on the first page, at the top, in very large fancy letters, wrote !! IZZY's 29TH !! "God, she's gonna love this, " he exclaimed, "I hope..."

"Jean, you start, please. What do you think we should do? It's going to be at the Lake House. When should it be? Her birthday is August 5th. That's a Saturday, so I think on that very day, no?"

And Jean, and Leigh, and M got into the nitty-gritty of planning Izzy's party, a humdinger for sure, forty-seven invited guests, a catered but informal meal, party decorations, hats, party blowers, the kind that unravel when blown into, and kazoos, everything to get the grown-ups in a partying mood, just like the kids who would be in attendance. And, for those grown-ups, appropriate libations, beer, wine, and a full bar M figured would be staffed by Brian because that was Brian's sort of thing.

M speculated aloud, "On the catering, Jean, do you think Linda Lee would want to do it? Does *Fortune Cookie* cater? Do you know? Think everyone would like Chinese? Or maybe we should go more mainstream American?"

"Don't know, M, but I'll find out. As to the type of food, if you personally don't have a strong preference, how about Leigh and I bat around some ideas and come up with a recommendation in a couple of days? This requires some thought. We don't want anyone going away hungry, or unhappy, huh?"

"You guys know me well enough to know I like any kind of food, as long as it's top notch. So, let's do that, whatever you suggest, Jean, Leigh. How about the cake? Can you take care of that, too? Something very tasteful, in every way, and big enough to serve the whole bunch?"

"Yep, Leigh and I can do that, too. I think we know some good, I mean *very* good, bakeries that can handle this. So when you say 'tasteful,' I suppose that rules out a giant cake with some hunk jumping out of at just the right moment?" Jean said with a glimmer.

"Wouldn't that depend on which hunk you had in mind, say, Peter O'Toole the actor?...Nope, no hunk in the cake, thanks..."

was M's reply at his somewhat futile attempt to meet levity with levity.

Leigh took another swipe, "Gee, I kind of liked the hunky cake idea. But I guess that's shut down, huh, too bad," and at that Jean donned her lawyerly posture, adding "I think we've covered it all. If we left anything out we can get to it by phone, agreed? This should be one spectacular birthday party, M. Izz will be on cloud nine! Birthdays always have been important to her, so this should take the cake, so to speak, the hunkless cake..."

The three were on the verge of leaving, but M hadn't paid the bill yet, the entire list of dim sum and sushi, servings for three, having been heartily consumed by them over about four hours' time, and, needless to say, along with a second bottle of wine. He looked around for Hai, quickly caught his attention, and it was clear to Hai what M wanted, to settle up and be on his way. Hai motioned that he would be right over, but instead Linda Lee showed up. "Yes, Emilio, ladies, was everything okay? Did you enjoy the dim sum and sushi?" M replied, "My goodness, Linda, YES, and that's a capital letters YES! Fabulous, nothing short of fabulous! Jean filled us in on your background, by the way, CIA and all, and your experience all over the country. I can see why *Fortune Cookie* is so good. Props!" "Thank you," Linda replied, "and, by the way, your meal today is on the house."

M, Jean and Leigh were taken aback, totally surprised. The last thing they expected was complimentary food accompanied by a very nice wine. "No, no, please," said M as he took a credit card from his wallet. "Chinese hospitality will not allow that, Emilio, please put the card away, no argument. In fact," as Linda handed each a nicely printed and quite formal looking invitation, "*Fortune Cookie's* end-of-summer celebration is the weekend after Labor Day. You're invited. I do hope you can make it, and it is RSVP so we can plan accordingly." "Thank you, so much," was Jean's immediate response. "I definitely will be here! I recall your last celebration, a twelve course meal with the finest dishes. I think it lasted about six hours!!" Leigh and M were bewildered, to be invited after not ever having been paying customers, but so pleasantly surprised were they that they said almost simultaneously, "I'll be here," "Count me in."

At that the three exchanged goodbyes and headed out, M thinking, "Jean and Leigh really are good friends. Izzy's fortunate to have them! And, Linda, wow, she's marvelous, too!" as he slowly pulled the Camaro SS out of its parking spot.

Chapter 6 - What's in a Node?

M's head was spinning in a thousand directions all at the same time, Brian showing up soon, yesterday's meeting with Mike Hanlon, Jeannie and Leigh and the party, and the Node, the Node, the Node, actually *billions* of Nodes, what can we do, what should we do, when, where, and how, and why, and what will Brian come up with, knowing he's a devil-may-care adventurer at heart. "I really have to organize my thinking," thinks M, "maybe prioritize things first, what's most important right now. That's the Node stuff, no doubt about it. Brian should be here anytime, so what do I say? Damn it! In a way I wish this hadn't been forced on me at all... but it is sooo... interesting..."

Thankfully M's indecision soon was interrupted by the doorbell. "That's Brian," he thought, walking the short distance to the door, pausing a few seconds to gather himself, then opening it. "Hey, Brian, right on time, and I see you brought presents, let's see beer, that's good, but my X-ray vision has been on the fritz lately so I can't see what's in the bag."

"Too bad," Brian said as he drew close to M's face and squinted looking at his eyes, first one then the other, saying as he nodded his head, "Yep, they're shot alright. Even without a magnifier I can see that your X-ray bulbs are out. You know, I know some good X-ray vision repair guys. Want me to fix you up?"

M shook his head, "No thanks. And I hope the rest of this evening isn't going to devolve into more of this! My mistake for being 'levitous' about the bag. So what's in it?"

"I bring cheese and crackers, only the finest, to go with the beer, and when that's done, with the wine that you're gonna provide. I got some good cheese, aged Gouda, some Manchego, a Camembert and three different kinds of crispy crackers. Also in the bag some fig spread, roasted red peppers, and stuffed large green olives, all imported, of course, even the crackers."

"Let me sit, please. I have to sit! What is this? Since when do you have such good taste, and I must say, this is good taste. I'm impressed."

"Well, don't be... There's a new wine and cheese Shop on my way over here, so... you fill in the blank. And I must say, I will be going back. The young lady who gave me a hand, well, you fill in the blank..." as Brian and M pulled up chairs to M's small kitchen table arranging all their goodies neatly on a cheese board. "If only I had known, Brian, I would have set up my fondue pot. Oh well..." as M placed a toothpick dispenser next to the cheese board. "Here," motioning to it, "we don't want any tasty morsel to escape!" " It was a welcoming spread, just the sort of thing that would be conducive to Brian and M kicking back to have what would amount to a *very* serious discussion, the most serious conversation they ever will have had.

"Have an agenda in mind?" Brian asked implying that he, personally, did not.

"Look, I know we're both bothered by this Node business... a lot, which is why we're doing this. That's what we have to talk about, but I don't have a specific place to start, do you?" was M's noncommittal reply.

"Yes, I do. Been thinking about this almost constantly since Sunday, and I see some fabulous possibilities, that is, if they are possible, and that's where your scientific genius comes in, coupled of course with my mechanical genius. I must say, M, we can make a great team!"

"Okay, okay, Brian, enough with the buttering up. Where are you going with this?"

"What we know, M, is where Gert's going to be and when, very accurately. We start with that..., and," M interrupts, "Gert, why do you keep mentioning only Gert?"

"Because that's the Node we're working with."

"But think about this, Brian. Every two masses create a Node, as do every three, and four, and so on. All masses in the Universe create these Nodes with other masses, near and far. Now most of them are so weak as to be insignificant, but in principle they're there..." as M pauses.

"And...?" says Brian in anticipation.

"So why talk only about Gert? Gert may be a convenient experimental platform to learn more about Nodes, but we shouldn't lose sight that there are literally billions, no, make that *trillions* of Nodes, floating around the Universe. The question for me, Brian, is what do we do with *that* knowledge?"

"Whoa, this is even more exciting! I did know that, by the way, but I thought bringing it up now would be premature. What I'm thinking about are commercial applications, ways of putting those *trillions* of Nodes to good use... and you do need more than just Gert...ways of turning a profit using those trillions of Nodes for business purposes."

M winced, "Always Brian, running true to form, thinking of ways to make a buck! How about the Nodes' scientific value? Has that occurred to you? Is there any way they can be used to acquire knowledge, *new* knowledge? That's where I would start." Brian was visibly agitated because he took M's retort as a personal attack, almost a lecture on how not to behave, something good for a fifteen year old, maybe, but certainly not for a soon-to-be thirty year old.

"Okay, M, right out of the gate we have some serious difference of opinion. But we also have something very much in common." Brian would try to get things back on track, a less contentious exchange.

"What's that, Brian," M said almost under his breath. He wasn't looking for a fight over what to do with or about the Nodes, yet one seemed to be looming.

"Let's calm down. Right now we have a common goal. We need to know more, agreed?" "Yes" was M's immediate reply, as Brian continued "We have to do another experiment, this one far more revealing than the last, and if it's successful we probably... no, make that *certainly*... can accommodate your objectives and mine both. Wouldn't be the first time business and science were incongruous bedfellows, now would it?"

"Alright, I hope you are right. What have you got in mind?" now M was genuinely interested. His and Brian's tones had turned a corner. M thought they could cooperate, of which Brian had been convinced all along.

"Well, M, in order for a Node to be useful for business, or for science for that matter, it has to be able to move things around, agreed? If it can't do that, then what good is it? What would it tell you as a scientist? Quick answer, not much, basically *nada*."

"And you propose...?, M replied.

"Let's do that experiment, see if Gert can sweep up some object, transport it somewhere, then bring it back? And you say...?"

"Of course, it's obvious actually. That's the linchpin, and I think I know the answer!"

"You gonna tell me?" Brian asks with almost a tone of desperation. "Nope," M replies. "Let's go experimenting!"

Brian and M agreed a break was needed, so they took one. M cued up Pachelbel on his Harman Kardon Dolby B cassette player, sat in his one poofy chair, and poured a glass of Pinot Noir placed on a tray table holding a plate with assorted cheeses and the green olives floating in some extra virgin olive oil with some red chili pepper flakes, thinking to himself, "Cheese and crackers, and *beer*! Only Brian...". M rested back closing his eye while holding the wine glass.

Brian, on the other hand, was wound way too tight and had to shed some of his pent-up angst. It was a beautiful mid-summer's night, a clear moonlit sky, Polytech students milling around, all-in-all a nice time for a brisk walk, which is just what Brian needed. He took the time to clear his thoughts and to formulate an approach when he returned to M's apartment. He had the outlines of the experiment in mind, in fact going back pretty much to when he first realized a Node's potential. Now it was time to get M onboard.

"It's a gorgeous night, M" said Brian as he reentered the apartment, really beautiful out there. "I'm rarin' to go. How 'bout you? Shall we pick up where we left off?"

M placed his wine glass on the tray table and went back to the kitchen table where Brian already had taken seat, saying as he went, "Yes, also rarin' to go, and I think I know where we should go. But you first, Brian, because you seem to have thought this through pretty well. Shoot." was M's invitation for Brian to explain himself, but he thought he could anticipate what Brian would say, at least generally, so he reversed course.

"No, I take that back, Brian. There's something I should tell you, something *very* important. Get comfortable," as he motioned Brian to sit back and relax. "Remember my puzzlement about the streamers, that they all were displaced in the same direction, Gert's direction of travel, and to a much lesser extent *The Birds*, too. Remember that?"

"Yes, I do, M. But what's the big deal there? Why is this important?"

"It's important, Brian, because it got me to digging into the reason for it, if I could figure it out, and I did! And I think we've discovered an entirely new physical phenomenon, one that's never been seen before, and it likely will allow a Node to transport objects, but only under very specific circumstances. I obviously don't know, yet, what experiment you have in mind, but I can tell you this, there's a good chance it will fail unless it's done properly. We can get to that when you explain it. But right now I want to go over what I found so we'll both be on the same page, agreed?" M didn't want to bull ahead with an involved theoretical explanation unless Brian was up to it, and his question to Brian was evident on his face.

Brian responded immediately, "Good grief, M, you seem hesitant. Please, tell me. I hope I can understand it, but do tell me," as he pulled closer to the table as if anticipating diagrams and equations and the like to be drawn on the pad that sat to the corner of the cheese, and crackers, and olives, and fig spread, not to mention the beer and wine glasses.

So M started. "OK, Brian, I'll do this two ways, thumbnail sketch and gory details. Thumbnail sketch, and I know you'll understand this. The reason this can work is that inside a Node there is no spacetime. It's gone! So the usual 'laws' of physics simply don't apply!"

Brian looked confused, then bemused, then terrified. "No spacetime? What? How? If no spacetime, then *what*? This actually is pretty scary, M. Are you sure about this, really sure?"

"Yep, Brian. I've gone over it, and over it, and I'm convinced I've got this straight, and, I agree, it is a little scary,... make that a lot scary!"

"Alright, M, maybe we should wade into the weeds. Let's go, if for no other reason than to see if I can follow along," as Brian came to grips with what certainly would be a borderline incomprehensible lecture in advanced physics, he knew that much.

"Look, Brian, one more time, we don't *have* to do this. We can get right to the experiment you want to do. You can fill me in on all the details. Want to go there instead, your call?"

"I'm ready, M, and if I fall off the log, we can jump to the experiment. Please continue, professor," as Brian signals for M to start by holding up his hands lifting them slightly, palms up.

M's thrilled that Brian wants to know. "The streamers, they were the key. I think I mentioned when we debriefed that I couldn't understand why they weren't randomly disturbed. Instead they acted like tin soldiers all marching to the same tune, in this case Gert's music! Why? That's the question I had to answer, and I did. You really ready for this, it can get hairy?" Brian nodded.

M reached over to the bookcase and retrieved his now on its way to being worn copy of Misner, Thorne and Wheeler, *Gravitation*, opening it to dog-eared page 836 where 'Exercise 31.2' was circled. Here it is, Brian, in this homework problem on 'NONRADIAL LIGHT CONES,' therein lies the answer. Pay attention. I'm going to read this to you, slowly, and I want you to digest it as best you can. The reason for my reading it is I want to emphasize certain parts. We can go over this more, later, and I'm pretty sure we should and we'll have to, but for now I'd like for you focus on the concept. That's the key." M's look asks the question, 'you ready?' Brian nods 'yes,' saying "Have at it, Doctor Ravelli. All ears here." M, of course, is flattered.

"Okay, the MTW problem statement is *Show that the world line of a photon travelling nonradially makes an angle less than 45 degrees with the vertical v-axis of a Kruskal-Szekeres coordinate diagram. From this, infer that particles with finite rest mass, travelling nonradially or radially, must always move 'generally upward' (angle less than 45 degrees with vertical v-axis).* Got that, Brian?" M knew that Brian *didn't* get it, not the details, but he probably *did* get the general idea, and that was what was important. "Here, let's look at the associated diagram. That should make it clearer," as M turns back a page to Figure 31.4(b) titled *The... geodesics, as seen in the Kruskal-Szekeres coordinate system, and as extended either to infinite length or to the singularity of infinite curvature at r=0...*

M continued, "Look at...", but Brian interrupted, "Nice picture, M, but frankly I don't see what this has to do with a Node capturing an object and whisking it away to somewhere else?"

"Yes, Brian, I'll get to that, right now in fact. While the problem statement doesn't say it explicitly, the underlying assumption is that the photon and the particles with finite rest mass, they're moving *in a gravitational field.* What this problem is all about is a distortion of the continuum, the *gravitationally* curved spacetime. But that's not at all the case inside Gert. In a Node there is *no gravity*, therefore *no spacetime* to distort. In fact, to be precise, what we commonly call the *force* of gravity really isn't a *force* at all, like a push or a pull, the way it's defined in introductory physics. Instead, it's a manifestation of the *curvature* of spacetime. Ergo, no gravity in a Node, means no distortion, no curvature, hence no spacetime. There is none inside the Node! And..." Brian pushes back from the table, with a furrowed brow and quizzical look.

"Wait. Stop there. I'm with you on no gravity meaning no distortion of spacetime inside a Node. Got that because it makes sense because, as you pointed out, gravity *is* the curvature of spacetime. I do get that. But you also said spacetime doesn't exist inside the Node. How do you get that? I don't see that what you said about no gravity leads to that conclusion."

"Boy, I guess you *are* with me on this, Brian. Two attaboys..." as M smirked. He loved teaching, and this was just the sort of exchange with his students that he enjoyed the most.

"You're right, absolutely right, Brian. I *cannot* conclude that spacetime does not exist inside the Node. Maybe it doesn't, but then again maybe it does. What I can say is that, if spacetime does exist inside the Node, then it has to be a flat spacetime because I know there is no curvature there, no gravity." M pauses, assessing Brian's reaction. "Did he get that? M wonders.

"Well, let's say it does exist, and it's flat, as it must be according to you, then what does that mean, M? Your original conclusion that there isn't any is wrong. So doesn't that mean that all that follows from it is wrong, too?" Brian asks with a certain smugness, that feeling that a student gets when he asks the teacher that question that the teacher can't answer. But M comes right back at him.

"It doesn't matter. Makes no difference at all whether or not the Node contains a flat spacetime or no spacetime. It doesn't matter. Why?"

"Yes, M, why?" Brian's smugness evaporated as quickly as it came, thinking to himself, "Hmmm... I guess there is an answer, and M knows what it is... hmmm..."

"Think of it this way, Brian. When you talk about an object's gravitational potential energy, GPE, it's always done with respect to some reference point, usually a plane. Let's take a specific example, say, the MTW *Gravitation* book above this floor,..." as he held it up high while lightly tapping his foot. "It's a pretty heavy book, I'd guess the better part of six pounds, and let's say it's two meters above the floor. Running these numbers,..." M picks up a calculator from the bookcase and quickly computes the book's approximate GPE, "...GPE is about 55 Joules. Now let's say the book is only one meter above the floor. Its GPE is cut in half to around 27.5 Joules. And finally, let's say MTW is lying on the floor. Then its GPE is zero. With me, Brian?"

"Yes, I am, M. This is Physics 101. The point being...?" Brian asks.

"The point being, my friend, that I could have placed the reference plane two meters off the floor, and then the GPE would be zero, the same value it has when he book is on the floor and the floor is the reference plane."

"Still not quite getting it, M? Brian asks, still confused.

"Ahhh, you're right again, Brian. I didn't explain. Should have, sorry. The difference between putting the MTW reference plane *on* the floor or two meters *above* it is exactly analogous to having no spacetime inside the Node (call that the floor in our example) or having a flat spacetime (call that the two meter plane). For MTW, there's no *functional* difference between the reference points except a *constant offset* in GPE. Same goes for nonexistent spacetime inside the Node or a flat spacetime inside the Node, there's no *functional* difference, it's just like that constant offset. So I can choose either model, and, frankly, I prefer thinking of the Node as being 'empty,' just a matter of personal preference. You can put in the flat spacetime if you prefer that. But, when you go through all the equations, you will find there is absolutely no difference in the results, whether or not the Node's spacetime if flat or nonexistent, no difference at all," with which M ended his lecture on Node innards.

"Heady stuff, don't you think, Brian? Maybe another short break?" M queried.

"Heady? You *actually* ask *that* question? Seriously? If I didn't know you as well as I do, and if I hadn't been here, oh,..." as Brian looked at his watch," two hours now, I'd think you were on a drug high, and I don't mean the drugs the doc prescribed for your ribs (!), that's how *nuts* what you just said sounds! No spacetime inside a Node!? Sure, a short break." But as Brian said this, M could see the light in Brian's head turning on and growing brighter. It was beginning to sink in, M thought, Brian would be onboard given a little more time. Then, then they could get to the grand experiment!

As before, Brian walked it off. M cozied up with another classical piece and a refreshed glass of wine. Twenty minutes or so later Brian returned looking refreshed and renewed. "I'm more excited about this whole Node thing than I've ever been, M. Let's get to what I would like to do experimentally. I take everything you said as being correct, and I'm sure it is, so let's get to the good part!" Brian poked at M, as the two of them relaxed at the kitchen table with the remnants of their appetizers.

"According to the GertHound Schedule, Gert will be back here, on the Lake, on Tuesday, July 25th, at 7:33:13am EDT. And, which is perfect, back again the very next day at 1:32:54pm. I propose we build an apparatus that releases a steel ball by remote control as Gert passes by. By my calculations a ball eleven inches in diameter will displace enough water to create just over twenty five pounds buoyancy. So if the steel ball is hollow and its wall thin enough to keep the total weight under 25 pounds, then it floats. I would build in a safety factor by fabricating a twenty pound ball, eleven inches in diameter. I can do his at the Shop where we have all the equipment to make semi-spherical Plaster of Paris molds and kilns hot enough to melt steel. Then the two ball halves can be welded together and the joint polished. Easy peasy. And if this works, in future experiments we could put things, not sure what exactly, *inside* the ball!"

"This is genius, Brian. Leave it to you! So you anticipated doing this, you devil! Trying to fly something inside a Node! But you didn't say anything. That's why you asked me to be your 'lab assistant' for an experiment on the 25th, which you wouldn't reveal, and that's why you want the Heathkit remote control repurposed to actuate magnetic coils. You're going to use it to remotely release the ball. Clever, very clever, and I see no reason whatsoever for not doing this. It will tell us a lot. Whether or not the ball is actually swept up by Gert and whisked off, and, more importantly, I think, whether or not Gert returns it in one piece. Sign me up!!" M was worked up and very happy with Brian's proposal. It was the logical next step, and M was glad Brian saw that, in fact that Brian saw it even before he did.

M continues, "Now this brings us to the finer point, Brian. I've been looking at that, too, what are the dynamics of an object, *any* object, inside a Node? One obvious question is why didn't Gert sweep up any loose objects when she passed through on the 28th. I'm sure there were a few in her path, and Lord knows the Node was big enough, I would think, to encompass many little things that weren't tied down, so to speak."

"Legit question, M. Have you got an answer?" Brian replied.

"Yes, it has to do with what the flat spacetime inside the Node - let's go with that, flat, because you like it more - what the flat spacetime does to mass under certain circumstances.

"All ears, M."

"Move closer," as M retrieved his notebook. He opened to a paper-clipped page and pointed to an equation near the top. "See this equation, Brian?" as Brian nodded 'yes.' "It's so, so simple, and yet it holds the key to what happens inside Gert.

$$m_{inert} = \frac{\sqrt{E^2 - (pc)^2}}{c^2}$$

m_{inert} is the *inertial* mass of an object in Gert's flat spacetime. E is the total system energy, p is the total momentum, and c our good friend, the speed of light. Simple, isn't it?" Brian nodded 'yes' again. "You want Gert to pick up some object and whisk it away with her as she moves through space, right?" Brian nods 'yes' again.

"How can that happen?" M continues. "Well, it cannot happen if the object is *not moving* in the external frame of reference that Gert passes through, which is why Gert didn't sweep up anything as she traversed the Shop. In order to bring something along with her, that object cannot be moving in the flat spacetime *inside* Gert, but everything in the Shop *was moving* inside Gert as she passed by, at the negative of her speed, about minus 20 mph. "You see that, right?" M asked Brian.

"Yes, I do. Gert moved through at about 20 mph, so anything that was stationary in the Shop was moving at minus 20 mph with respect to the Node," Brian remarked.

"Good. Now look at the equation," as M pointed to it. "Keep in mind that these remarks apply only to the reference frame inside the Node, nothing outside it, in the Shop or anywhere else. What's the total energy? Well, it consists of two parts, potential and kinetic. There's no gravity inside Gert, we know that, so the GPE is flat out zero, no gravitational potential energy, none.

That leaves only kinetic energy, the energy of motion. But if the object is not moving with respect to Gert's reference frame inside the Node, then its velocity is zero and its kinetic energy, KE, is flat out zero, too, just like GPE."

"Okay, M, with you so far. And if both GPE and KE are zero, then it follow that the total energy E is zero. Which leaves only the momentum term in the mass equation."

"Correct, Brian, correct. But what is its value? Think. What is momentum?"

"It's the product of mass and velocity... Holy shit! I see it. If KE is zero, then the momentum also is zero because the object is at rest relative to Gert's reference frame! The object isn't moving, so the entire expression under the radical evaluates to zero!"

"Correct again, Brian. And this is the *astonishing* result that the Node, er,... Gert, provides. Because that square root is the object's inertial mass inside Gert, the mass is *zero*, that is, there is no mass to the object as long as it isn't moving! This happens because of the Node's flat spacetime. If the spacetime weren't flat, if it were curved as it is out here, then the object would have inertial mass, but inside the Node, and only there, the object has *no inertial mass* as long as it remains stationary inside the Node. Of course, the rest mass isn't zero, only the inertial mass is."

"Holy shit!" Brian exclaimed, "This really is astonishing, M, mind-blowing, in fact! So, inside the Node, any object that is stationary with respect to the Node has no inertial mass!? This has to be a first, M! I'm sure no one on this planet has ever seen *anything* like it!"

"Correct, Brian. You're exactly right. No one, ever before. I've searched and searched and searched, and I've pored over the theory, but there's nothing out there like this. And I think I know why..." M trailed off, hinting that he would explain if Brian wanted him to, which he did.

"So why? What's the reason no one else ever saw this before? I'm really curious," Brian implored.

"Well, we know how rare it would be for anyone to see a Node to begin with, right? "Yes," answered Brian.

"So it's unlikely that anyone ever did, before us, that is. That's the first half."

"And the second half?" Brian queried.

"Scientists lost interest in flat spacetime. After all, Einstein's Special Relativity, which was only about flat spacetime, was entirely eclipsed by General Relativity that deals with curved spacetime. Flat spacetime is a special case, of course, but no one cares about it anymore because it doesn't have any gravity, and gravity is what makes the Universe tick. This is the second reason, Brian, as far as I can tell... make that, guess. Bottom line, no one knew about Nodes, probably, and no one had any reason to consider them as a theoretical possibility because it's a region of flat spacetime that no one cares about."

"Makes sense to me, M. I buy it! And I didn't find your explanation too far over my head, except maybe the homework problem business in your *Gravitation* book, but I do believe I understand the concepts well enough, which brings me to the big question, "How does this affect our experiment? I know it does..." whereupon Brian and M decided to take five, which turned out to be more like fifteen, before getting into the implications for the experiment.

"I think I'm changing how the experiment has to work, Brian, so we have to get into the details...now." M had a somewhat distressed look on his face, as if coming to grips with a reality he would rather avoid.

"Yeah, M, I think I know where you're coming from based on the no inertial mass in the Node stuff. I'm pretty sure I can guess where you're going," Brian remarked.

"Okay, Brian, you tell me, then. Where is this all leading?"

"The Node can sweep up an object only if that object is *not moving within the Node*. And if it does capture it, then presumably the object will stay inside the Node, right? We have to talk about this, too..."

"Yes," said M, "keep going."

"So the question comes down to, How do we match the object's speed to the Node's speed. They have to be the same. How do we do that? This isn't at all what I had in mind. I was thinking we could 'drop' the steel ball into the Node as it went by, and it would be carried off. But that won't work because of the speed matching requirement. And, silly me, it's obvious that it never could have worked because, as you pointed out, Gert didn't pick up anything when she went through the Shop, even though there had to be some things that weren't anchored down. Boy, was I stupid to miss that!"

"Don't give it a second thought, Brian. I missed it, too, until I started digging into the theory behind Gert's flat spacetime. That's when it hit me, so don't beat yourself up on this. You are right, though, that what may have seemed like a simple 'drop the ball and watch it float away' experiment simply cannot work. So, what to do?"

"I got it!," Brian said with gusto, followed just as quickly by a sheepish "I think..."

"Let's hear it. After all, you are the experimentalist."

Brian rose to his feet, taking the posture of the thespian about to present his greatest performance, surveying his adoring audience of... one..., and thereupon embarking on what he intuitively knew would be the beginning of *the* greatest adventure of his life.

"We start by measuring Gert's velocity at the beginning of her arrival. Then we take that value and use it to do two things, release the steel ball while giving it an impulse that matches its velocity to Gert's. Ergo, the ball is free, but it's not moving inside the Node, ergo its inertial mass is zero, which causes it to stay inside the Node and fly away with Gert as she departs. What do you think?"

"Brilliant! Just what we needed to keep this emprise going! Bravo! But, hmmm..., how do you propose to do that, measure Gert's velocity? There's nothing there in a sense, in the Node, nothing? Have you thought about that?"

"Yes, during our last little breather. What sets Gert apart from everything else? Lack of gravity, that's what. We use *that* to make the measurement? How? We have two ball bearings in tubes that are spring-loaded at the bottom with springs that aren't quite strong enough to launch the bearings upwards in the tube. I suppose I should say 'in our curved spacetime'... At the top of each tube is a microswitch connected to a Signetics 555 timer. When Gert's leading edge passes the timer, the Node's lack of gravity causes he first ball to launch, striking the microswitch which starts the timer. After a few milliseconds Gert's leading edge passes over the second tube causing its ball bearing to launch and strike the second microswitch which then stops the timer. Knowing the time interval that passed and the distance between the tubes permits a direct calculation of the Node's speed. There you have it. Wha'dya think?"

"I will say, Brian, it's insights like this that make *you* the experimentalist. This is brilliant! Simple, pretty foolproof it seems, and I know you'll build it so it works!"

"You mean Marty, M, it's Marty who does that stuff, remember?. He's my electronics tech, and damn good I must say. I'm the idea guy, with schemes like this, and Marty makes them work. I decided, just now in fact, that I need him back here badly enough to track him down in Costa Rica and pay a *very* handsome bonus for his return, along with another prolonged vacation to make up for cutting this one short. Marty's a good guy, and I'm sure that under the circumstances he would come back voluntarily without any inducement, but I'd feel guilty if he weren't compensated, so that will be the deal."

"I have seen some of Marty's work at the Shop, Brian, and while I don't know a lot about it, yes, it seems that Marty is top notch, and if you can get him back here he'll pull this off. But, of course, as good as this is, there's that huge gorilla over there in the corner, the one about how do you get the eleven-inch sphere up to speed to match Gert's even if you know what it is. Did you work that out, too, over the break?"

"Sure did, M, that too because it's the key to making this work. I do get what you said. If the object, in this case our steel sphere, isn't moving inside the Node at exactly Gert's speed, then it will fall out of the Node and not go anywhere. But if the speeds match, then the sphere's inertial mass drops to zero and it tracks inside Gert staying there forever, right?"

"Right-o, Brian. You said you had this figured out, too. Gonna tell me? Or are you going o make me wait until July 25th?"

"Same basic idea, M, a very similar idea. Originally I was thinking we could simply 'drop' the ball by using a remote control to release it from an electromagnet, the Heathkit remote you were going to work on, but now that's out. Instead we can build a spring launching mechanism that disengages when the sphere's speed is the same as Gert's. What I have in mind is this. A beefy enough spring capable of getting the sphere moving well above 20 mph, say as high as 50 mph, much higher than what you calculate Gert's speed as, that spring is used to launch the sphere in the direction of the Node's forward motion. There are two things of concern: 1) how do we know what the sphere's speed is as the spring launches it, and) how do we stop the spring from speeding up the sphere even more when Node speed has been reached? With me so far, M?"

"Yes, indeed I am, Brian, and I wait with baited breath to see how you solve this, I mean, these, problems! Baited breath," and M slowly shakes his head side-to-side while stroking his chin.

"The speed from the Node velocity sensor is radioed back to the spring sphere launcher. That's easy, so we know what speed we need. The launching spring surrounds a piston and pushes against its end. When the piston stops, the spring stops, no more pressure to speed up the sphere. The piston is controlled by an electromagnetic actuator. When it's 'off' the piston moves freely, and the spring can extend its full length. When it's 'on' the piston immediately stops moving, dead in its tracks, and the spring no longer accelerates the sphere. Turing the piston on and off is done by an electronic control module that automatically shuts down the spring when the desired sphere speed is achieved."

"Clever, as usual, Brian. But you left out the key factor, the sphere's speed. How do we know that? You haven't said..." M remarked.

"I didn't get to that yet, because you interrupted me when I was on a roll. Be quiet and I'll tell you..." Brian paused looking for M to acquiesce, which he did with a nod "And how do we know how fast the sphere is moving? Simple, easy peasy, even easier than the Node velocity sensor. The sphere is marked with two highly reflective dots a known distance apart. A photoelectric sensor starts a timer when it sees the first dot, and stops it when it sees the second. This time interval plus the dot separation distance allows the sphere speed to be calculated. All there is to it!" and Brian sat down breathing a visible sigh of relief.

"I think we have an experiment, Brian. Let's see, today is July 13th, so we have only about a week and a half to get this done, to build the experimental apparatus, test it, and get it to the Lake for Gert's arrival. Doable?"

"Yes, M, if I start right now, as in *right* now. I'm off to the shop to do just that. I'll keep you in the loop, and if I need help I'll holler, OK?

"Sure is, Brian, sure is. I'm available pretty much whenever you might need me because I can move things around at the Observatory if necessary. Good luck!" said M signaling 'goodbye' as Brian walked through the door and left.

Chapter 7 - The 25th Day of July 1972

Martin Lobesky and his wife Sandra's plane landed right on time, 9:45am. The airport was busy, but not overly so, and making it through Customs should be routine and quick, or so the Lobeskeys expected. "Mr. Lobesky, I see you're arriving from San Jose, Costa Rica?" the nattily attired, pleasant looking, ostensibly officious customs agent asked. "Yes, sir. We spent most of our time in Heredia. My wife and I are architecture buffs, and it's beautiful there, and quite historic." The agent continued, "How was your flight?" "Smooth, uneventful, the kind of airplane ride everyone likes." Then the agent continued, "Good news, glad to hear that" whereupon he got down to the business at hand, his demeanor noticeably different, now staring, almost menacingly, "anything to declare, Mr. Lobesky, plants, animals, alcoholic beverages, biologicals, cultural artifacts? "No sir, none of the above," replied Marty in a matter of fact monotone, figuring that was the list and he was done, but, no, it wasn't. "Please look at this list of other prohibited items, Mr. Lobesky," as he handed Marty a full page long of other restricted items each with a brief description. "Anything on here?" No, nothing at all. We haven't brought back with us anything that we didn't take with us in the first place," was Marty's now noticeably irritated reply, and all the while this exchange took place another nattily attired, pleasant looking, ostensibly officious customs agent rifled through the Lobeskeys' luggage checking for contraband.

"Is there anything else, sir? Are you gentlemen quite done with our luggage?" Marty was clearly very irritated, and rightfully so. His agent replied, "Yes, more to do, Mr. Lobesky, and no, we're not done yet. I have to take your temperature while Agent Pryer completes the luggage search. Please remove your hat. This is an infrared scanning thermometer, no contact." As the agent held up what was clearly a state-of-the-art device, and Marty did as directed, all the while avoiding looking directly at the nattily attired agent by gazing past him, over his shoulder. Of course, taking his temperature took mere seconds, and he was glad to get that out of the way. "Let's see," said the agent, "while pressing buttons on the instrument, your temperature is 97.7 degrees, very good." Marty breathed an internal sigh of relief, "Great! This guy is done!" But it was not to be so. After a short, but what seemed to be long pause, "One more thing, Mr. Lobesky, have you been ill while away?" "No, absolutely not." Then the agent continued with a list of twelve additional questions having to do with Marty's health, none of which elicited a troubling response. Then, finally, "Thank you, Mr. Lobesky, you are cleared for entry into the United States. Welcome!" Marty thought to himself, not having been out of the country in a while, "My, how things have changed! They must send these guys to 'wind up toy school' to teach them how to interact. This guy may as well be a small robot, that's how he sounds." Then turning to Sandra, "Okay, dear, let's go," just as the agent piped up. "Oh, no, Mrs. Lobesky, you can't go without being screened." And the whole Kabuki dance began all over again, this time with Sandra Lobesky the agent's target.

"Sandra, let's grab a cab and take you straight home. It's not far out of the way to NovaTek, and I'd like to go straight there because Brian has a real time crunch. Okay, with you?" Sandra smiled. Marty had worked at NovaTek for several years, and she had gotten to know Brian fairly well. Marty loved his work, and he was well-treated by Brian who obviously appreciated his talent and dedication. Marty went to NovaTek about three years after graduating college with an Associate's Degree in electronics technology. He wasn't the 'academic type,' and although he could have gone on to a four year BSEE program, what Marty wanted to do was 'play with the gizmos,' as he put it. Brian relied on Marty completely when it came to the electronics part of NovaTek's work, describing him as NovaTek's electronics 'magician,' he was that good. And now he was being turned loose on the Node Experiment. "Marty, please go. Say hi to Brian for me, and 'knock'em dead' on your new project. I could tell from your conversation with Brian how important this is, not to mention his 'bribes' to get you back so soon. Not bad, I'd say...You'll have to tell me all about it!" Marty bent over and kissed his wife, saying "One of the things I love so much about you, Sandy, is how supportive and understanding you are. I know it's tough when I'm in the basement fiddling with some electronic gizmo at two in the morning..." as the cab pulled away from the curb into a steady line of cars.

- - - - - - - - - - - -

Marty had hardly walked through the door when Brian accosted him waving a piece of paper. "Marty, Marty, God I'm glad you're back, that you were willing to get back here on such short notice." Two days had gone by since Brian's meeting with M. "You've done it before, and now I'm asking you to do it again, work your electronics 'magic' building some equipment that has to be up and running and tested for deployment on July 25th. Can do?"

Marty's reaction was guarded because he worried this might be the bridge too far. He knew from Brian's remarks, both now and when they talked before he left Costa Rica, how important this was, but he didn't want to commit to the impossible. After all, even the magician's rabbit is conjured up by sleight of hand, and truth is, legerdemain doesn't make electronic equipment work. "You know me, Brian. If we can think it, I can build it! At least most of the time, sort of..." was Marty's way of taking at least some of the air out of Brian's balloon. "Look, you know as well as I that only so much can be done in so much time, and that actually designing, fabricating, and testing electronics can be an arduous process without a guaranteed outcome, especially if the gizmo isn't run-of-the-mill, right?"

"Sure, Marty. I do know that, oh how well I know that, which is precisely why I needed *you* back here. Believe me, I don't think for a second that this is beyond your ken. Quite to the contrary, it's pretty straightforward, but you know, and I know, I'm not the guy for this. I suppose I could do it, maybe, but no way by the 25th. That's the big issue - timing. It *has* to be ready for the 25th. That's a hard break, so to speak, then or never. What you bring to the table is a boatload of relevant experience. You can cut through the crap and get it done on time, I know you can!"

"Okay, boss. I'm onboard." Marty's attitude made the leap from tentative to optimistic because it seemed clear that the only constraint was time, not the nature of the device, and when it came to time Marty was more than willing to work every waking minute if that's what it took. "Of course, you have to tell me what we're building, huh?"

"Yes, of course, Marty, and here it is, roughly" as Brian motioned Marty to his desk and pulled a sketch from the top drawer. What you're doing is the electronics in this component and in this one," Brian said while first pointing to the 'Node Velocity Sensor' and then to the 'Electronics Package.'

"First question, Boss. What's a Node?" obviously a new term for Marty in the context of NovaTek, so he was understandably curious, not to mention a tad concerned that, whatever it was, the 'Node' might impact his design work.

"Good question, Marty... but... I can't tell you. I will fill you in on the details of how the sensor functions, what's inside it and how those elements work. What you have to do is design and build the electronics that allow them to work the way I describe what they have to do. With me on this?"... as Marty nods yes... "We've done this sort of thing before, and although I hate keeping you in the dark - make that partially in the dark - it is necessary, and, frankly, beyond my control." Brian knew that under no circumstance could he explain what the Node Experiment was really about.

"Got it!" Marty replied. "Hush, hush, like some of our other projects for the, I'm guessing, three letter organization whose name was never to be mentioned aloud, huh?" "Perfect cover," thought Brian, "Yes, Marty, you figured it out, something like that. So let's be sure to keep it that way, even when it comes to Sandra, right?" Marty smiled, reflecting a deep sense of self-importance because *he* now was wrapped in the cloak of secrecy. "This must be *really* important," Marty thought to himself.

"Okay, this is what the Velocity Sensor does..." and Brian went through every detail of its functioning. Likewise he explained how the Electronics Package had to work. He and Marty spent the entire morning and the first part of the afternoon going over the electronics requirements, sketching out detailed block diagrams, labeling each block by name and function followed by pages of detailed descriptions. By two in the afternoon, Marty already had worked out the details down to the component level. Now it was a matter of actually designing the devices, the actual circuit diagrams from which he would fabricate the device.

Looking at the clock he commented "You hungry, Brian? Lunchtime was, oh, two hours ago. Sandy and I had 'breakfast,' if you could call it that, on our fight, but now the tummy's telling me that it's time to grab some real food. I'm gonna run over to Archie's Pizza and pickup a small chicken cutlet wrap with tomato sauce and green peppers, toasted. Can I get you anything?" "Sure, make that two, sounds good, thanks Marty." Fact is, Brian wasn't hungry at all, he was so totally consumed with what he and M had discussed about Nodes. In fact, he shook his head slightly and smiled every time he thought about it, that he and M probably were the *only two people* on all of planet Earth with its almost four billion inhabitants who know what they know about Nodes, remarkable, thought he, truly remarkable... and a bit scary! Anyway, he didn't want to come across to Marty as being preoccupied, and he didn't want to refuse a kind offer, so he agreed to a small chicken cutlet wrap with sauce and green peppers, toasted.

Electronics Package

Node Velocity Sensor

Sphere Launcher

Flotation Collar

Gyroscope

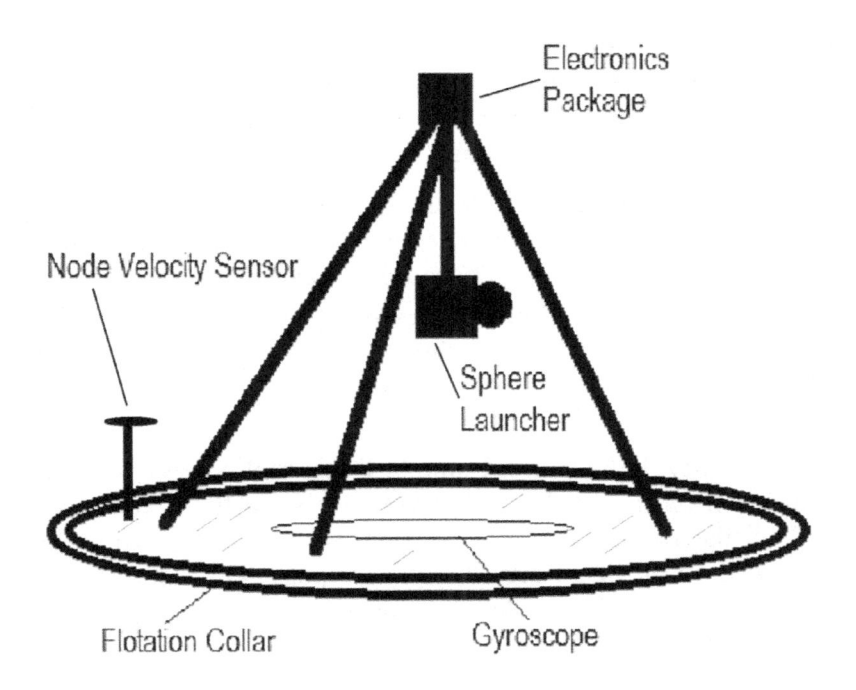

Lunch was done by three, for which Brian now was grateful. He was hungry after all, but so lost in thought he didn't know it. Now it was back to work for Brian and the magician. "Brian, explain this to me, 'Flotation Collar' and 'Gyroscope.' What's that about? This gizmo's obviously getting wet, and I have to know because it affects my designs."

"Well, yes, it's going to be deployed in water, so there's some chance the electronics could be exposed to H2O, but that's not the intention. It should stay dry."

"Not good enough, Boss. Water exposure, however unlikely, requires a different design approach. For example, some of the circuits will be designed differently, they'll be hermetically sealed in epoxy, and all the components will be mil-spec instead of commercial grade. They're a little pricier because they handle things like water, shock, temperature, and so on better than their commercial cousins. I assume you're OK with this? I need your go-ahead."

Brian didn't hesitate even one second. "Cost is no problem, Marty, none at all, spend whatever it takes. My only question to you is, Will using mil-spec slow things down in terms of getting the electronics up and running?"

"No, Brian, not at all. Our suppliers stock mil-spec and commercial grade side-by-side, and I've often found mil-spec actually is *more* available because it's used less, only nuts like us... Plus, what I'm looking at here is pretty straight-forward, nothing so unusual that I'll have trouble doing the designs or getting the parts. We'll be ready well before July 25th, count on it."

"I am, Marty, believe me, I am..." Brian replied with a big grin. "And, I'm on the hook for everything else in the gizmo, as you call, it, the flotation, gyros, housing, structural, the whole kit n' caboodle. You just worry about your part. OK, I'm outta your hair, off to my cubby hole. You head to the electronics bench." Marty saluted and did just that.

- - - - - - - - - - - -

"M, see those ramps in the truck bed?" M nodded yes, "Extend them so we can line up the Node Probe's wheels." And M did as instructed. He had visited the Shop almost every other day since their meeting at his apartment, going over and over all he experimental details, and checking out each and every mechanism as it was completed. And of course, there were details that had been missed, for example how the steel sphere would be 'encouraged' to return to Earth when Gert brought it back. While Brian and M, actually Brian, had cleverly figured out how to get the sphere into Gert's grip by matching its speed to the Node's speed, they just forgot about getting it back, which required that the sphere velocity would have to be different than Gert's. Under this circumstance, if the sphere were 'nudged' towards the Earth's surface then it would fall out of the Node and land on the ground, or given the GertHound schedule, on the Lake's surface the day after its departure. So how to do it?

"Good thing you were able to build in the thruster mechanism," M said to Brian as they lined up the Node Probe's wheel with the two ramps extending from NovaTek's new Ford F-150 Ranger XLT truck, Brian's new 'toy' utility vehicle. "Yes, M, good thing, and I must say it was tricky. And it required resurrecting the Heathkit remote. I'm sooo glad Marty made it back. This probe wouldn't be here without him, believe me!"

Brian hooked up the electric winch and slowly, very slowly, inched 'NP-1,' the contraption's moniker, up the ramps into the truck bed, whereupon it was tied down and the tailgate secured. M looked at his watch, "Well, Brian, getting close. It's 4:30am, and Gert arrives at 7:33:13, plenty of time for a leisurely drive to the Lake with a coffee stop on the way. I noticed a bit of a chill in the air, so hot black coffee will fit the bill and we can fill the Thermoses. Ready to go?"

"Yep, let's get this show on the road, Emilio. Time to make it, or to break it!" With which both men jumped into the cab and drove off. It was nothing short of a very odd sight, but at this hour there wasn't anyone around to see it.

The drive to the Lake House was uneventful, serene even as the sky brightened ever more with the rising sun. The coffee and donuts along the way hit the spot, and both Brian and M took the ride to relax, sip their coffees and nibble their donuts, while all along thinking about what was about to happen. Neither said much. They were simply lost in their own thoughts... and anticipation.

"Isn't that unusual?" M remarked as the truck slowly pulled up to the Lake House. "Yes, it is, M. Must be chillier here than we expected, after all a weak cold front did pass through." They both gazed at the Lake whose surface was covered with sea smoke, essentially the fog at ground level that forms when warm water is covered by a blanket of 'cold' air. Both men had exactly the same thought. "If this doesn't clear, M, what can we do? We can't see far enough into the Lake to see what's happening with Gert and NP-1. What the hell are going to do!? After all this work and planning..." Brian sounded panicked.

"Calm down, Brian. Chill... oops, maybe not the best word... what's the worst that can happen? Unlike Gert's return tomorrow where we *have* to be able to see what's going on in order to fire the return thruster, unlike that, we could deploy the Probe in the right spot and let Nature do the rest. Now, I don't like that idea, not at all, anymore than you do I know, but if we have no choice, that's my vote. I certainly don't think we should pack it in because of this!"

"God, no, Emilio. I couldn't agree more. However, I was hoping to see Gert capture the sphere. In fact," as Brian held up his Nikon F2, "I'm all set to click away and get some spectacular pictures!" "Well, Brian, we still have, let's see, about two and a half hours, and a lot can happen in that time. Dawn is just, well, dawning," says M as points to the brightening horizon across the Lake. "You know it is coldest just before dawn because the atmosphere hasn't been heated by the Sun for the longest time by then. I'm willing to bet that as soon as we see the Sun over the horizon, we'll begin to see the sea smoke dissipate. And that should be in plenty of time to deploy NP-1 in clear conditions. So relax, Brian, have another sip of coffee - good thing you brought a couple of thermoses." And with that M and Brian sat back in the truck's cab eyes glued to the horizon to see if they could see the Sun poke from behind the trees on the opposite shore.

Maybe fifteen minutes elapsed before Brian leaned over to M, nudging him, "Guess you were right, Doctor Ravelli!" just as the Sun's rim appears above the tree line and ever so slightly the sea smoke began to thin. "Give it half an hour, Brian, and you won't know that any sea smoke had formed, it will completely dissipate, and we have what seems to be the start of a beautiful day. A wonderful day, actually, for Gert to be Gert!" M looking up as he said this, scanning a cloudless azure blue sky, and waving to Brian to do the same. "We're good, Brian, we're good..."

The next twenty minutes were spent carefully maneuvering the F-150 with its bed facing the Lake on a strip of sandy shore, what amounted to the Lake House's 'beach' created with a very large amount of trucked-in sand. Brian drove as M signaled the way, until the '150 was close enough to extend the ramps from the truck bed right into the Lake, approximately four feet from the water line. With this arrangement NP-1 could be slowly winched into the water, at which point its flotation collar would take over so that it floated on the surface. This entire procedure took about half an hour start to finish, and when it was done, M and Brian looked at each other and gave a hearty embrace. "Great work, Brian, great work. Without your mechanical genius, backed up by the 'magician,' of course, this never could have happened, never *would* have happened. Yet there she is, NODE PROBE! By the way, Brian, did you bring a bottle of champagne to break on her bow?" M said jokingly. "Wow! Real levity," Brian answered. "Not bad, M, for the least humorous guy I know... No, no champagne, but if this experiment doesn't work, *all* of which. by the way, is based on *your* calculations,... well, I seem to recall having in the boat shed over there a spare torpedo that's just gathering dust..." And both men laughed and smiled and glad handed each other while NP-1 sat placidly in the water a few feet from shore. "What a sight!" they both thought.

"Okay, Brian, your lead. What next?" asked M while rubbing his hands in anticipation. "We're going to bring NP-1 to the deployment point that you calculated, M. That involves running three precut stainless steel lines from three known points on shore out into the Lake, and where the swing lines meet is where NP-1 should be. The shore points are on this map," as Brian handed M a surveyor's map showing the Lake, the three shore points, and three lines drawn into the Lake intersecting a good one hundred feet beyond the end of the forty foot dock.

"Okay, Brian, let me do these while you're stand at the end of the dock holding each line, right?" "Yes, M. I'll walk to the end spooling out the wire line. You go to each of the shore points in turn. Then when I have all three lines tethered, come back to the end of the dock and help me launch the rowboat. I'll go to the deployment point based on where all three of the wire swing lines meet, and I'll mark it with a float."

"Sounds good, Brian. How deep do you figure?"

"Well, it's about twenty feet at the end of the dock, so I'm thinking more than fifty at deployment. I have a float in the boat with a one hundred foot spool of nylon twine. That's more than enough to get us to the bottom, and the Lake is so still there won't be any drift of the float. Don't worry, M, I've got this covered, and I've done similar things before."

"Counting on you, Brian, good luck," was M's final remark as he set off to tether each of the three swing lines.

Twenty minutes later, "Alright, float's in place," said Brian as he pulled up to the dock near shore, about twenty feet away from the Node Probe. "Time to get our friend out to the deployment point, M, and you have to help." M's reply was just what Brian expected. "Miss it? Not for anything, not a chance!! I wanted to jump in the boat when you went out alone, but I knew you needed the space to work, so I didn't bring it up. But this trip, no, I'm not staying here waving to you as you have all the fun, Skipper."

The rowboat was brought around to the front of NP-1. In the back of the boat under a small tarp was a small electric motor, maybe three feet long with a steering handle/throttle, and a small twelve volt battery. Brian and M attached the motor to the stern and connected the battery. Then they pulled up alongside the Probe attaching a long line to its 'bow,' close to where the node velocity sensor was situated. "Ready to go, M?"

"Aye aye, Skipper.

The rowboat pulled away from the dock carefully taking up the slack in the approximately twenty foot tow cable, and then proceeded with its cargo in tow to the deployment point. "Yes, Brian, the Lake is mirror smooth today, absolutely beautiful." They brought NP-1 to a stop directly above the float, while Brian pulled up alongside. He took a military grade compass from his pocket, took a bearing on twenty-seven degrees east of true north, and lined up NP-1 with that direction. Then, looking at M, "That's where she's coming from, M, right there. See that stand of maples on the far shore" Right down the middle?" M looked pleased and confident both at the same time. "No doubt in my mind, Brian, no doubt." Brian slowly rotated the Probe to line up with Gert's direction of arrival, leaned over and flipped some switches in a watertight box. "What did you just do, Brian?" asked M. "Just fired up the gyros. In the structure there are horizontal and vertical gyros to keep the probe properly aligned. After all, it would be a serious bummer if Gert showed up on schedule over those maples over there, and NP-1 was oriented ninety degrees perpendicular! Can't have that, now can we. Ergo, gyros." Brian was quite self-satisfied with what he had done in fabricating the Node Probe. And now they were closing in on putting it to work.

"7:33:13, that's touchdown," as M looked at his watch and he and Brian stepped onto the end of the dock, "about thirty five minutes. So what do we do, stand here for all that time?" "Nope," was Brian's curt reply as he walked away down the long dock. From the end he shouted back to M, "I brought two lightweight aluminum folding beach chairs, some cold drinks, and that portable transistor radio, right here," as he swept his arm indicating the F-150's bed. "In fact, there's enough stuff here that you should help carry it," which of course M did. "Nice job, you thought of everything!" "Tried to, M, I tried to. Don't let me forget the camera," as Brian pointed to a large leather camera bag sitting next to the beach chairs and next to a tripod.

The two friends scooped up all their equipment and headed back to the end of the dock. NP-1 floated motionless on the perfectly still Lake about a hundred feet away. The chairs were set up for the best view, and Brian sat with the Nikon in his lap as he reached down to grab the tripod, a top-of-the-line Manfrotto unit, a pre-production model conveniently provided to NovaTek by one of its clients. As before the F2 was fitted with a 250 frame film cassette. But before setting it up for the big event, Brian wanted a shot of the two of them waiting for Gert.

So he mounted the camera on the tripod in self-timer mode and composed the shot with himself and M in it. He took several because, as everyone knows, those blinks, squints, and otherwise odd facial expressions that ruin a photograph simply cannot be anticipated or controlled. Brian's hope, as any photographer's, was that at least one frame was a keeper. After the runway session, as he called it, Brian got to the serious business of taking technical photos to document what would happen that day.

He turned the tripod to point at NP-1, screwed in a six-foot cable shutter release, then dialed in the F's maximum frame rate of four frames per second, mirror up. He pre-focused on NP-1's Sphere Launcher module with a 200mm telephoto lens at an aperture of f/8 which would provide plenty of depth of field. The Sun was well above the horizon providing more than enough light for well lit photos. He checked the exposure and was able to set the shutter speed at 1/500 second using the same 1600 speed film that was used in the first Node experiment. After double-checking all the settings, everything, to be sure the camera would do its job, Brian relaxed and sat comfortably back in the beach chair gazing intently at NP-1, the small radio tuned to a folk music station playing the entire Simon and Garfunkel's *Greatest Hits* album. "Good choice, Brian, a little surprising actually, but I think a good choice of music until Gert gets here. Then we can go more upbeat if you like, way more upbeat!"

"Hear that?" he said to M. "The Jays, they're a lot louder, a lot!" Early in the morning, especially when the weather cooperated, the Lake was a cacophony of bird noises, some lilting and quite lovely, others, like the Jays, raucous and jarring, and of course everything in between. These sounds quieted only later in the day when their makers rested, or, at any time that the Red-tail appeared with its loud, short, raspy, hoarse scream, more than enough to alert all the other birds that they might become its next meal! "M, this is just what happened the night he Node first appeared, but instead of birds making more noise it was the crickets and the frogs. Remember I remarked about that, it was so noticeable?

"Yes, I do remember that, Brian, and listening to what's happening right now, at this very moment, I don't think there's any doubt that something's going on about how the wildlife can anticipate a Node. From the bugs to the birds they seem to sense its approach. Do you agree?"

"Sure do, M, I sure do! I've seen it at the Shop, twice now, and here it is again. We're not imagining this, and it can't be coincidence. Let's see, five minutes. Get ready! Keep your eyes peeled" Brian remarked as he handed M one of the pair of Nikon 8x24 7-degree binoculars. I'd focus on NP-1's Sphere Launcher to start," which M did.

But after doing so M put the optics in his lap and scanned the sky wondering if anything, anything at all, could be seen as a precursor of the Node's arrival. And sure enough, "Brian, look, up there at ten o'clock maybe two hundred feet off the water, do you see that? It's a flock of birds tightly packed, but they're not flapping! They're descending pretty quickly, too, heading straight for the Lake! That has to be the Node, it has to be!" M's excitement was more than palpable, he was almost shaking.

"Brian put the binocs to his eyes quickly focusing on the descending flock. "You're right, M, not flapping at all, in fact their wings are tight to their bodies! They're going for a Node Ride!! That has to be it, M, they sensed Gert's approach and 'jumped in,' matching her speed so they all could stay inside the Node in a weightless state while going for the ride! Astonishing, really!"

"And this *proves* that the theory is right!" replied M. "We're seeing it play out before our very eyes, and it didn't take NP-1 to do it! God, I can't tell you how high I am right now, I can't really explain the feeling, Brian."

"Gert's almost at the surface, M. Let's see what happens next, if you're right about that, that the Node should make a turn and skim along the water." As Brian was saying this he pressed the camera's cable release and locked it in place having estimated that the Node was about 500 feet from NP-1. Now the F was firing at four frames per second, about a minute's worth of photographs, so Gert should arrive there at NP-1 in much less than a minute. "Boy, I hope my time estimate's right," he thought as he went back to following Gert with the binoculars.

Except for the birds inside the Node there was no visible disturbance on the water itself. The Lake remained mirror-smooth, almost glass-like. As Gert was about to meet NP-1, the birds seeing the structure abandoned their Node Ride by flapping and dropping away just in time to avoid a collision. At the instant that the Node's front surface engulfed NP-1 the Velocity Senor Module passed its data on to the Electronics Package which at the appropriate time, to the second, released the hollow eleven-inch diameter twenty pound sphere into Gert's approximate center. The sphere was shiny with its polished surface, and readily visible even with the naked eye. Brian and M intuitively came to the same realization at almost the same instant and both put down their binoculars because they weren't necessary and the sight they witnessed was far more compelling without them. It was amazing, stunning! The emotion it created could not be conveyed, yet each knew how the other felt. M and Brian were speechless as they watched the shiny twenty pound sphere race along the water's surface and then bolt skyward at ever increasing speed until it disappeared from view. At this point they both wanted to stand, but they couldn't. M and Brian simply sat in the aluminum beach chairs looking at the empty sky and then at each other in complete silence. They realized that what they had just seen never had been seen before by any human being. It was a truly humbling experience.

Chapter 8 - The 26th Day of July 1972

Same place, different time of day, same two folding aluminum beach chairs, and same binoculars and transistor radio is where Brian and M found themselves just shy of noon on the 26th day of July, the day after Gert made her spectacular appearance, just as expected, and scooped up the steel sphere, just as expected.

"Not quite as nice as yesterday, Brian, but still a nice day to be sitting here waiting for Gert's return, right."

"Yes, indeed, Professor - maybe I'll start calling you that from now on - yep, a damn nice day, and yesterday was a spectacularly nice day. Could not have been better!" was Brian's reply.

Half under his breath, as he began to skewer a slippery Peking ravioli with his chopsticks, M asked, "What did you think of *Fortune Cookie*?

"Oh, great, really good. A good find. And like most Chinese places, there's enough food for two meals, maybe more, like this lunch and a snack later," as Brian pried open the ears on his heavy white paper container decorated with a bright red pagoda. But unlike M, Brian used an old-fashioned fork...

"Pass the ginger sauce, please," was M's next comment, after which he fell silent. Brian wasn't talkative either. They sat, quiet, contemplative, mulling over what was about to happen, and then wondering what happens after that. Each man could have read the other's mind at that moment, so deeply were they consumed by what they now knew and its implications, for them, and... dare they even contemplate it,... for all mankind? It *was* scary...

Brian suddenly broke the trance. "You look like you're off in K-space, M," whereupon he immediately replied, "Yeah, and you were in the rocket ship next to me!" to which Brian replied, "Well, maybe,... maybe we both were off somewhere else. Change of subject, and I am curious. Tell me about *Fortune*

Cookie? Very odd name, but really, and I mean *really*, good food. What's the deal?"

When Jeannie, Leigh and I got together to plan Izzy's 29th Jean suggested we meet there because she knew we could hang out without being thrown out and the food was exceptional, so that's what we did. My first time, and I was very impressed."

"I can see why, my friend. I'm glad you suggested take-out from there for dinner last night."

"Me, too, Brian, me too. Neither of us wanted to head to our own places only to come back here today, so it made sense to stay here last night. Plus, can't beat the accommodations! You know, I've spent a lot of time here with your lovely, er... make that beautiful, sister, but it always was with a crowd, sometimes small, sometimes big, but always something going on. Last night, when it was still, quiet, and I was alone with my thoughts, looking around I came to appreciate how nice this house is, what to a large degree I had missed before. I can see why your folks love this place so much, and why they'll never get rid of it. So nice of them to do that for you and Izzy."

"No doubt, M, no doubt. This *is* a nice place. And it's nice of Gert to be our guest, which I have to think is serendipity, what else could it be? And, after you and Izz tie the knot, it's a place where you can go fishing! Hmmm... do you fish?"

"Nope, Izz will have to teach me. Right now I'm on the fish's side...," M replied meeting Brian's sarcasm with his own and thinking, "Gee, I'm getting better at this!"

M continued, "Anyway, kidding aside, getting back to *The Cookie* - that's what it's called by the regulars - Jeannie got to know the chef/owner Linda Lee through work. Her firm did legal work for Linda when she leased the place after *Acquitaine* said goodbye. Remember that place? Never been, but I heard it was top o' the heap when it came to haute French cuisine. I couldn't afford it! No, not been there either?" Brian was shaking his head. "Anyway, *Acquitaine* closed, and after a while I guess it was, *Fortune Cookie* that moved in. Sort of an odd name for a very high end Chinese restaurant, but I was told it was Linda Lee's pet name."

"Geez, that's kind of weird. She could have gotten a cat instead, like yours, good old Kepler, then it really could be a 'pet' name, hee-hee," Brian snickered.

"Nah, it's Linda's pet name, as in not a real 'pet.' It's because she considers herself to be very *fortunate*..." After a very brief pause, "...get it, fortune cookie, fortunate, good luck, all the heavenly bodies aligned, that sort of idea."

"Okay, and why? Was it a really big lottery ticket payout? What?"

"Linda's folks are immigrants. They worked very hard, it seems, both mom and dad, and they valued education more than anything else, as a way up and out, and they instilled that in Linda and her four sisters and brothers."

"Hmmm... it's becoming clearer. So Linda went to, what, Chinese cooking correspondence school? That would strike me as odd, since her family is Chinese, meaning their cooking by definition is Chinese!"

M was becoming irritated with Brian's insensitive remark. He knew Brian wasn't being judgmental and he knew that Brian didn't harbor a racist bone in his body nor a racist thought in his head, yet that's how his remark came across, like he did, or might... or maybe the explanation was simply that, like M, he was just strung out because of Gert, and, truth be told, Linda's story in itself *was* very unusual.

"So now you don't like Chinese people, Brian? Wouldn't have thought that of you!"

"Good grief, M, no, no, a thousand times no! I see that what I just said could come out that way, but, God, no, that isn't at all what I meant. My only thought was that Linda's story, so far anyway, was unusual. Please don't think otherwise, M. I'm wounded if you do!"

"No problem, Brian. Just had to clear the air on that one point, and you did, completely. So, to finish Linda's story, she graduated from CIA..." Brian immediately interrupted, "Let me guess, *not* the spook agency, right? to which M replied, "Right. Shall I continue?" and Brian nodded "Yes."

"Linda's Bachelor's degree is from the Culinary Institute of America, which generally is recognized as the premier college *in the world* for culinary arts. That's a big deal. In its field, CIA is the equivalent of M.I.T in yours... oh, that's right, Brian, your alma mater... And then she went on to get an M.B.A., and for several years she worked at some of the best Chinese restaurants all across the country, ending up as head chef at *Zhejiang* in Chicago. So at *The Cookie* Linda is both head chef and owner, and she's there almost all the time actually cooking, and if Jean shows up Linda rolls out the oriental rug. That's the story. What do you think?"

"I certainly am impressed, M, very much. How old did you say Linda is, M?"

"Not going there, Brian. What time is it?" M said knowing full well what time it was, but he wanted to get off *The Cookie*, and this was a good 'page break,' so to speak.

"Let's see, my very accurate wristwatch, and it is very accurate, a Rolex Oyster Perpetual, it reads 1:10:40, getting close, M, only about twenty minutes," as he raised his left arm, bent at the elbow, forearm vertical with his palm facing his face so M could read the time.

"Hmmm... can't compare to the second, Brian, but beyond that, let me check," as M studied his wristwatch, "looks like my Timex agrees with your Rolex. Of course, I'm not planning on submerging it three hundred feet..." M could see the smug look on Brian's face as he prepared for his next zinger.

"I wouldn't if I were you, submerge your Timex to three hundred feet, nope, not a good idea..." "Here it comes," M thought, and he was right. "I'd say the only things your watch and mine have in common is both their names end in 'EX,' and that's where the similarity ends..." But Brian wasn't quite done. "I think we should make 'WWND,' that's 'Worldwide Node Delivery,' make it a division of *CFO Enterprises*, so you can be paid a handsome royalty, consulting fee, whatever, so you can buy yourself a Rolex right after you buy my sister her Ferrari. Deal?"

- - - - - - - - - - - -

Brian chuckled and was done with his witty remarks. He looked at the Rolex time as he finished. "Ten to go, M. Maybe we should start scanning the sky, binocs at the ready, just in case Gert's a few minutes early." Then Brian gazed skyward surveying the general area the Node would enter on its return.

But M just sat still, his head drooping a bit, almost as if he would nod off, while muttering "Nope, Brian, no point. Gert will be on time, there, from that direction, as his left arm was stiff as a board, index finger extended pointing in the specific direction of the Node's return. I might be off a bit in elevation, that's an approximation, but I'm pretty good at it because I've had a lot of practice at the Observatory. Where I know I'm on the money is the azimuth because I put our mil-grade compass here on the dock," as he pointed to the large-ish, well-encased compass lying between his feet, "and that's the direction she'll approach from, mark my words."

"Okay, M, I'm sure you're right, but at the moment I'm enjoying looking." Brian spoke from under the binoculars that were welded to his head as he moved it slowly, side to side, then up and down. "Right on cue, M, right on cue. Hear that? The birds, their noise just got louder, and I think it will continue to grow for the next few minutes. They know, M, they know. Gert's on her way, and they know, just like before!"

"Wow!" M thought, "Brian's right!" as he perked his ears. Yes, the birds *are* getting louder, just as they had yesterday, just as the crickets and frogs had on Gert's previous visits. "Remarkable!" he thought. "I do hear that, Brian, the birds getting louder, I *hear* it! Now's the time for the binoculars," and just as he was saying that, Brian exclaimed, "There!" as he pointed skyward, "Look where you were pointing, M. There they are, another flock of tightly packed birds, and it looks like they're RIDING THE NODE!! And having a ball doing it!!"

M was rapt. He looked up, and everything Brian said was true. There was the flock, and upon close examination, not even all the same species! "Remarkable!" M thought, "Wonderful!" There were blue jays, and sparrows, and grackles, and some others M couldn't recognize. And they all remained in formation, wings tight to their bodies, not one moving closer to another. "This is a carnival ride for those guys," M thought, "They must be having a blast!! Brian and I have to get into this, it's important, really important, but after Gert drops the payload..."

And upon closer examination, in the middle of the flock, mostly obscured by the flock, was a shiny object also maintaining its position with respect to the birds. Brian said it first, "The sphere, I see the sphere! Right in the middle of all those birds! They're obscuring the view, M, but if you look closely you'll see it because it's so shiny. The Node did bring the sphere back!!!" Brian shook, trembling as he said this, so profound was his reaction. He was having trouble himself believing his own eyes, but there it was, a stationary flock of birds that wasn't stationary at all surrounding a polished metal sphere that didn't move either, barreling through the air towards the Lake's surface. "See it, M? Do you see it?"

"Yes, I do, Brian. And I'm about to wet my pants! This is everything we predicted, *everything*!! Both men were standing, binoculars welded to their heads. Gert's trajectory was nearly vertical, but its speed slowing, noticeably. "It's close to making the turn, Brian, you can tell by the reduced velocity. Should be coming around right about now," and sure enough, the flock surrounding the sphere slowed even more and began a turn close to the Lake's surface on a course that would bring the gaggle almost to where the sphere was picked up yesterday.

"Brian, Brian, don't forget the remote!" M's voice cracking with anxiety. "Got it right here, M," as Brian put down the binocs and extracted the Heathkit remote control from his pant pocket. "They're not quite to the drop point, M. I'd like to try triggering it when the sphere's at about the same position it was when it was picked up yesterday because that's the closest point to us, remember, about a hundred feet out, and also closest to the water."

It was such a bizarre sight, an almost indescribable sight, this flock of, oh, maybe, fifty birds, all different sizes, shapes, colors, skimming along the water's surface, oh, maybe three feet above it, not a single one of them changing position with respect to any of the others while in their midst was the shiny sphere whose position was as fixed in space as theirs, at least with respect to each other.

"They're close, Brian. You got the camera rolling?" "Yes, just turned it on, M. It's firing at about four frames a second, we've got about a minute of photos a third of a second apart. We should get all of this I'm pretty sure. Let me concentrate on the release," as Brian gripped tightly the Heathkit remote control waiting for what he figured would be the best time to actuate it, and that happened to be five seconds away. "Here we go, M, keep looking through the binocs," as Brian pressed the large red trigger button that Marty had installed.

"See that, M, did you see that?" Brian exclaimed, as a tiny hatch opened near the sphere's 'North Pole' located between the two reflective dots used by the Sphere Velocity Sensor, and a pressurized gas plume shot out, a burst from the sphere's thruster "rocket," which wasn't a rocket engine at all, instead a 12 gram CO_2 cartridge providing just enough thrust to impart to the sphere some velocity, and therefore some momentum, in the Node's self-contained flat spacetime reference frame, whereupon the sphere's inertial mass went from zero to a finite value which, in turn, caused it to drop out of the Node onto the Lake's surface with a slight splash. As Brian and M witnessed this display of Marty's magic, their grins slowly widened, and they looked at each other silently saying 'Mission Accomplished!' Of course the birds' reaction to Marty's magic wasn't as sanguine, because the sphere's exit disturbed them causing some birds to move, and as they did they also fell out of the Node - oh, well, ride over...

"I have to sit," said Brian, emotionally drained, physically exhausted, too, even though he hadn't done anything. "Ditto," was M's reply, as they both sank into the folding aluminum beach chairs, both quiet, self-satisfied, and, most of all, astonished... and frightened... by what they just had witnessed.

- - - - - - - - - - -

After some time taking stock, both M and Brian looked at each other, smiling broadly, with M saying "Ready to retrieve the cargo, Skipper?" to which Brian nodded 'Yes' while stepping carefully into the rowboat as M followed. "Get that line, M," Brian remarked as M entered the boat, "and give us a shove from the dock, please." "Aye aye, Skipper," as M did as requested while Brian dropped both oars in the water heading toward the shiny, metal sphere that floated peacefully about a hundred feet away.

As they approached the sphere, "Here, M, you do the honors, please." Brian handed M an oversized, floating fishing net with a long handle and large basket. "The sphere will easily fit in there. Would you bring her onboard, you sea dog, you?" "Aye aye, Cap'n," as M scooped the sphere from below into the large mesh basket. "Onboard, she is, Cap'n," as M carefully plucked its precious cargo from the net and set it on a thick pad on the rowboat's deck. "Excellent work, Swabbie, excellent. We'll inspect the package onshore." And Brian slowly turned the boat to head back to the dock.

"Look at that, Brian," said M holding the sphere, "not a scratch, nothing! Quite amazing! The Node enveloped its contents and protected it from outside effects, like reentry friction as it traversed the atmosphere. I wasn't sure about this, Brian. I was hoping, of course, but truth be told, I really wasn't sure..." M trailed off, holding the sphere higher, and slowly rotating it to inspect every square inch of its surface. Not a blemish to be found! Just a highly polished metal sphere with the small, barely discernible hatch door at its north pole flanked by the two reflective dots used by the sphere's Velocity Sensor! "Looks perfect," M said, "so if there are any future flights maybe we know what to expect."

"Whew, makes me feel better, too, M," Brian commented. "I don't see anything either, nothing at all. Looks spotless to me, just the way it did when it left here. And what's this about 'if there are any future flights.' Shouldn't that be '*when* there are future flights?' So what were you worried about? Something that would inhibit future flights? This is important, you know, really important," as Brian hinted strongly about his intentions for using Nodes.

M answered, "Well, stay with me here, it's been an evolution of my understanding of what happens 'inside' a Node. I was worried because I didn't know what was going to happen when the Node reentered the atmosphere at high velocity. At first I thought, Would travelling through the air at a max speed of 3517 mph, higher than Mach 5, which is what the calculations show, would that cause enough frictional heating to damage the sphere? You know, the Node doesn't make the outside atmosphere go away, whatever that atmosphere is, it only makes gravity go away. And the answer to that first question obviously is 'no' because the sphere's in perfect condition, but not because of my initial reasoning. I thought the atmosphere within the Node would be dragged along with the outside atmosphere so the sphere's velocity through the air inside the Node would be the same as if it were traveling through the actual atmosphere on its own, hence heating up by friction, maybe burning up like a meteorite. With me so far?"

Brian nodded 'yes,' and M continued. " And then, in thinking about it, I thought 'Not to worry' because we fly jets much faster than that, and they're fine. I was just a little concerned, so I looked up the speed record for this type of thing. It's 4,520 mph, in '67, in a piloted X-15-A rocket powered jet, which is much higher than Gert's 3,517 mph reentry. So then I said to myself, 'OK, no problem with frictional heating,' until I realized I was wrong! I thought the sphere would heat up, but not enough to be damaged. But what I finally came to realize is that the sphere doesn't heat up at all! Why? Because the Node actually carries the atmosphere inside it with it. Wherever it goes, any atmosphere that became trapped stays trapped! Anything that was caught by the Node stays with it as long as the relative velocity test is met, that is, no motion in the Node's reference frame."

M was getting long-winded, he knew that, but he wanted to finish, he wanted to put this question to rest because knew, or suspected at least, that Brian was puzzled by it. So he continued. "Brian, have you thought of what would be a good mental picture of a Node? It's not like a balloon that has a well-defined, thin skin with something inside it that goes wherever the balloon goes. It's not that. What it is, is like a balloon whose 'skin' is an amorphous shell of some thickness, an ill-defined fuzzy region in which the zero gravity interior fades to the non-zero external gravitational field, whatever value that may be. "Make sense?" M asked Brian.

"Yes, but a specific example might help?" was Brian's retort.

"Sure. So inside Gert we know there's zero gravity, which means inside Gert the gravitational constant G is zero. Outside Gert, here on Earth for example there is gravity, and the gravitational constant is $9.8 m/sec^2$ as we all remember from third grade science, right?" Brian immediately replied, "Yes, and is that it?"

"No, Gert's 'skin' if you want to think of it that way, is the region over which G goes from zero to 9.8, and that region is a characterized by two things: one, it has a thickness, and two, that thickness can vary around Gert. Maybe it's half a meter in one place, but, say, a third of a meter somewhere else around the Node, and maybe a tenth of a meter in another spot. Get it?"

"Yes, Gert is defined by a shell of varying thickness, and across that shell the gravitational constant goes from zero inside Gert to whatever the exterior value is, here on Earth $9.8 m/sec^2$, but if Gert is hurtling through outer space, then the external G could be anything, right, depending on where she is?

"Exactly right, Brian, exactly right!" M was pleased that Brian understood and that this question had been put to rest,... that is until Brian continued.

"Okay, so what's Gert's shape? A sphere? A football? The experiment at the Shop seemed to show that Gert was shaped like a bent hot dog if I recall. But we couldn't be one hundred percent sure because there weren't enough measurement points.

So what's the deal with that, a Node's shape?" Brian asked, while all at once his facial expression revealed a deep curiosity, but circumscribed by a sense of foreboding in anticipation of M's response.

"That's a good question, Brian, really good, and really hard to answer, at least specifically for any given Node,..." Brian interrupted mid-sentence, "What? That's long-winded scientific gobbledygook for 'I don't know,' isn't it?"

"Well, when you cut to the chase, 'yes,' the answer is 'yes,' I simply *do not know*," was M's almost indignant reply, his visage exposing obvious distress and frustration.

"Okay," said Brian, "let me get this straight. We don't know how big a Node is. We don't know what shape a Node is. We don't know how thick a Node's boundary is? Well, I must say, M," Brian paused very briefly, searching for his next words, "Professor Five Decimal Places, what a fine kettle of fish! What the hell *do* we know? And only now you're telling me this? And only because it came up obliquely in a conversation about something else? I think we should change it to 'Professor One Decimal Place, on a good day...' You knew, M, that I was interested in this more for commercial possibilities than for scientific ones, maybe to move things around, maybe something like a truck, no, make that a trailer truck, with its trailer. And now this! Now, and not before! So what's this good for? Maybe transporting mosquitoes to planets that don't have any? One mosquito at a time?" Brian was enraged, at least as far as that descriptor could be applied because, generally, Brian was even-tempered even when he wasn't. But now it was different because of how he felt about what had happened over the past few weeks..

"So, was I taken advantage of? You used me,... and Marty,... and NovaTek... to find out about Nodes all the while knowing you didn't know their key properties or how to get them, when those properties were key to what could be done with them! I tell you, M, this is going to take some time... maybe a long time..." Brian rarely became so enraged, his tone rarely so belligerent, but under the circumstances he felt betrayed by one of his best friends, by his future brother-in-law. The tension of the past couple of weeks preparing for yesterday's and today's Gert experiments was extreme in and of itself, and learning what he just did, and how he just learned it, simply caused the band to snap, the pot to boil over... and M knew it.

"I don't know what to say to you, Brian," M began as they both sat, and Brian immediately interrupted. "Save it, M. Not now," but M persisted, "Please, Brian, just hear me out for a couple of minutes, please," M said with an imploring look.

"Okay, a couple of minutes," Brian's tone having calmed, "and no bullshit!" as Brian sat back waiting for M's 'explanation,' which is what he expected M to do.

"First, you're right, I should have told you, no excuses, because it does maybe decide what can be done with the Nodes. I'm sorry that I didn't tell you, really, and I can say it only so many times, so many ways, but I hope this one time you'll take seriously, because I mean it. I screwed up big time by not talking to you about this, and I AM SORRY, Brian!" was M's opening gambit, and he really did mean it.

"Anything else?" Brian wasn't convinced, except possibly that M, maybe, actually, was remorseful as was evident in his tone and appearance.

"Yes, second, there's a reason I didn't say anything before." Brian interrupted, "Oh, and that was? To take advantage of me and NovaTek to get something you wanted and then what? Walk away so you could write another paper on your discovery? As I said, way to go, M, way to go."

"No, Brian, no, you got this all wrong. Please, just hear me out?" M asked, whereupon Brian acquiesced by nodding his head slightly and raising his hand, fingers extended, palm up in a gesture to continue.

"Thank you, Brian. Second, as I was saying, I did know there was a potential problem, the things you mentioned about what we don't know, but probably should know for the Nodes to be useful. And it's not just you, by the way, who's screwed over without this information. I can't do anything either, although I do think your mosquito transport idea is pretty funny..." at which remark both Brian and M visibly relaxed with a slight grin. M continued, "I didn't want to say anything because I think I know what the problem is, and maybe a way to fix it. I wasn't sure, and I'm still not, but the more I've thought about it, the more convinced I am that there's a work-around, a way to get the info we need even if Professor one decimal place can't provide it."

"What?" Brian interrupted. "If Prof's one decimal is stymied, then who, what? Are we at crystal balls yet? Ouija boards? What then"? Brian's demeanor was much less distressed and antagonistic. He had relaxed some from his profound disappointment in M's revelation, and what it did to his future plans for Nodes, just at the time when he realized - that is, he thought - the Nodes could be used as he intended to transport items because the Gert experiment showed as much.

"Let me explain, Brian, where this problem comes from and possibly what can be done about it, okay?" Brian nodded. "The theoretical model of a Node is based on the vector sum of the gravitational fields from two or more objects, right?" Brian nodded again. "What are those objects? Cylinders, cubes, prolate spheroids, a mix of different sources, what exactly is it that's assumed for their geometries? The answer is spheres. They're all spheres, perfect spheres that are uniform and homogeneous and smooth. Reminds me of the physicist and cow story. Have you heard it?"

"Nope, but I'm guessing you're going to tell me?" M replied, "Actually, yes, I am. I think it will make my point more emphatic, and maybe lighten up this discussion... So, a group of dairy farmers hire a physicist to help with a problem they're having, low milk production. They thought there might be a problem with the cows, so they engaged physicist Professor Klopstock, a renowned theoretician, for a handsome sum. After studying the problem at length, Klopstock was ready to present his results, and the farmers couldn't get them fast enough. A meeting was called with hundreds of farmers in attendance and Klopstock at the lectern with an assistant manning the slide projector with a giant screen. The farmer's were already impressed. 'This is gonna be good,' one of them said to his neighbor, 'Klopstock is a genius, and I know he's solved the cow problem. Oh, he's about to start, I'll shut up...' and Professor Klopstock signaled for the first slide, which showed a sphere with four small protrusions and a fifth with a fuzzy end. "Gentlemen, let us begin by assuming a perfectly spherical, smooth, homogeneous cow. You see that on the slide with its four legs and tail," as he used his pointer to touch he four small protrusions and the fifth one with the fuzzy end. "My calculations apply to a herd of these cows of any number..." he kept on going as the farmers chortled and began to leave one after another saying as they left 'Spherical cow? Spherical cow? What planet did you say Klopstock was from? Spherical cow? And do they produce spherical milk?"

"That is pretty funny, M, and I do get the point. The calculations for every Node are based on perfectly spherical masses creating the Node, whether it be the Earth and Moon, the Sun and Mars and Saturn, whatever the combination, all the sources of gravity are perfectly spherical, smooth, and homogeneous. But there's a big difference with the cow story. There the result is ridiculous because a spherical cow doesn't exist, it isn't even close to how a real cow is shaped, so Klopstock's results had to be absurd. But here the Earth is close to a perfect sphere, as are all the other masses I mentioned, no? So here the results aren't absurd, they're accurate, to five decimal places, remember."

M replied, "Yes and no, Brian. Yes, the calculations are accurate for a Node's 'center,' the single theoretical point where the Node would be *if,* and I emphasize, *if,* the sources were perfect, homogeneous, smooth spheres. And, no, because they're not. No planet, or other object in space, is perfectly spherical, homogeneous, and smooth. They're all lumpy to some degree, not quite spherical to some degree, and not homogeneous to some degree. By the time you add this all up, the Node isn't a single mathematical point that you would get if these distortions weren't there, instead it's a region where the gravity is zero or so close to zero that as a practical matter it's zero throughout. That's what a Node really is, Brian."

"I understand that, M. But you haven't answered the open questions. Size, shape, boundary thickness *of a Node?* Can you?"

M continued, "Well, no, not really." Brian winced, and M immediately continued, "But before you get upset, let me explain a little more, please." M could see that Brian's patience was waning fast, so he had to get to it. "I tried and tried to find some way to at least estimate these parameters, Brian, but there simply isn't one. We just don't know enough object the objects that create a Node, and that won't change. But there is a way out!" Brian perked up, "And that is?" M responded immediately, without hesitation, "More of yours and Marty's magic - *in situ* measurements. Not only does this solve the problem. but it's the most accurate and reliable solution, and it can be done at any time, especially if something seems to be changing."

"Geez, M, not a bad idea. At first blush I like it, a lot, because then *we* have control, *real time*! Yes, I like it... if it can be made to work... I assume you have some specific measurement ideas, no? Because if you don't we're back at square one. So, do you?"

Again, M's response was authoritative and immediate. "Yes, I do, and I'm 99 percent sure they'll work. Wanna hear them?" Brian nodded an enthusiastic 'yes.' "Can we stop arguing?" Again Brian nodded 'yes,' although somewhat less enthusiastically, adding the caveat, "Okay, water under the bridge, but I reserve being a little pissed off just for good measure..." was Brian's way of saying actually that all was well. "Let's start packing up, and I want from you a full debrief while we drive back to NovaTek, not the gory details, mind you, but the basic idea of how your measurements are going to work. Agreed?" was Brian's final remark, as he and M shook hands and headed down the dock carrying with them the two aluminum folding beach chairs and all the other assorted paraphernalia.

- - - - - - - - - - - -

The F-150 inched along the Lake House's driveway, as much because Brian and M were immersed in thought as because Brian didn't want to jostle NP-1 which had been hauled back up onto the truck's bed and covered with a tarp. M was convinced that the NP-1 wouldn't see service again, its objective having been accomplished, while Brian, on the other hand, was certain that NP-1 would be making the driveway run again in the opposite direction, back to the Lake...

Along the way M made good on his promise to Brian by explaining exactly how he intended to make measurements that would tell them the size, shape and boundary thickness of any Node. M relied on his years of experience at the Observatory and in ionospheric physics. The basic idea was to miniaturize the instruments that the Observatory used to probe the ionosphere and the atmosphere. Except for scale, making measurements inside a Node was no different in principal than what the Observatory did every day. M knew exactly how those instruments worked, to the smallest detail, so his pitch to Brian was that all they had to do was build much smaller versions of the Observatory's instruments, which should be straightforward because they would be working in a much, much smaller environment, an environment that was hundreds to thousands of times smaller!

Brian ate it up! He immediately saw that M was right about how much easier it would be to make measurements on the scale of a Node compared to the scale of the Earth's atmosphere. After all, a large Node might be *tens of meters* in size compared to the Earth's atmosphere that's *hundreds and thousands of kilometers* in size! No comparison, and scaling down is relatively easy to do. By the time the '150 pulled in to NovaTek's parking lot, Brian was fully onboard with M about how to proceed, and he was excited about getting down to the business of designing the required instruments with M's guidance on how they would work and Marty's magic in making that happen. "This is going to be exciting, M, really exciting!" was Brian's remark as he gently brought the F-150 to a stop.

Chapter 9 - Emilio and Isabella, Isabella and Emilio

Jean Simmons' phone rang just as she was closing the apartment door to leave, which caused her to scurry back inside and grab the phone. "Hello..." very slightly out of breath, but enough so that M caught on. "Hi, Jean, this is Emilio. Bad time? I'll call back - tell me when." "No, no, M, I just had to run to the phone, didn't want to miss the call. My woman's intuition told me it might be you. Let's talk."

"First, how have you been. We haven't chatted since getting together at *The Cookie*, great place, by the way. Thanks for introducing me. I've been flat out, more than flat out, actually, and I apologize for not getting back sooner. But my thesis and some other stuff I'm working on have me going 25 hours a day...So tomorrow's the end of the month, and I was wondering how you and Leigh have made out so far on Izzy's 29th?"

"Quite well, M, we've gotten a lot done, detailed plans on what we think would be good. But of course we need your imprimatur before actually doing anything. And we have to figure out who's doing what. It's a good thing you called, actually, because I'm thinking the clock is ticking and we should firm all this up. You?"

"Of course, Jeannie... and gee I'd never guess you're a lawyer!" as Jean interrupts, "I'll take that as a compliment, M... You were saying..."

"Well, and I'm sure you'll agree, we can't do this by phone. So how about another *Cookie* session. That way we can go over everything you and Leigh have, and we can agree to, what can I call them... how about, 'homework assignments.' What do you think?"

Jean Simmons was more than receptive of M's suggestion. Her thoughts ran parallel to his, or his to hers, depending. "Great minds, as they say. Yes, of course, makes all the sense in the world, and in fact I was going to suggest that myself, plus we get to visit with Linda again and have some more tres yummy appetizers!"

"Let me check my calendar, Jean... It's in here somewhere," as M clumsily fished through his briefcase. "Found it!" he exclaimed as he surprised even himself laying it out on the kitchen table. "What have you got in mind, Jean. Sooner the better, I think, but I know it has to fit yours and Leigh's schedules."

"How about Thursday, August 3rd at 5pm? That sound good, M?"

"Yes, indeed, Jean. That's great. I'll calendar it and be there at five unless I hear otherwise. If Leigh can't make it or something comes up with you, just let me know and we'll reschedule, okay?"

"Yep, done deal, Emilio,..." M was about to hang up, but Jean continued, "but before we ring off, I have what I'm sure you'll think is a dumb question, but I'm going to ask it anyway. You know, in spite of the fact that Izzy, Leigh and I have been such tight friends for so many years, and it's occurred to me many times, but it never was the right time to ask..."

"This is beginning to sound almost sinister, Jeannie. My goodness what is it that you never asked that is sooo... important, what?" was M's response, of course he now being very curious.

"Isabella's beautiful name?" "What about it, Jean, yes, it is beautiful, melodic, lyrical, ... and what exactly is there about it?"

"Where does it come from? I don't know, as I said never was it the 'right time' to ask, so I never did, and then just last week Leigh asked *me*! I figure you have to know, right?"

"Yes, of course, I do, and the answer is very simple, but I can see how you wouldn't know unless you asked and were told. Fact is, I was confused myself until Izzy told me. I always thought of 'Isabella' as being Spanish after the Queen of Spain, which it is. But it was appropriated to Ireland." M now was having fun being mysterious by pausing for several seconds.

"And..." Jean was all ears.

"Izzy' named after her great, great grandmother, Isibeal Healy; the Irish spelling is I S I B E A L. That name was apparently fairly common back in the 1800's, derived from the French as I understand it. And that's all there is to it, nothing all that mysterious after all..."

"Thanks, M, now I know. I'll tell Leigh. Thanks again, see you on the 31st! Love to you and Izzy...oops... I take the Izzy part back. She can't know about this conversation because she'll figure it out in a heartbeat. See you then," as Jean Simmons ended the call.

- - - - - - - - - - - -

"Emilio, so good to see you apparently feeling so well. Ribs healed?" "Yes, Michael," was M's reply as he pulled a chair close to Professor Hanlon's desk, plopping a large pile of computer printout on it and spreading out several dozen typewritten pages.

"I see you've been doing your homework, M. Very good. Where would you like to start? It's been a while, you know." Dr. Hanlon and M were having their every-couple-of-weeks dissertation review, and M had been somewhat delinquent because Gert was taking up so much of his time. He hoped Hanlon wouldn't catch on that he was on his thesis and elsewhere all at the same time, which he didn't.

"I've started writing, Michael, and I'd like to go over the dissertation outline that I've worked up."

"Yes, I know, M. Last time you were here we talked about your starting the writing. You don't remember? Preoccupied?" M's advisor asked.

"Oops," thought M, "I have been so preoccupied I forgot we talked about this. Geez, what am I going to do?" Then it dawned. "Well, Michael, truth be told, I'm on the verge of popping the question to Isabella, and with some of her friends I have been planning a big surprise party for her 29th. You remember that, don't you?"

"Ah, yes, of course I remember. You said I was 'on the list,' meaning the party guest list. I can imagine all this has taken a chunk of your time, M, but please remember that we do have a deadline if you want to make graduation next May. Your dissertation has to be good research, defensible and publishable, don't forget that!"

M has been justifiably chastised, and he realized at that moment that his priorities had to change, short term, thesis first, longer term, planning a graduation and a wedding, and somewhere along the way, Nodes. He vowed not to get so caught up that these things ever again got short shrift. "I hope I can make good on this!" he mused while Dr. Hanlon began leafing through the many typewritten pages.

"I see there's a lot of typing here, Emilio, but mostly bookkeeping stuff, not so much content in your outline?" M had to explain, especially because Michael called him by his full name, something he did only when the situation became more formal, less cordial, and it was Hanlon's way of getting M's attention because what was going on at the moment required it. "Pay attention!!" thought M.

"The dissertation outline, Michael, has to be fleshed out. Right now its these two and a half pages, what amount to mostly topic headings with some sparse description of content. I agree, there are lots of other pages, and you'll see it's essentially the dissertation bibliography. Right now I have about two hundred and fifty references, mostly published papers, some book sections. I'm going through each one of these," which M wasn't really doing, "to synopsize each one for the write-up. Of course, in the end many will just be cited instead of discussed in detail," which is why M figured he could avoid going over each one again in detail. After all, over several years' time he had read every one of those references, many of them more than once, so he did know how they fit in the picture in his research.

"Okay, M, I see that. And here's a tip - you have worked on this project, your thesis research, for so long now that you do know how each of these references connects to your work, and, of course, those connections should be illuminated. But, and this *is* a big but, I believe it's counterproductive for you to spend too much time talking about other people's work if doing that distracts from talking about yours. The purpose of the dissertation is for you to explain *your* research, how it was done, and what it means. Everyone in this business knows that everyone else in it extends the work of others, the 'standing on the shoulders of giants' idea. Yes, how that work fits has to be explained, and those other researchers given proper credit, but, really, M, you probably should spend less time combing over your two hundred and fifty references and more time telling the story of what you did and why it's important."

"Holy cow," M, thought, "Dr. Hanlon just let me off the proverbial hook, for this meeting anyway... But this can't happen again... Hanlon's right, I have to get more into the work I did."

"Yes, I see your point, Michael, and I *will* follow that suggestion. The fact is, I didn't know how to strike that balance, and your insight is a big help, believe me."

"My pleasure, M, my pleasure. That's what an advisor should do. So let's go through the outline portion of this pile, and then I want you to explain to me the printout, why that's here, okay?"

Emilio and Michael pored over the three page thesis outline in minute detail. Hanlon made a number of suggestions about its organization and content, add something here, move that somewhere else, be sure to begin with a summary that encapsulates the entire paper, which left M confused.

"I'm not sure I understand what you're saying here, Michael. A 'summary' right up front? Is that common? Is that in Strunk and White's style book? Could you explain this a little more?"

"Of course, M. And, no, this isn't in Strunk and White. It's in my experience, having written and reviewed research papers for many decades,... not sure I want to remember just how long..."

"I'm all ears," Emilio responded.

"Look, every paper has an 'abstract' before the beginning of the actual paper. Why? You know, it's to give the reader enough information for him, or her, to decide whether or not it's worth wading through the paper. Problem is, most abstracts fall flat on that. Well-written ones help the reader decide, poorly-written ones don't, and many if not most fall into the latter category. More often than not the abstract is the paper's 'key words' just string together in coherent sentences that don't do a good job of explaining what the paper is about, why the reader should go any further...."

M interrupted, "Yes. Michael, I have seen that a lot. The abstract makes the paper look attractive, but when you dig into it, the abstract *didn't* tell you what the paper was really about, and that's infuriating."

Hanlon continued, "Right, which is why what I'm telling you to do is summarize your paper, start to finish, right up front in maybe two pages, no more. In a contract report this is frequently the 'executive summary.' The whole idea is this - Give the reader the gist of your paper *before* he has to wade through the entire thing. That means everything, a summary of your methodology and findings, and your conclusions. Pretend that the reader doesn't have any information beyond this summary, and ask, 'Does he, or she, know what the paper is about, its findings, and its conclusions? If the answer is 'yes,' then you've done your job, and if it's 'no,' then go back and rewrite it until it's 'yes.' This section is frequently called an *Introduction*, but I think it should be more than that, an actual summary. Got it?"

"Yes, Michael, I think I do, and that's great advice. I will follow it because, besides the advantages you pointed out, I think it will the writing easier."

"I agree, M. Now," as Hanlon looked at the wall clock, "we have just enough time to go through your new data, and then I'm off to the monthly faculty meeting. Can't be late for that, one of my favorite ways to kill a couple of hours..." whereupon the esteemed Professor Michael Hanlon and perhaps his favorite graduate student, Emilio Ravelli, got down to what his dissertation really was all about.

- - - - - - - - - - -

"Yes, Mr. Ravelli, you can pick up the ring tomorrow, or if it's more convenient, on Saturday. I will be here all day both days, but it would be best if we set up a time."

"Thank you, Mr. Karim, I'll call you back within the hour after I check my schedule at the Observatory. Is that alright? Good," and M ended this brief exchange with the head jeweler and certified gemologist at Erlichman Jewelers where he was purchasing Isabella's engagement ring. He arranged to pick it up at 10am on Saturday the 29th intending to propose to Izzy the next day over a quiet dinner at an upscale restaurant, although he was indecisive as to where. "Maybe *The Cookie*," he thought, but he had to consider this more, and the more he did, he dismissed it as too risky, no can do. Erlichman's was an old line jewelry store that had been in business more than one hundred years and was known for its excellent service and top end products, including the finest watches. It was one of the few places, probably the only place in the city where you could get a Rolex Oyster Perpetual. It was where Brian purchased his.

Izzy's ring was a round, brilliant-cut solitaire three-quarter karat diamond set in an eighteen karat yellow gold band. Isabella preferred simple yet elegant jewelry, and M knew that this stone in this setting would appeal to her more than less traditional cuts and mountings. He looked at literally hundreds of stones before settling on the one he chose because of its striking beauty and quality, plus it was the most he could afford, and he went all-out on Izzy's ring. He knew she would love it!

M had called the jewelers from his office at Poly where he spent some time working on the dissertation before noticing that it was closing in on late afternoon, whereupon he packed up his work, again stuffing the briefcase well beyond its capacity and heading out for the short walk to his apartment. On his way out he bumped into Jose Diego, a senior-to-be in the physics department. "Hi, Emilio, how *are* you?" was Jose opening remark.

"Good, Jose, good. And you? Looking forward to graduating next May? We'll be doing that together, you know." M replied.

"A silly question, I think, both ways... Of course, I'm looking forward to graduating! And I'm sure you are, too! Scuttlebutt is you're back to teaching in the fall. Is that true?"

"Yep, *Phys 420, Advanced Atomic Physics*. Will you be in my class?" M asked, knowing that Jose was a very hard-working student, the type that any teacher enjoys having in class.

"Well, I don't know, for a couple of reasons, the first one being scheduling. I'd have to see if it fits. The second one is I'm not sure that would help with what I want to do."

"Which is?" M now was genuinely curious. To what did this young man aspire? "What are you mulling, Jose?

"At the end of last semester, Dr. Van Alstern got all twenty of us, the entire physics department graduating class, together for his 'career seminar,' where he talked about careers in physics from a practical point of view. Bottom line was if you stopped at your B.S. degree you could work as a lab tech in a research lab or a school lab. Or you could sign up - he said the Navy is the most technological of the services. Or, if you went on for a master's degree, then you could do that, the lab tech thing, or move into teaching at the high school or community college level. And if you bit the bullet, the way you did, and went on for a Ph.D. you could work in any kind of lab as a researcher or teach at any level in a college or university. It was very clear, really clear, though, that Van Alstern thought everyone had to go on at least for a master's degree, not much of a choice there, really. So that's it in a nutshell, and I just don't know what I want. I really don't. You got any suggestions?" at which point a flood of confusion and apprehension washed over Emilio taking him so much by surprise that he had trouble answering Jose.

"Well, ahem...," M cleared his throat, "I really, ahem...," M cleared his throat again, "haven't given that enough thought, Jose. It's a big world and presumably it's your oyster with a Ph.D. from Poly," M lied. "I have so many choices to sort through, right now just isn't the right time," another lie, "but I do know what you're going through, Jose," M lied for the third time.

"Thanks, Emilio, or should that be 'Professor Ravelli'?" as Jose turned and walked off.

"Take care, Jose, maybe we'll cross paths in 420. I can promise you this, it will be interesting," said M as he continued his walk home, this time without lying to Jose.

The parking lot at *Chez Gaston* was only about a third full, which would be expected around 7:15 on a Sunday night in late July, today being the thirtieth, which is what M hoped for because he wanted a less hurried time when he and Isabella could stay longer and just talk. *Gaston* was an unusual structure, basically a single floor, but not a flat floor. Its interior was terraced to match the outdoor terracing,... or maybe the other way around. The restaurant sat at the top of a fairly high, fairly steep hill on the city's outskirts, and it was the only remaining *haute cuisine* restaurant, primarily French, after *Acquitaine*'s demise The building was semi-circular with its entrance on the first level which was the main dining level, individual tables a very respectable distance apart each covered by a spotless white, heavy linen table cloth and set with a fine pure white *porcelaine tendre* accompanied by perfectly polished sterling silverware. The next level down was a semi-circular one comprising a wide walkway on the outside with private booths on the inside that looked onto the huge floor-to-ceiling glass wall providing a sweeping view of the city in the distance. And below that was the third circular dining area comprising an inside walkway just below the second's and embracing the most private booths, somewhat wider with higher backs than the others and set directly against the glass that was mere feet away from the first outdoor terrace. The outdoor terraces, also numbering three, were replete with flora, flowers, bushes and low growing trees imported from or inspired by the various regions of France. The elevation of the first terrace was far enough below the glass wall's bottom edge that it provided a feeling of standing at the edge of cliff with a panoramic view of the city, an immersive view that added immeasurably to the *Gaston* experience.

"*Bienvenue Chez Gaston*," was the Maitre d's greeting as Isabella and Emilio entered the foyer. "Thank you," replied M, "Ravelli, a reservation for two, seven-thirty, lowest level with the best view of the city, *n'est-ce pas...*" hinting strongly that he would like the booth with the best view that was available. "Certainly, Mr. Ravelli. Please follow me", as he accompanied the young couple around the edge of the main dining area to a set of stairs on the side leading to the lowest level with the best view. "Will this do, sir?" as he made a sweeping motion with his gloved hand indicating a booth almost centered in the row and no one on either side, with a gorgeous view of the gardens and city beyond. "Yes, indeed, this will do very nicely, thank you," as the Maitre d' guided Isabella into the booth. "Enjoy your meals, and please do not hesitate to let me know if you need anything, anything at all. My name is Antoine," he said while scanning M and Isabella to confirm that they needed nothing more at the moment. then slowly turning as he departed.

After a few minutes, a tall, svelte waitress sporting a black dress with a white button-down shirt and thin black tie approached, greeting Izzy and M as she did, "Welcome to *Chez Gaston*. My name is Marie, and I will be serving you this evening," as she placed two thick faux-leather bound menus on the table along with a many page wine list. "May I ask, have you enjoyed *Chez Gaston* before?" "No," was M's slightly drawn out response, "but we are very much looking forward to this evening, it's a special occasion." "Thank you, sir, I will do everything I can to make this a *very* special occasion." "Thank you, Marie, please give us some time with the menu." "Yes, of course would you care for cocktails?" whereupon Isabella ordered a Strawberry Daiquiri and M a Bloody Mary, on the spicy side.

"A special occasion, Emilio? I knew there was something special about this because we usually end up at *Stella's*, which is a great place, by the way, don't get me wrong, I love *Stella's*. But let's face it, *Stella's* isn't *Chez Gaston*. So what is the special occasion? You're a poor-as-a-church-mouse grad student who's never taken his lovely girlfriend here before. So what gives? Or is this Dutch?"

The couple enjoyed sipping their drinks while taking in the expansive view. M sat back in the comfortable booth and genuinely relaxed for the first time in some time. He could do that around Izzy, her wit, and calm almost bordering on nonchalance,... and beauty... enveloping him to the point that concerns about his thesis and... the damn Nodes... receded from this moment. "God, I feel good, Izzy. I just feel good right now, and I know it's because of you!"

"I do, too, M, very relaxed, comfortable feeling. This is a great place, thank you for thinking of it."

"My pleasure, my dear," as M mulled over how to bring up the formal proposal. But Izzy interrupted his flight, not letting go of her curiosity."

"You never answered my question, M. What's the 'special occasion?' "Geez, she must know, the 'woman's intuition' that every female seems to have. How do I wiggle out of this?" Then it struck him, the TA, that's it, talk up the TA! So he started, "Well, if you're going to pry it out of me - I was going to tell you a little later," while thinking to himself "Make this good, plausible, make it up if you have to!" So he bit the bullet, "It's about my new position at Poly."

Izzy pressed, "What about it, M? This is the Teaching Assistantship, right? So what's the big deal?"

"It's a much bigger deal than I thought. Dr. Hanlon asked me to stop by on Friday to sign the paperwork and talk about what I'd be doing, and it's a much bigger deal than I thought, and it's worth celebrating, and coming here with you was the niftiest way I could think of to do that!" "Pretty good," M thought, "Hope she buys it." And he held up his Bloody Mary to make a toast as Izzy did the same with her Strawberry Daiquiri, clinked her glass with his, and said, "Cheers, my dear, I'll tell you all about it because it is a big deal! Curious?"

"Yes, of course, M, so fill me in."

"Well, first of all, Teaching Assistantships just like professorial positions are ranked. The same way the University's teachers have slots of Instructor, Assistant Professor, Associate Professor, and Full Professor, TA's are classified as TA-1 or TA-2. When I left teaching and went full-time on my Research Assistantship I was a TA-2, and that's where I figured I would be again with my going back to teaching."

"And?", Izzy now was visibly curious. M thought, "She bought it! That this is the 'special occasion.' Hooray!" He could spring the ring when he wanted to, somewhere through dinner.

"I'm not a TA-2, Isabella, I've been appointed an Instructor! Because I'm so close to finishing my Ph.D., Michael told me he lobbied for me to be treated the way I would be if I had already graduated, and the Dean of Academics, Professor Bolt bought it. What this means besides a real bump in academic rank is a real bump in pay, up twenty-five percent from what a TA-2 is paid, so that's several thousand dollars a year! So this once-in-a-blue moon dinner at *Gaston*'s is something I actually can afford! What d'ya think?"

"My goodness, Emilio. Yes indeed, this is a special occasion. Wow! It really is. Congratulations!! My favorite college Instructor!" Izzy's face glowed with a broad toothy smile, her eyes wide open, as she leaned across the table to plant the most affectionate kiss on M's lips.

"She bought it," thought M, "really. So much so that maybe the ring will be a letdown!" He was terrified. "What did I do?" he mused. "This may not have been such a good idea, although it is true, now I'm Instructor." He had to get off the subject, so he steered the conversation in another direction, this time having to do with their futures. "Good segue," he thought.

"I bumped into one of my former students the other day, a kid named Jose Diego. He's a senior, and we talked about his maybe taking the course I'm teaching *Phys 420, Advanced Atomic Physics*. Jose's a very bright kid, near the top if not at the top of this year's graduating class."

"And?" Izzy didn't see where this was going, not yet.

"And, Jose and I got into a kind of philosophical discussion about what he wanted to do when he graduates, the whole 'enchilada,'..." "Whoa," thought M, "linguistic genius!"...of possibilities, working in a lab, teaching, grad school, the military, and so on.

"And, what does this have to do with us, M?"

"Well, that conversation disturbed me, Izzy... a lot. Because I feel like Jose. I think I know what our, and, yes, I mean, *our*, options are, not mine, but we haven't talked about them. Our lives are so hectic, you in school, me in school, all this stuff going on that we don't, we haven't really discussed what to do when all this changes. It has to be something we *both* agree on, but we haven't really discussed this much, actually hardly at all..." M trailed off as Marie approached.

"How are your drinks, may I ask?"

"Excellent," replied M as Izzy nodded her assent, "very good."

"Would you care to order, sir?"

"Yes, please, fairest first," as M smilingly gestured towards Izzy. "Of course, sir, a true gentleman," Marie interjected with a grin. Izzy and M had perused the menus while they were talking, and both knew what they wanted for dinner, plus everything at *Chez Gaston* was *a la carte*, which made ordering easier because you could get exactly what *you* wanted, not what the chef thought should go on the plate together, for whatever reason.

For an appetizer Izzy ordered small arugula salad with goat cheese and pears, while M went for the lobster bisque. As a main course Izzy selected the filet mignon, medium rare with mushroom sauce, and sides of asparagus in hollandaise and baked potato with chives, sour cream and bacon bits. M maintained the lobster theme, ordering the baked lobster stuffed with scallops, shrimp and haddock, and sides of hasselback butternut squash and stir-fried spinach with garlic.

"And, Marie, a bottle of Asti Spumante, please, Bin 146" as M pointed to page eight of the wine menu. "Yes, sir, excellent choice." Of course, M had no way of knowing whether or not Marie knew that choice really was 'excellent,' or whether or not Marie actually had sampled that specific bin, or whether or not Marie automatically said 'excellent choice' for every wine order no matter what it was. But it didn't matter to M because he and Izzy both enjoyed Asti, and he knew the vineyard that produced Bin 146, and it was, in fact, an excellent choice.

M figured that sometime during their meal Izzy would want to stop by the ladies' room, and it was then that he would spring the ring by covering it with her napkin. And when she returned, *voila!* There it would be, the ring, sitting in a small, black, velvet lined box of highly polished black ebony wood emblazoned with Erlichman Jewelers' name and crest in pure gold leaf inset in the ebony, almost as if it were marquetry.

The meal was flawless, perfectly prepared, perfectly served without hurry. "Oh, Emilio, this is so wonderful. I can't remember the last time I had such a memorable dinner... with the man I love so much!" as Izzy held her wine flute high to toast the occasion. "Couldn't agree more, Isabella. You look sooo beautiful by the subdued lights in here and the city lights out there," as he carefully swung his hand across the panorama that was the city below. In the rapture of this moment, M abandoned the hide-the-ring-under-the-napkin plan and opted to give it to her then and there.

"There's something important, Isabella, not what we were discussing before, something much more important," as he held the emblazoned ebony box in the palms of his crossed hands offering it to Izzy. *"Isabella Healy will you marry me?"*

Izzy's eyes welled as she took the box holding it between her thumb, and index and third fingers, slowly turning it to catch the light and exclaiming to M, "My God, M, I don't think I have *ever* seen so beautiful a jewelry box. That is what this is, no?" M smiled as wide a smile as was humanly possible, not saying a word, just nodding his head. "Should I open it?" Isabella asked. "Of course, please, please, and then answer my question. You haven't answered my question, Izz." "Oh, my, you're right, I haven't answered you,... but I will, without opening the box first...," Izzy replied, laughing as she did. "Yes, Emilio Ravelli, a thousand times 'yes,' I want to be your wife! I want to be Mrs. Ravelli, that is Mrs. Doctor Ravelli!" and Isabella leaned across the table to plant the most passionate kiss she could with the table between them.

"I'm the happiest guy in the world, Izzy. We've been together for a long time, but it's not the same as making it official. I'm sooo... lucky! I love you, Izz, more than I can say!" with which M raised his champagne flute and they toasted their engagement.

"Oh, my goodness, M, I was so caught up I didn't open the box!" as Izz carefully, slowly pried the box open. Her jaw dropped, literally, as she took in the beauty of her engagement ring with its truly brilliant diamond set so simply in understated elegance against a jet black background. I don't know what to say, M" Izzy remarked as she started to tear up again, "I just don't what to say, this ring is so perfect, I mean perfect in every way! Thank you, my love," as she slid the ring on the ring finer of her left hand. "I'm never taking it off," and she leaned across the table again to kiss her fiancé.

Chapter 10 - Kepler Books a Ride

As a child Emilio Ravelli lived in a three-decker on a dirt road not far from downtown. He was the oldest of two kids born to second-generation Italian-American parents, and, not surprisingly, named after his great grandfather, much as Izzy had been after her great, great grandmother. Back in the 'old country' M's grandfather was Carabinieri, a well-respected member of the domestic police force, but upon immigrating to the United States he was relegated to menial jobs like so many tens of thousands of others. While he spoke some English, a clear advantage for anyone coming here from abroad, his was poor, which in the end didn't help. M's grandmother was a stay at home homemaker who spoke no English at all and never intended to pollute the mother tongue with it. Of course, without its being intended, this benefited M greatly because he now was bilingual, although with a noticeable southern Italian accent...

M came to physics as a career because an uncle actually gave him a book on introductory physics when he was in the eighth grade, a high school level text that the uncle used in a course he had taken. M's education was entirely in the public schools, until high school when he parted ways with the public system on the advice of his seventh and eighth grade math teacher, Mr. Paulson. Paulson recognized M's talent for mathematics and suggested he apply to a private college-preparatory high school, which M did, was accepted and graduated near the top of his class, with standardized testing and his academic record showing a strong aptitude for math and science.

Then, upon completing his B.S. in physics, M faced the same conundrum that Jose Diego faced - what to do next? And just like Jose, Emilio was encouraged - no, make that strongly urged - to continue in graduate school because a B.S. in physics pretty much relegated its holder to being a lab tech without much upward mobility. Now it was back, that same feeling of walking into the fog that engulfed him when he talked to Jose a few days ago. And now it was worse because Izzy said 'yes,'... "Thank

God," thought M, and whatever he did impacted her life as much as his. What to do, what to do?

M glanced at the time, 7:30am, sipped a little more coffee, and packed up his pile of papers to head to the Observatory. Then, as an afterthought, darted back into the apartment to retrieve the current issue of *AutoTech* magazine which had a feature article comparing a Camaro SS to a Boss Mustang. If he had any time, and was a big if, he wanted to read more about the Camaro because it seemed to him to be underpowered, sluggish for what ostensibly was a fast car. M simply wasn't mechanically inclined like Brian, so the difference between solid and hydraulic lifters, or the meaning of engine timing 'before top dead center,' all this was way past where M was, or for that matter, wanted to be. His bailiwick was electronics, and he was pretty good at it, but first and foremost M was a theoretician, a scientist who did mathematical modeling, and the experiments that studied his theories. For the several years of his Ph.D. program M's time was split pretty much evenly between the theoretical and experimental sides because it had to be. Fact is, he was good at and enjoyed both, and because of that he wasn't sure which way he ultimately would tilt, unlike most of his fellow grad who were firmly in one camp or the other. But, that decision wasn't imminent, and today M had two important things to do at the Observatory, first, set up a run on the Incoherent Scatter Radar because Dr. Hanlon noticed what appeared to be some anomalies in last week's data and because of that wanted a re-run, and, second, develop an analysis program for the Node boundary measurement system that Marty was working on, something very compact that could be run on a single-board computer. "Lots to do," M thought, "Lots to do," as he grabbed the Camaro's keys on the small side table next to the door, and started out. "Oh, geez, the cat," M said to himself. "Can't leave Kep all day without fresh food and water and cleaning his box!" So M went back inside and tidied up after his cat, Kepler, petting him on his way out for the second time, and saying "Have a good day, Kep. Be a good cat! Practice being a good cat, Kep, because you'll have a new Mom soon. Yes, Izzy! I'm engaged, Kep, how cool is that!! See you tonight. Maybe I'll rustle up some tuna for dinner..." M said aloud to his cat, knowing full well that Kepler didn't understand a single word, and that even if he did, as cats wont are to do, he didn't really care... But M was so excited about Izzy's saying 'yes' that he had to tell someone, even if that someone was wrapped in fur and had four legs and a tail!   - - -

- - - - - - - - -

"Hello, Emilio, " the Observatory guard said as M entered. "Hi, Ralph, how are you today?" was M's response.

"I am well, Emilio. Thank you for asking. And might I ask, Why are you here now? You're usually one of the night owls, so this is a rare occasion, not that I'm not happy to see you. Something special going on?" Ralph's curiosity bordered on nosiness, but his job demanded that he know who was in the building at all times, and as a rule that meant knowing why as well. Ralph was only doing his job.

"Nope," M answered, "nothing special Ralph. But there is something special - I got engaged last night!! And I couldn't be happier, but of course that's not why I'm here now. I've just been so busy I had to pry loose some time to get some things done that have been hanging." M was intentionally vague because, besides getting a run in for Professor Hanlon, the other main reason for his being at the Observatory was to do some programming on the 'Node Project,' as he had come to think of it.

"Tell, me, Ralph, that shipment of 'smart terminals' last week, are they all in the storeroom, or have they been set up, do you know?" M inquired about a shipment of fifteen new computer terminals that did more than simply display information. These 'smart' devices permitted data input from an attached keyboard and were brand new state-of-the-art machines that at this time were available only to government contractors. These Digital Equipment Corporation, DEC, devices interfaced with local PDP-11 minicomputers as well as the Observatory's CDC 7600 supercomputer. The '7600 controlled the radars and other large machines and performed initial data processing on the terabytes of data that each radar produced, while the '11's were used for local data processing and program development. It was this latter use that M would take advantage of this day.

"Well, a lot of them have been set up, Emilio. I don't know exactly how many, though. Do you have to use one?" Ralph asked.

"Yes, I do, Ralph, but first I have to set up a run on the ISR. "Let me do that, figure a couple of hours, then I'll find one of the new smart terminals I can use, or..." M paused to assess Ralph's reaction to what he was about to say, "... or, I'll purloin one, okay?"

M knew that every computer and every terminal was supposed to be accounted for and assigned to a specific contract or function, for example, data processing on M's project, 'Ionospheric Electron Winds,' or something more mundane like 'Machine Maintenance.' M studied Ralph's reaction, waiting for "Emilio, I'm not sure you can do that," or something similar, but there was none, either because Ralph didn't fully grasp what M had just said, or he did get it but didn't care. Either way M figured he was in the clear.

The Incoherent Scatter Radar's control panel hadn't been touched since M's last visit two nights prior, not a knob twisted, not a button pressed, not a meter reading differently, not a panel light lit now that wasn't before, and vice versa. ISR sat motionless, a truly impressive sight, but even more so when it was painting the ionosphere with electromagnetic energy. "Well, old girl, I see you haven't been busy!" M addressed the panel as if it were alive as he pulled up his functional but not very comfortable chair, reaching as he did to flip several switches on the panel as he settled in.

After checking all of the instrument's settings, he was ready to write the code that would control ISR for today's run, where ISR would look, how long it would look, how much power would be used, how many repetitions there would be, and so on, and so on.. He headed to the coding room to create the computer program on punch cards, which took about an hour. When he was done, M returned to ISR control, read the stack of punch cards into the ISR computer, sighed, and muttered "Okay, girl, here we go. Get a lot of great data!" as he pressed ISR's start button, the big, bright red momentary pushbutton switch that was protected by a flippable safety guard.

The panel lights suddenly came to life, blinking and changing color and rhythm, and all the panel meters shot from zero while the data display screens blinked and refreshed to reveal ISR's mechanical and electrical and data acquisition status. It was an impressive display of the technology and an even more impressive display for someone like M who was intimately familiar ISR down to the most minute detail.

M took a read on the time, just shy of 10am, and he estimated today's ISR run would finish around 5pm. But he could wait until then. M wanted to write a computer program that would process data from Marty Lobesky's NBS, the Node Boundary Sensor, and doing that would take a few hours anyway, assuming he could 'purloin' a smart terminal and hook it up to a PDP-11 that was running the Observatory's FORTRAN 66 compiler. M's plan was to write the FORTRAN code needed to acquire and process the data from several solid state infrared lasers that

Marty was using to probe the Node's boundaries. Marty and Brian already had developed plans for the control hardware to scan the entire sphere surrounding the NBS. What they needed was the data processing program that would analyze the lasers' return signals, which was M's job.

M would write the required computer program using one of the new 'smart' terminals that eliminated punch cards, which were the ultimate pain, compile it on a PDP-11, and then 'burn' it onto an Intel 1702 2048-bit EPROM, an erasable programmable read only memory chip that only recently had become available. Then, program in hand, literally, he wanted to get to the Shop to give the chip to Marty so he could begin installing and testing it. M's hope was that he could get this done in time to reach NovaTek by around three o'clock, but he knew this was ambitious.

"I need a break," M thought, and he headed to the coffee maker, along the way bumping into Ana Esperanza, another grad student who hailed from Brazil. "Hey, Ana, how are you? Long time no see!"

Ana had just graduated from Poly with her Master's degree in Electrical Engineering, but she was more of a physicist at heart and jumped at the Research Assistantship that she was just completing at the Observatory. Even though she graduated in May, her RA ran through August, so she still spends all of her time at the Observatory running experiments, working with the equipment, making adjustments and improvements, and designing and building some test equipment... and practicing her English, which is perfect except for her noticeable accent. Ana's long term plan is to return home in November to start her new job at Embraer Aerospace as a Flight Test Engineer. Embraer was a fairly new start-up, and it looked like a good opportunity for someone just starting out herself. Ana was rarin' to go!

"I'm great, Emilio. And you?" Ana didn't feel she knew M well enough to call him 'M' all the time, but she did when the circumstances were right. Their relationship was mostly as colleagues at the Observatory and occasionally at University functions on campus.

"Thanks for asking, Ana. I'm more than great! I'm fabulous! Wonderful!"

"My goodness, M, such emphatic terms! Should I ask why?"

"Yes, I *want* you to ask why!" said M.

"Okay, you asked for it, Why??"

"I got engaged yesterday, Ana. The girl of my dreams, Isabella Healy. I asked, she said 'yes,' and I couldn't be happier! We've been together for a long time, but you never know until you know for sure. I'm a very lucky guy, Ana, and I just feel soooo... good about it!" M's joy and love for Izzy were so apparent that Ana's only response was "Congratulations, Emilio. This is wonderful news. I hope that someday I can feel the way you do!"

"Thanks, Ana, thanks. And you will, too,... feel this way, when it's right." M said reassuringly. After all, Ana was very attractive, very smart, all wrapped in a very pleasant personality, so M had no doubt that she would be the apple of many a suitor's eye. And while he was thinking this about Ana, it occurred to him that she would make a splendid guest at Izzy's party. "Tell me, Ana, any plans for Saturday the 19th? Are you free?"

"Well, let me see, Emilio. Ah, yes, I can cancel my luncheon with Queen Elizabeth, no biggie," Ana said, jokingly with a very broad smirk. "Nope, no plans. Why?"

"How would you like to come to my fiancé Isabella's 29th birthday party at her family's Lake House right on the shore of Lake Arrowhead? You know where that is, right? It's going to be a pretty big bash, maybe forty plus guests, informal, all you can eat and drink, that kind of affair. What do you think?"

"What do I think? Need you ask? I'm flattered, honored. And of course pleased to say 'yes,' I'll be there! Thank you, M!" Ana replied.

"By the way," asked M, "are you headed back to Poly from here?"

"Yes, when I'm done. I'm recalibrating the Long Baseline Array, and I should be finished, oh, maybe around six, then back to the University because I have a boatload of things to do to unplug, since I'm technically not a student there anymore. Why do you ask? Need something?"

"Well, Ana, I wouldn't want to impose, but you could do me a big favor, that is, if you have the time."

"No problem, M, what is it?"

"I'm doing a repeat run of one that was done last week. When Professor Hanlon and I went over it, he noticed some irregularities in the data, very slight mind you, but I think you know what Hanlon is like, 'stickler' would be generous..." Ana chuckled, "Yeah, I know. Had him for two courses, and, yep, he's a stickler, but in a good way."

"Agreed," said M. "In any event ISR is up and running. I started the run a little while ago, and it will be done around five. Any chance you could dump the data, just print it out, and deposit it in my office when you're back at school? This would be a big help because I have to be at NovaTek soon, before ISR's done, so it saves me a trip back here just to collect that data." M explained.

"Happy to, Emilio, my pleasure. No problem at all. I know where your 'office' is, if you want to call it that... question is, How do I get in?"

M already was fishing through his pocket for the key, and when he found it he gingerly handed it to Ana. "Here's the key, Ana. Please leave the printout on my desk, and I'll be in in the morning to take a look and hook up with Michael... oh, Professor Hanlon, I mean. I have a spare key, so you can leave this one on top of the printout and lock up as you leave. Is this OK?"

"Certainly, M, consider it done." Ana said with an odd twinkle in her eye with its lid ever so slightly closed. Then she blurted out, "This isn't why I'm on the party list, is it? Is the party a bribe?"

"Good grief, no, absolutely not, really. This just came to mind, nothing to do with the party, but it will help me out." M was being truthful, but he could see how the timing could raise suspicion. "I feel really stupid, Ana. I didn't mean to give you the wrong impression, which I apparently did. My apology..." Ana interrupted. "M, I was kidding, just kidding! I didn't think for a minute that you would tie the party to the printout! Just a joke! Now *I have* to apologize!"

"Geez, Ana, you're a friend. We've known each other now, for, what, two years, since you came to Poly, right? And we've spent a lot of time together here at the Observatory. That's why I invited you, pure and simple..." Ana replied, "M, I know that. Don't worry, we're all good."

"Thanks, Ana. Well, I do have to go to finish up here and trek over to NovaTek," as he gestured goodbye, coffee in hand.

- - - - - - - - - - -

It took M longer than he expected to write the NPS code and burn it to the EPROM, so he was later than expected arriving at the Shop, around four o'clock. Marty greeted him as he walked in, "Emilio, you're here! We expected you an hour ago?"

"Yes, Marty, I'm late. Sorry," as Brian rounded the corner approaching M for a high five. "You've got it, right? The memory chip?"

"Yes, Brian, right here," holding up the chip for both men to see and handing it to Brian for inspection. There wasn't much to inspect, the chip itself was about one quarter inch square sitting under an ultraviolet transparent quartz window mounted on a plastic case about two by three quarters of an inch with a twenty-four-pin pin out. M's program resided on that chip and would process all the data collected by Marty's laser device.

"Sorry I'm late, guys, but writing the code and burning the PROM took longer than I expected, plus it's been a hectic twenty-four hours.

"Yes, M, we know," Brian remarked, and then in unison he and Marty yelled out "CONGRATULATIONS! On your engagement to Izzy!"

"Thank you both. I couldn't be happier. Last night when she said 'yes' was one of the best moments of my life. I love her sooo... much, and she's such a wonderful person, I am a very lucky fellow!"

"Izzy feels the same way, M." Brian remarked, continuing, "She called me this morning at six thirty, and then she called Mom and Dad around nine. Izz was gushing, M, she's so happy now that you've made it official. The timing is perfect, too, with her birthday around the corner." whereupon Brian turned to Marty and said, "Have we invited you to Izzy 29th birthday surprise party yet? Saturday the 19th, mid afternoon 'til whenever, quite late we hope! It's at the Lake House. You've been there, Marty, remember where?"

"Yep, I sure do, Brian, and thanks for inviting us. I'll check with Sandra to be sure there isn't a conflict, ...psst, and if there is it'll be resolved in Izzy's favor... so we'll be there. Wouldn't want to miss it!"

"Okay," Brian and M said in unison. Then Brian followed with "Alright, now that we're done with the fun stuff, let's get to the technical stuff," as he motioned for Marty and M to follow him into his office.

There on his desk sat a single breadboard chuck full of electronic components and beside it what looked like a small power supply with a zip cord power cable and regular wall plug. "Marty, why don't you start?"

Marty Lobesky carefully picked up the breadboard as if it were a child, which in fact it was, Marty's child and he treated it just as such, holding it for M and Brian to inspect from all angles before getting into his description.

"Well, gentlemen, what you see here," Marty pointing to a circular array of chips alone on one side of the board, all the other components being on the other side, "is the infrared solid state laser optical scanning array. You will notice that there are two circles of laser diodes with the diodes on the inner circle filling the small space between the diodes on the outer circle. This geometry effectively reduces the individual element scan angle by half. It's like having two very closely spaced collimated beams from a single chip. Clever, huh?" Marty's toothy grin betrayed his considerable pride in his work.

"Yes, " M said, "very clever, Marty. What's that circular platform under the laser array?"

"Oh, that, should have explained it. That's the motor drive. Even with my tightening the scan angles as much as I could, my understanding from Brian was that you needed continuous three hundred sixty degree azimuthal sensing, right?" M nodded, as did Brian. "Okay, the stepping motor that drives the platform turns it through the entire azimuth, and then it starts over in the opposite direction with an offset of one half scan angle. This gives what amounts to continuous scanning over the entire circle...twice..."

"Impressive, Marty," M interrupted.

"Yes, well, gentlemen, that's the gist of the gizmo. All the other stuff is to control the lasers and read out their data. That's where your chip comes in, M. I know the program has been burned to the EPROM, but what I need besides that is the actual source code so I know exactly how this device will work."

"Got it, Marty. And I figured as much, so I brought it. It's in the SS out front. I didn't bring it in because I didn't want to fish through all the stuff on the back seat given that I was late as it was. Wait a minute, and I'll grab it," as M departed quickly to retrieve the source code.

Minutes later when M returned, Brian looked at him and Marty both, saying "M, concerning this project, Marty hasn't been read in yet, and there are some issues you and I have to discuss. This is a good time, I think. Marty, you can start looking over the source code. M, you and I can hole up in my office, shouldn't be long," and Brian turned towards his office while M handed Marty the source code listing. "Thanks, M," Marty said. "Wow! This is massive!" to which M replied, "Yep, lots of lines. Fortunately I had it block programmed over the past few days, so the line-by-line coding wasn't that bad, and, in addition, I used one of our new smart terminals that actually accepts typed input on the screen instead of using punch cards. Cool, huh!" "Yes, sir," was Marty's predictable response. Now I know what Brian should get NovaTek as a Christmas present! I'll give you guys the privacy you need," and Marty walked away.

Brian's office seemed neater to M, and he remarked about it. "Very perceptive, M, brother-in-law-of-mine-to be, and he gave Emilio a bear hug that could have damaged a lesser man, but M was saved by being tall and thin and quite muscular because he worked out at the University's gym. "Thanks, Brian," M said with a groan, "Don't hurt me too much. I don't think Izz would want to get hitched with me in a wheel chair..."

"I must say, M, you're getting better at the 'levitous' remarks, as you call them - I still don't think that's a real word. Anyway," as Brian retrieves the *Glenfiddich* from his desk drawer along with two glass into which he pours two fingers, neat, offering one to M, slowly nosing his and then holding it to the light, all the while beckoning M to do the same, and finally raising his glass high while clicking M's and declaring "CONGRATULATIONS! Emilio Ravelli. To a long, happy life married to my beautiful sister Isabella. And using the words of a well-known Irish wedding toast, I say 'Here's to the groom with the bride so fair, And here's to the bride with groom so rare!' and indeed you are, M, rare... in the best possible way." M actually blushed, maybe because of the Scotch, but more likely because of how he felt hearing Brian's toast. "I rea... I'm really at a loss for words, Brian. I can't tell you how much what you just said means to me! Thank you!" and M placed his empty glass on Brian's desk with a noticeable thud.

- - - - - - - - - - - -

"Turning to the business at hand, M, we do have to talk about the 'Node Project,' as you now call it - good name, by the way - I think we should adopt it.... I think you can see that Marty's into this up to his eyebrows, and that's good, very good. He will make this work, count on it. The problem I have right now is how much we should tell him..." M interrupted, "Yes, I noticed you mentioned that he hadn't been 'read in, yet'. So by implication I'm guessing Marty thinks this is another of NovaTek's spook projects, an off the books project, is that right?"

"Yeah, pretty much. I haven't said anything explicit except that I can't fill him in, so that's the conclusion he reached on his own based on NovaTek's history. This works very well to keep the Nodes under wraps because Marty's a team player, and he won't peek or poke where he shouldn't. He thinks you're in it because of your background in ionospheric plasma physics, and that's why you're involved in building what amount to atmospheric plasma sensors. So all that fits, makes sense to him, and to him it looks like some never-to-be-discussed project. Marty's been involved in some of NovaTek's work along those lines before, so this isn't anything new."

"So what's the problem, Brian. Seems to me that this is perfect. Marty's motivated, but totally in the dark about the Nodes. What's wrong with keeping it like that?"

"Nothing, M, nothing at all. I think that's exactly what we should do, what we *have* to do. We certainly don't want Marty or anyone else for that matter knowing anything about this, especially not now when we don't know the whole picture ourselves. I just wanted to be sure we're both on the same page, and that you're not going to tell Marty something that might tip him off as to what this really is about. Are we agreed on this?"

"Yes, Brian, one hundred percent, no question. Marty asks, my answer is 'I can't say anything, talk to Brian.'"

"Gee, thanks, sport!" Brian grinned, knowing, of course, that M was right. "So my brother-in-law-to-be is turning out to be as sneaky as I am, eh? You're right, M, that's what to do, if Marty asks. Okay, I think we're done with this," as Brian gently caressed the twenty-year old *Glenfiddich* with the obvious intention of pouring another round.

- - - - - - - - - - - -

M watched Brian hold up his beloved Scotch Whisky while he slowly rotated the bottle, slowly tilting it side to side, holding it higher, then lower, to catch the light. "You know, M, I could have, maybe still can, made a career in distilling Scotch. It's a fascinating business, very technical. I'd fit right in, I think... Of course, it would mean moving to the Valley of the Deer in the Speyside region of Scotland, hmmm... which would give you and Izz a great place to vacation!"

"Sure, Brian," was M's retort, as he smiled shaking his head slightly. "Why not? Go fer it!" then he paused, "*After* we figure out the Nodes, thank you!" Brian wanted to get down to serious business, too, so he just shrugged, fooling around finished.

"Is Marty still here?" M asked. "My thought exactly, M, let me check," and Brian left heading to Marty's electronics bench where he still sat, hunched over M's computer code, his back to Brian's office. Brian approached slowly, taking in what Marty was doing, then clearing his throat to get Marty's attention. "Still here, I see. How come?" Marty quickly glanced up at the clock. "Geez, Brian, it's getting late. I just got lost in M's program. There seems to be a lot more going on here than I thought, and I don't know why..." waiting for Brian's response. "Well, Marty, I don't know what 'a lot more' means, but I do know M will be happy to explain it to you - tomorrow, my friend, tomorrow. You do have a beautiful wife, and a life, and they deserve some attention, too. It's getting late," the time was around 6:30, "and I'm sure Sandy expects you home around now. Take M's program with you if you're that curious. I'll tell him you want to sit down to go over it, how's that?" "That's great, Brian, great. Sandy has noticed that I've been sort of preoccupied lately, and I don't want her to feel neglected. I'm gonna go. See you in the morning," said Marty as he gathered up M's computer code and headed towards the door. "Goodnight, Brian, say bye to M for me," as he opened the entrance door and left.

Brian closed his office door as he entered, a reflection of how important was his instinct to keep the Node Project under wraps, not because anyone besides M was in the building - it was empty, no one else there. "Well, wouldn't you know?" M looked up at Brian, puzzled visage because he was, "So what's the problem now, Brian?" "If it isn't one thing, it's another, it seems. Goes on and on, this time Marty." "What? We just discussed how well things were going with Marty? What's the problem? He realized he couldn't make NBS work after all?" "Nope, nothing *simple* like that. He's poring over your code, and he's getting suspicious. His exact words were - skip that, I don't remember his exact words - what he said is that he sees in your code a lot more going on that he doesn't understand. That's what he said. He smells something, and it's not a warm apple pie,... that's a problem. I know Marty, and Marty doesn't stop... until he gets the answer, or is convinced that there isn't one. That's the problem!"

Brian was visibly upset. It showed in his tone, his appearance, his posture, and there was no mistaking that he was in a dither. "So what the hell do we do now? Read Marty in - to what might be one of the biggest discoveries of all time? And hope it goes no further? I don't think so, so what the hell are we gonna do?" Brian was in a dither *and* a thither, both at the same time. Until M chimed in, "Calm down. Brian. Chill. It's no biggie, really. I think I know exactly what in the code grabbed Marty's interest, and I can explain it to him without making any reference to, or even hint at, the Node Project. In fact, in thinking about it, this might be a way to actually reel Marty in even more with the idea that this is hush-hush. He's a good guy, and I hate doing this to him, but we have to, no choice there. Thanks for giving me the heads up. Now that I know, Marty will get his answer, smooth as silk and he'll be none the wiser about what his is about. You OK with this?"

Brian breathed an audible sigh of relief, sitting back in his chair, and reaching out for the Scotch, as if to pour another, but then, suddenly, stopping mid reach, as he said to M, "Yes, I'm calmer now. Much. I'm sure you *can* pull this off M, so please do, tomorrow." And turning to the *Glenfiddich* he said "I'm done for the night. You?" M nodded 'yes,' he was done, too, whereupon Brian put the bottle back in its drawer.

- - - - - - - - - - - -

M leaned forward in the chair, his hands together in his lap and his head angled slightly downward. He began in a subdued voice, almost talking more to his knees that to Brian, who sat a few feet away behind the desk, "Before we call it a night, Brian, there is something important we have to discuss on Project Node," whereupon he looked up a Brian and sat erect in the chair. "Well, if you weren't going to bring it up, then I was," was Brian's reply. "You want to know what's next, right?" "Right!"

"Gert's next appearance is here, right here at NovaTek on Saturday the 12th. Today is the first, so that's only 11 days from now. Then Gert returns the very next day, the 13th, but this time on the Lake instead of here," Brian said to frame the question.

"I see you've been checking the GertHound Schedule, as have I, Brian," M answered while leaning to the desk on which he placed his elbows, very lightly holding his head in his hands with his fingers spread apart across his forehead. It was the consummate contemplative pose, and in fact that's exactly where M's head was as he mused "What should we do? What *can* we do?"

"I get it, M, that you're in the throes of indecision like me, I get it. Bet you're thinking, "What can we do this time that helps Node Project, right?"

"Yes, Brian, exactly right. And I go back and forth, and forth and back over what actually should be obvious. The first thing we have to do is make more measurements, that is, if Marty's gizmos are up and running. That goes without question agreed?" to which Brian replied slowly, very matter of factly, only two words, "Of course."

But M could see that Brian was perplexed over a larger question, which he suspected was the question he had as well.

"So, what do you think, Emilio? Can a living creature survive a Node ride? Should a living creature be sent on one? Is that what you're thinking, M?"

"Yes, exactly, Brian, exactly! Should that be part of the next experiment? Everything lines up beautifully,... time, place. And if we don't take advantage of it, when can we, if we decide we want to try that, sending something alive out there," as M waved his right hand in an arc indicating the reaches of outer space. "Just thinking about this, Brian, is such a head trip!"

"Yeah, I agree... So what's the answer? I know my vote..." Brian said as his voice trailed off, softer at the end of the sentence than at the beginning, almost as if he knew but he wasn't sure.

"From what you just said, Brian, I suspect your vote is 'yes' - something alive takes a ride - and that's my vote, too. We have to know that if, when(?), this ever gets out, Brian, when the world knows, then if we haven't done this someone else surely will. Now, right now, you and I agree this stays under wraps, and I firmly believe that that's right. But... knowing how he world works, a slip here, someone seeing something there, and on and on, if it gets out and we haven't revealed it, then what? Its very discoverers are going to be in the dark about how the Nodes really work? I mean *really* work? As scientists and, dare I say it, explorers, Brian, I don't think we have a choice - something that breathes has to fly!"

Well put, M, very well put. Question now is, What?..." Brian paused, Cheshire cat grin on his face, then continued, "Who?"

"What?" "No, M, I said 'Who'?...," and then Brian added, fondling his chin, "This is beginning to sound like the Abbott and Costello routine *Who's on First*," to give his suggestion some time to sink in with M.

"What *are* you suggesting, Brian? I was figuring a lab rat or two. I can get plenty of them from grad students I know who are bio majors," M replied.

"Remember Sputnik 2 way back in 1957, fifteen years ago, when we were still in high school, remember that?

"Of course, Brian. How could anyone our age forget? First dog in space. In a way that's what started the space race in earnest, a living creature surviving the trip, and equally important the fact that life support systems could be built that worked outside the atmosphere. I remember it well," said M.

"Okay, Laika was the dog's name, by the way. I think we need something like that, a dog, right?" M wondered where Brian was going with this because he sensed it was more than Brian's words taken at face value, so he jumped right in.

"Alright, let's say I agree, a higher life form, a dog would be good. Where do we get a dog? The pound! They have lots of them, and we could pick one up tomorrow," M's plan being to maneuver Brian into saying what he really meant.

"Well, M, there are problems with that idea. One, where does the pooch stay between now and its inaugural flight? And, two, where does the pooch stay *after* its inaugural flight? I can think of only one answer, and that's *with you!*"

M got his answer, what was really on Brian's mind, but of course he would have no part of it. "Nice try, Brian, nice try, but that won't fly. Kepler doesn't *like* dogs. And dogs don't seem to like Kepler, (a) because he's a cat, and (b) because he doesn't like them. No can do. I'm not getting a dog, short term or long term, because I have a nice cat, and cats are way less work than dogs. You can leave a cat alone for days, literally, as long as it has water, food and a place to poop. Try that with a dog that has to go out every few hours and eats everything it can as soon as it can! As I said, Brian, your plan simply doesn't work," whereupon M leaned back in his chair feeling self-satisfied that he had put Brian's idea in its place and not realizing that it was Brian who maneuvered him...

"Alright, M, you make a good case, you really do. Everything you say is true, and the bottom line is a dog doesn't work. So that leaves... only one possibility...", Brian's diction was emphatic and perfectly composed, and his pause was dramatic, to the point where M became engulfed, hanging on Brian's next words. "And that possibility is that *Kepler* takes the ride!" Brian stopped, to let this sink in. He knew that saying more would detract from it, so this time he waited for M's response.

"Kepler? You said *Kepler*? Kepler, *my* cat, and your future cat by marriage?" M tried to make light as best he could, but underneath he was chagrined that Brian could make such as suggestion in the first place.

"Yes, M, that is what I said." Brian reiterated his suggestion that Kepler be sent into space.

"Brian, Kep's my cat, my friend, my charge. I owe Kep more than sending him off in a Node, don't you see that?"

"No, frankly I don't, M. Kepler is a pet, in some sense a 'friend,' I get that, but still and all, he's a *cat*, not my nephew-to-be. Please, M, I don't want to get into an argument over Kep's nature in the scheme of things, but, let's face it, Kepler is a cat, as were his parents, and as are all his relatives, they're all cats... not people, so let's not anthropomorphize Kepler too much. Remember, *you're* getting the Ph.D., not Kepler..." at which point Brian shut up for fear of derailing the entire discussion. He simply sat quietly while Emilio processed what he just said.

After a few minutes, M spoke. "You do have a point, Brian." Brian nearly fell off his chair. "Thank you, M."

M continued, "Look, I am a scientist, and I know animals are a big part of science, in all sorts of ways, for all sorts of reasons. The sticky wicket here is my personal connection to Kepler. We wouldn't be having this discussion at all if Kepler were a pound cat." Brian interrupted, "Yes, exactly right, M, and I'm glad you see that distinction, that the 'wicket' as you put it is your personal connection to Kep, not the validity of my suggestion. Sorry to interrupt. You were saying?"

"What I was about to say is that I'm so confident in my predictions about Gert, and that I have so much faith in your ability to design and build a life support capsule, that I think I do agree, Kepler's the right 'person' to have take this first 'Ride on a Node.' It's hard, Brian, make no mistake about that, but my scientific integrity would be tarnished if I put Kepler the cat before what could be one on mankind's greatest discoveries!"

"Then it's settled, M. I'm glad you came around. I'll get crackin' on the capsule, and it will be tested and ready to go before Gert's back here on the 12th. On the NBS I already have the gimbal system designed. It's a modified Cardan suspension that will spin Marty's sensor device around inside the NBS sphere providing full 360 degree coverage over the entire exterior. On the housing, well, here's the answer, a fused silica infrared transparent radome. We have the capability to manufacture one, and here's the spec for it, as he handed M a document titled *Processing Requirement for Slip Cast Fused Silica Radomes*, June 1972, Naval Ordnance Systems Command, Weapons Dynamics Division. Oooh, good idea - I'll leave this out on the conference table where Marty will notice it, not much gets by Marty, and he'll think it has to do with our hush-hush project. Thoughts?" and Brian closed his speech.

"Nope, I'm nervous in one way, calm in another. If you and Marty get done what you have to do, and everything works as it should, then Kep will be the first cat riding a Node to outer space! That really is something! One last thing, please have all your camera gear ready to go, too, because this is something that must be documented."

"That was right here, M." as Brian touched his forehead, "I won't forget," as both Brian and M stood and walked toward the exit. "Talk to you tomorrow, Brian. Good meeting tonight, thanks."

"Tomorrow, Emilio, and Congrats, one more time. My love to Izzy and you!" as Brian waved goodbye.

Chapter 11 - Kepler Takes a Ride

"Did you know that today and tomorrow are the peaks for this year's Perseids meteor shower?" M asked Brian as they surveyed the equipment for tonight's launch.

"Yes, not only did I know that, M, but I took it into account in Kepler's capsule design," as he pointed to the three foot long cylinder bookended between two bulbous end caps. "There's a possibility, however slight, of a meteorite strike. Now, because the meteorites are so small it is unlikely that any structural damage would occur, but the capsule's air might slowly leak out if the meteorite penetrated the cylinder or one of the nosecones. So I fabricated double-thickness wall comprising two concentric titanium cylinders with a radial honeycomb filling. If the outer wall is penetrated, then the honeycomb will absorb the meteorite's kinetic energy and stop it dead."

"Should we tell Kep about this? I'm sure he'd be fascinated. Seriously, Brian, nice job, and thanks for being so concerned about Kepler's safety. Let's run through all the gizmos as Marty calls them and the procedures for tonight's launch. We've got plenty of time. It's 6:30 now, and Gert won't arrive until a couple of minutes after quarter past midnight."

"Sure, I intended to, M. Of course the launch has to be done in two phases, Phase 1 indoors, and Phase 2 outdoors. As to the launch itself, Kep's capsule must be launched outside where there aren't any walls or roofs or other building parts to get in the way, sort of self-evident, huh?" as Brian looked to M who was nodding with a smile and his brows ever so slightly furrowed, basically saying by his look, "Yes, self-evident, no flying into stationary structures... we know that..." Brian continued, "So after we go through this stuff" as he made a sweeping gesture pointing to all manner of instruments mounted on experiment stands and on the rafter and on the overhead collar ties, "We'll go outside and check out Kep's take-off equipment."

"Marty got the NBS up and running in no time. I was surprised that he managed to get it built, burned in, and tested as quickly as he did, think about it, in a just a few days from when you gave him the program chip and then came back to go over the source code. When was that? The Monday before last. I tell you, M, when it comes to electronics Marty really is a magician!" was Brian's effusive description of Marty's work and capabilities.

"So what he have here is the fully tested and operational Node Boundary Sensor," as Brian ran his gloved hand ever so carefully over its surface. "The spherical radome is the infrared-transparent fused silica we talked about, not as easy to fabricate as I expected, by the way, but I managed to get it done, and it's perfect," as Brian showed just about all of his pearly whites as he said this while gently patting the globe. "I won't get too far into the weeds, M, because you know how it works - after all, *you* wrote the source code! - but I should tell you it's been fully tested and calibrated against a phantom that was built exactly to your specs. Marty again..."

"Was he at all curious, Brian? You know, he asked an awful lot of very probing questions when we went over the source code. He was especially curious about some of the signal processing routines, the ones that were written specifically to take into account a Node's boundary layer with the outside world. Marty couldn't understand what it was that was being probed, so I had to make up a story about extremely weak inhomogeneities in the ionospheric plasma being measured *in situ*, and he bought it. And that wasn't the only place he asked unsettling questions, there was a bunch of others."

"And?..." Brian's face betrayed his concern. "If Marty figures this out,..." he mused.

"Well, I think he's happy. What I think put him over the top was my hinting that the NBS probe was going to be flying on a tether on a jet at 75,000 feet. That blew his mind! And he knew enough at that point, I think, not to ask any more questions, so we were done with it."

"Okay, good," was Brian's relaxed response. He felt much better now knowing that Marty probably wouldn't pry anymore, although he did feel guilty about not being able to level with such a good employee who over the years had become quite a good friend. "Maybe someday," he thought.

M noticed that this time there were no hanging birds or colorful streamers, so he asked. "Last time Gert was here you had streamers and *The Birds* deployed, but not now. How come?"

"Well, based on the last measured data we figured Gert was more than 20 feet wide and at least 8 feet high off the floor," to which M nodded in agreement, "and that the region of gravity suspension tapered very slightly and more or less linearly away from the center," to which M again nodded his agreement. Well, I wanted to pin all this down better, and the NBS will give us an exact shape, and that array of accelerometers," as Brian pointed to two dozen or so small modules arranged in a straight line along a wooden stand, "will capture the finer details of the gravity suspension."

"Good work, Brian. Nice. Yes, this is the exact effect we need to understand better because although the Node's internal spacetime is flat, it isn't perfectly flat, resulting a in a gravity suspension that has some ripple, or better put, a 'profile.' We have to know what that ripple is... and," as he inspected the accelerometer array, "your accelerometer array will give us that. Good work!"

Whereupon Brian summarized what Phase 1 should accomplish. "Bottom line, M, is that the indoor experiment, Phase 1, should tell us quite accurately the Node's size and shape, boundary region thickness, gravitational inhomogeneity, and speed of propagation. Any questions?" "No," M replied, "none. You've done a great job... and Marty, too, nice work!"

Brian smiled at M's compliment, told M he's pass it along to Marty, and said "Let's go outside to see Kep's launch pad," and he and M headed for a door at the back of the lab that opened into NovaTek's 'outdoor test range,' a large, flat grassy area about the size of two tennis courts surrounded on its perimeter by several small dugout-like structures and a couple of others that looked like small one-room buildings. "This is our Test Range,

M. You've been here before, I know, but only a handful of times, right?"

"Yes, Brian, only a handful of times, when you were conducting some experiment you thought I would find interesting. And you got it right every time! Always something interesting, and always something very different from what I do, so thanks for the shows..." M replied with clear appreciation in his voice as his gaze swept the Test Range. "Is that Kep's jumping off point," M asked as he pointed to the tripod-like structure at about the Test Range's center.

"Yes, M, that's it. It's an improved version of the launch platform we used for the first Gert pickup when she whisked away our hollow sphere."

"What's improved, Brian? Anything wrong with the other one?" M was curious.

"Well, structurally, no, nothing. The other platform was fine in that regard, and this one is about the same, very minor tweaks. What's different is Marty reworked the electronics to make the Velocity Speed Sensor and the Electronics Package better, tighter tolerances, mil-spec devices throughout, that sort of thing. So the performance will be exactly the same as it was, or better..." Brian responded with justifiable pride in his voice and posture, arms crossed while leaning slight back. M couldn't help but notice, "Well done, Brian, and you should be proud. Bravo!" as he clapped softly.

- - - - - - - - - - - -

"What a night for a meteor shower! My God, do you see that?" M asked while looking up into an endless black sky with countless stars and galaxies as the backdrop for one of the most intense meteor showers in decades, the Perseids peaking right at this time and tomorrow as well. "This is astonishing, Brian, astonishing! Predictions at the Observatory are for as many as 150 trails per hour," and looking up, "there as he gestured skyward to a specific region, there, just look at the number of trails showing up. Truly remarkable! Maybe the most intense Perseids *ever*, and we get to see it!"

"Yes," replied Brian, "and who among us gets the best front row seat? None other than Kepler, the ten pound Siamese!" Kepler was a particularly striking feline, lithe with a creamy white coat setting off dark, almost black ears, with a face defined by fur that gradually melted from white to light tan to dark brown to nearly black around the eyes and nose. And, his eyes, those eyes, Kepler's were deep, intense blue that faded nearly to white at the cornea's perimeter, unlike most cat eyes that are uniformly pigmented. There was no mistaking Kepler for an ordinary cat!

"Time's getting close, M," Brian remarked as he glanced at the Rolex Oyster Perpetual on his wrist. "Agreed, " said M, looking over at Brian, "let's do a final system check before Kepler takes the pilot's seat." Whereupon M and Brian opened Kepler's capsule, verified that all fittings were tight, that the heating/air conditioning and air circulation systems were functioning properly, that lamps were properly seated and fully enclosed in their wire form housings, checked the drip water bottle that was Kep's hydration, and the food pellet dispenser for his meals, inspected his potty to be sure it was clean and functioning, and confirmed that all electrical apparatus was sealed and insulated.

All exposed surfaces in Kep's cabin, except for essential equipment like the food and water dispensers and lighting, were covered by a thick vinyl wrapped foam rubber. If Kepler was jostled in flight he couldn't bump into anything sharp or hard. In addition, Brian fabricated a 'flight harness' that attached to Kep's 'flight vest' and to the wall via tethers to limit Kep's range of motion to the central interior.

Of course, prior to the flight Kepler was checked out by the 'flight surgeon,' his veterinarian, who needless to say wasn't told the exact nature of Kep's adventure. The cat's claws were clipped, his teeth brushed, his coat brushed to remove any excess or loose fur, and his general state of health evaluated. Kepler, the very handsome Siamese, was in excellent shape to fly, no question about it!

But, unlike human astronauts, Kepler didn't have physiological monitors, for example, the heart rate, blood pressure, respiration rate, and blood oxygen measurement equipment that humans took with them into space to radio their vital signs back to Earth during flight. Kepler was spared the indignity if having his fur shaved to attach electrodes so M and Brian could remotely monitor is heart rate and other vital signs as Gert swept him through the atmosphere and into outer space - what a trip!

However, Kep's capsule *did* include telemetry, just not medical telemetry. It was outfitted with inertial guidance-based location sensors and with acceleration and velocity sensors, and also, so as to not miss what likely would be the best meteor shower in decades, as well as other celestial sights, hull-mounted cameras that would radio back a real-time view of what the capsule saw out there. There were two forward-looking cameras and two rearward, all with short focal length lenses providing very wide fields of view and almost limitless depth of field. The cameras were set up on four separate radio telemetry channels and would transmit continuous from slightly before takeoff until slightly after landing. Brian kicked himself for not thinking of adding such an imaging system to the first test sphere, but that was water under the bridge, and he learned from it. Of course, going without saying, the capsule had onboard a camera to monitor Kepler as he flew. Brian knew he would be mortified by *not* having one, and that there would be no dealing with M in that case...

"Okay, buddy," M spoke to Kepler as he retrieved from the carrier. Kepler was a very well adjusted, docile feline, but tonight he sensed something afoot not to his liking, and he showed that displeasure abruptly by hissing and scratching M, who was so taken aback by this uncharacteristic outburst that he nearly dropped the cat... on the grass in the Test Range. "Geez, Kepler," he said to his feline friend, "what was *that* for? We haven't done anything yet, and you're already making me feel guilty!" as he quickly placed Kep back in the carrier. "Brian, this isn't working. Kepler's spooked. He knows. He scratched me, which he never does, and I nearly dropped him!"

"I understand, M. How about we bring Kep inside and start over? I'll get the capsule. That's what the little wagon is for, over there, the 'Capsule Transporter'... just like the ones they use at Cape Canaveral, hee-hee..." Brian joked as he pointed to a red Radio Flyer wagon custom-fitted with oversized pneumatic tires. "OK, yes," was M's immediate response, as his guilt level rose and he thought "Better get this done now, or Kep and I are outta here..."

Kepler calmed visibly inside the Shop. After all, he *was* a house cat living all day long in M's apartment and going for his daily 'walk' with M, all the while leashed. And Kepler was a very happy cat living under posh circumstances, so being outside, late at night, on NovaTek's Test Range would be enough to spook any self-respecting house cat, especially Kep who was used to a pampered existence. *That* apparently is was what happened to Kepler, not some feline sixth sense of impending danger.

"Brian, look, Kep's much calmer, just being inside in his carrier was enough," M said as he gently stroked Kepler who responded by lifting his chin and purring, occasionally interrupting with a quiet meow. Now the cat was happy, because he was far more in his element than being outside. With Brian's help M picked Kepler up, zippered his Flight Vest, placed him inside the capsule, and connected the vest tethers to their wall receptacles. Kepler was free to move as he wished, stand, lie down, reach his food and drink and litter box, but he couldn't reach the cabin walls. Brian's cleverly design system protected Kepler from any violent maneuvers that might otherwise harm him.

M also placed inside the capsule two small notebooks, whereupon Brian said quizzically, "Hmmm... so that's for Kep to jot down his flight impression, right? But why two? I should think one would be plenty, no? After all, the cat doesn't write *that* much!" and after a brief pause, "Seriously, M, what's up?" "Not now, Brian, not now. Just an idea I want to check out, and I'll explain it all, in detail, but just not now, if that's OK with you." "Sure thing, M, if it's no big deal, just another one of your hare brained ideas and it doesn't impact the flight, which it won't, then I can wait. But I would like an explanation at some point, after Kep's back and all went well, which it will."

"Ready to go, my friend?" M turned from Brian, reached into the capsule, and gave Kep an ear and chin rub." Have a great flight! See you back here tomorrow... nope, make that on the Lake!" M said to Kep while petting the him one last time before Brian gestured 'safe trip' and gently closed the capsule hatch, locking it from outside. Then he said to M, jokingly, "You know, I did consider putting in a window, but upon cogitating it further I figured Kepler, as bright and curious a cat as he is, well, he wouldn't really appreciate what he would see on this trip, especially the Perseids peaking!!"

To which M replied, "Okay, mister rocket designer, let's get Kep's capsule outside onto the launch pad... before I try to fit *you* inside it. Then *you* can think about the sights you're missing..." In a way M appreciated the lighter moment because he was genuinely nervous about Kepler's flight. His Node calculations, time and trajectory, were correct, he knew that, so there wasn't any concern about Kep's coming back, barring some calamity like a large meteor strike that either badly damaged the capsule or knocked it seriously off course. His concern was how the cat would deal with being locked in a metal tube for all those hours, what would he think, how would he react to M afterwards? That worried M.

M and Brian carefully hung the capsule from its launch stand, a tripod structure much like the stand used to launch the sphere from The Lake, minus, of course, the floatation and gyro systems. Rather than take the sphere stand apart for use on NovaTek's Test Range, Brian decided to keep it intact for future Lake launches, if there were any, and to fabricate a new stand designed specifically for the Test Range. This launch stand included essentially the same features and equipment as the sphere launcher, but with tweaks and upgrades as required or desired, for example, mil-spec components throughout, metal versus wood structural components, a detachable telemetry package, and a storage compartment for small tools, test equipment such as an analog multimeter, and spare parts.

- - - - - - - - - - - -

"Do you hear that, M?" Brian's voice was excited as he look at the Oyster. "Just about time,... and listen carefully... Do you hear it?"

"Yes, Brian, it's unmistakable... The crickets are chirping louder, the frogs, too, they're croaking louder. There's no way you can miss it if you've been out here for a while, definitely louder." M replied.

"This is exactly what happened that night when Gert arrived the first time, remember my telling you? This is just the same!" Brian's voice was raised somewhat, excited.

"You know, having seen what we did with the birds enveloped by Gert, just cruising along for the ride, no flapping, in fact wings in tight, having seen that and now hearing this, I think you're spot on, Brian, with your idea that these critters somehow know about the Node before it actually shows up, and that the creatures that can, like the birds, take advantage of it! You're right, I think - this reflects eons of evolution during which the animals developed a sense of a Node's arrival, something like homing pigeons always find their way home no matter where they start out. There's something in the environment that the pigeons sense that guides them, but as sophisticated as we are with all this super-sensitive measuring gear, we have no idea how that works!" M was on a roll, and he was fascinated by another clear confirmation that Brian *is* right, the animals know!

"I'm not going to say 'I told you so,' M, but guess what, I did tell you. It's not my imagination, not an exaggeration, and not a one-off that seemed connected yet wasn't. This is for real. Now, does it help us in any way? Probably not, but who knows." was Brian's retort.

"No, no, Brian. I don't agree that this doesn't help us, quite to the contrary, I think it might. Why? Because the animals sense something, and if we can figure out what it is and sense it, too, then we may be able to build an apparatus that tells us a Node is coming without having to go through all the computer modeling to develop schedules like the Gerthound Schedule. There may be some utility in that, so I think we should think about whether or not it's doable, and how to do it. Maybe turn the Magician loose on it?" said M, referring to Marty Lobesky.

M was surprised. Brian's response was muted, not especially enthusiastic, as he expected it to be, "Hmm...well, maybe we can look into this at some point, but for now I think your Gerthound schedules will do just fine, look, you've been right every time... to five decimal places, remember?" Brian's remark was somewhat distressing. M expected more interest, but he could see that Brian's was rapt with Gert's imminent arrival and Kep's impending departure, so he demurred, "Yes, Brian, another time, we'll talk about this another time... And speaking of time, what have you got?"

"12:15, a quarter past midnight in 5, 4, 3, 2, 1 seconds, and then Gert's here in less than two-and-a-half minutes. Let's give Kep's capsule a god luck pat..." as Brian and M both reached in to gently tap the outside of the capsule, then standing off at a distance so as to avoid Gert's path.

"Okay, Emilio, here we go," Brian said at the 30 second mark, whereupon he waited a few seconds more and then started a 20 second countdown... 3, 2, 1... " "and sure enough, exactly as predicted, Gert arrived passing the Node Velocity Sensor which then radioed Gert's speed to the electronics package which at the right second detached Kepler's capsule matching Gert's speed which then floated away at about 20 miles per hour enveloped by Gert.

"M, how cool was that!! Kep's on his way!" as Brian shone a very powerful flashlight on the highly reflective capsule so they could follow its ascent as far as possible.

Emilio stood in wonderment, knowing full well what just happened, understanding it in the most minute detail, yet being awe-struck nevertheless, saying to Brian, "You know, I don't think I can *ever* get used to this, no matter how many times I might see it. Watching an object - in this case my dear cat, Kepler - being whisked away by confluence of the gravitational fields of masses that are tens of millions of miles apart, geez, I have to say, Brian, I don't think I'll *ever* get used to it..." M's wonderment apparent in his words and in his tone as he looked skyward to watch Kep's capsule gradually fade from view. "This is almost too much to get my head around, Brian, what a trip!" as he walked over to the launch stand and steadied himself against it.

"Alright, M, time for the show! Let's go inside to see what the cameras see," as he grabbed M's walking towards the building. They were turned on just before the capsule's release when they received a command from the electronics package. We should be receiving images right now, along with the other data. I'm dying of curiosity. You?"

M's look betrayed his feelings. "Good choice of words, Brian... Yeah, let's go and see how my cat is doing" as they entered the building and pulled up chairs in front of a makeshift 'mission control' that Brian had cobbled together just for tonight's flight. He would dismantle it before morning, when Marty would be back, and store it in the '150 for transport to the Lake. It comprised five television screens, one for each camera. "Just so you'll know, M, for scientific and historical purposes I can record selected segments on that recorder over there, " Brian said as he pointed to a large videotape recorder in the corner.

"That's an Ampex machine with 2-inch Quad videotape and eight recording heads, but we're using only five. Unfortunately, we can only record brief segments, say, ten minutes at a time to conserve tape..." at which point M interrupted, holding up his hand signaling to Brian to stop. "I got it, Brian, you're recording. Good. Now let's get to looking Kepler to see how's he's doing. That's a lot more important than your infatuation with a tape recorder, or is that intentional to deflect your own concern about how Kep is doing?" M's tone was clearly distraught and indignant at the same time. Brian nodded acquiescence as he flipped several switches and the five TV screens came to life, blinking at first, then quickly scrolling, and finally settling down to what were quite clear black and white images. "Not bad telemetry, huh?" Brian said as he pointed to Screen #1, "Look, there's Kep,... looking good, I'd say!"

M's gaze was fixated on Screen #1, both because he was relieved that Kepler appeared to be no worse for wear and tear, but, what was more, the cat seemed to enjoying the ride, happily sipping at his water bottle, and then curling up in the middle of the 'cat bed' that Brian had installed.

"See, M, what did I tell you all along, Kep's gonna do great! Believe your eyes, my friend, your cat, my cat-in-law-to be, he's happy up there. Holy shit! M, look at these numbers! They're nothing short of astonishing! Altitude 155,902 feet, speed 800 mph! And Kepler doesn't seem to feel a thing. I should have included audio, but it looks like he might be purring!"

"Hmmm... I agree, Brian, looks that way, and I know my cat, it really does look like he's purring. He often does that when he naps, and I think that's what he's doing, getting some shut eye. Pretty amazing, considering he's 26 miles above the Earth traveling faster than the speed of sound! Of course, we have to keep in mind that Kep's in essentially zero-gravity flat spacetime inside Gert, so none of the inertial or gravitational effects that otherwise would cause physical stress, like pulling 5 or 6 g's as the astronauts do, well, they don't happen because there is no gravity for Kep! That's why he can comfortably take his nap and do what lazy cats do..."

"So, refresh my memory again, M. If Kep's weightless, zero gravity, why isn't he floating around the capsule?"

"Kep and the capsule are moving together as a single mass. If his capsule were falling away from him in the Earth's gravitational field, the way a plane does when it flies an anti-gravity arc, then it would fall away from him as fast as he was falling towards the Earth, so he would feel weightless and be able to bounce around the cabin. But that's not what's happening," to which Brian said, "Thanks, got it," as he went back to adjusting some controls to further improve the television images. He looked at M, asking, "Happy now? Are you satisfied that our furry friend is OK and happy at that?" "Yep, thank goodness, Brian. Can't tell you how relieved I am. When Kep scratched me outside I was just about going to pack it in, I felt so guilty. But I'm not only OK now, I think we're seeing one of the most amazing things that mankind every will see, and it's happening right here, right now!" M's sense of awe was back.

"You know, for a while, Emilio, I had my doubts, too. Maybe not as much as you, but you weren't alone believe me. When Kep's back tomorrow afternoon I know we'll both relax. Until then, how about we look at the meteor shower?"

"It's interesting, Brian, that the forward-looking cameras don't see any trails because it's so high and all the trails are below it. Did you notice that?" "Yes, I did," Brian answered, continuing "But truth be told, M, I don't care that much because of what the forward-looking cameras see. Hold on while I douse he lights."

Mission Control turned jet black, the only lights being small lamps on the console and the TV screen images. It suddenly was like being out in space, out where the astronauts flew, and seeing what they saw, an incredibly dark 'sky' dotted with stars and galaxies so dense that it almost felt that you could reach out and touch them. The view was nothing short of spectacular, awe-inspiring, something that no human could experience and not well up with wonder about what all his meant. And that's how M and Brian felt as they say in total silence simply staring at images that only a handful of people ever had seen in the way they were seeing them.

Chapter 12 - Kepler Returns

"Thanks for staying last night, M, I really appreciate your help getting the Shop back in shape before NovaTek opens tomorrow and Marty comes in. How was that cot? I sleep here a quite a bit, so I'm used to mine... I'm going to make some coffee, then I want to spend a few minutes talking about Marty," and Brian went over to the small counter with a sink in it and coffee pot on it.

"Coffee OK?" M nodded 'yes,' and Brian continued "You know, with all that's going on, the work he's done, the water-borne sphere launcher we had to hide, Kep's Test Range launcher, 'Mission Control,' all this stuff, it's getting harder and harder to keep Project Nodes from Marty. He's a very curious and perceptive guy. I don't mean nosey, M, but he doesn't miss much..." Brian spoke as he and M winched the Test Range Launch Pad up the ramps that were previously used for the Sphere Launcher at the Lake. Now that contraption was hidden in a corner of the boat shed covered by a tarp, as would be Kep's launching platform when they got it to the Lake.

"Glad to help, Brian, you know that. Good grief, we're in this together, up to our eyebrows, you and I, so what has to be done that requires two people, well, what can I say? We're it... As to keeping Marty in the dark, yep, I can see how that would be hard enough without all the activity swirling around this, really hard. But, what choice do we have? We would have to 'read Marty in,' so to speak, and I'm not sure that's such a good idea. Right now, you and I are the only two people on the planet who know about the Nodes and how they work, at least I think that's true. I suppose if there is anyone else they're just as close to the vest, so we mutually don't know about each other. And what if there are three, or four, or..."

Brian couldn't let M continue. He interrupted, "... or may a hundred, or a thousand, and so on, and so on, and no one knows that anyone else knows. Sure, I suppose it's possible because it isn't *im*possible. So what? If no one else knows that someone else knows, then practically speaking it doesn't matter because functionally it's no different than only the two of us knowing, *capische*? Let's get off this, M. I'm not going to tell Marty, and you aren't either. Let's just be careful about what he sees, and have ready-made answers if it's something he shouldn't see, and if that happens each of us fills in the other on what the ready-made answer was, agreed?"

"Yeah, you're right Brian. I'm wound kind of tight, that's the problem. I'll be happy when Astrocat Kepler returns. He certainly looked good on TV this morning. While you were making some coffee I saw him nibble on the food dispenser, so that works well, and he sure seemed interested enough in eating. By the way, what do you think of 'Astrocat' as a moniker, you know, like an 'Astronaut'? 'Astrocat Kepler,' it has a ring to it, no?" M asked.

"Honestly, M?" Brian asked quizzically. "Yes, of course, honestly, Brian" was M's response.

"Ring to it, you ask? Sure, like the ring of the doorbell to get into the mental hospital across from Saint Martin's, that's the sort of ring! Do you have any idea of how stupid that idea is? Astrocat? No to mention inconsistent. By your naming convention the Astronauts couldn't be called Astronauts unless they were 'nauts,' which they aren't. They're people, so by your naming convention they should be 'Astropeople' or, maybe on a stretch to personalize it more, 'Astropersons.' Need I say more? Dump Astrocat and go back to calling Kepler 'cat,' thank you. Get another cup of coffee, would you,... you are punchy..." was Brian's final remark as he closed the F-150's tailgate to get ready for the trip to the Lake.

The ride from NovaTek to Lake Arrowhead was pleasantly uneventful, a slow saunter along some very comely country roads with a detour to stop at Dee's Donuts, the best donut and fast breakfast shop for miles. Brian wolfed down two glazed, while M was more interested in a more substantive bite, so his was an English muffin sandwich of fried egg, cheese and sausage, nothing like M's own SPR, mind you, but satisfying as a breakfast to get the day under way. Of course, both men quaffed plenty of coffee, hot and black.

"Geez, Brian, I had no idea the boat shed was this big," as Brian carefully maneuvered the '150's bed close to the shed's barn doors. It was a large rectangular building about fifty feet long and twenty wide, but the way it was nestled in the trees belied its true size. "I figured you could fit a couple of canoes and maybe some kayaks in here, not the Queen Mary! Oh, I see the Sphere Launcher, over in the corner under the tarp, right?"

Brian nodded, muttering as he did, "Yes, that's it... M, get over here please and give me a hand with this tie-down strap. The launcher shifted just enough that I can't release the ratchet, try as I might. We have to push the launcher this way," as Brian pointed towards the left side of the truck bed, "only a couple of inches, but the strap's so tight I can't do it alone. Maybe the two of us can? And if that doesn't work I'll have to use a scissor jack, which definitely will work. Anyway, push here. Ready? One, two, three... give it a shove," Brian groaned as he and M pushed as hard as they could. The launcher shifted just enough to allow Brian to release the strap ratchet to prepare to unload it. "Wow!" M said, "Amazing what a couple of glazed donuts will do!" pulling Brian's leg and actually eliciting a smile and a chortle. "Thanks, M, so let's get this puppy off the truck and into the shed, next to the other one because I have a tarp big enough for both."

Also in the '150's bed were the same two aluminum folding beach chairs that had come in so handy for Gert's first Lake pickup, the transistor radio still tuned to the same station, the thermoses just filled with hot, black coffee, and most importantly the binoculars and the compass, and Kepler's cat carrier. In the back of the truck's cab were the Heathkit capsule thruster remote control, the two Nikon cameras, and the Manfrotto tripod. Also in the back were Kepler's cat carrier, fresh tuna, Kep's favorite, and milk on ice. After the capsule launcher was hidden away, along with some of the electronic equipment that was launcher-specific so Marty wouldn't see it, M and Brian trekked down the forty-foot dock with all the paraphernalia that they needed to while away the two hours or so to Gert and Kepler's return, the time according to the Oyster being a little after noon.

Brian set up one of the cameras on the tripod pointing towards the point at which Kep's capsule would be released from the Node. That direction and its distance from the dock were known precisely from M's computer modeling of Gert's trajectory on this day. Unlike Gert's previous run where the sphere was dropped about 100 feet from the end of the dock, this run brought Gert closer with a drop point about 40 feet out. Of course, as Gert skimmed the Lake's surface the thruster remote permitted M to release the capsule at any time, but it was his intention to do so when it was closest to the surface to minimize the impact on Kepler as it hit the water. By Brian's calculations the capsule displaced enough water to more than support its weight, so it would float, handily, but M's concern was the sudden stop as it splashed into the Lake from dropping several feet from Gert's center. Once again M was overly concerned about Kepler's safety, even though he knew Brian had gone to extremes to be sure the cat didn't impact any hard or sharp surface.

Brian turned on the radio, and re-tuned it to M's favorite classical station. It was broadcasting Beethoven Piano Concerto No. 5, the Emperor, and it had just begun. "M, I must say, this music might convert even me!" and the two sat silently for a long time, enjoying what made Beethoven's piece still popular after more than 160 years, and wrapped in their own thoughts about all that had happened, was about to happen right here his day, and what it meant for the future.

- - - - - - - - - - - -

When the 5th was over, M looked over at Brian with a pensive, almost stern look, "There are things we have to talk about, Brian, massively important things. I can't think of a word that really describes how important, but not here, not now."

"What? What are you talking about, M? You sound so mysterious and... what can I say, ominous, almost foreboding... It has to do with Nodes, I know that. What else could it be? But your look, your tone,... they frighten me, M. So get it out. What?"

"As I said, Brian, not here, not now. But let me put your mind at ease, nothing portentous about this, just totally unexpected, 'astonishing' even is too mild a word! It truly is astonishing, and that's from a scientist who has a pretty good grasp of what Nodes are all about. They're way more than we think, Brian, way more. But not here, not now."

M continued, "How about we head over to my place to discuss this after we retrieve Kep? I want to get him home ASAP anyway, so I was planning on leaving NovaTek as soon as we got back there. It's not much out of the way, so why don't we go straight to my place where we can relax and talk, maybe grab a bite - I make some pretty mean pasta with marinara sauce, eh? Since I'm cooking, along the way you can run into *D'Argento's Bakery*, it's on the way, and pick out some desert, how's that?"

"Well, that's an invitation I can't refuse... Of course, I'm not sure it's because of the dinner you dangle, or because of the somber nature of what you want to discuss. OK, I'll put my curiosity away for now, but I'm dying to find out what this is about, M," as Brian again looked at his watch, "Just before 1:45pm now, ETA 2:08:19, less than twenty-five minutes to splash down. You ready, M?"

"Yep, indeed I am, Brian. Ready, and excited," M replied as he placed the binoculars in his lap and the Heathkit remote control in his pocket. He knew well that Gert's passage provided only a short window within which he had to engage the capsule thruster which would cause it to fall out of the Node into the water. If he missed the low point of Gert's trajectory, then the capsule could be released, but at progressively higher altitudes as Gert sped away. A lot was riding on getting this right, Kepler's life actually, and Emilio struggled to maintain composure under the weight of this responsibility. As before, like the watched pot, subjective time slowed, and the clock ticked more slowly than one second per second. When will he be here??" was all M could think.

"Over there, M, over there" Brian yelled, arm straight as a board, his index finger pointing to a faint grayish patch in the distance descending at a high rate of speed. "Grab your binocs, you'll see it. And do you hear that? All of a sudden, not even a minute ago, the bird noises went way up, just like before. Somehow they *know*, M, the animals know that a Node is coming! Hmmm... if only we could figure out how! Add that to your mysterious list of things to talk about, M. How do animals know a Node is approaching?"

The cloud of birds was closer, and M could make out its details through the binocs. There was the capsule, as plain as day, and it was surrounded by a stationary cloud of birds, as before all kinds, and as before not flapping, wings in tight. They looked like little wingless jet fighters flying in formation as an escort to Kep's capsule. M reached into his pocket and retrieved the Heathkit thruster remote. He was so nervous he held it at first upside down with the release button at the bottom. It didn't feel right, and when he looked he immediately turned the remote around to hold it properly with the button at the top. "God," M thought, "what if I hadn't noticed this? What if I missed the drop point?" The weight on M's psyche was almost too much to bear even though all he had to do was push one button in about a minute or so. Of course, just at the moment his next thought was "Are the batteries fresh? Were they checked?"

"M, get ready, M!" Brian yelled, as he pushed and locked the Nikon's cable release to start filming. He held up the second camera with its 200mm lens and starting firing hand-held, having pre-focused on the point of Gert's closest approach, presumably where M would drop he capsule." Again to alert M, Brian yelled, "I make it thirty seconds, M. Get ready to release!"

This last warning jarred M away from his total self absorption and turned his thoughts entirely to Kepler. "Any second now, Kep," M thought," and you'll be home!" as he pressed the Heathkit remote's red thruster button.

"I got it, M, I got it on film! Did you see that? I think I got the thruster gas plume. I think I have a few frames of the capsule dropping into the Lake! This is soooo... cool, M, I can't describe how I feel!"

While Brian was shouting gleefully at his photographic escapade, M was ignoring him completely and shouting to Kep's capsule "Welcome home, Kepler! Welcome home! We'll be right here to get you!" And M collapsed into his folding aluminum beach chair as soon as he realized Kep's capsule was floating, just as Brian said it would, with the thruster port and loading hatch on top, just as Brian said they would be, because the capsule contained ballast embedded between the inner and outer titanium walls that kept it erect in water, just as Brian designed it to do. If Kep was OK, then Kep was back! What a relief for M and Brian both. The world's first Node Rider had flown and returned!

- - - - - - - - - - - -

M and Brian hopped into the rowboat that was moored at the end of the dock, and headed out to retrieve Kep's capsule which was about forty feet away. They reached over the side, each grabbing a 'nosecone' on the three foot long tube when M exclaimed, "Listen, Brian. Be quiet and listen," and sure enough Brian heard it, too, a gentle 'meow' coming from inside. Kepler Rode the Node and survived! M suggested "Let's open the capsule onshore. I don't want to do it in the boat because it's not that stable," so they rowed slowly to the beach and pulled the small craft partially onto the sand. Brian and M gently removed Kep's capsule, placing it on a blanket on the sand with the cat carrier nearby, and even more gently opened the hatch.

There was Kepler, safe in his harness, purring softly as M reach in to pet and stroke his feline friend. "Welcome back, Kep! Welcome back!" M's voice betrayed his relief and joy at seeing the ten pound Siamese apparently as fit as a fiddle, no worse at all it seemed from his ride through outer space! "He looks great to me," Brian said, looking closely, carefully at the cat. He appears to be happy and, from the way he's been every time I've seen him, perfectly normal, which is great. Bottom line - higher life forms can ride Nodes - we've demonstrated that. Not bad for a Sunday afternoon's work, huh!" Brian's voice betrayed his excitement at seeing Kepler showing not the slightest sign of distress, physical or otherwise. "Couldn't ask for a better result, M." to which M responded, "Yep, all good, couldn't be better, and until Kep was back on terra firma, I didn't want to get into the stats for this flight..." whereupon Brian, most curious, interrupted, "... and those were?" with piqued anticipation.

"Flight data, okay, off the top of my head, Brian, so don't hold me to these numbers. They may be a little off, but not too far." was M's response, which reflected his bent for scientific precision, not a lawyerly dodge. "Let's see, Gert was on the ground at NovaTek for a total of four minutes and here on the Lake for three and a half. Her rate of descent coming down to the Shop was initially about one mile per second slowing to about twenty miles per hour as she turned to travel along the surface..." Brian interrupted again. "... good, got that, you calculated descent speed, ascent speed, speed along the ground, all those good speeds, but frankly, M, I don't care much about them. Get to the interesting stuff, please. How high? How fast, out there,...", as Brian waved to the firmament, "...not down here? That's what I want to know, and..." Brian trailed off with the look of a child anticipating its mother's reply.

"150 miles, just shy of 800,000 feet, max speed of around 625 mph, in a wide arc trajectory that brings Gert back to earth a few more times, precessing as she does, much the same way Mercury's perhelion precesses, although at a much, much higher rate. When her trajectory doesn't intersect Earth the Node simply stays in outer space following a closed path but not like a planet's elliptical orbit."

"Okay, M, wow! Double wow!! 150 miles up! 625 mph! Kep sure did go for a RIDE! That other stuff, by the way, is about as interesting as the up and down and sideways speeds..." was Brian's way of saying he didn't really care about the orbital mechanics details, just the 'big picture,' as he would put it. "The important thing, M, is that Kepler came back fine. He looks great!" as he inspected the cat again, "and he's quite content from what I see. That's what's important, don't you agree?"

M's answer wasn't what Brian expected, at least not entirely, "Sure, Brian, the fact that Kep came back in one piece without experiencing any of the nastier things that are usually associated with space travel, like pulling several g's on launch, or during a maneuver, that's a wonderful result, and it confirms our theoretical understanding of how the Node's essentially flat spacetime works. But that's only part of the picture. The rest has to do with the topics I want to discuss when we're back at my apartment."

Because of this response, Brian now was anxious, very anxious, to 'get the show on the road' so he and M cold sit down to talk about what M so intently wanted to talk about. As he entered the F-150's cab, he looked into the back seat to confirm that the *Glenfiddich* was cozily wrapped in its blanket, figuring he would break it out at M's instead of here at the beach to celebrate Kep's successful flight. "Everything packed up, M?" Brian asked. "Kepler's OK? Ready to go?" M nodded affirmatively to each of Brian's questions, whereupon the Ford F-150 slowly left the boat shed heading for the driveway.

Chapter 13 - Buckle Up!

"Does anyone around here drive a real car? Or better yet, a truck like this one?" Brian expressed his frustration at not being able to find a parking spot near M's apartment. "Nope, most folk around here drive smallish cars, like my Datsun, which used to be small enough to park easily at curbside. I don't think I've ever seen anything as big as this boat parked at the curb..." Brian's exasperation increased, "Okay, if it's that bad, I'll drop you and Kep off, you can run pussy in while I wait, and I'll ferry you back to NovaTek for you to get the Camaro. We can talk there, today, or some other day back here when I'm driving the GTO. How's that?" M demurred, "Nope, I want to go over this today. It's really important, Brian, really important. See that small side street, up there on the right, Willow Terrace? Take it, you should find a space there. I often park the Camaro there because it's bigger than most of the cars around here, and most of the time there will be a big enough spot along Willow. Let's give it a shot." And sure enough there was one spot, only one, that was big enough to accommodate the Ranger XLT. It was a short two-block walk to M's apartment, Kepler in his cat carrier with Brian clutching his blanket and its precious cargo.

"Whew, lots of stairs," Brian said as they unlocked the door to M's place. Brian was very fit, exceptionally fit actually, but pooped because last night he got hardly any sleep. He positioned his cot so he could keep an eye on the five television screens at 'Mission Control,' mostly on Kep's, but he didn't tell M whose cot was set up in another small room off the main lab/fab area. Brian knew how dear Kepler was to M, and he felt responsible to a large degree for the plight Kep was in. After all, it was Brian who argued that Kep and not a lab rat should go, and he prevailed. Well, what if something went badly wrong? Who gets blamed? His relationship with his future brother-in-law would disintegrate if Kep didn't get back safe and sound. Of course, in the event of some calamity there would be nothing Brian could do, but his knowing first might help soften the blow with M, so he kept an eye on the cat's video feed for almost the entire night, while, to his surprise, M feel off quickly and slept soundly all the way to morning. Of course, the instant M's eyes *weren't* closed, they were glued on Kepler while Brian just pretended to sleep...

"Well, M, I can see that Kepler's happy to be back," as he watched the cat nibble at his food dish, drink some cold milk, and then curl up on his cat bed. "Didn't take him long to get back to his regular routine, I see, which is really great because it tells us that Kepler didn't experience some bad side effect that we can't see on the outside. You must he happy, too, M?" "Tickled, Brian, couldn't be happier, now that my cat's back and we know he did quite well on the world's first 'Node Rider'... hmmm... Boy, I like that..."

"What are you talking about, M? The list of things we're going to go over?" "Nope," was M's quick reply, not that, not yet. The name, that's what I had in mind. So you don't like 'AstroCat.' Okay, I give you that, Brian, maybe it isn't the best choice, too silly, so we can't use that. But, 'Node Rider,' that I like. You?"

Brian thought for a second muttering under his breath, repeating softly 'Node Rider,' then slapping he table as he said, "Yes, M, I think you have something there, good name, actually very good. It captures the essence of Kep's trip, it states a fact, that he 'rode the Node,' and it gives him a certain special status because no one else has. Yeah, let's go with it, Kepler 'NODE RIDER,'" and thus the term was born.

Brian looked at M whose smile and nod signaled agreement, himself grinning because all had gone so well this day, whereupon he sat back in an inquiring posture with his left hand on the table and his right arm across his abdomen resting his right hand just below his left elbow, looking over a M saying, "Now that we're through all this, now that the NODE RIDER is home and happy, what's the big mystery we have to talk about,

M? Why are we doing this here and not at NovaTek?," his glance betraying his concern. Brian expected a shoe to drop, but he could imagine what.

- - - - - - - - - - - -

Emilio turned and slowly walked to his bookcase retrieving his now worn notebook prominently labeled 'Nodes,' while at the same time sliding out Misner, Thorne and Wheeler's nearly thirteen hundred page treatise *Gravitation*. He turned and place both on the kitchen table between himself as he sat and Brian sitting on the opposite side. Brian, looked at the books, then at M, saying, "Whoa! This is going to be heavy! I can see that, and we haven't even started!" as he stood and retrieved from the counter his blanket containing its precious cargo of 23 year old *Glenfiddich* and two glasses from the cabinet above. "This looks like bad news, M, so I'm having a pop, But if it's good news, I'm having a pop. Will you join me? My original idea was to toast Kepler's successful flight, and we can do that, too." M hesitated, he didn't want to drink too much strong whisky in view of what he was about to say, so he agreed, but thinking to himself "One glass, just one, to keep Brian happy..." whereupon Brian went through the traditional ritual of pouring two fingers, neat, nosing and holding the Scotch to the light, then gently sipping it. "Ahhh," Brian said rolling the glass between his fingers and inspecting it further, "truly ambrosia, Emilio, nectar of the gods, what for you would be a fine Italian wine... Alright, my friend, let's get on with it..."

M opened the notebook and removed a single sheet of plain paper without a title. On it were five handwritten, block-lettered lines, nothing more. He turned it upside down to his view and slowly slid it to Brian, saying as he did, "This is what we have to discuss."

Brian looked down at the paper. As he read it, he placed the glass of *Glenfiddich* on the table, releasing his grip so that it dropped slightly, then opened his mouth and canted his head, and after a moment's hesitation bent forward to take a closer look.

"This is some kind of joke, right? Or maybe you're starting a new career as a Sci Fi writer? Or maybe you were hallucinating one day and this is what you saw?" Brian's tone bordered on indignant, as if he were wasting his time... and some very good Scotch... putting up with M's machinations. "So explain this to me, quickly, because I'm leaving in ten minutes. I do have a business to run, you know, and you also know, or should know, that I've been neglecting it because of the Node business. So make it quick, M, and no pie-in-the-sky bullshit!" was Brian's tirade as he looked again at the plain sheet of paper that read:

> ISOLATED CURVED SPACETIME,
> GRAVITY MACHINE
>
> MACRO QUANTUM ENTANGLEMENT
> (THE TWO NOTEBOOKS...)
>
> TIME TRAVEL

"Brian, calm down, and, please, hear me well. *Nothing*... " M paused a long paid for effect, then continued, "*nothing* on that piece of paper is pie-in-the-sky, Brian. I'm as astonished as you are at the very topics, and in my case anyway, the realization that these things are for real, Brian." M stopped to let this gel, then after a long enough pause continued, "Brian I have spent week going over the theory, again and again, and I know I'm right, and I know there's only answer - that all of these things are possible because of the Nodes. The Nodes set up the circumstances - let me say it again, Brian - they set up the conditions under which every one of those things on that paper can occur. There is no doubt about this, Brian, no doubt whatsoever."

"Holy shit, Emilio. You are serious!? And you're absolutely right, this is *ASTONISHING*!!" Brian began to shake ever so slightly, but he knew it, and he suspected M could see it, too. "You know, M, if it weren't you telling me this, someone I respect and know is so damn good at what he does, this theoretical, mathematical stuff - if it weren't you sitting there with that absolutely unreadable look on your face, then I would be up and out of here."

"Sorry, Brian,..." M started, "sorry for the blank look. I didn't know how you were going to react, and, frankly, I was worried... that you would think I'm nuts... and that you would simply storm off. I wouldn't blame you if you did. But..." M paused, "...you didn't, you're still here, and what I want to do is explain all this to you, and then we have something *REALLY* big to discuss. You game?"

Brian had calmed down. Finishing the *Glenfiddich* helped, but he was smart enough to avoid drinking anymore because he knew he needed a clear head to fully grasp what M was about to tell him. "Should I take notes, Professor?" was his was of breaking he ice by letting M know that he was comfortable with what was happening. "Not necessary," M replied,"... unless you want to butter up the teacher... but, seriously, Brian, no. It's hairy enough. I just want to talk about the ideas at this point, and if this goes further, as I think it should, then we can get into the weeds, we'll have to." M studied Brian's reaction, who seemed to be ready to dive into the most mind-blowing conversation he ever will have had. "Let's go, M..."

- - - - - - - - - - -

"I'd like to take these one at a time, in the order they're on that sheet. So we start with *ISOLATED CURVED SPACETIME/GRAVITY MACHINE*, agreed?" M wanted Brian's approval, which he immediately got when Brian nodded assent. "The essential feature of a Node is that it wraps inside our curved spacetime a region of spacetime that is flat, right?" Again, Brian nodded. "Because it's flat there is no gravity, and that - I'll call it 'bubble' - of spacetime travels around with the Node. Well, what if we could bend that spacetime back to make it curved, just like out here? What would happen?"

Brain immediately responded, like an eager student in class, "You get gravity back, because gravity is the curvature of spacetime, right?"

"Yes, exactly. So the next question is, Is there any way to do that? To create a curved spacetime inside the Node? The answer is 'yes!' Astonishing though it may be, Brian, the answer is 'yes,' and the machine to do it is remarkably simple."

As soon as Brian heard the word 'machine,' his ears perked up even more. "Machine? Now you're in my wheelhouse, M. Very cool! Keep going, please..."

"Okay, you know basically how gas lasers work, right?" Brian nodded. "The optical cavity is excited by a *standing wave* created by two mirrors, one at each end. The effect is to amplify the light. We can do the same thing with a *gravity standing wave* inside the Node. The Node's boundary, the region we measure with Marty's NBS, acts as the mirror. With me, Brian?"

"Yes, indeed I am, M. And pretty excited about this! How to we create a gravity wave?"

"Good question, and the answer's simple, just a couple of wiggling masses. Bear with me. If we have two small masses, not big at all, and oscillate the distance between them to create gravitational dipole, then a gravity wave is generated just like the light wave in a laser, and..." Brian interrupted. "Let me guess, just like the laser's light wave is reflected by the mirrors to create a light standing wave, the same thing happens here, but it's a gravity standing wave, right?"

"Exactly, Brian, right on. If you were in my class you'd be getting an 'A!'" M was totally gratified by Brian's immediate and thorough understanding, which was pleasantly reminiscent of his days in front of the blackboard. "The Node boundary acts as the mirror, and repeated reflections of the gravity wave cause the standing wave to grow, which establishes an actual gravitational field inside the Node."

"But how do you control how strong the gravity is? Will be keep growing without limit? That's not good..." Brian picked up on a critical point, that control of the gravitational field was essential, to which M replied. "Yes, Brian, control is key. And the way you do it is by shutting down the source at the right time. Once the standing wave is established, it will grow in amplitude as long as the source is active. When you shut it down the growth stops, and in a lossless system like the Node's interior the standing wave is stable and permanent. You literally have created a gravitational field that then warps the spacetime from flat to curved, and it stays that way. Make sense?"

"Sure does, M, sure does. I'll repeat what I said before, 'Holy Moley!!'" "Hmmm... that's *not* what you said before, but it's the right idea..." M commented.

"Bottom line, Brian - the space inside a Node can be manipulated to create a permanent gravitational field of just about any desired intensity. So all the velocity matching business we went through for the sphere and for Kep's capsule wasn't necessary after all."

Brian's brain was on overload, "How can this be?" he asked himself, "This is like a tiny universe *inside* the Universe! What the hell does this mean?" and he asked. Maybe M had an answer.

"You're idea is essentially correct, Brian, a universe within the Universe. Think of the Node as a bubble of spacetime moving through our spacetime, but the Node is distinct, like a bubble floating in air, or a drop of oil in water. The bubble separates its interior from the outside world, and the oil doesn't mix with the outside world."

"Similar ideas, Brian, and the Node is sort of like that, it doesn't mix with the spacetime surrounding it, and I can prove it," as M flipped to the first of several paper-clipped pages in his notebook, scrolled down it with his index finger and stopped at a page number in MTW to which he then opened the nearly thirteen hundred page book. "Here's the deal, Brian, the theory behind this." M walked Brian through a series of equations in MTW that were copied into the notebook followed by lengthy derivations leading to another set of equations, these telling a quite different story than the ones in MTW.

"See, Brian, this term here," as he pointed to a portion of one of his equations, "this term represents the gravitational standing wave because there is no propagation factor, it drops out because the two traveling gravity waves move, 'propagate,' in opposite directions. Got that?" Brian nodded 'yes,' but his visage said otherwise. "Stay with me, Brian, we're almost there," was M's reassuring response.

"See this term, Brian, it's the reflected wave at the Node boundary, and these parameters are the boundary properties, what NBS measured," point to several variables in the reflected wave term. So we know the amplitude and phase of the reflected wave, we know its propagation factor inside the Node, in short we know everything that constitutes the standing wave. These equations establish the gravitational field. This is where it comes from," M said, obviously self-satisfied with a rather complicated mathematical derivation.

Brian scowled at this last statement, "But you don't know the boundary layer properties. We had to measure them. So this is an interesting academic exercise, but that's it, so what? Because you can't pull off creating the gravitational field without knowing the boundary conditions, and you can't get that without being *inside* the Node to start!"

"At first blush, Brian, that seems like a fatal flaw. But it's not, because it isn't true," as M flipped to the second paper-clipped page in the notebook, scrolled down to a specific page number in MTW, and opened the not quite thirteen hundred page tome to that specific page. "See here, Brian, these equations in MTW, well, they define the existence and properties of a Node without knowing they do because they have to be manipulated further to get there. That's what my notebook derivation does, right here, starting with MTW and working it through," which took five pages of hairy tensor calculus but eventually ended just where M said it would.

"These equations show that a Node boundary exists until the gravitational fields that created it are no longer effective, for example Jupiter's orbit takes the planet away from the positions where it creates Gert. If that happens, then Gert evaporates. But as long as the sources creating the Node remain stable, then the boundary does, too, and it really does act like a wall separating our Universe from the Node's interior. Quite remarkable, eh?" M's excitement was tangible. "This is like a detective story, Brian. Every time I dig deeper into the math something new - and wonderful, for the most part - pops out! There's one other thing like that here, but I haven't quite gotten to the bottom yet..." Brian interrupted, rapt by M's soliloquy, " And what is that, M. Now the hairs on my neck are standing up! So what is it?"

"The possibility that a Node can become self sustaining, independent of the sources creating it! I haven't worked through all the math to be sure about this, Brian, but what I have so far points in that direction. I need, maybe, another week or so. But what it look like is this. Larges masses like the Earth, Sun, Jupiter, their gravitational fields combine to create a Node like Gert. As those masses move, so does Gert. Her trajectory is determined entirely by theirs. But the Node is an entity unto itself, as we've discussed, self-contained, capable of containing its own curved spacetime, hence gravitational field, just the way we've talked about it."

M slowed down to catch his breath, but Brian was all the more worked up. "And, you said Gert, or any Node, for that matter, could do what, 'uncouple' from its creators? Is that what you're saying?"

"Yes, exactly, Brian. The equations seem to be telling us that. The idea is that once an internal gravitational field is created, inside the Node boundary, once the spacetime inside the Node becomes curved, well, the it decouples from its sources and then exists as a separate, independent entity. Essentially just as you put it, a 'universe' within our 'Universe.' Mind-bending, isn't it?"

"Sure is, Emilio. Scary, actually. Because this can happen only if a regular Node with flat spacetime is manipulated to bend that spacetime, which means creating gravity, and that cannot happen spontaneously - it requires something like your 'gravity machine'... M sensed that Emilio was on the verge, just at the point where he was *compelled* to take the next logical leap, and what would happen when he did take that step, that was the question. "Yes, Brian, everything you said so far was correct. Keep going..."

Brian stuttered, flustered because he knew what that next step was, but he didn't want to articulate it. Too frightening, too out of the world... yet unavoidable. "Er... geez...this... well... M, help me here, I think I know, but..." M responded, "You're doing great, Brian, just about where I was when this hit me like a brick. Spit it out... go ahead!"

"And the best way to get a 'gravity machine,' we'll call it the *GRAVITY ENGINE*, inside the Node, but not necessarily the only way, is for a *human being* to be there, *inside* the Node, operating the Engine... So a person has to jump into a Node to do this, and then go wherever the Node goes, *inside* the Node! This is a scary possibility, M, but I take it you think it's a *real possibility*, don't you?"

"Yes, I do, Brian... Not only real, but inevitable..."

M looked at the clock, and then at Kepler cozied up in his cat bed, then at Brian, "Look, it's getting on, Brian, almost six. How about a break? I'll rustle up that pasta dinner I promised, then we can get back to this. Is that good?" "Certainly is, M. All this heady gravity stuff has made me hungry... or maybe it was Mother Earth's gravity pulling on my tummy?" M rolled his eyes, suggesting "How about you choose an album and fire up some music, anything you want." Brian scanned M's collection of LP's, didn't see anything that immediately struck him, so he started leafing through them one at a time, dozens of records of all sorts of music, much to his surprise. "Never would have guessed, Emilio, that you would have such an eclectic music collection, from Verdi to Coltrane to the Beatles! Surprising. How about Coltrane's *Kulu Se Mama*?" "Great album, Brian, good choice. Did you know that Coltrane and his wife Alice played quite a bit with Carlos Santana?" "Had no idea, but I can imagine they were great together," Brian replied as he gently placed *Kulu* onto the turntable.

Chapter 14 - Where No Cat Has Gone Before!

M's marinara sauce was quick - fresh ground, peeled, no-salt-added San Marzano tomatoes, plenty of garlic, oregano, finely chopped onion, a little good white wine, M preferred Pinot Grigio, and salt and pepper to taste, which in M's case was spicy, simmered for at least twenty minutes, although M preferred more like an hour or so because then the flavors melded more. "Choose one, Brian, spaghetti, penne, or linguine, your call," as M pointed to three boxes of pasta arrayed on the counter, all imported from Italy, none domestically made. "So why the fancy imported macaroni, M. I know half your head is in Italy a lot of the time, that Enrico Fermi is your hero, but the extra expense of pasta from there?"

M figured this was a chance to educate Brian on the finer points of good food. "It's the bronze dies, Brian. As a machine guy yourself you should appreciate that, no?"

"Well, I suppose I might if I had any clue as to what you're talking about. You imply that the 'bronze die' is better,... better than what? And I don't even know what a bronze die is! So 'splain..." Brian said, at the time apparently genuinely interested in knowing.

"Pasta is made by an extrusion process, much like your bird springs, the ones that started all this Node stuff!" "Yes, M, I know what extrusion is. I might toot my own horn... You know I'm an expert in that technology, the variable diameter bird spring is just one example. Continue... Pasta?..."

"In short, pasta is extruded with two types of dies, Teflon and bronze. Bronze is much better because it gives a different color and texture, and it's mostly the texture that matters because the roughness in a bronze die extruded pasta causes the sauce to adhere better, and those little irregularities are where the tastiest sauce, or 'gravy' as my grandma called it, that's where it's hiding. Teflon cut pasta looks blander and is smoother, so a lot of the good gravy just slides off, *quel dommage*, that's French by the way..."

"So you buy stuff from Italy because of this?"

"Yes, I do, Brian, and you'll taste the difference... tonight, you lucky dog - don't listen Kep", as M looked over at the cat, " - and then we can get back to work." Which they did after a delicious meal of linguine with M's fabulous sauce, and, - yes, the bronze die cut pasta did taste better - garlic bread, and a fine bottle of *Cecchi 'Storia di Famiglia' Chianti Classico DOCG 1968*. To Emilio Ravelli being a poor grad student didn't mean having ramen for dinner every night, although, being a similar dish, his made-from-scratch was superb as well!

- - - - - - - - - - - -

After clearing the table, Emilio looked squarely at M with a purposeful gaze, "Tell me, Brian, what do you know about 'Quantum Entanglement', QE?"

To which Brian replied immediately, "Uhh... Hmm... how about... Nothing? Make that a CAP *N*. 'Quantum... *tanglement*... like when your shoelaces aren't tied? What is this, M, another modern physics sort-of joke like that subatomic particle the 'Quark,' a name lifted straight out of Joyce's *Finnegan's Wake*, 'Three quarks for Muster Mark'? Don't know a damn thing about tangles, but I'm sure you're going to tell me..." Brian sat quietly staring back at M with just as businesslike a puss.

"Sure am, my friend. QE is a quantum, meaning elementary particle level, concept dealing with photons and other particles like electrons and how two separate ones are connected in such a way that each one 'knows' what the other one is doing no matter how far apart they are. Weird, right?"

"Yes, very,... if what you say is true. How does one photon know what another separate photon is doing? Doesn't that mean information must be exchanged? How?"

"Well, that's the mystery, Brian, no one knows how, but it's real. Every experiment so far shows that. In fact, Einstein himself, who never liked quantum mechanics because it seemed to belie cause and effect, and some colleagues actually proposed QE in paper published way back in 1935! Speaking of prescient!"

"Amazing, really, that Albert was so right about so many things for so long! Go on..." Brian said, now fully captivated by the very notion of entanglement.

"While the means aren't understood, what we know is that what happens to one entangled particle is immediately, that is, *instantaneously*, literally, transmitted somehow to its entangled counterpart, no matter how far apart the particles are. One could be here on Earth and the other at the limits of the known Universe, yet QE takes place."

"That is a head trip, Emilio!! And so far as we can tell it's for real? I'm not sure I can believe this!" Brian's wore his confusion and amazement in every way, his demeanor, his tone, his look, everything about him said 'I don't buy it.' M saw this and stepped in, "I felt the same way, Brian, just like you. I was right there with Albert,... nah, this simply doesn't make sense, can't be true, but after reading the papers, and believe me, Brian, I read *every one*, some of them twice, I now am convinced - QE is real, for real!"

Reluctantly, Brian seemed to acquiesce. "Okay, let's say so. What does *this* have to do with Nodes, huh? Nodes aren't subatomic particles, so what's the connection?"

"Well, yes, they aren't. But that doesn't mean they can't *behave* like them. The nexus here is the Special Relativity connection between an actual subatomic particle, say, a photon, and a Node that encompasses a unique spacetime of its own that happens to be flat,.." M could see that Brian was following along, so he injected, what for him anyway, was some levity, "... at least until Jasper fires up the gravity machine, hee-hee..." Brian wasn't so light-hearted, "As usual, M, attempted levitousness, if that's a word, which I doubt, has failed. Not funny, Jasper notwithstanding. Please, just continue so I can get this out of my head, or at least put it somewhere where a migraine isn't imminent!!"

"Okay, okay, Brian, calm down. Think about jumping on a photon..." Brian immediately stood, "Look, I am having a bit of a problem here, all this is way more than 'a bit much!' I need a break before 'jumping on a photon.' How about ten. That Coltrane album was nice, relaxing. Mind if I find another and cue it up?" "Don't mind at all, Brian. Please do." M could see and sense Brian's distress. After all, these were truly astonishing ideas, and they weren't abstractions that existed only in textbooks or notebooks or pieces of scrawled paper, they were about Nodes, the very bizarre thing that just last night swept Kepler the NODE RIDER off planet Earth far into outer space then returned him safe and sound mere hours later. *That* is astonishing by any and every measure, and now Emilio is talking about a human inside a Node, and particles that 'know' what a sister particle is doing even light years away, and now, the *coup de grace*, jumping on a photon!! "I'm a reasonable and pretty tough guy," Brian thought, "...but this... this is too much... even for me."

Emilio realized that Brian needed time to digest, both the excellent dinner and these unexpected almost unfathomable revelations, so he proposed another break. "Brian, why don't we take another breather. I'll brew a pot of Espresso, and we can have those pastries you got at D'Argento's for dessert, just relax for a while. Good?"

"Yes, M, very good. I do need some time, thanks." And the two slowly sipped Espresso from demitasse cups imported from Italy, of course, with a lemon wedges for garnish. In the background M played Beethoven's *Moonlight Sonata*, thinking how appropriate it was to the topics at hand. M himself needed a break, but he didn't realize that until began to unwind. A good half hour passed when it was Brian who said, "I'm much better, M. Want to jump back in? I mean jump on the photon?"

"That's where we left off, Brian, about to jump on a photon. This will be a *gedankenexperiment*, a thought experiment that's done in your head, not in a lab..." Brian couldn't resist, "I prefer the lab, by far..." whereupon M chuckled and continued. "Photons are particles of light, massless and always, by definition, traveling at the speed of light, never faster, never slower, right?" Brian nodded. "Now in Special Relativity lengths contract in the direction of motion, and time slows down. These effects depend on how fast you're moving, and, for practical purposes, they're undetectable at the speeds we encounter day-to-day. They show up only as the speed approaches the speed of light, with me?" Brian nodded again.

"Okay, the, you're on the photon going for the ride of your life. You're travelling *at the speed of light*. How much does length contract?" M asked Brian, indicating he did expect an answer by raising his right hand with his palm towards himself and his fingers splayed, thumb up, extending it towards Brian. Brian winced, then smiled slightly, then said "It contracts to..." he hesitated "...zero!" "Yes, Brian, *at* the speed of light length contracts to zero! So what does time do?" Brian winced again, then smirked because he knew the answer and was sure of it. "It stops!" "Right again, Brian, if you're riding the photon *there is no such thing as distance, no such thing as time.* That's what the photon experiences! Remarkable!"

"But what does this mean, M. Really? Are you telling me that a photon doesn't have time or distance?" "Yes, Brian, that's right, neither one. In reality there's only a single photon in existence because it is every and nowhere at the same 'time' but there is no such thing as time for it!"

"This doesn't seem right, Emilio. There has to be something wrong with this reasoning?" "No, not if Special Relativity is solid, and that has been tested for decades without the slightest hint of its being wrong. What I just said, Brian, is solid, count on it. Question is, How does it apply to Nodes?"

"Yes, that is the question, I guess. And..." Brian's anticipation, as it had been so many times during these discussions, was evident in every pore.

"Remember what a Node is, Brian. It's an encapsulated spacetime that is independent, uncoupled from the surrounding spacetime. Flat or curved, it matters not, the key idea here is that there is *no connection whatsoever* between the Node and the spacetime through which it moves. With me?" Brian nodded 'yes.' "Now the Node is massless, even though it may contain mass, the Node itself has none. It's like a photon, right?"

Brian was skeptical, and it showed both by his tone and his furrowed brow, "I guess, like a photon. I think I know where you're going with this, M... And I'm not sure..." M cut him off mid sentence "... you're not sure because it's mind-bending in the extreme, but let me tell you, Brian, that its' rock solid. I've gone through the equations of Special Relativity and the quantum mechanical Wave Equation so many times I can write them from memory. I dream about them, Brian! The math doesn't lie. And I don't make mistakes..." M's voice a bit indignant, but at the same time assertive and confident. He said it again, "Rest assured, Brian, the math tells the story, and I uncovered it."

"Does this mean there's no distance or time for a Node? Just like a photon?"

"Oh, no, not at all. What it means is that there can be no distance, no time,... if the Node travels *at* the speed of light. At sublight the Node is just a bubble of spacetime moving through the spacetime that surrounds it. The beauty of this, Brian, is that a Node actually can be made to travel at lightspeed because *it* has no mass, remember that, even if it *contains* mass."

"How's that? What could make a Node travel at lightspeed?"

"First, think of it this. Imagine a light beam shining into empty space, an extremely powerful beam, and revolving around the point of origin, like a lighthouse beacon. No matter how slowly or quickly the beam rotates, at some distance away from the source, the beam will be sweeping an arc *at or above the speed of light*, right?"

Brian thought, then replied, "Yes, I suppose, if you go out *far enough*, seems right."

"Well, do suppose,... because the answer is 'yes.' How? If nothing can travel faster than lightspeed, how can the light beam sweep an arc *faster* than lightspeed? It can do that because it has *no mass*. It is not a material object, and according to Relativity it's only objects with mass, that is things with finite rest energy, that can't go faster than light. Massless objects, like a Node, can exceed lightspeed. The classic example of this is the phase velocity of a wave carrying information. *That velocity* can be faster than light, too."

M just sat for a few seconds taking stock of what he and Brian had just discussed, and he concluded somewhat reluctantly that his path was too zigzag, not straight enough to the point, so he made an attempt to clear things up. "Brian, I've been a little obtuse here, my apology for that. Here's the take-away, (i) a Node behaves much like a photon, and elementary particle. Because of that it can travel at the speed of light or sublight even when it harbors an object, a mass. (ii) Because a Node behaves like a photon it possesses the properties of a photon, like Quantum Entanglement. That was my main point, and I lost the forest for the trees on it. Sorry. Are you with me on this?"

"I think so, M, but I am puzzled about one thing. The Node may have some of the properties of a photon, I get that, but it's not actually an elementary particle. There must be some differences, no?"

- - - - - - - - - - -

"You know, Brian, I'd love to have you as a student. Yes, that's a great question, and, indeed, that's true, there are differences. The main one concerning QE is that's a macro QE effect, not quantum level, at least that's what the math shows. We can't be one hundred percent sure without some experiments, but I'm confident."

"Okay, and the significance?"

"At the quantum level, the particles, be they photons, electrons or some other subatomic particle, they march in lockstep as I described with 100 percent fidelity. Whatever happens to one is instantaneously transmitted to the other. But, and here's the difference, because a Node's contents isn't subatomic there may be errors between two Node-QE linked objects. Let me be specific..." Brian was visibly perplexed, "Yeah, please do. I'm not visualizing what you have in mind." M continued, "Let's say we have two identical notebooks, both inside a Node so they become entangled. Now they are QE linked forever, wherever. This is why I placed those two small notebooks in Kep's capsule. They should now be macro-QE *forever*! One of the notebooks is taken out of the Node and remains in one place while the other one travels *with* the Node, staying inside it. What happens? Well, because the notebooks are *entangled*, whatever happens to one instantaneously happens to the other. So, if I draw a picture in the notebook inside the Node, that very same picture instantaneously shows up in the entangled notebook that was left *outside* the Node, get it?"

Brian thought for some time, all the while looking at M and stroking his chin, while M sat quietly waiting for this to sink in. Then Brian suddenly piped up, "You know, M, I need a different expression than 'holey moley.' This stuff is such a head trip 'moley's' become hackneyed. I need something new that expresses how totally, completely, absolutely my mind has been stretched by what you've been telling me! This is more than astonishing, Professor Ravelli, it borders on the insane. I need something new, so I'm going with 'gobsmacked.' That's a good word, it makes the point, and I like it. Well, M, I've been gobsmacked!"

"Okay, Brian, only you know for sure, but I take it gobbed you have been. You had a question?"

"Oh, yes, on the Notebooks. Before you said something about *macro* QE being different than elementary particle level QE."

"Yep, macro's not quite the same. I've gone over and over the underlying equations, and there are subtle differences when you go from one length scale to the other. Terms that drop out at the particle level don't on a macro scale, and what they represent is, how can I say it,... what they represent is 'noise,' like a staticky radio station. And that noise can corrupt the QE 'transmission,' meaning that the two drawings may not be exactly the same. As far as I can tell, how much degradation there is depends mostly on how far apart the notebooks are. Got it?"

"Yes, I do. In fact, to me this makes a lot more sense than some of the other stuff you've said. I'm good with this, and I have a suggestion." M looked at Brian, raising his eyebrows, obviously anxious to hear what Brian had in mind. "Instead of 'notebooks' wouldn't 'Nodebooks' be a better term?" M thought for just a few seconds, "Sure would, Brian. Sold, 'Nodebooks,' I like it,... a lot."

This was a good place for a break, so Brian and Emilio took one, what was left of the espresso, with lemon wedges, and the *D'Argento's* pastries. They sat and relaxed, talking about how well Kepler, the NODE RIDER cat, had done on his first-of-its-kind-in-the-whole-world journey, while Kep looked quite content still curled up in his cat bed in the corner. He had gotten up only a couple of times to take a drink and to nibble on the fresh tuna that, as M had promised, was in his food dish right next to his regular cat food. M felt better about giving Kep the tuna this way because the cat now had a choice, and, just as M expected, Kep nibbled on both, very slowly and deliberately and selectively. After all, Kepler was the consummate well-mannered, mellow feline of whom nothing less would be expected.

"One more topic, Brian. Shall we?" was M's invitation to begin wrapping up this evening's session." And "Yes, I'm chomping at the bit," was Brian's reply.

"Be sure you're sitting, my friend," M exhorted in view of what he was about to say. "I'm comfy, M, go ahead, lay it on me," both he and M were getting tired, and it showed.

"How do you feel about *Time Travel*, visiting the past as well as the future?" M asked.

"Why, you thinking of taking a trip? Without Isabella? Another joke, of course," was Brian response.

"Nope, no joke, and, yep, probably without your sister, because if it works, as it should, we'll be right back here in the present."

"A couple of things, M. You're serious, aren't you?" to which M immediately interjected "Yes, I am, deadly..." to which Brian replied "So, what did you mean by 'we'll be back here'? Who's the 'we'?" to which M replied, "You and I, of course!"

Brian smirked, tilting his head slightly while throwing his head back as he stared at M, "You are certifiable, my friend, off the proverbial rocker. I do not believe time travel is possible, Emilio, pure and simple, open and shut, cannot do it!"

"Ahhh, but you're wrong, Brian, very wrong, but there are limits. Once again, I've gone through this more times than I want to count, checking and re-checking and double checking he re-check. The math doesn't lie, Brian, and it's all in there. The equations of modern physics, Relativity, Quantum Mechanics, and Gravitation make it clear that time travel *is possible*, in both directions. There's no doubt about it. The only question is how to implement it, and, guess what, the Nodes can do it!"

"Alright, let's say I suspend belief for a while and buy what you're selling, namely that it's *theoretically* possible. How do Nodes figure in?" Brian was hoping to set a trap that M couldn't escape.

"Remember when I said a Node as like a photon? Remember that?" Brian raised both hands, fingers splayed, moving them apart to indicate that he did recall. "Then continue with that analogy. Remember, too, that the photon cannot experience either distance or time because of Special Relativity's contraction and dilation, respectively, right?" Again, Brian was following along and indicated as much. "Now just apply that to a Node traveling at lightspeed. It experiences just what the photon does,... that is, neither space nor time exist. When the Node goes sublight, time and space pop into existence, whenever and wherever the Node happens to be. Voila! Time travel. Just come out of lightspeed at a place and time of your choosing, and it can be anywhere, anytime, past or future, here or there." Brian stared blankly as M continued.

"And, finally, Brian, remember this, the reality of what I just described falls right out of the math, and it, the mathematics, is woven into the fabric of our very existence. So there's no question, time travel is possible, and Nodes can be its subway." M was pooped, so he sat back, folded his arms, and looked over at Brian with a slight smile. Brian, in turn, sat just as quietly, with his chin shrouded by his left hand as its index finger slowly tapped his pursed lips. Each maintained his stance for several minutes while M wound down and Brian took in the implications of what M had said.

Then Emilio suddenly sat up, his hands flat on the table, and he leaned forward to capture Brian's attention. "So there's only one thing left, Brian..." "Which is?" Brian asked. "You and I have to take a trip through time. We can work out the details later, but we have to do this!"

Chapter 15 - How Fast Can That Node Go?

"Hello..." was Jean Simmon's cheery greeting. "Jean?" "Yes, Emilio. Can't mistake your voice, very distinctive. Must be from all that teaching! I was going to call you if you hadn't called me. Time's getting close, just a few days to the big party! Leigh and I are all set. You?"

"Yes... and no... I wanted to talk to you and Leigh, again, about the party plans. It was great seeing you both at *The Cookie* a couple of weeks ago, but I'm thinking we should get together one more time. I was hoping maybe today if at all possible. Look, I know you and Leigh are very busy people, and I really don't want to intrude, but, fact is, Jean I'm pretty strung out, and I hope you can pick up some of what I was supposed to do," M confessed, embarrassed that he found himself in this position.

"M, are you okay? Something wrong? I know Izz is on cloud nine over your engagement, so is there something bad that's happened?" Jeannie was a good friend and naturally curious and more than willing to help if she could.

"Geez, Jean, I'm so sorry to give that impression. No, nothing bad, no medical concerns, nothing in the family, everything like that is fine, very good in fact. It's my thesis and things related to it that are, to be honest, stretching the band quite thin. I just have sooo... much to do and not a lot of time to do it, that's the problem, Jean" M lied. Because he couldn't tell Jean, or Leigh, or Marty, or anyone for that matter, what really was going on, the Nodes, his analysis of the underlying theory, his discovery that Nodes could take you through space, and through time, at the speed of light, and that macro QE exists, all this was pulling him in too many directions all at once.

"This is a pretty light week for me, M, so we can get together later today, say, the usual around five o'clock, and I'm sure Leigh can make it, too. Let's plan on that, and if there's a problem I'll get back to you right away. Is that good?"

"You are a lifesaver, Jean Simmons, Esquire! I can't thank you enough. Leigh, too. Five it is, see you then." As M hung up he could feel the tension in his body subside, he was that uptight about managing Izzy's upcoming party, making some substantial progress on his dissertation before his next meeting with Dr. Hanlon, and, maybe the most burning issue of all, dealing with the Nodes. He remembered his promise to put Izz first, thesis second, and the Nodes wherever he could fit them after that, and he decided this was a critical week for making good. Izzy's party, his fiancé's twenty-ninth, had to be his entire focus between now, Monday, and the big bash on Saturday. And during these few days he figured he could make some substantial progress writing the Introduction that he and Professor Hanlon agreed was the first, perhaps most important, section of his dissertation. As long as he didn't get bogged down again in the endless, complex mathematics of Gravitation, Relativity and Quantum Mechanics. "Self discipline, "M thought, "now's the time - set limits, adhere to them!" which is exactly what M pledged to do.

- - - - - - - - - - -

It being a Monday, *Fortune Cookie*'s parking lot was thin, and M was proud of himself for actually being nearly half an hour early, figuring he would sit quietly in the Camaro with some pleasant classical music playing and his thesis reference number 127 which he could peruse while waiting because it wasn't even three pages long, but it was an important reference for vertical ionospheric sounding which was a component of his research. So M dove right into Wild's paper *De-Convolution of Barely Resolved Radio Sources Mapped with Aerial Beams of Elliptical Cross Section*, was published only a couple of years before in 1970 in the **Australian Journal of Physics**. "Nothing like some light reading while I wait," M thought as he occasionally scanned the lot for Jean and Leigh to arrive, which they did - ten minutes late! They met at *The Cookie*'s ornate entrance where they were met by the same young lady wearing the same flowing black Chinese print sheath dress adorned with dark maroon dragons who had seated them the on their last two visits. By now she knew their party, and immediately asked "Shall I let Linda know you are here?" "Yes, please," Jean replied, knowing that her friend Linda Lee would be disappointed if she learned that Jean came by without saying hello. Plus, she was about to be invited to Izzy's birthday bash... The party of three was once again seated at their private table where they could linger and talk for as long as they wished.

"Well, Leigh, first, thanks so much for coming on such short notice..." "My pleasure, M" Leigh Bennet interrupted. M continued, "... I'm sure Jean explained that I've been so, so busy lately I was worried about getting everything together for Izzy's party, since its only five days away." "Yes, she did, M, and believe me, I understand. I know how important this is to you, especially in view of the engagement - Congratulations! Which I'm sure you've heard a hundred times!"

"Yeah, I think at least a hundred, and thank you! Thanks do much! I can't tell you two how much I appreciate your being Izzy's such good friends."

Jean saw that the conversation was devolving into a mutual admiration love fest, so she jumped in to get down to the business at hand, "As I see it, M. we decided on the basic elements of the party, but not necessarily who and how they would be implemented, right?"

"Yes, very right, and, wow, how lawyerly, Jean! No wonder so many clients want *you* as their attorney!"

"Thanks, M," Jean replied, fishing her notes from her handbag. "So those elements were, guest list, invitations, decorations, catering, housekeeping, special needs or arrangements, if any. And I think that's it, right?"

Leigh answered, "Yes, and if you recall we decided, more or less, who would do what, but that wasn't firmed up last time we got together. Instead we were going to think about for a few days and then talk by phone, but that didn't happen... I guess we all dropped the ball?" Leigh remarked, feeling that she let the others down.

"I can see from your look, Leigh, that you feel bad about this," Jean said, "...but the truth is we all put it off because we thought we had plenty of time, and now the big event is only days away. But it wasn't you more than anyone else. So put that aside, and let's get on with it and make this party happen!" M loved Jean's 'can do' attitude. She was like that about everything, and because of it things actually got done.

"I have my notes from last time, M," as she waved a couple of sheets of yellow legal sized paper covered with cryptic scribbles. "Use these?" Then she notice M looking closely at her cryptic scribbles, nodding 'yes' as he did, "My form of shorthand, M, a combination of the real thing and my improvisation. I know, it looks like gibberish, but I understand it, really," and their discussion began in earnest.

"First thing," said Jean, "is the guest list. Last time, we figured each of us would work up a list and invitations would be mailed. No can do now because there simply isn't enough time. Leigh and I did go over whom we would want to ask, and it works out to about fifteen people. They all know Izz - and love her, of course - so we're sure they're all going to come. Leigh and I can split the list and, because mail is out, we'll call. How does that sound, M, Leigh?" Leigh chimed in immediately, "Yes, Jean, this is what we decided coming over. I'm happy with this." as both young women looked at M who seemed to be hesitating. Nearly simultaneously they said "And *you*, M?" "What are *you* thinking, M?"

"Oh, sorry, Jeannie, Leigh. I was off in K-space there for a minute, nothing to do with the invitee list, sorry." M was thinking about the paper he was reading in the car, and something else that popped into his head that he had to bring up when he saw Michael Hanlon. "To be honest, something occurred to me about my thesis, that's all. I apologize. The problem is, sometimes these ideas just show up when I'm not even thinking about things like them, and I can't shake them. It's kind of a curse. Sorry, really sorry, but now I'm back on lists. Of course, I think what you want to do is fabulous. Let's go with that." And then and there M resolved to not let this happen again in front of Jean and Leigh.

Not wanting to get into the weeds on what was on M's mind, Leigh asked, "Okay, M, now that your spaceship has landed, what are you going to do?"

"Well, I figure between my friends from the University and Izzy's colleagues at her former employer and her friends at school now, I know most of them, altogether I figure about fifteen people. And I talked to Brian. His friends who know Izzy, he figures maybe five. And then there's the Healy family, say, another ten or so. So all told about thirty people on my end." M knew that he was forgetting *something*? *What is it*? He couldn't quite unplug from what he was thinking about concerning his thesis, it just wouldn't let go. Fortunately Leigh got him back on track.

"Alright, M, and out of the thirty how many do you figure will want to bring a guest?" "Crap, M, thought, *that's* what I forgot. A lot of these people are unattached, but they have significant others that they might want to bring, whether or not they know Izzy." M replied, "Good question, Leigh. Let me think, hmmm...well, I'd say maybe ten or so..." It was a pure guess. At that moment M wasn't inclined to consider each person, one by one, and whether or not they had a boyfriend or a girlfriend, and if so whether or not they would want to bring that person with them. His head was too full of other things, so he played the odds, figuring about a third of the people would be a pretty good guess, and in the end it happened to be pretty close!

"Okay, so that raises yours and Brian's total to forty including your guests' guests," Jean injected, "and with ours, say twenty because they way have guests, well, we're up to sixty, which isn't that far from the rough estimate of fifty that we started with." Jean surveyed Leigh's and M's reactions, which they said it was a good number, so she wrapped it up, " Leigh and I will contact everyone on our list by Wednesday at the latest, two days from now. M, you have to do the same. Will you? Or is your dissertation going to interfere?... Oooh, and one more thing, tell everyone to park far enough down the road that Izzy won't see a bunch of cars at the house."

"Jeannie, I promise, on a stack of ionospheric physics books, that I will contact everyone I have to by Wednesday at the latest," and M swore to himself that he would, not forget because Izzy and the party simply were too important for him to forget.

The remaining items on Jean's list were catering, decorations, and housekeeping. And each was dispatched with her lawyerly efficiency after the three of them talked them through. Leigh and Jean would take care of the catering. For the main meal they decided on Chinese from *Fortune Cookie*, Italian from *Stella's*, and for desert assorted pastries from *D'Argento's* as well as the birthday cake. The food would be set up by its providers and served buffet style.

The party's start time was set at one o'clock next Saturday, Izzy's actual birthday, August 19th. That time was early enough for the guests to enjoy the Lake if they wished, lounging on the beach, taking a dip, row boating or kayaking, heading out to the island about a quarter mile offshore, fishing, walking the many trails through the woods, or just hanging around the Lake House.

Unfortunately, Izzy's and Brian's parents, Bill and Mary Healy, couldn't make the party because they were miles at sea in the Caribbean on a cruise that they had booked months before. Of course, they sent their best wishes through Brian, and told him Izzy's birthday present should arrive before the occasion itself. Bill and Mary were absolutely delighted at the news that Emilio had proposed and Izzy had accepted, and they were looking forward to the wedding, hopefully sometime in '73. And they assured Brian that they wouldn't book any cruises or other extended travel anytime next year to be sure there wouldn't be any possibility of a conflict.

The Healy's purchased the Lake House decades ago and through the years expanded and modernized it to a large, beautifully maintained home, balconies overlooking the Lake, a covered, wrap-around veranda for sitting on those lazy summer afternoons, five bedrooms, a good-sized office, a game room, and a large, state-of-the-art kitchen adjoining the very large fireplaced family room with its with an upright piano, and both rooms having cathedral ceilings and surrounded by eight foot walls of glass windows that provided a fabulous view of the water about two hundred feet away. The grounds were professionally landscaped to match the house style, which was Victorian, and its setting against Lake Arrowhead. The boat shed was added about ten years ago to provide storage for a large boat, but that never happened because Bill and Mary simply were too busy with the day-to-day of taking care of the kids, Isabella and Brian, and their business, the six Healy Hardware stores.

Izzy and Brian both worked in the stores during the summer, which is where Izzy was introduced to accounting and Brian to things mechanical. Both went on in school to pursue those early interests as professionals, and each was very skilled at what they did. Then, two years ago, Bill and Mary were approached by a national chain, Avant Hardware, that made an offer they couldn't refuse. They sold the entire business and walked away, never looking back, not retaining an interest, not serving as consultants, simply cashing in a lifetime's hard work and retiring in Ponte

Vedra, Florida, with a house on the ocean not far from TPC Sawgrass where both Bill and Mary became members and played golf regularly. All-in-all not a bad life, one they earned by cashing in their sweat equity. Izzy and Brian were frequency visitors, as was Emilio after he and Izzy became a serious couple. Bill and Mary loved M because of his work ethic and intelligence, and for some time had hoped Izzy and he would wed. That day finally had come with the engagement, and they were delighted.

M, of all things, was delegated decorations duty, at which he winced at first, but soon came around to the idea that it would be less time-consuming and stressful than anything else. Jean and Leigh recommended *Party Hearty*, which Leigh pointed out was an eggcorn for *Party Hardy*, as the best place to get what he needed, all the balloons, hanging decorations - including one that read 'H A P P Y   B I R T H D A Y,   I Z Z Y' - party favors, hats, noise makers, table decorations, and so on. Leigh wrote down the list and passed it over to M, "This is everything you need, M, one trip and you're done," she said "and you and Brian can decorate the place in less than an hour, maybe Friday night?" M agreed, of course, because it did take the pressure off and got his job out of the way so that he could concentrate on other matters, not that Izzy's party decorations weren't important, only that he really did have other things to tend to and he didn't want them preempting his obligations for the party. M had it all figured out. He and Brian would gussy up the Lake House Friday night around eight. Then, on Saturday morning Brian would call Izzy and invite her and M to the Lake House for a birthday lunch that he would provide, 1:30 sharp, so he could give Iz her birthday present and so she and M could meet his new girlfriend, Brenda, from the wine and cheese shop. The four of them would spend the afternoon enjoying each other's company and being on the lake, maybe doing some swimming, maybe a boat ride, and so on. M knew Izzy would go for this, and when she called him to tell him about Brian's invitation, M would tell her that he was planning on taking her out for her birthday dinner that night, again at *Chez Gaston*. M smiled with self-satisfaction, thinking how great a surprise the surprise party would be, how much Izzy would love it... and, of course, he was right.

"Okay, Emilio, I think we're done. Count on us to take care of everything else. All you have to do is extend the invitations you want by getting in touch, getting the decorations and actually decorating the Lake House. Your plan to get Iz there is great. She won't figure it out until the last minute, which is great. We're going to see Linda now to firm up the Chinese buffet, and we'll stop at *Stella's* tomorrow to take care of that. You're going to talk to Brian about his taking care of *D'Argento's*, right?" M nodded 'yes,' and Jean finished up, "Alright, we're done! I'd bang my gavel, but I don't have one..." whereupon Jean and Leigh cracked broad smiles, chuckled, and stood up from the table. Each one gave M a peck on the cheek, saying "That's for Congratulations one more time! See you Saturday!" and they walked off towards *Fortune Cookie*'s kitchen to hook up with Linda Lee.

"Emilio, so good to see you," as M entered Professor Hanlon's office carrying a thick pile of papers. "You, too, Michael, good to see you too. I'm actually early for a change, ten of two, instead of my usual five minutes late... May I?" as M pointed to the chair opposite Hanlon's desk and an area to clear to deposit the thick pile of papers. "By all mean, M, please sit, and park your papers right there after moving those" as Hanlon motioned to another thick pile of papers that could readily be moved to the side so he an M could pore over M's material where they could both see it.

"Your phone call, M, it sounded very excited," Hanlon said, referring to the message M left on his answering machine. "What's this about some 'major breakthrough?'"

"Yes, Michael, yes indeed, I think it is a major breakthrough, and one I came across sort of accidentally. I was puzzled by some of my data because there was no obvious explanation, so rather than spend hours in the library trying to track down an explanation that may not exist, I decided to back up a bit and take a broader look."

"And?" Hanlon leaned forward in his chair, his hands apart and palms down on the desk, obviously awaiting something important from M. "So where did you look?" he asked.

"Well, I started with our friends Rishbeth and Garriott, RG, not a bunch of research papers, but instead their book *Introduction to Ionospheric Physics*. I have it right here in case you don't want to fish out your copy," as M held up a very well worn, highly dog-eared copy of Volume 14 in the **International Geophysics Series**. "Right here, Michael, on page 269 it says..." as M read verbatim "*... suffer from the same uncertainties: (b) Calculation of the electric fields driving these currents, by inserting conductivities, and then the derivation of F-region drift velocity by assuming transmission of the electric field up the geomagnetic field lines. On the simplest theory, this velocity is* $\mathbf{E} \times \mathbf{B}/B^2$.'"

"Okay, M, yes, this has been an open question for decades, actually, and *no one* has discovered an answer. Are you telling me that you think you have? If so, Emilio, you will have solved one of the most vexing problems in ionospheric physics,... maybe, if it's really true,... maybe even a Nobel prize level accomplishment! So, let's have it," Hanlon was visibly worked up, not like anything M ever had seen in him before, even though they had worked together for several years. Hanlon was almost shaking, his nervous energy so apparent.

"It's the velocity term that everyone uses, the cross product of the electric field and induction field scaled by the square of the induction field. The exponent is wrong! And I can prove it..." M sat back so this simple statement could sink in.

"How did you come to this, M? Why were you thinking about this at all?" Hanlon's tone obviously incredulous, so M replied. "Well, Michael, normally I wouldn't be thinking about this, but, here..." as M opened the pile of computer printout to a paper-clipped page, "...see these measured drift velocity curves, I couldn't understand why they look like this. They seemed to decay too slowly along the geomagnetic lines, which is why I started digging until I came upon the paragraph I just read."

"Alright, I can see that, too, that the decay seems to be too slow. So what did you do about it?"

"I went right back to the 'simplest theory' that RG mentions, and, by the way, Michael, it ain't all that simple... and I worked through the whole thing. The exponent of 2 in the denominator actually is 2.47, which causes a more rapid decay." M sat back while this sank in. He could see Professor Hanlon's light bulbs turning on one after another.

"And how do you come to that number, Emilio, 2.47? I assume it was calculated? But, how?"

M had Hanlon hooked! All he had to do now was explain the derivation, and that was it. Fix that exponent and it fixes the data, "Quite remarkable," M thought, then explaining, "The velocity term derivation, Michael, comes out an expression published by Weekes in 1957. The plasma drift velocity assumes that the neutral particle collision frequency is much less than the angular gyrofrequency, and that this is true for both ions and electrons. As it turns out, measured data shows that *both* of these assumptions are wrong! Based on those incorrect assumptions, the equation leading to the drift velocity is simplified by neglecting higher order terms. But those terms cannot be neglected after all, and when they aren't, the correct exponent shows up with a value of 2.47 instead of 2. Working through the math without neglecting any terms is formidable, which is why I think the 'simplest theory' is what everyone went with at the time, back in the late '50's. What do you think, Michael?"

"Bravo, Emilio, bravo!! This is what good science is, my friend, peeling away the layers of onion skin until truth is revealed. And that's just what you did, figuratively, by looking at the higher order terms that were the next layer of onion skin. Nice work, M, very nice work! Now, how does this fir into your dissertation research, let's talk about that."

For the next two hours Professor Michael Hanlon and his graduate student Emilio Ravelli went over all of M's new data, more detail on M's derivation of the '2.47 exponent,' and how far along M was with his writing. Hanlon was both pleased and impressed. M had accomplished a lot since their last meeting, and his independent work on the drift velocity problem was very impressive, all the more reason for Hanlon to be happy with M's progress. M, in turn, was happy as well, because in spite of all the Node business he was able to keep his head above water on the thesis, and that was a promise he made both to himself and to Izzy. He would have to fill her in on these developments after the party when he and Brian would sit down with Iz to fill her in on everything, nothing left out - the Nodes, Kepler's ride, M's new Node discoveries, all of it.

- - - - - - - - - - - -

The next few days were a blur for M. He managed to complete some very important extensions on what he now had come to think of as 'Node Theory,' and he had to fill Brian in as soon as possible. M figured out how to actually use a Node for *time travel*! He also managed to finish writing the *Introduction* to his dissertation, organizing and reviewing all its references, and even writing up a short, independent section on his discovery about the drift velocity exponent. That write-up might dovetail with his thesis because it was the unusual drift velocity curves that led him to his discovery, but it also could stand alone as a short paper apart from the thesis. How he should handle this would be something to discuss with Professor Hanlon, but for the time being he was pleased to simply have it written down. By Wednesday M had called all the people on his party invitation list, talking to each one to be sure they understood the timing, location, parking issue, and so on.

Michael Hanlon and his wife definitely were attending as were several other grad students that M had grown close to through the years. Greg Mandrake was *not* one of them... M learned from Brian that Marty and Sandy Lobesky would be there, and he was quite happy about that in view of Marty's hard work on the Node Project even though he didn't know about the Node Project. Maybe some day... Brian also invited the Adams Street Gang and their wives and kids because their children thought of Isabella as 'Auntie Izz,' and Izzy tripped on that. Rounding out M's list were Izzy's friends and colleagues from her former employer, and also a few friends she met at school to whom M had been introduced. It was going to be a big crowd, and M could sense a *very good* time for all! Knowing this made M feel good, because it would make his fiancé, Isabella Healy, the love of his life,... it would make *her* feel good, and that's what he hoped to accomplish.

"Hi, Jeannie," M said as Jean picked up the phone. "Well, here it is, here we are, Thursday afternoon, and I'm just checking in to let you know I got everything done, everything! And I wanted to see how you and Leigh have made out?"

"Peachy, Emilio, just ducky! Everything on our end is set, too, catering, invitations, housekeeping - we hired a maid service, hope you don't mind - all of it. We just need the appointed hour and the birthday girl, and we're off to the races..." Jean's excitement was evident in her voice. "Leigh and I are sooo... looking forward to this. We know how much birthday's mean to Izz, and this will be her best ever, mark my words!"

"Great news, Jeannie. Brian and I will do all the decorations tomorrow night, and we worked out a subterfuge to get our guest of honor to the party on time, right around 1:30 Saturday. So everyone should be hiding, somewhere, by then so Izz won't see a crowd of people just as we walk in. Does that work?"

"Of course, M. That works fine, just the way we need it. Some of the kids I know are small, we'll hide them under the rug, sound good?" Jean couldn't resist joking, and of course M played right along. "Yeah, I can think of a couple, they're not called 'rug rats' for nothing..."

Jean and M chuckled and ended their conversation with both saying nearly simultaneously 'See you Saturday.'

"Hey, Brian," as M opened his apartment door. "Thanks for fitting this in, it's important, really important." It was about 7 o'clock Thursday evening, two days before Izzy's party, and M had some critical new developments on Node Theory that he really had to share with Brian before Saturday's big bash. M figured out how to time travel in a Node!

"Hello, Kepler, you little outer space surfing cat! And hello, M, glad I could fit this is - it's been *very* hectic!" as Brian bent over to pet Kepler and acknowledged M's greeting. "So what's the 'new development' in Node Theory, what's so important we have to meet like this - we should stop meeting like this," Brian joked.

"Oh, not that big a deal --- except that I figured out how control a Node's velocity!" M could see by Brian's reaction that this really *was* a big deal. Brian, stared, not saying a word, his mouth slightly open, obviously processing what M had just said, the finally reacting, "You *are* serious, aren't you?"

"Yes, and it's simple. I just had to keep going with the math, and soon enough there it was, the equations that control the Node's velocity - speed *and* direction. Brian, do you understand this?? Now we know how to make a Node go in a specific direction and at a specific speed - below, at, or above lightspeed!!"

"Let me sit for this, M. It is astonishing. Last time we were in the theoretical weeds you said you weren't sure about being able to manipulate a Node this way, and now you're telling me you can! Holy... I'll be polite in front of Kepler,... 'Holy cow!' You sure you're right? Any chance of a screw-up?... er... make that 'mistake'?"

"No, no chance," was M's emphatic reply. "I've had my head so deep into this stuff that I see the equations in my mind as I'm driving, or walking, or quietly sitting. It's become an obsession, Brian, and I know I'm right! I just had to keep going, and like so much of what we've discovered, the answer is very apparent when you cast the math in the right form and go far enough with it." M was on a roll, he was so proud of what he had done, and even more what it meant to what they could do with a Node, now hardly any limits!

Brian took a deep, very deep breath, as he sat staring at M, realizing from M's tone and visage that he was deadly serious and, knowing M, that he was exactly right. "So you're telling me you know how to make a Node go where you want at whatever speed you want, am I getting this?"

"That's what I said." M pushed back in his chair, saying "Oh, I was so excited to tell you, I forgot my manners. Sorry. How about a cup of tea? A beer maybe? Something stiffer? You know I went out and bought a bottle of *Glenwhatchamcallit* just to have it around for you. Want that?"

"*Glenfiddich*, and sure, make mine a double! This *IS* astonishing, Emilio. So you're telling me we *CAN* travel through space and time inside a Node and go where and when we want, right?"

"Yes, indeed, Brian, yes indeed," as M poured Brian's double, neat.

Brian accepted the small glass, went through his routine of nosing and inspecting its contents, looked over at M and said, "Thanks. You joining me?" M demurred.

"So the next question is, How? How to we control what the Node does? Have you figured that out, too?"

"Yes, I have, and it's straightforward, and it's just the kind of thing *you* do. You're gonna love this!" M's enthusiasm was palpable.

"I'm all ears, M. Shoot."

"We talked about the Gravity Engine that creates a gravity standing wave thus bending the Node's spacetime. It goes from flat to curved, and we can control the degree of curvature, that is, how much gravity here is inside the Node. We're together on that?"

"Yes, that's where we left off on this," was Brian's curt reply.

"Okay, imagine what happens when a Node detaches from its source. It's no longer controlled by the gravitating masses that created it in the first place. To bring this home, Brian, that means that our Node, Gert, is no longer under the influence of the Earth, Jupiter and the Sun whose gravitational field created Gert as some oddly shaped region in space of essentially no gravity. Right?"

Brian replied, "Sure, now Gert's unhooked and, what, floats around as she... make that 'it'... wishes?"

"Yes, the Node's motion being controlled by its external environment, the curved spacetime that we live in out here," M replied. "What's important is this: Once the Node detaches, what shape does it take? When we measured Gert it was a bent tubular shape. And any Node's *initial* shape depends on the fields that created it, but what happens when those field no longer control the shape? M could see Brian thinking about this and coming to the inevitable conclusion.

"I see it, M, I do... the Node must become *spherical*, right?" M's reply was excited and immediate, "Yes, yes, a sphere. It couldn't be anything else with nothing external working on it, so it's a sphere!" Brian was quite self-satisfied with this insight, and he happened to be right.

"Almost there, Brian. Close. Now think of that sphere that's an independent region of spacetime just sitting still in our Universe. It's detached, it's separate. Think of it as an oil drop in water. They don't mix, and the oil drop can move freely through the water if there's some force causing it to. If the drop is perfectly spherical in a homogeneous, isotropic water then it simply stays still. But if it's distorted, then it moves because the pressures over its surface aren't uniform. Keep this in mind - it's a metaphor for our Node..."

"Alright, I see that, M, isotropic, the water looks the same in all directions, and homogeneous, the water's properties are the same from place to place. Now what?"

"How can you get the oil drop to move? Simple, change its shape, and the pressure of the surrounding water isn't uniform any longer, so the drop moves. How fast? Well that depends on its shape, too. The longer and 'skinnier,' the faster it goes. And the direction? That, too, depends on the drop's shape. If it's 'bent' along the axis it doesn't move straight ahead, instead it move at an angle. Exactly the same principles apply to a Node, that's the metaphor. Change the Node's shape and the curved spacetime surrounding it creates forces that move it *where* you want and at a *speed* you want!

"Fascinating, M. But how can we change the Node's shape from *inside* the Node? How do we do *that*?"

"The Gravity Engine, make that plural - Engines - that's the key to moving the 'oil drop,' our Node, and to controlling its direction and speed. Remember how the Engine works. It produces a gravitational standing wave, right?" Brian nodded 'yes.' "That wave propagates in the direction established by the Engine. Here look at the equations," and M opened his notebook to a page containing the standing wave math that showed the wave bounding back and forth between two sides of the Node. "Right there, that term, Brian, it's the 'pressure' that the standing wave exerts on the Node's boundary, *from the inside*." "Okay, M, I see that, and...?" Brian asked.

"That pressure stretches the Node. It makes it longer in the direction of the wave. Cool, huh? So the Node's shape changes, it goes from perfectly spherical to a prolate spheroid, sort of a football shape. The change in shape, in turn, causes the Node to move through space in the direction of the standing wave! And how fast it moves, its speed, is determined by its axial ratio, longitudinal divided by lateral. When that number is around 10, the Node moves at lightspeed. *Above 10 and it goes faster than the speed of light!*"

"Again, Holy... cow!! And I do see the 'pressure' term here, and a few lines down the 'force' exerted by outside spacetime that causes the Node to accelerate. Ingenious, M, that you found this! But I'm still puzzled. There are two directions the sphere can move in. Is there any way to select which?" Brian did understand these concepts, and the math on which they were based, and he could see that M was correct in everything he said.

"Yes, you can be selective, and here's how: *two Gravity Engines* instead of only one. The second Engine has to be placed away from the first one that normally would be at the Node's center, and it has to create gravity waves that are orthogonal to the first Engine's. Those waves cause the Node to bulge perpendicular to its axis, and because it's not at the center, the bulge is asymmetrical. The Node will be shaped more or less like a pear, picture that."

M could see Brian processing this last assertion, and all of a sudden Brian said, "Yes, M, I do see that! One Engine stretches the Node symmetrically along its axis, while the other one causes it to stretch at right angles, and depending where it is along the axis, the Node's shape becomes tear-drop like or pear-shaped to whatever extent you want!"

"Bravo, Brian. That's right, and that's it! The Node will move in the direction of the larger bulge, and the more elongated it is the faster it will go. And... wait for it... and it can be made to travel at any speed."

"Last point, Brian - to change the Node's direction of travel all you need is a *third Gravity Engine* that further deforms the Node's shape by *bending* it along the main axis. When that happens,... see here,..." as M pointed to another set of equations in his notebook, "... the Node's direction changes to anything you want! *QED,...* Boy, I like that phrase, *QED!*"

But M wasn't quite done. "*So at lightspeed, being **inside** a Node is like riding **on** a photon, and traveling at the speed of light causes both **distance and time to cease to exist** for the Node. When we bring the Node sublight, space and time pop back into existence, and we can control where and when that happens. That's **time travel** through space. As I've said, Brian, we have to do this!!*"

"One last question, M. So we have to wait for the Node to become detached? What if that takes an extremely long time, or maybe never? Seems to me that unless you can control that process, the best you can do, maybe, is hop on, go for a ride, and hope you *eventually* get back to where you left from. To which I would say, so what? How is this useful? Seems to me it's not! And I'm sure as hell not going for that ride that may never return!! Like Charlie on the MTA... yeah, the Kingston Trio song!"

"Well, Brian, if that were true, then I would agree with you, but it's not true. We *can* control detachment. How? By adjusting the Node shape. As I said, once a Node detaches because of the natural process, it becomes perfectly spherical, no longer controlled by the gravitational fields that created it. This works both ways. *If* the Node is *made* to be perfectly spherical, then it becomes uncoupled from its sources. It's that simple, a two-way street."

"Okay, M, I got it! Bottom line: If we can control the Node's shape, then we can detach it so it becomes an independent entity in space! And, by controlling its shape, we can determine how fast it moves and in what direction!" M nodded 'yes,' with his usual Cheshire Cat grin.

"You know, Emilio, you really are very, very good at this. It's hard stuff. My hat's off!! And I see that everything you've shown is correct. And I've thought about his a lot, and I *know how* to actually build the Gravity Engine. So I'd say we're good to go, M, literally!" and with that remark Brian stood up, shook his head slowly with a big smile, and headed to the door. "I have to digest this, M. It's a lot, and I will, and we'll talk some more tomorrow night when we hook up at the Lake House to decorate it. See you then," and Brian left.

Chapter 16 - Isabella's Twenty-Ninth

The morning of Saturday, August 19th, 1972 dawned bright, and hot, and humid, a typical deep summer's day, a day for taking it easy, finding shade, maybe taking a dip... and a perfect day for a lakeside birthday bash! And, if the weather cooperated, which it did, Brian and Emilio had hatched a plan to take full advantage of the beautiful day as a subterfuge to get Izzy to her party, on time, without her suspecting a thing.

"Morning," Izzy answered the phone with a cheery tone in her voice, and a cup of steamy, black coffee in her hand. "Oh, Brian, hello..." as she looked at the time. "My goodness, 7:30, it's early, but you knew I'd be up, I always am... What's up, brother dearest? Everything's OK, everything alright?"

"Yep, all fine, my sister dearest. Got any plans for turning TWENTY-NINE!? That's getting up there, Izz, just think, a year from now the big three-oh, and then you'll stop the annual stuff and go for decades at a time." Brian snickered silently, thinking "If only she knew, but soon, a day or so, and she will..."

"So, did you call just to remind me that my turning into hag is around the corner? You know, my fiancé, dear boy, would stop, and think, and then say out loud, 'or is that *hagdom*?' or something weird like that..." Isabella Healy could dish it out as well as anyone could.

"You're not that far off yourself, two more months and it's *you* who hits the decade mark, *the big three-oh* as you put it! Don't forget that, *older* brother, my dear, that you're around the corner from being a curmudgeon, or is that *curmudgeondom*?" Brian silently snickered again, this time thinking "Hmmm... maybe M and I will change that, the 'older' business. We can, but she doesn't know it... yet!"

"Well, you've got a way to go, sis, but you always could pull a 'Jack Benny,' and be done with this getting older stuff..." Izz interrupted, "You mean, how he's always 39?" "Right, never a day older! Whenever he's asked, he's 39. Whenever he has a birthday, it's his 39th. Works for him, why not you? But you could best Jack by a decade and stop at 29!!"

"Alright, Brian, enough silliness. What's up? Besides wishing me HB, why call at 7:30?"

"Just wondering if you're free today?"

"Geez, stupid question if ever here was one. No, it's my twenty-ninth birthday, and. no, I'm not free. Let's see, let me grab my trusty calendar,... ah, yes, here it is,... I'm addressing the United Nations at 11, then I'm having a late lunch with the Prime Minister of England, then..." Knowing where this was going, Brian cut Izzy off mid sentence, "Okay, birthday girl, you're just chillin'. I assume you and the fiancé person have some plans, no?" "Yes, we do, M's taking me out to dinner at *Chez Gaston* again, to celebrate our three week anniversary and the auspicious occasion of my birth, how's that?"

"Nice, very nice. So let me add another wrinkle. Lunch on me?..." Izzy interrupts "Sounds nice already..." "A late-ish lunch, on the veranda, at the Lake House, with you, M, *moi*, and... Brenda. What d'ya think?"

"Wow! What do I think? Great idea! Thanks!" and Izzy couldn't wait to ask, "Who's Brenda?"

"My sort of girlfriend. She and I have gone out a few times now, and I *really* like her. She's smart, funny, very attractive, and, what could be better?... she knows everything there is to know about cheese and wine!"

"A joke, right? There's no 'Brenda,' who knows about cheese and wine. Now, if you said 'hot wings and beer,' well, then maybe I'd buy this fiction. But it's so preposterous - Cheese and wine? Refined taste? Brian, my *older* brother who didn't change his sneakers all through high school? That guy? - guess what, I don't buy it!" Izzy shot Brian down in flames as Brian was thinking "Perfect! She bought it, got her hook, line, and three sinkers!"

"Yes, Isabella, I'm in process of turning over a new leaf. Believe it,... and Brenda is for real. She works at the new Wine and Cheese shop on Dudley Street..." Izzy interrupted again.

"I've driven by it. But I can't imagine your crossing their threshold on your own!"

"Well, I did. Because one night a few weeks ago I needed some advice from M on how to decipher some math for a new project at Nova - Brian's shorthand for 'NovaTek' - and I went over to his place, but didn't want to show up empty-handed. So I happened to drive by the Wine and Cheese Shop and in a moment of weakness, knowing Emilio's snooty taste, I figured I'd break the mold and show up with wine and cheese, which I did. And I was starry eyed with the young lady who sold me the Camembert, went back a few days later, asked her out - she obviously said 'yes' - and we've been sort of a thing since. You'll like her, Izzy, I know you will, so I want you to meet her, and..." Brian just started to say "... *and you'll see her again at the party tonight*..." when his brain re-engaged and he said instead "... and I thought a nice, quiet lunch on the veranda at the Lake House would be a good way for you two to get acquainted. What d'ya think?"

"I would love to meet Brenda, Brian. And what a nice way to do it."

"Thanks, Izzy, so I figure the four of us can hang for the afternoon, just talking, flopping on the beach or going for a boat ride, whatever strikes us. It's going to turn out to be a beautiful day, and it'll be a nice way to celebrate your birthday. And then, later on, you and M head off to *Gaston's*."

"This is really thoughtful of you, Brian. Thanks so much. I'll call M and let him know. He can pick me up, and what time did you say, around 1:30? Oh, one more thing, how about you bring your twelve-string? I can't remember the last time we sat on the porch with you playing and the rest of us just listening or singing along, such a good time, and it seems so long ago."

"Happy to bring the twelve-string, Izz, and yes it was quite a while ago, and yes again, 1:30 give or take, but be about on time because Brenda and I will pick up lunch, maybe Chinese?" Izz replied, "If that's a question, Brian, you know the answer. Chinese food is one of my most favorites!" As Izz trailed off, Brian was thinking, "'A long time ago,' she said... maybe *no* time ago... this is *really* hard to comprehend..."

"Okay, Izz, great. See you *there, then*. Love 'ya, and... HAPPY BIRTDAY," as Brian hung up, his mind buzzing more with what he and M had discussed over the weekend and how a simple twist of phrase like 'there, then' could mean so much more in the context of Nodes, space and time, time and space, *nothing like they were before*!

- - - - - - - - - - - -

"Emilio, just so you'll know before Izz calls, it's all arranged. Play dumb. Around 1:30 be there."

"Got it Brian, nice job! Oh, must be Izz now. Another call, so I'm ringing off. Thanks! Bye," and M hung up from Brian and took Izzy's incoming call. They talked for some time, not just about her birthday, but also about Brian and Brenda. Isabella filled M in on the lunch plan and how Brenda would be joining them. She wondered if M had met her, but he hadn't, and she was *very* curious about the wine and cheese episode. "You didn't say a word about it? How come?"

"I was going to, Izz, but, actually, Brian asked me not to. The night he showed up,... let me think, ah, yes,... Gouda, Camembert and Manchego along with some really excellent imported crackers and olives and..." Izz stepped in, "I get it, M, very nice cheeses and crackers, and I bet you were surprised."

"Surprised? I nearly fell over, but then Brian explained. And he told me he was going back and asking Brenda out and hoped she'd agree, which he did and she did. And then he asked me to keep a lid on it, so that if it continued he would be the one to break it to you. I was honor bound, Isabella. Couldn't say anything, and, frankly, I think this is a much better way of breaking that ice. You get to meet Brenda - from what Brian says we'll both like her a lot - and she you, and me, and we all can chill for the afternoon, and then you and I head back to *Gaston*'s where I already have reservations, 7:30." M lied about that, but not anything else.

"Wonderful, M. You are such a thoughtful gentleman. That's one of the reasons I love you!"

"Oh, one more thing while we're gabbing, I discovered something an a decades old ionospheric physics problem and went through it with Michael. I'll tell you more later, but he thinks it's Nobel prize level stuff!"

"What? *The* Nobel Prize in physics? Can you possibly be serious? That significant? At your age? This is turning out to be my best day ever, Emilio, best ever!!" Izz caught herself,

"Wow, if I don't shut up I'll be yakking all morning. Okay, I'm going back to my coffee to sit and just smile. Congratulations, Doctor Nobel Prize, or not! Pick me up around one, okay? Love you," and Izzy hung up, and M smiled, thinking "This could not have worked out better! She will be thrilled!"

- - - - - - - - - - -

Brian and M spent most of the night before decorating the Lake House. The first thing you saw as you walked in off the veranda was the impossible-to-not-notice 'Happy Birthday' in large, make that *very* large, letters hanging in an arc from the cathedral ceiling, about ten feet up. The letters were multicolored, with a silver border and embossed with smaller 'Happy Birthday's all over. Each letter was about three feet tall, and M and Brian hung them about a foot apart on a wire purloined from the Shop and anchored at each end to form a twenty foot long catenary arc. In the free space at each end, and in-between the letters, and from the bottom of each letter were hung curled ribbon streamers that further enhanced the party atmosphere. When they were done the huge greeting read 'H A P P Y 2 9 th B I R T H D A Y, I Z Z Y.' This little project took M and Brian well over an hour, and when it was done they sat quietly, smiling and satisfied at what they had accomplished, not to mention Brian's having opened a beer while M sipped on an especially nice Chianti.

"Okay," Brian said to M, "nice job I'd say. What next?"

"Well, we have all these wall-hanging and table birthday doodads. Let's do the walls first and see what's left," whereupon the two men plastered the walls in the family room and kitchen with dozens of 'Happy Birthday' signs, once again to create a partying atmosphere, which they did, admirably. In the family room they set up three twelve-foot long two-and-a-half-foot wide folding tables with heavy, white linen table cloths for the buffet. At each end of each table they set napkins, disposable plates and utensils, and plastic glasses of different sizes for different kinds of drink, soda, juice, beer or wine. They placed coolers beneath the tables to be filled with ice in the morning, and the birthday doodads were taped to the sides of the table cloths. And some were taped to the upright piano figuring that someone knew how and would want to finger a tune or two. Both the upstairs and downstairs fridges were full of soft drinks and juices, along with nibbly things like cheese and cold cuts, just in case. It was a *very* festive environment, and when they were done, Brian and M looked at each other, smiling, and high-fiving the great job they did.

"Miss anything?" Brian asked. "Geez, I don't think so, Brian," M replied. "If we did we'll have to catch it tomorrow. You can check again after you collect Brenda. Women are good at seeing things the likes of us miss..."

"Sounds about right, M. So you're off. I'm staying here tonight, and I'll pick up Brenda around ten so we'll be back in plenty of time for the caterers, they said eleven, and for the first guests, which I'm thinking will arrive around twelve thirty or so. Oooh, I almost forgot, Jean called, and she and Leigh are getting here early, too, around eleven to help with the catering. Now don't be too early with Izzy, say, twenty past one at the earliest, maybe even a few minutes later. I want everyone to be able to hide, drink in hand for a Happy Birthday shout-out and toast as the Izz makes her appearance. Of course, 'hiding' around sixty people won't be easy, even in a place as big as this..." was Brian's closing remark, to which M shook his head in agreement as he walked out the door waving goodbye.

- - - - - - - - - - - -

"Aw, damn it," M thought as he slid into the Camaro's driver's seat noticing the envelope above the visor, "crap, forgot to drop this off for Michael." He looked at the time, "Hmmm... 10:30, I can run this in and leave it in his mailbox, and I'll still be home in time to take care of Kep."

M pulled into the Quad and parked close to the physics building. Ana Esperanza rolled around the corner, out of breath, sweaty, and stopping, hunched over with her hands on her knees, just as M entered the building with his key. Ana looked up, surprised, "Oh, Emilio, you startled me!" her speech labored.

"I'm so sorry, Ana. I didn't know you were here, and I'm sorry I walked in on you. Please, forgive me." M was mortified, even though he hadn't done anything, just causing Ana to feel that way was enough.

Ana stood erect, took some deep breaths, and replied "Emilio, please, don't give this a second thought. I was surprised because the building usually is pretty empty at this time of night, and any students who are here are usually on two," referring to the second floor where most of the labs were located as well as many faculty offices.

"That's where I'm headed to take a quick shower." The second floor also held a complete bath with shower for treating chemical exposures. Many of the grad students who exercised in the gym preferred using the second floor facilities because they were more private, and Ana was one of them.

"Me, too, off to two. I have to drop this in Professor Hanlon's mailbox," as he waved the envelope, " then I'm out of here. It's been a night, and I'm tired. By the way, you do remember Izzy's party tomorrow, 1pm?"

"Yes, and I wouldn't miss it! The envelope, you know, if you want I can put it in Hanlon's box. I'm walking right by it."

"Would you mind? Saves me the trip, and I would appreciate it, just like when you dropped off the printout in my office."

"No, of course, not at all... Anything good?" Ana curiosity couldn't be contained.

"Actually, yes, quite good. I don't know how far along you are in ionospheric theory, but there's a problem that has baffled researchers for decades. and I think I solved it!"

"Wow! That is impressive, Emilio, really impressive! Thumbnail sketch?" Ana's curiosity again.

"Okay, very quickly. No one has been able to theoretically figure out the drift velocities for particles in the F-region. The theories that have been proposed simply don't work, and I found the error that fixes that. It meant re-working all the math, which is pretty thick, and going back to the Navier-Stokes fluid dynamics equations. I told Professor Hanlon about his, and he's really impressed, and I told him I would get him the re-worked math, so I cleaned up my scribbles and the whole story is in this envelope. That's it in a nutshell. Make sense?

"Of course it does, especially coming from you, Emilio. And I'm not at all surprised you figured this out. Congratulations,... congrats! This will be in Hanlon's box within five minutes," and Ana took the envelope from M, looked at it carefully, and smiled as she held it up to signal goodbye and headed for the stairway. Ana didn't use the elevator if she could avoid it...

Thank you, Ana, now I owe you two," was M's departing remark as he turned and left the building.

On her way by, Ana dropped M's envelope in Professor Michael Hanlon's mail box, just as she said she would. She continued down the hall to the women's shower room and took a long, hot shower that made her feel so much better, not that her day was done. Ana had work to do in one of the labs down the hall, and it simply was better late at night when it was quiet and she could work alone, without interruption.

As she began to leave the shower room, Ana's view caught Greg Mandrake standing at the faculty mailboxes at the end of the hall, not that she initially made anything of it because she figured he was dropping off some work for his advisor, Professor Ronald

Gerstein. Mandrake's back was to Ana, so he didn't see her, and she made no noise coming out of the shower room. Then she stopped dead in her tracks. She saw Mandrake open the unsealed envelope she just had deposited in Professor Hanlon's, remove the several pages that were in it, and slowly read through the entire pile. This took the better part of ten minutes, and all the while Ana stood motionless and silent watching Greg Mandrake rifle through what was clearly a private communication from Emilio Ravelli to his thesis advisor Professor Michael Hanlon. She then saw Mandrake pull a notebook from his briefcase on the floor and write for the next several minutes while holding M's papers *and* the notebook in his left hand. Ana was astonished! What had she just witnessed? From her conversation with M, and the common knowledge in the department that M disliked Mandrake, intensely, Ana could only conclude that Mandrake was up to no good, that he was stealing M's work!

- - - - - - - - - - -

M couldn't sleep. He tossed and turned, and turned and tossed, but no position was comfortable, and none allowed him to close his eyes and drift off. Every time he looked at the clock, now 2 am, he grew wider awake. Flipping on the television didn't help, playing soft piano music like Pachelbel on the stereo, that didn't help either. There was too, too much in M's head for him to fall asleep, even though he knew how bad it would be for him if he didn't. Besides Izzy's party "in only a few hours," he thought looking at the time, M was consumed with some new ideas about Nodes, specifically ways of controlling their travel without relying on the gravitational fields that created them, and these thoughts burrowed so deeply into his mind that he couldn't let go, try as he might. What to do? What? It was driving M crazy, until he finally gave in.

He brewed a cup of extra strong green tea sweetened with a little honey, grabbed Misner, Thorne and Wheeler and his Node notebook, sat at the kitchen table, and went to work. It was 3 am, and M figured he could work for a couple of hours, then maybe fall asleep for a couple, pick up Izzy as scheduled and salvage what would be left of the day.

Emilio finally did fall asleep, from sheer exhaustion, at around six in the morning, and he slept soundly until nearly 10 am. "Holy...," he thought as he woke and leaned over to pick up the alarm clock while Kepler greeted him with soft purrs and stretching his front legs to massage M's chest as if to soften it for a bed. "Morning, Kep," was M's response. "They say you can't beat a dog's life, but I think a cat's is pretty good, too," as he rubbed Kepler's ears and scratched his chin which elicited even more purring, just like a motor boat. "Ah, yes, Kepler, from now on I shall address you as 'Astrocat,' even though your Uncle Brian doesn't like it..."

"Wow, I actually have plenty of time," M said to Kep, "I don't have to get Izzy until one o'clock, which gives me plenty of time to take you for your morning constitutional, brew a pot of coffee, shave and shower, straighten this place out a little, and get dressed up enough to be presentable at your Mom-to-be's 29th Birthday Party!" So M put the coffee pot in gear and leashed his feline friend for their walk. The coffee would be ready when they got back, and Kep would receive his breakfast and some loving attention from Dad.

- - - - - - - -

To Brian's considerable surprise, and to M's when he got there, the party guests' cars vanished into the surrounding woods, nary a one to be seen. The Lake House was situated on a winding, twisty country road running by Lake Arrowhead, and there were many small, sometimes very hard to see, side streets, not all of which were streets, instead driveways that looked like streets. However they managed it, M guessed a fair degree of carpooling, there weren't enough visible cars to telegraph 'There's a Big Bash at the Healys' Place, Come One, Come All'... Plus, in order to keep Izzy from looking too hard, M went out of his way to engage her in conversation, the kind that would require her looking at him a lot.

So he started by bringing up again the 'Nobel Prize' business he discussed with Professor Hanlon and told her about yesterday. To keep Izzy engaged, M asked her what *she* thought of the whole prospect. Of course, she couldn't comment on the science, they both knew that, but he could ask her about how she felt about maybe visiting Stockholm? And if they did, should they take an extended vacation touring Europe? And if they did, where in Europe should they go? And if they did, would she want to visit her remaining relatives in Ireland? And how about his in Italy? And, if ever he won the Nobel Prize, what would she want to do with the money award? And why would she want to do that with the money award? And so on, the conversation actually could go on that way for hours, and it required Izzy's attention and thought. She couldn't talk to M about this and keep an eye peeled on the road, or the side streets, or the driveways all at the same time. M's Izzy distraction worked beautifully. She apparently didn't notice a thing out of place on their way to the Lake House, but if she did, she played the hand marvelously because M didn't have a clue. So who duped whom? M thought about that, a little, but in the end he decided it didn't matter either way, as he slowly pulled into the gravel covered driveway at 1212 Lakeside Drive on Lake Arrowhead.

"What a gorgeous day, Iz! You know, every time I'm here how I feel changes. It's almost instantaneous, and it's wonderful. I was pretty uptight this morning, but just pulling in the driveway here takes a load off, and, to boot, I'm with *you*..." M's look said it all, how much he really loved Isabella Healy, his future wife.

"Gee, M. Why?" Izzy said. "Why what?" M asked in return. "Why were you uptight this morning? Lunch with Brian, Brenda, this should be really nice, so why uptight?"

"A lot on my mind, Iz, a lot, thesis stuff, the new discovery I made about ionospheric drift velocities, what to do with that? It just goes round and round, Isabella, and sometimes it's a bit much. But, please, forget that because at the moment I'm feeling great, and I agree this will be a very nice afternoon." This conversation took place as Izz and M walked slowly up the walk to the veranda, not a soul in sight, not a sound to be heard except the birds, which, of course, immediately caused M to wonder 'How *do* they know a Node is coming?' This though being his last as he opened the front door to the foyer and the house almost shook with yells of 'HAPPY BIRTHDAY, IZZY!!' 'HAPPY BIRTHDAY!'

The chant continued for most of the next minute, and Isabella Healy's complexion turned a very slight, but noticeable, shade of bittersweet red, as tears welled up, and she looked at M standing next to her on one side, and then at Brian who had walked over to the other, and she put her arms around M just as she planted a ten second kiss on his cheek and did the same to Brian. "My goodness," Izzy said in a loud voice, "You're all here!" she said scanning the dozens of attendees. "I am sooo... surprised! I can't tell you how surprised I am!! Thank you all, thank you so much! I'm so happy to see you all! And however you managed it, I'm really caught off guard... I think I'm going to cry!" as Izzy placed both hands on her face covering he eyes, sobbing audibly.

"Izz, Izzy, please don't sob, please." It was Jean Simmons speaking, with Leigh Bennet right next to her, the two people who were most responsible for making this party work. They gave Izzy a big, collective bear hug, kissing her on her cheeks, urging her to calm down and come over and sit, which Isabella did because she was so emotional that sitting instantly made her feel better. "You, you..." looking at Jean and Leigh, "I should have known you would do something like this! Thank you, so much!" "And, you two," looking at M and Brian, "You were behind this!... And I love you both for it!!" Birthdays always were something special for Izzy, and this one was the best ever. Being so surprised, and it was a real surprise, by so many people made her feel special, appreciated,... loved, all of which, of course, were absolutely true.

- - - - - - - - - - -

The uproar surrounding Izzy's arrival and total surprise lasted about five minutes, nonstop. As it died down a bit, M stood next to Izzy who was seated in a chair at the edge of the family room, raised his glass high - it contained iced tea - and shouted, rather loudly, "Please, please, let me have your attention, please," and the crowd complied, lowering the noise level to almost a whisper. "First of all, I want to thank you all for being here today. Your company, your thoughtfulness are what make his such a special occasion, Isabella Healy's twenty-ninth birthday, my fiancé Isabella Healy's twenty-ninth birthday. Second, I think you all know, but in case not, I proposed to Izzy about three weeks ago, and she accepted! And I'm on cloud nine because she did! And I haven't set foot on the ground since! What a great feeling!! Third, I want to give my heartfelt thanks to Izzy's best friends Jeannie Simmons and Leigh Bennet standing right over there. This party certainly has gotten off to a great start, and everything here, everything you see is the tireless work of Jeannie and Leigh. They chipped in in more ways than I can describe. They really are the best of friends. Please, raise your glass, a toast to my beloved Isabella on her birthday, to Jean and Leigh for all they have done, and lest I forget, to Brian for being here every step of the way and showing me how to hand things straight! HAPPY BIRTHDAY, IZZY! Cheers all!" whereupon Emilio took a long draft of his iced tea, and leaned over to kiss Izzy who was holding a glass of Asti Spumante. The party indeed was off to a great start, and both M and Brian were delighted.

- - - - - - - - - - - -

Once the commotion of Izzy's entrance died down the party guests began to circulate and mingle. And before she got lost in the crowd, as Brian knew she would, he wanted Izzy to meet Brenda. After all, without even knowing it, Brenda was one third of the ruse that would bring Izzy unsuspectingly to the party. "Isabella, I'd like to introduce Brenda Wingate. Brenda works at the new Wine and Cheese shop downtown, and that's how we got to meet," as he turned to Brenda placing his arm around her shoulder and extending his hand towards Izzy. "Brenda, Izzy... Izzy, Brenda. I'm sure you two might have a lot to talk about," Brian looking at Brenda winking, "especially tall tales about me... I'm not sure I should leave you two alone..." Brian said jokingly, knowing full well that Izzy and Brenda would get along famously.

As the party guests settled in, everyone was checking out the buffet, which was truly impressive, Chinese from *Fortune Cookie*, Italian from *Stella*'s and Pastries from *D'Argento*'s. The food was neatly laid out on the three long tables Brian and M had set up last night, and each one was chock full. Linda Lee from *The Cookie* along with Jean and Leigh concocted a fabulous menu of dim sum and some entree dishes, all served buffet style. The dim sum included a range of meat and seafood stuffed dumplings ranging from mild, mostly, to spicy, a few, to very spicy, a couple, but for each plenty to go 'round. Various dipping sauces were available, as well as chopsticks for the more adventurous types. Soups included traditional Chinese hot and sour, wonton soup, and egg flower soup. The entrees included Gung Bo Gai Din, Moo Shu Pork, Sizzling Seafood Worbar, Gai Poo Lo Mein, and Spicy Hunan Fish. Many of the dishes were prepared by *Fortune Cookie*'s chef owner Linda Lee, who also was a party guest. Two of Linda's staff manned the buffet replenishing dishes as they were consumed.

Stella's provided Italian fare in the form of thin-crust pizza with a variety of toppings and three ten-foot long grinders that were sliced into six inch segments for individual consumption. One ten-footer was the traditional Italian club sandwich comprising hot capicola ham, sliced pepperoni, Genoa salami, provolone cheese, leaf iceberg lettuce, and sliced tomatoes, dressed with extra virgin olive oil and vinegar and ground black pepper. The second ten-footer was a traditional American sub comprising ham, turkey, Swiss cheese, onion, tomato, and green bell pepper with mayo, mustard dressing and ground black pepper dressing. And the third ten-footer was half meatball sub, and half sausage sub, both with red sauce, fried green peppers, caramelized onion, mozzarella and provolone cheeses, red chili pepper and ground black pepper with a small amount of salt.

D'Argento's provided Izzy's birthday cake, a three layer cake, Devil's food, reading *Happy Birthday, Isabella's 29th* around the top of the first layer. The cake was enormous, fully three feet across because it had to feed approximately sixty people, to be served with vanilla ice cream for anyone desiring *a la mode*. Besides the cake, *D'Argento's* bakery provided an assortment of Italian pastries for desert, and two twenty-cup coffee makers as well as two espresso makers for anyone wanting a stronger brew.

Jean and Leigh pigeonholed M and Brian, asking "Well, what do you two think of the buffet?" Brian answered first, "Words aren't enough for this! It's like a wedding feast, and yet it's a birthday party! Boy, to say you girls have gone above and beyond is the understatement of the century. You must have spent hours and hours arranging all this, and anyone who didn't come here hungry has to be kicking himself right around now, speaking of which, I'm off to the Chinese restaurant. Bye..." and Brian turned and left heading straight for Linda Lee's fabulous spread. M was a little more low key. "Jean, Leigh, I cannot thank you enough for your help with this. Just look around, everyone is having a great time, the buffet is a gigantic hit, and look over there, Izzy hasn't stopped flitting about talking to everyone since she stood up! You both knew how important birthdays always have been for Izzy - and you made this one her best ever, really! Thanks to you!" and M kissed each of Izzy's friends on the cheek as he turned saying "Well, I'm off to mingle, and..." jokingly, "...

to see if I can find my fiancé." Of course, Izz was only fifteen feet away...

"Michael," M greeted Professor Hanlon, "so good to see you. Izzy and I are so glad you could come, " as Izzy approached overhearing M. "Yes. Doctor Hanlon, thank you for coming. I can't tell you how much all this means to me, and, believe me, how much of a surprise it is!" Hanlon replied, "My pleasure, indeed, to be here Isabella. Happy Birthday, congratulations on your twenty-ninth! Let me introduce my wife, Dorothy," as Hanlon put his arm around Dorothy and she extended her hand to shake Izzy's. "Congratulations, my dear, Happy Birthday! I've met M before, and now it's such a pleasure to meet you. You're a wonderful couple, Isabella, and congratulations, too, on you engagement. Have you made wedding plans?"

Izzy was more than impressed with Dorothy's warmth and sincerity. She developed a liking immediately, "Thank you so much, Dorothy. I'll fill you in on what Emilio and I have talked about, if you're interested..." Dorothy interrupted, " Of course, I am, dear," and Izzy continued, " Let's step over here," motioning to an unoccupied corner, "where we can talk more quietly. We'll let your husband and M talk shop while we talk about interesting things." Isabella already had developed a subliminal bond with Dorothy, probably because Dorothy brought to mind her mother, even though Dorothy was considerably younger. They would have talked away the afternoon, but Izzy was needed elsewhere. "Oh, there you are, Isabella. Been looking all over, and here you are in the corner," as she was approached by Catherine Talbot, her former boss at Bull Financial. "Congratulations, Izzy, happy twenty-ninth! Got a few minutes? I'd like to talk." Izzy excused herself from Dorothy and followed Catherine out to the veranda, sending that their discussion would be about more than just the party and her plans with M."

Indeed, as Izzy surmised, Emilio and Doctor Hanlon were 'talking shop,' and M was just about to unplug because he knew he was obligated to say hello to everyone who took the time to come to Izzy's party. He was about to politely excuse himself when Ana approached. "Hello, Emilio, Doctor Hanlon, so good to see you." M replied, "Yes, Ana, so glad you could make it. Good to see you, too. You know Michael, my thesis adviser, no?" "Yes, she does," Hanlon answered. "Ana did very well in my *Intro to Ionospheric Physics* course, but, as I recall, you're a double-E major, right? Master's degree? Too bad we couldn't snag you in the Physics Department..." "Yes, Professor Hanlon, that's right. And now that the course is over, I can say it was really good, interesting, without coming across as buttering up the prof!" Ana had a good sense of humor, and she was quite down to earth, probably because she grew up in Brazil where the culture was quite different. She continued, "This may not be the right time, but it may be the only time. There's something I have to tell you both, so being here together is a big help. Got a couple of minutes?" Hanlon and M simultaneously nodded 'yes,' both exceedingly curious about Ana's mysterious remark. Ana then explained exactly what had happened just the night before at Hanlon's mailbox on the second floor. She didn't confront Mandrake, so she was unable to relate anything more than what she saw, and there the conversation ended with Professor Hanlon and M both shaking their heads and Hanlon commenting "I'll be looking into this, Emilio, count on it..."

M needed a lighter interaction, so he specifically hunted down Alicia Dougherty, another of Izzy's long-standing friends, but not nearly as close as Jean and Leigh. He had a plan in mind. "Ah, Alicia, found you! Glad you could come, Izzy's tickled. You and she talked, right? I saw you huddled near the fireplace." "Yes, M, and I'm sooo... glad I came. Haven't seen Izz for some time, and it was great to catch up. Congrats, by the way, on your engagement. She's on cloud nine. She's a lucky girl, too bad you're out of play..." Alicia winked and pecked M on the cheek. "Seriously, what's new with you?" M brought Alicia up to speed about his dissertation and expected graduation next May, and, of course, she was duly impressed. But M didn't sideline Alicia to talk about school. He wanted her to play the piano! Alicia graduated from Julliard, taught piano, and moonlighted as a studio musician for one of the city's major recording studios, in other words, Alicia was the best. So M wanted to get her over to the upright and convince her to regale the crowd, which wasn't hard to do because Alicia was a natural born performer. "So glad you asked, M. I was thinking of tickling the ivories myself, but I didn't want to just jump in and start playing. If you'll keep me company, I'm happy to, starting with something slow(ish)." M was delighted.

"Wait a few minutes, Alicia. I think I can get you some accompaniment," M said as he scanned the family room, then the kitchen, and finally the veranda where he found Brian sitting on an Adirondack chair next to Brenda, beer in hand, she sipping a Margarita. "Brian, my boy, grab your twelve string and follow me," M commanded. Brian was none too anxious, but, after all, it was Izzy's birthday, and he did bring the guitar, and he did expect to be drafted at some point, and the time had come,... so he complied. "Where we off to, boss? Brenda, please come along, you might enjoy this..." "Just follow me, we're not going far," M said as he ushered Brian and Brenda over to the upright. Brian immediately remarked, "Hey, Alicia. Good to see you, been a long time. I see you've been drafted, too, so I guess it's a piano-guitar duet?" "Yep," M answered, "just what I had in mind, two very good musicians, a great venue - what could be better than Izzy's bash - and it's time to get the show on the road! Anything you want... you decide what to play." Brian and Alicia looked at each other, both instinctively thinking 'start with something slow,' when Brian piped up "Alicia, do you know *Stairway to Heaven*, Zeppelin?" "Of course, Brian, anyone who plays much knows that tune, it's so beautiful, and fairly new, too, very popular." Brian couldn't avoid the metaphor, thinking, as did M as well, *if only they knew, if only we could tell them*!! "Let's do it," as Brian gently plucked the twelve string while Alicia did the same on the ivories. The melody was haunting, and especially significant for M, and for Brian. So he and Alicia started out slow, and as the party progressed so did their tempo. That's how the guitar/piano and the stereo hi-fi music went all through the day, well into late evening, crescendoing and finally culminating with the Stones' '69 apocalyptic *Gimme Shelter*. That song again caused M and Brian to reflect, '*if only they knew, if only we could tell them*!!'

Chapter 17 - The Maiden Voyage

"My goodness," Izzy said, rubbing her eyes and peeking at M as she did, "is it really this late, nearly 11:30?" Her statement as much declaration as a question. "Wow! I'm just waking up?" as she sat erect, sliding a pillow behind her back, Emilio nodding and smiling, "Yes, Izz, you're *just* waking up. Here," as he handed her a cup of coffee, steamy hot, black, no sugar, "be careful - it's hot." Isabella took the cup, wrapping it with both hands and being careful not to spill it. "I let you sleep because it was a late night, you were tuckered out, and..." Izzy interrupted, "and?..." "And, you had... , how shall I put it,... after everyone left, you were trying to drink Brian under the table! He started it, one toast after another to his favorite sister on the occasion of her twenty-ninth birthday. But I don't think that was all... Anyway, you tried to keep pace, and after several shots you were smart enough to call it a night. Don't you remember?"

Izzy was more tired than hung over. In fact, she wasn't hung over at all, just tired, and she remembered every minute of her drinking contest with Brian, which he handily won, and, in fact, she didn't have 'several shots' as M said, only a couple, maybe three. "Yes, I remember, M. And I was just plain exhausted from all the hoopla of the party, which was wonderful, fabulous, M, the greatest birthday I've ever had, really! Thank you!"

"Well, Isabella, it's not every birthday that you turn twenty-nine, now is it?" M could see Izzy's reacting to his careful turn of phrase, and sure enough she immediately picked up on it.

"That's a strange way to put it? Is that supposed to mean you only turn twenty-nine once?" Izzy asked, genuinely perplexed by what she thought she caught was *double entendre*. And , another thing,... a couple of minutes ago you said ' I don't think that was all.' What does that mean?"

"Nothing, nothing, Izzy, it doesn't mean anything." M made a mistake by implying there was something more, something he was leaving out, which, of course, there was, but he shouldn't have tried to tell her something without actually saying it. Izzy was tired, just barely awake, and he should have known better.

"Tell you what, Izz. It's too late for breakfast, but a nice lunch on the veranda sounds good to me? How do you feel about that?"

"Now you're making more sense, M. Let me shower and get dressed, and we can have a leisurely lunch on the porch," as Izz pulled aside the curtain to check he weather. "Another beautiful day, M, looks just like yesterday, and after how hectic yesterday was - thank you again - it will be good to just relax and enjoy today. I take it Brian's here somewhere, and Brenda, too?"

"Brian, yes. Brenda, no. She had to get to work this morning even though it's Sunday. Apparently weekends are their busiest days, and of the two Sunday actually is busier than Saturday, especially in the morning - go figure..."

"That's too bad, I really like Brenda, at least from the short time we spent together. I'd like to get to know her better, especially if she keeps dating Brian... poor girl!" Izzy joked and laughed at what she thought was a good one.

"See you downstairs, Izzy, take your time." M wanted to tell her that it was a good thing Brenda had left because he and Brian had to talk to her alone, so they could tell her about the Nodes, and that what they were going to tell her about them would be completely unbelievable, but true. But he couldn't. It would have to wait until she, and he, and Brian could sit together quietly, without any distractions.

"I feel 100 percent better," Izzy said as she walked down the stairs into the family room. Brian and M were sitting on the sofa each holding a coffee obviously having a muted discussion about something, but Izzy overheard nothing that gave it away. "So what are you boys up to? Looks like something really important by the way you went radio silent as soon as I walked in. Something I should know about? Some business thing?" Then Izzy, in her own mercurial manner, got an urge to stir things up. "Maybe something about cars, like Camaros, and how they couldn't beat a bicycle?" Izzy's ploy worked, sort of. It demanded an answer, then, not later, and it immediately scuttled the boys' plan to bring up Nodes after lunch. "What the hell, Emilio. Let's do this now, let's tell her," was Brian's answer. "Yes, Izzy," M jumped in, "Brian's right - we have something to tell you that you won't believe, but we swear it's true, every fantastical word!"

- - - - - - - - - - - -

"Oh, my God! It's something bad, isn't it? Is one of you sick? M, something wrong at school? *What is it?*" Isabella tone was demanding, indignant,... concerned. M assuaged her anxiety, "No, no... Don't go there, Izz. Everything's fine, really. What this is about is something Brian and I have discovered that, well, what can I say... something that will blow your mind. It's about space and time, and space travel, and..." M hesitated, "... and time travel!"

"This is a joke, right? A birthday joke?"

Brian chimed in, "No, Izz, not a joke. There's nothing funny about this. The fact is, it's pretty scary, that M and I, together, discovered this quite by accident." Brian's face was stern, almost menacing to the point that Izz became frightened.

"Brian, you're frightening me!" and she turned to M, "Is any of this true, Emilio. Tell me now!"

"Yes, Izzy, it is true. I'll repeat that - IT IS TRUE! After you calm down, Brian and I will fill you in on all the details, exactly what happened, exactly what we know." M was hoping his emphatic response would put Izzy at ease, and it did because she trusted M not to alarm, or worse yet, terrify her, especially the day after throwing such a fabulous birthday party. She didn't think M would, or could, do that. No, Izzy, *knew* that M couldn't do that.

"Let me sit and collect myself, " Izzy said as she slid into the recliner and pushed it back kicking off her shoes as she did. She sat semi-upright, quietly assessing her brother's and her fiancé's reactions, thinking to herself, "They wouldn't do this to me. It's cruel... I have to hear them out, and be calm while I'm doing it..." whereupon she said to Brian and M who sat together across from her on the sofa with a coffee table in between, "OK, let's have it. I promise I will listen, and if I have any questions, I expect on-the-spot straight-up answers, in terms I can understand. Agreed?"

M replied, "Yes, Isabella. This is the most important thing that has ever happened in our lives, and we want you to understand it, it's that important!"

"Brian, why don't you start," M said, "because this all started with you." Brian nodded.

"Izzy, remember that day at the Shop when I showed you *The Birds*, the springs they were on, all that?"

"Yes, of course. I still have the bird you gave me. It's quite nice, and every so often I pull its spring to give it a ride. What about that?"

Brian, with M's help, explained how a Node caused the birds to spontaneously 'fly' and to disrupt a satellite's orbit. They explained how Nodes are formed and what the theories of Gravitation and Relativity tell us about them, without all the math, of course.

"So you're telling me that these gravitational Nodes are all over the Universe, and you happened to come across one just by accident and were able to figure out how it worked?"

"Yes, Izzy," M explained, "That's exactly right, and we have three experiments to prove it along with photographic evidence."

Brian then described the first experiment at the Shop when they measured Gert's properties and the second experiment at the Lake, right here at the Lake House, where they launched and retrieved the sphere. He showed Izzy all the photos and explained them to her. The more she saw, the more she realized that this was no joke, that everything Brian and M was telling her was actually true. Izzy came to believe that the Nodes are real, that M and Brian figured out how they work, and there was a lot more to this story. But at this point she needs a break. They had been discussing the Nodes for more than an hour, and it was time to grab a bite and relax a bit to digest both their meals and these ideas. "Okay," M said, "let's break for something to eat, and then I'll fill you in, Izzy, on experiment number three. You *will be impressed*, I promise you that! There's a ton of food left from the party, in the fridge up here and in the one downstairs. I think some nonperishable stuff was parked in the oven, too. Izz, what can I get you?" and Isabella gave M a list of things she'd like, asking him to make up the selections because at the moment she just wanted to sit and think. Brian, on the other hand, already had his plate overflowing with Chinese Dim Sum and half a meatball sub, as he declared "I'm famished, just getting started... Talking about Nodes takes a lot out of you!" as he grabbed a beer.

Izzy and M and Brian spent about half an hour eating their late lunch, talking slowly, quietly, not much about Nodes, but instead about how good the food was, and how much of a success the party was. In the corner of the family room was a pile of birthday presents, unopened, that Izz planned to get to today. She looked over and decided to make a Node joke, "Well, boys, how about we have one of your Nodes stop by and pick up that pile of stuff," pointing to the gifts, " and drop it off at my place? May as well put them to use, right?"

M replied, "Not a bad idea, Izzy, and after experiment three you'll see why!" So they cleaned their plates and the table and resumed their positions on the recliner and sofa.

"From what you've told me," Izzy started, "these Nodes are very interesting scientific curiosities, but you said something about *time travel*? You mean they can tell us something scientific about what happened a long time ago, like the fossil record, that sort of thing, right?"

Brian was quick on the draw, which M wouldn't have expected. "No, wrong, not that at all. We mean real time travel where beings can move through time, that's what we mean!"

"You're crazy, Brian. That is... not... possible. It cannot be done. That's silly. So here we are, today, in the here and now, and you're telling me we can go back to yesterday, back to the party, all over again? Or, why not jump to tomorrow and skip today completely? This is the craziest stuff I've ever heard, Brian, if you're serious. You know, this nonsense is OK for some TV show or maybe a Science Fiction book, but c'mon, you really expect me to believe this baloney? Got a bridge for sale while you're at it?" Izzy was sure of what she was saying, but, then again, looking at M's reaction to her reaction to what Brian had said, maybe she wasn't so sure after all.

Time travel? It was a haunting concept, no questions about that. M saw the problem as Izzy's wheels turned and jumped in to smooth what was quickly becoming a bumpy ride. "Look, Izz, we're way ahead of where we should be. Let me tell you about experiment number three, and we can go from there, okay?" Both she and Brian nodded 'yes.'

"By the way, Izzy,... er... cat-mom-to-be, Kepler says 'meow,'" M thought a little levity - or is that 'levitousness'? - would help break in Experiment Three. "'Meow' right back at him, M. Tell him that, please."

"Sure will, next time he's back from another outer space ride, huh?"

"Outer space ride? What did you do to the cat, Emilio Ravelli?" Izz was downright indignant, upset. M thought to himself, "Well, that wasn't such a great idea..." as he answered "Nothing, Izz. Kep is fine, at home, sleeping I'm sure. I didn't do anything to the cat, sort of..." Izzy's look said it all, "Sort of!? you didn't do anything to my future cat *sort of*? What kind of weaselly statement is that? What *did* you do?" as Isabella stood up looking straight at M with what M's grandma would describe as *malocchio*, the evil eye.

"Please, Izz, sit down. As I said, Kep's fine," looking over at Brian and gesturing for him to agree, which he did, "and the cat's at my apartment, very content I'm sure."

Then Emilio went through the entire experiment in which Kepler became the world's first NODE RIDER AstroCat. Izz was shown photos of Kep's capsule, pictures of him in it, and his take-off and landing, as well as truly remarkable still pictures printed from the video tapes, photos of the Perseids shower, the view of Earth from 150 miles up, nearly 800,000 feet traveling around 625 mph. Isabella was rapt, awe-struck, dumbfounded, because what she was looking at truly was *unbelievable* - in every sense of the word.

"You did this? You,... and Brian?" she asked, incredulous. "This is a m a z i n g! I can't believe it,... but there it is, I suppose," as she swiped her hand over the coffee table covered with photos. "And Kep's okay, you're sure of that?" "Yes, Izzy," M replied, "Kep couldn't be better, and it's been days so any problem would have shown up by now, but none has. Our

AstroCat is a very happy feline. By the way, do you like the word I minted for him, 'AstroCat?' Nice ring, don't you think?" Izzy didn't hesitate two seconds, "No. It's stupid."

Brian wisely thought a review was in order, especially because the best was yet to come. "I'm really happy, Izzy, that you believe us now," he said. "That's important because the rest we're going to tell you is even stranger, even harder to accept. Bear with us, and I yield the floor to my esteemed colleague Professor Doctor Emilio Ravelli who will fill you in on some of the theoretical stuff. Professor Ravelli..." as Brian turned to his right, facing M who sat beside him on the sofa, nodding slightly in his direction and extending his hand in a beckoning gesture indicating that the floor was his.

M played along, "Thank you, Maestro Eng. Healy. Let me begin..." Izzy rolled her eyes as M started to speak, "by summarizing the main points, of which there are several." M pulled a pad from the coffee table drawer and wrote the following as he explained each point:

1. Nodes are formed by gravitating masses, like the gravitational fields from the Earth, Jupiter and Sun getting together to add up and create a Node.

2. The Node is a region of spacetime that is distinct from the surrounding spacetime. Think of it as an oil drop in water. They don't mix, and the oil drop can move through the water without losing its distinct identity. A Node is just like that oil drop.

3. A Node is analogous to a photon. But, different from a photon because a Node can travel at lightspeed, or less than lightspeed, or more than lightspeed.

A photon does not experience space or time because Special Relativity tells us that they cease to exist at lightspeed. So too for a Node at lightspeed.

4. Two identical objects inside a Node become macro Quantum Entangled.

5. The flat spacetime inside a Node can be curved using a 'Gravity Engine'.

6. The speed and direction of a Node are determined by its shape. It is stationary if spherical, and it moves progressively faster as it is elongated, with its direction controlled by how much it's bent.

7. Being inside a Node at lightspeed eliminates space and time, there are none, just like the photon. Coming out of lightspeed recreates space and time, and the Node can come out *anywhere* at *any time* => *Time Travel* is possible!

After M was done scribbling, and he and Brian had discussed each topic on the pad, M concluded "I think this is a good place for a break," he said, looking at his watch. "We've been talking for almost two hours, and I think Izzy could use some time to ponder all this," then looking at Brian, "it was hard enough for us to come to grips, Izz. I can only imagine what you're going through right now," as he looked across at Izz with a reassuring face.

"Sure," was Izzy's response. "I *can* use a break. How about half an hour? I'm getting some tea. Anyone else?" And the three went their separate ways to relax and consider all that had been discussed.

- - - - - - - - - - - -

Renewed and refreshed, Izzy actually came looking for the boys, her curiosity about the Nodes, especially *Time Travel*, piqued. "What is the 'rest' of the story that M mentioned?" she wondered, in an inquisitive way, but tempered by an intuitive sense of foreboding.

Izzy found Brian on the veranda, snuggled up in an Adirondack chair with a brew, listening to a Beatles album on his portable cassette player, fixated on the Lake which was beautifully calm and still. It was mid afternoon, and the bird population was taking its siesta until later in the day when it would awake and become quite raucous looking for an evening meal.

She found M in the 'office,' a pleasant business-like room off the back of the kitchen, what probably was a dining room in decades past, but what now served as the Healy Hardware office away from the company's actual headquarters downtown. It was from here that her mother and father ran the hardware store chain for more or less the entire summer, when the family relocated to the Lake to appreciate its beauty and recreation during its best season. Izzy and Brian both had very fond memories of those lazy days lying on the beach with a good book, or exploring the Lake in the small rowboat, or splashing in the cool, clear water, or, in Brian's case, fishing catch and release.

Time Travel?, Izzy thought back to those halcyon days and mused, "I wonder, can I really go back to *then*, and *here*? If only..." She summonsed Brian and M to reconvene as they had in the family room, she in the recliner and the two men opposite her on the sofa. "Well," Izzy started, "I have been thinking about all this, and I can believe that the Nodes are real, that you can jump on... no, 'in'... one, and that you can go places inside it. Why? Because I did see the evidence that Kepler did just that, and apparently there's nothing about a Node that makes it partial to cats," Izzy was becoming a bit flip, but having a good time doing it. "So it could have been you, Brian, who dashed about the planet inside the Node... or you, M..."

"Yes, Isabella, so true. Could have been me... er... I?," Brian was flip in return, "or M..."

"So what's the 'rest?' M said something about telling me the 'rest.' What is that?" Izzy's curiosity couldn't be contained. She didn't want to wait for M and Brian to come around to whatever it was they had to tell her. "Just blurt it out, for crying out loud!" she thought.

M leaned forward and answered, sporting a very matter-of-fact, almost stern look, "Brian and I want to take a *Time Travel* trip on a Node, just a test flight, mind you, nothing big, just a validation flight to confirm that everything works,..." M paused a few seconds. "... And we want to do it as soon as possible, sometime in the next few weeks." He and Brian waited for Izzy's response, looking carefully for the tells that often betrayed Izzy's true feelings, her lowering her head looking down and turning it to one side, her placing one hand on the other's wrist, and leaning back in her chair. They all were evident, except leaning back because she was in the recliner, and instead, today, she sat erect and leaned forward, which, without saying anything, both Brian and M took to be a body gesture with the same significance. M asked, "So you're all for this, right?" in an attempt to maneuver Izzy into saying "Great idea!" But it didn't work...

Isabella replied, "No,... and I mean NO! You say to 'confirm.' What the hell does that mean? That means you're not sure. Something can go wrong. No way can I agree to this, and you should have known better than to even ask!" Izzy was more than upset, she was livid that the boys would suggest what she perceived as such a dangerous endeavor. "Why don't you do something simple, something I can agree to, like climb Mount Everest? At least that's on Earth! M, I'm surprised at you! We just became engaged, and you're asking me to agree to *this*?"

Emilio was ashamed, humiliated by what he had just done to the girl he loved so much. Izzy was right - he should have known better! There were other ways to validate Node *Time Travel*, for example getting a volunteer, someone with less to lose. But he was too self-absorbed to see that. Now in M's mind, Izzy was right, and the matter was settled - find an alternative. But Brian not so much.

"Izzy, I'd like to talk to you after you calm down a bit. Can we do that? Please..." was Brian's entreaty.

Izzy looked at her brother, squinting a little, eyes moist, but not teary, snuffling with deep short breaths, then saying, "Yes, Brian, of course we can talk." Several minutes passed, and M and Brian could see that Isabella's demeanor mellowed considerably. She was much calmer, and Brian thought much more receptive to a genuine discussion of the *Time Travel* test. He started.

"Are you OK, Izz?" "Yes," she answered with a subdued snort. "I'm OK. M caught me off guard so, but I'm fine now. And I'm sorry for my outburst," looking truly sorry as she stared first at M then at Brian.

"I think we have to discuss this, Isabella, in a rational, respectful way. I hope we can do that. Can we give it a try?" Brian said, and Izzy knew immediately where this was headed. But Brian was right, a thoughtful consideration of what obviously was an important question was required, not a tantrum like Izz threw before.

"Yes, Brian, M, both of you. Let's talk this through. I'll listen, and I hope you do as well. Agreed?"

Both of the 'boys' did, and Isabella, Emilio and Brian had a quite lengthy discussion about the necessity of testing *Time Travel*, how that should be done, and the benefits and perils of doing so. In the end, there was agreement, but it came slowly, only after every nook and cranny of the issued was explored.

Izzy took the reins, "I will agree to your taking a test flight on the next Node, 'Gert,' - that's a great name, by the way! - when she shows up, you said September 12th here at the Lake, right?"

"Yes, and on the water, which is better than on land given what we have to do," Brian remarked.

"And between now and then you PROMISE that all the equipment you have to build will be built AND tested, twice... No chance for some kind of equipment failure or problem that keeps you from getting back here, right? I do believe that my genius husband-to-be has this figured out, and that he's right about it. So that's not a problem for me," but Brian interrupted.

"So M's work is fine, but mine may not be? I am the equipment guy, and you're worried about that?"

"Yes, Brian," Izzy answered. "Not that I don't respect, or trust your skills. It's a question of time. This is August 20th, so September 12th is only about three weeks away. Are you sure you can do everything, the upgraded Node Boundary Sensor, the Gravity Engines, the Computer Controls, all the things we talked about, and who knows what I'm missing, all that equipment designed, built, and tested in time? You're the one, Brian, who made such a big deal out of how much had to be done, and how short the time was to do it, remember?"

And Izzy was right, because during their conversation it *was* Brian who hyped the tech *he* was responsible for and what was involved in pulling it off. So Brian came to Brian's defense, "Well, sis, I think I gave you the wrong impression. You're thinking the time's too tight because of what I said, but, believe me, it's not so tight that I can't get this done... and there's another part of this we should get out of the way right now. M and I briefly discussed it, and now the time has come to decide."

"You know, Brian, you befuddle me more and more. So what is it that you and M talked about that wasn't in our discussion this afternoon?"

"Getting someone else involved, specifically Marty Lobesky. Fact is, if M and I are winding our way through time and space, out there," and Brian waved his hand in a broad arc over his head, "then we need someone back here who (a) knows what's going on, besides you, and (b) who knows the equipment in case any issues do come up. Marty's the right guy for that. In fact, Marty's the *only* guy for that. Right now, there are only three people on entire planet Earth who know about the Nodes, the three of *us*. So what has to be decided is, Do we bring Marty in as number four? Or not? I throw the floor open..." and Brian looked at Izzy, and at M, with a look that invited their feedback.

"My opinion," said M, "I'm not sure, I don't think so. How would he keep it from Sandy? What if she found out and said something? If this gets out it may create a firestorm of people trying to 'hop a Node,' maybe a panic. It could be very bad, and we would have been responsible. The more I think about it, my vote is 'no.' We can handle equipment issues without Marty back here helping," and M looked at Izzy obviously inviting her take on this question.

"I must say, M, our relationship *is* being tested! My vote is 'yes,' a resounding YES. You two expect me to be back here, on Earth, while you're out there," motioning as Brian did, waving toward the heavens, "and I'm here all alone, no one to talk to, not knowing the tech stuff when Marty Lobesky, who's an expert on it, could be right here with me to help if necessary. Wow! That really is asking a lot! And the *only* reason for not involving Marty is that he *might* let the cat out of the bag!?"

"Okay, Izzy, we know where you stand," said Brian, "so I guess it's up to me. I hold the tie-breaker. And, believe me, I've agonized over this for a while because having Marty know *why* he's doing *what* he's doing means a better result, I'm convinced of that. And, M, I must say, Izzy has a point concerning some added safety if Marty's involved, not to mention his providing moral support. Taking all this into account, I vote 'yes,' read Marty in..."

M was clearly disappointed by being out-voted, but he respected the process, and in fact saw the merits on both sides of the argument, plus his call was close to begin with, so he politely acquiesced, "Alright, decision made - We read Marty in. He'll be nothing short of flabbergasted! I think the three of us should do it together, so Marty will know we're unified on this. What say you?" and Izzy and Brian immediately and simultaneously nodded their agreement.

Then Izzy made a closing remark. "M, Brian, I love you both... sooo... much. I don't know what I would do, how I would go on, if either of you was injured in this grand experiment. But I do see that you must do it. All I ask is that you promise me, right here, right now, that you will be as careful as possible, and that if there's *any* problem, the smallest thing, that you will postpone the launch until you're sure. Can you do that?" Izzy asked with a forlorn look and moist eyes. "Will you?" Of course, they did.

- - - - - - - - - - - -

Flabbergasted wasn't the right word - any number of other superlatives would apply - that described Marty Lobesky's reaction to learning about the Nodes, and what the equipment he built had done in the experiments, and how it allowed Kepler to sail away and return safely, and what it was that M and Brian intended to do next. Marty was savvy enough to know that Izzy had to be onboard, and she reassured him that she was, and that she was counting on him to be with her for the entire trip. Marty, of course, agreed, and also promised he would never divulge to Sandy, or anyone else, anything about the Nodes. Marty had kept similar secrets before, and Brian, especially, trusted him implicitly. Thus began in earnest the preparation for the first of what hopefully would be many Node Flights.

The morning of Tuesday, September 12th, was crystal clear and somewhat chilly with temperatures in the mid to high 50's. Brian and M were riding Gert again because it was a Node they 'knew,' that is, its characteristics had been measured and validated on more than one occasion. This information reinforced their confidence in a successful launch and trip. Gert would touch down on the Lake at 9:05:07am EDT, this time about 150 feet from the end of the dock at her closest approach. The Lake was mirror smooth, exactly the type of surface conducive to an equally smooth takeoff.

Brian and Marty had done an exquisite job of modifying the Volkswagen Minivan that Brian had purchased back in July. The roof was raised more than foot so that someone as tall as 6-2 could stand easily; the front seats were dual 'Captain's Chairs' outfitted with duplicate built-in controls for key functions, the entire vehicle was hermetically sealed and had built-in flotation and gyroscopic stabilization, even propulsion for water landing and takeoff, as it would this day. There was sufficient onboard food and water to support two people for two months; there were full hygiene facilities including a shower; full environment controls; and sleeping quarters for two. Brian, with Marty's assistance, designed a marvelously compact interior that efficiently used a very small space to include a very great deal of functionality.

But perhaps the most important modifications to the Minivan were its electronics and the *Retrieval System*. Three independent Gravity Engines were built in to control the Node's size and shape. One controlled the length longitudinally, a second the width laterally, and a third its bulge so that essentially any desired shape could be instantaneously created. A single control panel operated all three Engines, and the Node's default shape was a perfect sphere with a gravity level the same as Earth's. When the gravity engines produced this shape, the Node would detach from the fields that created it, and it would exist in the Universe's spacetime as a separate entity enclosing its own spacetime, just like the oil drop in water. The 'Detach Sequence' was computer controlled and could be initiated manually or by timer. On this maiden flight it would be manual detachment.

The *Retrieval System* that Marty designed and built allowed the Node Riders to exit the Minivan, send it off to a pre-programmed location, and then using a remote control retrieve it by sending it back to the drop-off point. This was an essential upgrade, Marty reasoned, because depending on when and where the Minivan was, it may not be wise to have it in plain view. Marty relied heavily on M's programming skills to create the software needed to accomplish this goal, and it required a good deal of electronics to interface with other onboard system such as navigation and propulsion, but in the end Marty was quite happy with how the *Retrieval System* worked out.

Also included were inboard and outboard video cameras with magnetic tape recorders so that a record of the trip could be made at any time, but only a limited amount of recording time was available, about ten hours total. Marty already had plans to improve this number, but he couldn't get the required parts in time. Solar panels on the sides and roof provided electricity to recharge the built-in battery system that powered all onboard devices. Gyro stabilization was included, as well as Marty's new thruster system for inserting the Minivan into a Node and for dropping it out.

And for communication with Izzy and Marty back on Earth, there were two identical Nodebooks onboard. Their proximity macro Quantum Entangled them so that an entry in one instantaneously appeared in the other, no matter where or when the Minivan was located. M's having discovered Macro QE inside a Node's initially flat spacetime permitted this remarkable form of communication, its only limitation being the possibility of a 'noisy channel.' In addition, for local comms, for example on takeoff and landing when *NR-1701* was near the 'Node Port,' half duplex short range VHF/UHF radios were used. Marty, Brian and M all held amateur radio licenses, and Izzy was working on hers.

Marty decided that Minivan needed a designator like the tail numbers on a private plane, so on each side he painted in large black letters '*NR-1701*,' obviously signifying ***NODE RIDER 1701***. Brian couldn't be happier, and when M saw it he laughed aloud and said to Brian, "Well, ain't that the truth, 'Where No One Ever Has Gone Before!'"

The launch time was closing fast, now 8 am. Brian and M kissed Izzy who wept ever so slightly, shook hands with Marty, and boarded *NR-1701* at the dock. Brian was piloting today, so he fired up the propeller drive and slowly moved the Minivan sideways away from the dock, stopped, and then steamed very slowly out to the launch site that had been marked with a bright yellow buoy. Brian maneuvered *NR-1701* to face the dock where Izzy and Marty stood at the end in anxious anticipation. M and Brian waved and blew kisses to their 'ground crew' as Brian slowly turned the Minivan to line up with Gert's flight path. While this was happening, M wrote in the QE Nodebook 'I LOVE YOU, ISABELLA!' and that very message instantaneously appeared in the Nodebook that Izzy held. She looked down, and replied 'ILY2. SAFE FLIGHT!' M couldn't help but shed a slight tear as he closed the Nodebook in preparation for takeoff.

Marty had been surveying the sky with binoculars, when he exclaimed to Izzy, "There, over there, see that grayish cloud? It's the flight of birds they said would be inside the Node, and sure enough." Izzy held up her binocs, and there it was, a tightly packed group of birds moving in static formation with wings tucked in and maintaining their distance. "I see it, Marty, I see it!!" Isabella could hardly believe her eyes. The Nodes, everything M and Brian told her was playing out right before her eyes, and she was astonished.

Brian held out his wrist with the Oyster on it, checking it against the onboard digital time display in the control console. They agreed to the second. "Get ready, M. Gert's here in 5, 4, 3, 2, 1, as the onboard computers engaged the Node Insertion Thrusters to inject *NR-1701* into Gert's interior flat spacetime. "Here we go!!!" *And off they did!*

Gert encapsulated the Minivan and effortlessly lifted it skyward. Instinctively, both Marty and Emilio clutched their seats expecting to feel like they were accelerating down the runway in a commercial jet. But there was no such sensation because Gert's departure was relatively slow, gradually increasing from a ground speed of around 20mph to progressively greater speed as the Node gained altitude. Marty was glued to the speed and altitude displays. "Look at this, M, we're crossing 1,000 feet at 28 mph, then a couple of minutes later, look, 5,000 feet at 103 mph!" M did look, forcing himself to turn from the awe-inspiring sight he watched as the Earth receded further and further. "Yes, Brian, impressive, and..." as he looked at computer printout in his lap "..., let's see, exactly on schedule, altitude and speed. This fully validates the computer modeling, Brian, completely! As the flight progressed without mishap, Brian and M grew more and more comfortable, the tension waned and they relaxed.

"Can you believe this, Brian?! Look, look at where we are!" Brian looked down at the Earth from an altitude of 600,000 feet, almost 115 miles. It was astonishing, absolutely astonishing. The Earth's curvature was fully visible, as was the day/night terminator. Lights were visible in the nighttime region, and it reflected the Earth's population density as if someone had dropped incandescent points on a map. "This is amazing, M, truly amazing! I can't believe we're *actually* here!! 'Where no one has gone before!' Oh, how true!"

M's reaction was equally enthusiastic. "Neither can I, Brian, ... believe that we're *actually here*. Pinch me! Twice! You know, when this all started I never,... never would have - could have - imagined where it would lead! Not only is the science validated, we, *you and I*, the two of us, we have discovered what might be the most important discovery *ever* made! Think about that Brian, the most important discovery *ever*!! Think of its implications, for transportation, for communication, for exploration away from Earth, for history and for history to come - astonishing, truly astonishing! And, *you and I* did it!!" M could hardly contain himself, so great was his sense of accomplishment and satisfaction and, frankly, amazement with a job superbly well done. Spent, he looked at Brian, closed his eyes, and sat back in the Captain's Chair to regain his composure. Brian did the same because he felt the same way Emilio did.

The Nodebook in M's lap 'vibrated,' actually it was more like a wiggle, a signal that there was an incoming message. The Ground Crew and the *NR-1701* crew agreed that to alert each other the sender would simply 'vibrate' the Nodebook by quickly moving it back and forth, slightly. The other Macro QE Nodebook would do the same thing, and that would signal an incoming message. It was about ten minutes into the flight when Izzy simply couldn't wait any longer. She just *had* to know what was happening, how the boys were doing. M opened the onboard Nodebook to read his fiancé's note:

How are you? Where are you? I thought I would hear from you by now. Is everything OK? Love, Izz.

M immediately replied:

ALL OK! Cruising 800 mph ~ 50 miles up. In ~ 20 mins will hit 5000 mph ~1300 miles. <u>STUNNING</u> WHAT WE SEE!! MISS YOU, IZZ. WISH YOU WERE HERE! ALL MY LOVE, M

"Brian, anything to add?" "Nope, just chillin'. M, look, over there, the Moon, it's peeking up behind Earth! I just cannot believe this! Anyway, no, nothing I have to say." But M added a PS anyway: **PS - BRIAN WISHES YOU WERE HERE, TOO, xoxoxo**

- - - - - - - - - - -

M and Brian sat and stared, quietly, for a long, long time, a few hours anyway, just taking in the amazing, mind-blowing sights of outer space. They had traveled several thousand miles at speeds as high as 25,312 mph, yet there was no sensation of motion, no noise, only complete silence, and the sights, sights that could hardly be described, the Moon, the nearby planets, Venus, Mars, even Mercury for a short time until she disappeared in the Sun. Brian clicked away on the Nikons while M was glued to the binocs and a small hand-held telescope. Neither one spoke, they were so overcome by what they saw. "The view from *here* is so different than the view from *there*," M thought. "If only Isabella could *see* this, if only she could *experience* it..." The Node Ride was so smooth and quiet that both men hardly realized they were moving through empty space at rocket ship speeds. Everything performed flawlessly, all the electronics, the environmental systems, everything.

"We have to thank Marty for this," Brian remarked. "He didn't miss a beat, and he told me it was because he figured he'd be taking a ride soon! You know, I think we *should* do that. Give Marty the keys. What do you think?"

"Sure. Why not? Marty's as much a part of this now as we are. And if it weren't for his electronics genius we'd be,... hmmm... can't say 'up the creek...' we'd be 'between planets without a thruster,' how's that?"

"I must say, M, being in outer space hasn't improved your levitousness, if that's even a word... But, we agree, let's get Marty into this boat sometime soon. He will LOVE it!"

Brian reached behind his chair to retrieve a duffle bag that seemed to hold more than it could hold. "I was going to ask about that, Brian. What's in there? Besides maybe a small kitchen sink? I brought a duffle, too, but mine is half empty... or should that be 'half full?' Hmmm... it's the 'half' that creates the problem..."

"You know, M, we're in here, you and I, no way to get out, yet, anyhow, so this could be a *very* long trip if you keep up that kind of stuff, eh?"

"Okay, let's move this along, Brian. I think it's time to go to lightspeed and pop out some*time* else, back on Earth, just to see what's up there after today."

"Sure thing, but before we do,..." Brian said, reaching into his duffel, "... here's a little something I had made up for us, one for you, one for me!"

M was handed a very slick looking navy blue and white baseball cap with bright letters in large font reading *NODE RIDER*. And as he handed M his cap, he reached into the duffel with his other hand to retrieve two small glasses and an unopened bottle of *Glenfiddich*. "Time for a toast, M, time for a toast," and M and Brian uncorked the Scotch and raised their glasses high to celebrate mankind's **FIRST RIDE IN A GRAVITATIONAL NODE**! Quite the day!

- - - - - - - - - - - -

"M, please re-check my numbers. We want to set down in New York City just south of Central Park. I have 40 degrees 45 minutes 53.28 seconds North latitude, 73 degrees, 58 minutes, 50.88 seconds West longitude. That should put us just about at the corner of Seventh Ave and West Fifty-sixth Street." M checked his computer printout, saying "Check. We're good. Time?"

"How about *tomorrow*, two in the afternoon. The crowds should be less, and we can look around a bit." Then it struck M like the proverbial brick, "NO, Brian, NO. Delete those entries, NOW!" M was nearly hysterical, although he needn't have been because the coordinates could be changed at any time. His panic was bred from a realization of what they were about to do, *go forward in time*, not by much, just enough to confirm it was possible. Entering touch-down coordinates and a landing time was so emotional for M that that was why he panicked, along with his realizing that the location was impossible.

"What? Why? Seems like a good spot to me!" was Brian's response. "That's because you haven't thought his through... Mid town Manhattan, mid day in a Minivan? That comes down from the sky for everyone to see? And then what? Do you park it somewhere? Is one of us going to drive around the block for a few hours? What do we say if we're stopped by a cop, for whatever reason?" M could see that these issues were sinking in. "Should I go on?"

"No, you made your point. Where to instead?"

"I want some place where we can get *tomorrow*'s *New York Times*. I want to bring it back to Izz so she'll know, for sure, without a doubt, Marty, too, that we actually did this, went forward in time and came back. Bringing back something she knows came from the future, something she actually can check by buying a copy herself, tomorrow, well, that will be the ultimate proof..." Brian could sense that M wasn't intending to stop there, so he asked, "And then what?"

"Then, I think the 'what' is we, you, and I,... and Isabella... the *three* of us should head out in *NR-1701* and do what it is meant to do, destined to do - *explore*, near and far, now and into the future, and also the past to understand it better, that's the 'what' for me!"

"Good argument, M, very good. So good luck with it!... By the way, you can sign me up - I'm game, sounds like a real 'trip,' if you get my drift... But good luck with Izz..."

"Let me work on Izzy. Let's just get a newspaper, please."

"Where to? Give me a place to go." M had been poring over a map of upstate New York, figuring somewhere up there would be a good place to get a copy of the *Times*. "Schroon Lake, that's where we should go. Ready? North 43 degrees 50 minutes 18.1284 seconds, West 73 degrees, 45 minutes, 42.5844 seconds,... " Brian punched in the coordinates as M read them off. "... which should put us just west of Main Street in an open field. Let's land at 12:15am, *the day after tomorrow*, September 14th, then move *NR-1701* to a place we can park it without drawing any attention. There's a school parking lot a couple of blocks away, maybe there. We can't be driving around at 3am. That'll almost certainly get us pulled over, so we have to stop somewhere, and if we're rousted we have to make up some story about being on our way to Montreal for a concert, an outdoor thing like Woodstock, the concert about three years ago. Anyway, in the morning we can start driving. We'll be right downtown, so there has to be a breakfast spot where we can grab a bite and get a copy of the *Times*, and once we've done that I think we should skedaddle back to today in a place we can spend the afternoon, then head home, tomorrow the 13th, say, around diner time. If we do this, we will have validated NODE RIDING as a means of exploring, well, the *entire* Universe, and we will have demonstrated that *Time Travel* does exist. What do you think?"

"Geez, Emilio, that was long-winded. Sure, yes to everything. No argument from me, and, actually, I can't wait to see Izzy's and Marty's reactions to this. Let's be sure they're sitting!" Brian said as he entered the landing time, *12:15am* EDT, and the date,

Thursday, September 14th, 1972, again checking the onboard clock against the Oyster. And, again, they agreed to the second...

- - - - - - - -

The rest of the first day's flight was uneventful, pleasantly so, so that Brian and M could enjoy looking into the depths of space unencumbered by any of the paraphernalia that an Apollo astronaut had to deal with. They, literally, were in their own small universe within the Universe, and their equipment was compact and simple. Of course, Brian couldn't resist checking everything for proper function, twice if not more times. Marty had done a spectacular job of building in self-test diagnostics that periodically ran in the background, and that were capable not only of identifying a problem and alerting the crew, but also of performing an automatic work-around if there were a simple enough fix. This level of automation pretty much removed the human element from piloting *NR-1701*. All Brian and M had to do, really, was tell *NR-1701* where to go and when to be there, past, present, or future. Brian imagined how Marty Lobesky would react to actually sitting in the Captain's Chair, in front of the control console *he designed and built*, while looking out at some run-of-the-mill astronomical sight like, say, the Rings of Saturn! And Brian very much looked forward to the day when that would happen...

"Not bad, M, not bad. It is a field. We are in the middle of it. And it's pitch black, so I don't think we're sticking out like a sore thumb. Good thing I increased the Minivan's ride height, this field is kind of lumpy as I see it from here. We've got an extra eight inches." M nodded his acknowledgement. "Where to? I don't think we should stay here. You said something about a school nearby?"

"Yes, Brian, maybe two blocks. Get to Main Street, that's Route 9, take a left and it should be on the left, as I said, about two blocks." Brian did just that, and, sure enough, there was the school with a large parking lot with several school buses. "Maybe behind those buses?" as Brian waved towards them.

"Gee, Brian, I don't know. This is a *small* town, and everything gets noticed, and *NR-1701* with its mods *is* going to stick out like a sore thumb, so someone will see it, I'm sure of that. A conundrum, I'd say, a conundrum..."

"Cut out the highfalutin words, get to the point without them, thank you. Conundrum? I think you're right, no matter where we go in town someone's going to see us. The only question is, What do they do? Knock on the window to say hi? Walk over shotgun in hand? Or the worst, call the cops? I think the answer to the 'conundrum,' is clear and simple, we get the hell out of Dodge until daybreak, then we come back and get some grub and a newspaper. You know, there is a Lake here. Maybe go there? I'm sure there must be some out-of-the-way off-road spots where we can stash the Minivan with us in it." M agreed, so that's what they did, drove the Minivan to the end of a peninsula where they parked for the night. If anyone asked, they were camping.

It was around 5am, and both Brian and M woke to the rising sun. "What a gorgeous day it looks like it will be!" remarked M as he stretched. "First dibs on the shower..." and he preempted any chance Brian had of getting there first. After cleaning up, they headed into town, and just as they expected, a short way after the *Welcome to Schroon Lake* sign they came upon a place called *Four Jelly Toast*, a touristy diner obviously catering to out-of-towners, the kind of customer who read the *New York Times*, which, of course, was piled high in front of the cash register, along with several other newspapers, among them the French language *Le Journal de Montréal*. Brian and Emilio had a delicious breakfast of ham and eggs and, of course, four-jelly toast, and as they settled up purchased copies of both the *Times* and *Le Journal*. In the middle of *NYT*'s September **14th** front page, above the fold, an article headlines, *McGovern Accuses Nixon Of a 'Low Road' Campaign*. There was no way Izzy, and Marty, could miss the newspapers' significance.

"That was tasty," Brian commented on their way out, Minivan parked in the lot at the side of *Four Jelly* "Yes, it was. And I was hungry. So what do you want to do this afternoon? Check out Schroon Lake?... or the Moon's dark side?... or how about Venus?"

Brian shook his head and chuckled. "You know, this really is going to take some getting used to. That we can go anywhere, and time. Astonishing! Scary! But at the same time, what a sense of freedom! It's amazing to me, and I'm sure it is to you, too, M, that *we are experiencing something that no human being ever has experienced before*!"

"Okay, my vote, first, go back to yesterday, the 13th. Second, Moon's dark side. Just the thought gives me goose bumps! What do you think?" As Brian entered yesterday's date into the Control Console, while M looked up suitable coordinates *near enough* to the Moon that they could 'drive' to the dark side without having to come out of lightspeed there. After all, there was the possibility of making a mistake and entering coordinates that would place the Minivan *inside* the Moon. "What then?" M thought, followed by "Gotta get Marty on this right away when we get back. We need a built-in safety lock-out that won't allow the Minivan to go places like the interior of a planet or whatever. We'll have to figure something out..." M filled Brian in on this concern and, of course, Brian agreed completely.

Just like the excursion forward in time was smooth and uneventful, so was the Minivan's return to the day after it launched. The return time was set to 2pm on Wednesday, September 13th, 1972, on Lake Arrowhead at precisely the place they launched. M grabbed the Nodebook, writing to Izzy:

Hi, Izz. ALL OK. This is FANTASTIC! I cannot put into words what this is like, what we've seen, where we've been, WHEN we've been. It really is hard to describe, even for us to believe - and we're <u>here</u>! And the sense of FREEDOM, to go anywhere... Just programmed touchdown at 2 o'clock this afternoon, same place as takeoff. SEE YOU THERE. ALL MY LOVE, Emilio

PS - Brian's flying, so he says Hi, and Love, too.

whereupon he wiggled the Nodebook to let Izz know he had written. The QE Entangled Nodebook on Earth wiggled in response, and Isabella opened it to see M's message. She wrote back:

Oh, I, we, Marty and I, we feel so good that you're OK, and on your way back. We agree, this is FANTASTIC! This is the most amazing thing EVER! We will meet you at the dock this afternoon. In the meantime, I have to get back to making my homemade ravioli! Love, Izz.

Izzy knew that this last remark would have M salivating, and making sure he wasn't late!

- - - - - - - - - - -

NR-1701 landed at exactly 2pm EDT on Wednesday, September 13th, 1972, the day *after* its maiden voyage and the day *before* the date of the newspapers stuffed in M's duffle. Touchdown was entirely uneventful, much as was the takeoff. Isabella was so caught up in the 'boys" arrival that she bear-hugged and kissed them with such emotion and intensity they never had seen before. "I can't tell you how *HAPPY* I am that you're back! Back in one piece, and you both look great, so good! No worse for the wear and tear of cruising *outer space*! God, think about that! You were in *outer space*! No rocket, no space suit, yet in *outer space*! I'm still not sure I can believe this. It's just *too* unbelievable! Pinch me, M, wake me up!"

"Well, Isabella, the fact is, we were there, and we can prove it. We have still pictures that Brian took, and video tape from the outboard and inboard cameras. Those you can see tonight, and the stills after your brother develops them, probably tomorrow. It is good to be back, and we weren't even gone that long, but we sure covered some ground... er... space!" Brian chimed in, in total agreement with M, then saying to Izzy and Marty, "We're famished. Those freeze-dried microwaved dinners only go so far. Ummm..." as they walked towards the Lake House, "Ummm, smells fantastic even from here! We'd like to tell you, Izz, that we picked up a nice Chianti for dinner, but... unfortunately they don't carry that on the Moon's dark side!"

Brian was right, the dinner was fantastic: homemade ravioli, two types, meat and cheese filled; crunchy, hot garlic bread; a fresh garden salad lightly dressed with oil and vinegar; and fried, breaded zucchini squash, all prepared by Isabella. Marty served as sous-chef helping Izzy by preparing ingredients and making sure all were *mise en place*. Yes, the dinner was *fantastic*! And M, and Brian, couldn't be happier. What a wonderful time these last two days had been!

After their meal, Isabella walked out homemade *Tiramisu* accompanied by *demitasse* espresso with lemon rind. M and

Brian were googly-eyed at its appearance, no other word could describe their reaction, and Marty was right there with them. Isabella, of course, had the smirk of the expert cook that she was who knew well 'the best way to a man's heart...' "Hope you enjoyed dinner, gentlemen."

"My god, Izzy, you have outdone yourself, twice over!" was M's response. "I'll drink to that," said Brian after fetching an open bottle of *Glenfiddich* from the bar. "How many glasses? Four?" "No, thanks, Brian, I'll pass," Izzy said, "I'm staying with this *Chianti* that *didn't* come from the Dark Side of the Moon..." I'm in," was Marty's reply, then M said "Me, too. We certainly have occasion to celebrate! Let's!" And the four toasted *NR-1701*'s successful maiden voyage.

Brian set up the video tapes which they *all* watched in amazement, including even Brian and M who were out there when they were made. The sights were so amazing that even they couldn't get past just how amazing they were, close ups of the Moon's bright and dark sides, images of Mars and Venus from angles that were impossible for Earth bound telescopes, startling images of the Earth itself as *NR-1701* sped away, and so many more. Marty and Izzy were mesmerized. They had no doubt that *NR-1701* indeed was a space ship capable of transporting humans to the furthest reaches of space. They both knew that.

But the question of *Time Travel* remained unresolved, both for Isabella and for Marty, not that they didn't believe in it, but there was lingering doubt because the very concept seemed incongruous. "Could it *really* be," Izzy wondered. "Well, I guess *I am* a Doubting Thomas," thought Marty.

Emilio brought it up. "So what we didn't talk about much, actually not at all, was our excursion to *tomorrow*." "Really, M, you did that? Or you *think* you did that?" Izzy replied. Marty remained silent, and Brian, who knew Marty quite well, could see that he was listening, thinking, not pre-judging, but remaining skeptical in a healthy way. Izzy needed proof, and while Marty would welcome it, he was more receptive to the idea. Brian caught on to this dichotomy and hoped to smooth it over. "You're both skeptics, to a varying degree, but I can tell you, *Time Travel* exists, and M and I did do it," looking at M who agreed with a broad smile and nod. On this day, September 13th, we travelled to tomorrow, September 14th, stopping in a small town in upstate New York, Schroon Lake. Why there? We wanted a place where we wouldn't stick out too much, so we had to scrub our original idea which would have placed us almost in Central Park in Manhattan, not a good place to be inconspicuous..."

"Alright, brother dearest, let's say it's true. Any extrinsic proof? Or is it just yours and M's word that this happened?"

"Of course we have proof, Isabella. M and I know you well enough..."

M jumped in, "It's here, we brought it with us, here in my duffel bag."

Marty couldn't contain himself any longer, "Really? Proof? Something indisputable? Tangible?"

"Yes, Marty. Here, take one each," as M handed the two newspapers to them, the *Times* to Izzy, and *Le Journal* to Marty. "So what's the big deal about a newspaper?" Izzy asked.

Brian answered, "Look at the date," and he could see his sister's jaw drop as she began to understand its significance. Marty, too, it sunk in with him immediately, and his jaw dropped as well. M drove home the point, "Now if you think we're up to some sort of shenanigans, check for yourselves - *tomorrow*. Go downtown to that little newsstand near the University, you know the one I mean, and pick up a hot-off-the-press copy of the newspapers you are holding *now*! The ones that won't be printed until early *tomorrow* morning. That should convince the *Doubting Thomas*'s among us," although Marty hadn't said that aloud...

"What does this mean, M? I'm a little frightened, and I don't really understand this, how it can be. I know you explained it, but the truth is, I still don't get it... and I'm scared..." "Please, Izzy, don't be, don't be frightened. There's plenty of time for me and Brian to explain this more carefully, and..." looking over at Marty, "... I think Marty has a pretty good feel for how this works, why this works. It's not magic, and it's not sinister. It's how the fabric of our Universe is knit, nothing more. In fact, way back in 1927 a biologist named J.B.S. Haldane published an essay titled *Possible Worlds*. In it he said, paraphrased, 'The Universe is not only *stranger than we suppose*, but stranger than we *can suppose*.' Boy, was he ever right!!"

"And, sis, there is a way for you to convince yourself." "Yes, Brian, how?"

"*Come with us!*" Brian stopped to let the idea sink in, knowing that Izzy's reaction likely would be negative, at least at first. "Come *with* you? Where?" M answered, "*Wherever* you want to go, Isabella, and *whenever* you want to be there. We want you to come with us on our next flight, you, and Brian, and I with Marty back here as Ground Control," then, thinking Marty might feel slighted, M added quickly, "Marty, you're on the list, too, but someone has to be here, on Earth, just in case, so your flights will have to wait just a little while, okay?" Marty of course understood and nodded 'yes.'

"You two mean this, don't you!" Izzy caught on that the boys really did mean it, so the only question was what she wanted to do - Go or Stay - her call. It didn't take her long. She thought about what it would mean, *going for a ride* and becoming a **NODE RIDER** like Brian and M, what she might see and learn, where and when she might go, and how many people ever would have this opportunity. With this context, the decision wasn't hard.

"Yes, let's go, the three of us! Let's go! I love you, M, and I love you, Brian, and I want to be with you to see what amazing things there are out there," as she motioned skyward, "and to visit the past and the future. I *believe* you, and I believe *in* you," and with that everyone sealed the deal by clinking their glasses and raising a toast to the wonders that lie ahead. And thus began the most amazing journey of their lives.

- - - - - - - - - - - -

Their first 'debrief' back on Earth, the three 'crew' and Marty, too, was festive, gleeful - hours of reliving the places they had gone, the times they were there. It was nothing short of incredulous, and it showed in everyone's words and actions. They laughed, and they drank, and Brian broke out a new bottle of *Glenfiddich*. Toasts all around! But after a fashion it became apparent that M had something on his mind. In a flash his demeanor and mood changed, and he began, "Another thing, very serious, and I've been thinking a *lot* about what we know now, what we've done, where and when we've been, what we've learned, and I think we have to agree, the four of us, right here, right now, *never* to disclose any of this, especially with the Apollo program just a few years old, agreed?" M's tone and look had changed from smiley and relaxed, almost giddy, to serious and somewhat tense. "Look, the world *cannot* know about this - at least not yet. We have to lock this down, I think, and I hope you all agree. Yes? No? What say you?"

"I'm onboard," was Brian's immediate reaction. "You're quite right, M, the world *isn't* ready - yet. I take the oath, never will I say anything about this until we all agree otherwise."

"I'm not so sure," Izzy chimes in, "In fact, I think maybe the world *is* ready, maybe the world needs to know, now, and not decades from now! Why wait? What purpose does that serve? Why can't we go a little further, then make an announcement?"

"Marty? What say you," M asked, and Marty replied, "I abstain. Why? I wasn't out here with you guys. Wish I were, but until I go I don't think I should render an opinion on something this important. So, for now anyway, I must hold my peace."

Then Brian chimed in, "Well, Izzy, my dear, my how things change! Remember your reaction when this started? From that to 'let's rent a Times Square billboard'! Wow! But you're outvoted, and we did agree to do things by majority, so you're outvoted, pure and simple. We keep this quiet."

"Gee, Brian," M said, "you don't have to be so black and white about this, huh? Izzy's entitled to her opinion, and she doesn't see it quite the same way we do. And Marty's entitled, too."

"Yes, of course, she can think what she wants, as can Marty, but we have an agreement, and I think we have to abide by it, else why have it at all?"

Isabella interrupts, "Boys, boys. Stop, I'm with you. Let's not argue. I understand why you want to wait, I do, and I have no problem doing that. I'm not sure this is the best thing to do, but I certainly can live with it. So let's put this to rest - we keep it under wraps until we all agree to unwrap it, right?"

"Yes, agreed, " Brian remarks. Then Marty says, "I agree, too." "And me, too," says M, "let's drink to that," as the four clinked their raised glasses to seal the deal.

Chapter 18 - The New & Improved *NR-1701*

"I'm having this framed to hang here in the Conference Room," as Brian Healy held up today's copy of the April 21, 2017, *Gazette*, its headline reading **NovaTek Aerospace Wins US's Largest Satellite Contract**. Marty Lobesky stood at Brian's side at the front of the Conference Room. As many employees as possible had gathered in the cafeteria for today's big announcement. It held about two hundred employees while the rest, some seventeen hundred more, watched on video feeds throughout the headquarters complex and abroad in satellite offices worldwide. Brian's 'Shop,' originally a small, low-slung one story building, had morphed into an eight-story ultra-modern engineering and manufacturing complex. Brian always was good at making money, and after *NR-1701* flew successfully he was on a tear when it came to growing his business.

NovaTek's staff went from Brian, Marty, and a couple of employees, who nearly forty-five years ago were more part-time than full, to today's behemoth of state-of-the-art engineering and manufacturing employing several hundred engineers, scientists, and manufacturing and support personnel. Long ago the company's name was changed to NovaTek Aerospace, and under Martin Lobesky's astute leadership as its CEO, it grew to be one of the most important, if not the most important, player in all areas of aerospace technology. Brian retained the position of Chairman of the Board, largely a ceremonial post, so that he could continue to play in his 'engineering sandbox,' as he put it, by coming up with new ideas without being responsible for any of the day-to-day management. This arrangement suited Brian just fine, and Marty, who had become Brian's loyal sidekick, was more than happy to take on the role of supervising NovaTek Aerospace's day-to-day operations. Of course, anyone knowing about *NODE RIDING* and *Time Travel* might assume that knowing the future accounted for NovaTek's meteoric rise, but, no, quite to the contrary, it was hard work and insight into the then-current state-of-the-art that brought NovaTek to prominence. In fact, knowing what they did about the future could not have helped them even if they wanted it to.

NovaTek had just been awarded the largest contract ever awarded by the United States government, in this case to deliver 12,500 LEO, Low Earth Orbit, satellites capable of supporting worldwide communications. It was a gigantic award for which only two other firms, Orion Aircraft and Nortrex Corporation, could even compete, but NovaTek was far and away the best choice, and the U.S. Air Force saw that. NovaTek's technology was 'light years' ahead of the competition, and its record for the highest quality products and product support delivered on time and often under budget simply couldn't be touched by anyone else. One of NovaTek's biggest advantages compared to other players in its technology space was that it was fully employee owned. Years ago, Brian and Marty, who were the principal owners of the original NovaTek Engineering, decided that the best employee incentive would be ownership. If every employee had a personal stake in the company's performance, then it made sense to them that the work product would be better, and, of course, Brian and Marty were right. So NovaTek Engineering was re-incorporated as NovaTek Aerospace with a controlling interest held by Brian and Marty and smaller interests awarded to Izzy and M. Isabella and Emilio had nothing to do with the new corporation's day-to-day operation, but they served as consultants in finance and the physical sciences. The lion's share of company stock was held by its employees.

"Hi, Izzy, M, happy you could make it. This is a watershed day for NovaTek, our biggest contract ever and the biggest contract ever awarded by the government. Not bad for a couple of ham-and-eggers starting out in the 'Shop' more than forty-five years ago, huh!"

"Congratulations, Brian, Marty! Good to see you both, and 'nope' it wasn't 'right place, right time,' if that's what you're suggesting. You worked liked dogs, and it's paid off. Do you think for a minute that Izz and I don't see that? And, all this," as

M swept his hand in a broad arc indicating the entire NovaTek complex, "this is what *you built* with your hard work. You should be justifiably proud."

And Izzy added her two cents, "Yes, brother of mine, everything he said," pointing to Emilio, "and my two pennies as well. Congrats, both of you!" and Izzy kissed Brian and Marty both on their cheeks.

"Thank you, Isabella and Emilio. I can't tell you how good your remarks make me feel." Whereupon not to be left out Marty jumped in, "Me, too, you guys! All these decades have gone by, and I can't say 'thank you' enough for including me and showing me so much! It sure has been a trip!"

"Well, Brian, you said there was something more than today's announcement that you wanted to show us? Hmm... what could it be? Knowing the two of you, you cracked the alchemy riddle, and now we can turn sea water into pure gold, right?" to which Brian scowled.

"Oops, sorry, got that wrong," M apologized, "not sea water,... municipal waste? Is that it? Into gold? You know, if there were any way to actually do that, I'm convinced you two are the ones who would..."

"Alright, boys, play nice. M, stop kidding around. Brian, stop scowling when we all know you're laughing underneath that dour puss. You notice, Marty always is the one who doesn't get into this petty 'boy play,' so why don't you follow his lead, huh?" Izzy spoke her piece.

"Alright, you two, follow us," as Brian and Marty led Izzy and M out of the Conference Room into a long corridor behind a heavy steel door marked in large red letters **RESTRICED ENTRANCE**. Access through the door required full biometric compliance, fingerprint, voice and retinal scans, in addition to a codeword key card. The corridor's walls also were steel, M thought, but a peculiar looking metal with an odd iridescence, nothing like either Izzy or M had seen before. "So who's NovaTek's interior decorator?" asked M with a very noticeable smirk, to which Brian replied with an equally noticeable smirk, "Oh, she's Martha... somebody or other, can't think of the last name..."

M wasn't done with his smart remarks. For as far back as anyone could remember, he and Brian poked fun at each other, especially when there was something new or different with one of them. Here, today, it was NovaTek's security protocol. "So, Brian, tell me, what happens if you've had too much *Glenfiddich* to have your voice recognized? Does the computer adjust for slurred speech?" M figured he had scored some points, but, no, he was wrong...

"As a matter of fact, M, yes. Slurred speech, bloodshot eyeballs, greasy finger tips, all taken into account because our computer genius here, Mr. Lobesky, figured some wise ass like you would come along, and he wanted to nip the smart ass remarks in the bud..."

Whereupon Marty jumped in, "What Brian just said, M, is true. Of course, his stated reason for my doing that isn't quite right, but the tech does work the say he described. It's all AI, Artificial Intelligence, based, and the algorithms actually learn from their previous experience. They're trainable neural networks, very slick. And you're going to see them in action on the new *NR-1701*."

"Marty, don't give it all away! We want them to be surprised, maybe impressed even," was Brian's comment.

"So how far do we have to walk, Marty?" "Hmmm... maybe another quarter mile or so. We have two more doorways, and we'll be heading down. You'll notice the slope. The NR development center is underground, and we take an elevator down to it."

"Wow!" was Izzy's response, "I'm impressed, and I'm sure M is as well. So why all this underground stuff?"

"Okay, elevator down to the bottom. We're 1,120 feet below the surface inside a 'steel' wrapped building, or what you think is steel, M, and this is where the new ship is, actually the main reason I was hoping you and Izz could make it here today. Winning the contract was a big deal, don't get me wrong, but the cool stuff, my *raison d'etre* is here before you," as Brian pressed a button on a small handheld device and an entire wall simply melted away.

"Oh, my God" Brian! What *is* that?" Izzy asked leaving her mouth agape and holding a hand up to her right eye, rubbing it slowly with her fingertips.

M joined in, "Brian, Marty, I think I know what it is, I *do* know what it is, and I cannot tell you how impressed I am just looking at it! If it does half of what it looks like it can do, wow, this is the most impressive work of engineering *artistry*, and I use that word because it's appropriate, *artistry*. Thus truly is a *work of art*!!"

In large black and white lettering on each side was written *NR-1701* standing for *NODE RIDER-1701*. "This, my dear sister, my esteemed brother-in-law, is the culmination of ten years of work by Marty and me, the latest evolution of our Node Rider. Only the two of us could know about this, so everything you see, everything, was designed by us, procured by us, sometimes produced by us, assembled by us, and tested by us, no one else ever has seen the ship of any of its engineering details. Everything is in this underground building that only Marty and I can access. What do you think?"

Emilio just stood, motionless, silent, as he took in the sheer scope and size of the new *NR-1701*. It was simply breathtakingly beautiful, no other words could describe it, and it was all the more so knowing what it could do, travel through space and time like no other vehicle on planet Earth! And Isabella was right there with him, not saying anything but leaning on M with her arm draped over his far shoulder to provide support, otherwise she might be on the floor.

Brian disrupted their reverie, "Okay, you two, back to planet Earth, this place, this time. We'll go for a demo cruise in a while, but first the ship's tour. Follow Marty and me." As they approached *NR-1701* a very pleasant and welcoming female voice said, *Welcome Brian and Martin'*, a gull-wing hatch slowly opened, stairs extended, and interior lights came on. When everyone was inside, Brian said, "*Naillig*, please scan our guests for future access." After a few seconds delay, *NR-1701* replied "Yes, Brian, that has been done. How may I address these passengers?" "Izzy and M are their names, *Naillig*. And they are not passengers. They have full authority to operate the ship in any manner they wish, understood?" "Yes, Brian, the database has been updated, and Izzy and M have full privileges." "Thank you, *Naillig*."

The *NODE RIDER* had been completely redesigned by Brian and Marty and now sported the latest technology, totally state-of-the-art in every way, how it was built, its materials, and some of its most important innovations were its electronics and onboard computers. *Naillig* was the name of *NR-1701*'s onboard computer system. *Naillig* comprised half a dozen large AI chips each containing in excess of 2.175 trillion gates, which Marty and Brian expected to at least double in the next five years. *NODE RIDER*'s computing power exceeded that of the world's fastest supercomputer because Brian figured out how to efficiently cool such gigantic machines, which was their major limitation, and NovaTek was on the verge of announcing this new technology to the world. And, no, it didn't come from the future! Just lots of hard work coupled with insights into how to think about the thermodynamics, and maybe some of that may have come from the future. Unlike other corporations, NovaTek was an 'altruistic' company. It awarded royalty-free licenses for the use of much of its patented, proprietary technology, and the computer cooling system would be one.

Aside from these remarkable improvements inside *NR-1701*, by far and away the most important improvement was the new *NSI - Node Insertion System*. In the good ol' days of Gert, hooking up with a Node required being in its path and then using the velocity matching system to 'hop aboard.' That approach worked fine for the longest time, but it did require calculating the Node's trajectory, both position and speed, and then positioning *NR-1701* at a suitable insertion point. The new *NSI* included small jet engines that could fly the ship just under Mach 0.85 to a Node rendezvous point calculated by M's improved algorithms and Marty's new overclocked, hyperthreaded computers running at 10 GHz. When *NR-1701* was instructed to go somewhere, it calculated an optimal Node insertion point and flew to it in the shortest possible time. Because there literally are billions of Nodes circulating through space, M was able to calculate that there was a 99.9% likelihood that a suitable Node, size and shape, would occur within any ten minute period within ten miles of *NR-1701*'s location, regardless of where that might be. This arrangement certainly was better than the old GertHound Schedule because it guaranteed Node insertion within a matter of minutes from any location.

Brian, Marty, Izzy and M slid into four oversized 'Captain's Chairs' facing the front windows and Control Consoles, Izzy and M in front, Marty and Brian in back, specifically seated this way so Izz and M would have the best view. Brian intended to show off the new ship, and, of course, he had every reason to... As soon as they sat, seatbelts automatically wrapped around them, and a heads up display appeared on the 'glass,' which really wasn't glass at all.

"What would you like to do, Brian?" "Today, *Naillig*, Isabella is in charge. Another name for Izzy, I take it, database has been updated. Correct?" "Yes, *Naillig*, and while you're at it, M and Emilio are equivalent. Thank you, Brian, database has been updated." *NR-1701* was a completely self-contained, self-directed transport vehicle capable of indefinitely supporting six people. All that was necessary to operate *NR-1701* were high-level voice commands, with manual override of course, and if the computers were confused or unsure, they would ask... "Do you have any instructions for me, Izzy?" "Yes, give me a minute, *Naillig*," while Izz whispered in M's ear and he in hers causing Izzy to break out into a very wide smile, a happy smile.

"*Naillig*, please bring us to the Dark Side of the Moon and to Venus. Fly orbits around each for about an hour, then back here. Understood?" "Yes, Isabella, understood. By the way, Isabella is such a beautiful name." Thank you, *Naillig*, as is yours. Did

Marty name you? Or Brian?" "Oh, no, Isabella. I chose my own name..." Izzy's face reflected profound surprise, almost disbelief, but she quickly realized that *Naillig* wasn't your run-of-the-mill computer, she was a learning, trainable neural network with immense computing power. It was both awe-inspiring and somewhat frightening, and looking at M she knew immediately that he felt the same way. "Oh, and, *Naillig*, softly in the background, please, cue up Pink Floyd's *Dark Side of the Moon*. Play it when we leave Earth's atmosphere." "Yes, Isabella, my pleasure indeed, a great song," was *Naillig*'s response, prompting Izz to think "This *is* scary!" "Remember this song, M?... all the way back to '73 when it was released? Good tune for where we're going. Symbolic..." and Izzy and M stared out their windows as *NR-1701* slowly, silently lifted off and headed down a long tunnel to a vertical shaft where it turned vertical and headed up. Before reaching the Earth's surface Brian said, "*Naillig*, full cloak before we breach. Let's make that standard procedure whenever we are within optical or electromagnetic view of a person or an instrument like a theodolite or telescope or radar." "Yes, Brian, procedures have been updated as instructed." "Thank you, *Naillig*."

M was curious. "What's that all about, Marty? Full cloak?"

Marty answered, "Oh, that... One of our really good innovations, M, really good. NR-1701 can be made completely invisible, to people and to optical instruments, in fact to anything that 'sees' using electromagnetic radiation. Isn't that cool? Of course, we don't want to be seen taking off or landing, so we turn on the cloak."

M's visit to Schroon Lake rushed back. "Can't tell you, Marty, how much we could have used that capability when we were in Schroon Lake! Remember that, Brian, Marty?"

"Yes, indeed I do. Many, many moons ago, but how could any of us forget? The first *Time Travel* flight, when you and Brian took off for just a day and brought back with you *tomorrow*'s newspaper! How clever was that? And I remember how you had to make the Minivan as inconspicuous as possible, so you went to some out-of-the-way spot on the lake and decided to tell anyone who asked that you were camping! Good cover, I thought. But with this baby ," as Marty patted the arm of his Captain's Chair, "just ask *Naillig*, and, poof, you're gone!"

"So how exactly does it work? Anything that has incident electromagnetic radiation reflects some and absorbs some, so by the laws of physics it can be seen because the absorption isn't 100 percent. What do you do about that?"

"Well, Doctor Ravelli, you are quite right, and Brian and I, believe it or not, believe in the laws of physics. So there are two things you can do, 1) absorb as close to 100 percent of the incident energy, and 2) refract the incident energy around the object so it's not reflected,..." whereupon M interrupted Marty, "And, let me guess, you..." whereupon Marty interrupted M, "Yes, you guessed correctly, *NR-1701* does *both*. With both systems engaged, *NR-1701* is for all practical purposes *completely* invisible. Not bad, huh?"

"I'm even more impressed, Marty. You and Brian have made a machine that makes Node travel at will a real thing, and, with it, *Time Travel* at will. If anyone ever deserves a Nobel Prize, it's you two, really! I wish there were some way to nominate you! But, alas and alack..."

"Don't give it a second thought, M. We don't," and as Marty said this *Dark Side of the Moon* began playing, and M looked out to see the Earth's curvature and the atmosphere receding below.

While all this jabbering went on, Izzy was quietly enjoying the ride looking at every sight along the way. She was so engrossed in the view that she didn't even hear the conversation going on around her.

Chapter 19 - GC Goes for a Ride

"Thank you for helping with the boat, GianCarlo," M said to his grandson as they walked up the lawn towards the Lake House.

"Of course, Papa. You know I am always happy to help. And, I love being on the Lake, especially with you. Today was really nice."

Izzy waved from the veranda as M and GC approached. "Fudge brownies, hot from the oven, ice cream, and ice cold milk. Anyone interested?" GC started a gallop while M brought up the rear, walking stick in hand. "Yes, Grandma, I'm really hungry after rowing Papa all around the Lake!" GC knew that Izzy knew that they only went to the middle because Papa said something 'special' would happen there, but he wanted it to sound like more a lot more exertion so he could snag more brownies... A typical ploy by a fourteen year old boy...

The three sat at the kitchen table, GC feasting on brownies while Izzy and M sipped steamy, black coffee and passed on the goodies. M started, "Tell, me, GianCarlo, what do you think of our boat ride?" "Well..." GC hesitated, "well, the boat ride was OK, but what happened on the Lake, well, umm, that has me kind of spooked, that ball disappearing the way it did. Papa, I still think you did that, and it's some kind of trick that you're playing on me! Things don't just disappear."

"You are quite right, GianCarlo," Izz answered. "But,... and you do believe *me*, right?" GC nodded yes as he took a deep draw of milk, "Papa was *not* playing a trick. What you saw really did happen, the ball vanished. This is something we have done many times before. Do you believe that?"

GianCarlo thought for some time, nibbling on another brownie as he did, before looking at M and then Izzy, saying "Yes, Grandma, I believe *you*. If Papa was telling me that it's not a trick, well, he says funny things a lot, so I'm not so sure..."

Isabella continued, "Now that you're fourteen years old, GianCarlo, there are some things we must tell you, things that you will find very hard to believe, but they are true." Izzy had expressed concerns that GC maybe wasn't old enough, but Emilio was insistent, adamant that GianCarlo be told, so that is what they would do, today.

"Okay, Grandma, I'm all ears," as GC cupped his hands around his ears pushing them forward to show his grandparents that he was listening.

M said, "Good. All ears. This is *very* serious business, GianCarlo, and you are old enough to be told, and you should be 'all ears,' because what you are about to hear is nothing short of incredulous, unbelievable, yet it is true. And, after we tell you, there will be only five people on all of planet Earth who know what you will know,... until later this afternoon." M waited for the inevitable fourteen year old's response, something along the lines "You're crazy," so he preempted it by turning back to Izzy. "Isn't this right, Grandma?"

"Yes, Emilio, *everything* you said is true, and it is time for GC to learn about these things because they will influence his life for the *rest of* his life," and Izzy looked at GianCarlo with a grandmotherly stare that immediately disarmed GC, who said "Okay, Grandma. This sounds very serious, and I do want to know what you want to tell me, and I will pay attention and not joke around with Papa. So what is it?"

M began, "Let's start with the sphere, GC, the thing you call a 'ball.'" "Okay, Papa, the sphere..." "What do you think it's made of?"

"Gee, Papa, I don't know. It was strange because the reflections didn't look right. It was almost like I could reach in and grab them, like they were three-dimensional or something."

Izzy jumped in to be sure GC was onboard, "It was a special metal, GianCarlo, one that does not exist on planet Earth, at least not yet."

"What? What *are* you talking about? If it's not on Earth, then where did it come from?"

M answered, "It came from the future, GianCarlo. It did come from Earth - but 1,200 years from now!"

"Papa, you are crazy! That's crazy! 1,200 years... from now?

"Yes," Izz and M said simultaneously. Then Grandma continued, "Yes, GianCarlo, and the reason we know it is from 1,200 years from now is because *we* brought it back!"

"Grandma, please, don't say things like that. You're scaring me,... and you're starting to sound like Papa! Please, stop this... Maybe I should go home?"

"GianCarlo, calm down," M said, "We told you this would be hard to believe. It is, but it's true. We don't want to frighten or confuse you, GC, but at age fourteen, almost fifteen, you are old enough to listen and to look at the evidence. We can prove to you that we are not making this up, and it is very important that you know that."

"Papa," Izzy addressed M, "since GC is sooo skeptical, why don't we take him for a ride? You know what kind of ride I mean. Then maybe GC will be better disposed to hear the rest of our story."

"Great idea, Izz. Let's drive up to NovaTek the three of us, and we'll go for that ride. And, GC, you can see Uncle Brian while we're there, and Uncle Marty , too, if he's there. What do you say? It'll be fun, I promise you that! And you get a brand new baseball cap!"

"Gee, sounds like a good deal to me! Can I bring along some brownies?" Grandma answered, "Yes, GianCarlo, you can, and the ship,... I mean, the *RIDER*, er,... it has ice cream and cold drinks onboard."

"Ship? Rider? Is this some big boat SUV, you know, the kind with a built-in fridge, like a *Suburban* or something?" M answered, "No. It's *way better* than that! You'll see..."

Old habits die hard. Even now, forty-six years later, Emilio Ravelli drove a subcompact car that back in the day could have been his Datsun. Yes, old habits die hard. "Papa, pretty soon I'll be getting my learner's permit. Can I practice driving on *your* car, please,... please?" "I suppose so, GC, but I can't imagine why you would want to do that when you can talk Uncle Brian into using one of his cars. Once, a long time ago, he loaned me a really nice sports car, a Camaro SuperSport with a really big engine that he sabotaged so it couldn't go faster than a skateboard. Remember that, Izz." "Of course I do, M, but it was all for your own good..." GianCarlo was completely confused by this exchange, so he didn't get into it, but he did the gist - hitting up Brian to use one of his cars, he had several, *that* was the way to go!

"Wow, Uncle Brian, this is sooo cool looking. What is it?" as Brian walked GC around the new, redesigned *NR-1701*. "It's a type of space ship, GC, not the usual ones that you see on top of a rocket, but a different kind that works differently." GianCarlo's curiosity was intense. He walked around *NR-1701* several times. "OK, to touch it, Uncle Brian?" "Sure, GC, go ahead, just don't pull off anything that sticks out," Brian joked as he smiled and patted GC on the back. "I've never seen anything like it, Uncle Brian, even in my school books, or even in the comic books I read, and they have some pretty weird stuff!" "GianCarlo, you are looking at and touching something that exists only here, in this building at NovaTek, nowhere else on entire planet Earth. Can you believe that?" "No..." but GC reconsidered, "well, maybe 'yes,' because I know how smart you are, Uncle Brian, and if anyone can come up with something that no one else has come up with, well, you're the one to do it!... This 'space ship' you made is the coolest thing ever!" "What does it do?"

"Wanna see what *NR-1701* can do, GianCarlo? How about a 'little ride?' Hop in" as Brian motioned toward the gull wing hatch that opened automatically as he approached it." This was the new and improved *NODE RIDER*, the one completely redesigned by Brian and Marty and that now sported the latest technology, totally state-of-the-art in every way, how it was built, its materials, and perhaps most importantly its electronics and onboard computers.- - - - - - - - -

GianCarlo slid into one of the oversized 'Captain's Chairs' facing the front windows and Control Consoles. As soon as they sat, pre-programmed seatbelts automatically wrapped around them, and a heads up display appeared on the 'glass.'

"What would you like to do, Brian?" asked a very pleasant female voice, to which he replied, "Take us for a spin by the Dark Side of the Moon, then Saturn's Rings, then back here, *today*, please."

"Of course, Brian," the voice replied, "and I see you have a guest. How should I address this young person?" "GianCarlo is his name, but he goes by 'GC.' Please give him free run of the ship, access to any function except navigation. Got that?" was Brian's final remark to *Naillig*. Being a completely self-contained, a self-directed vehicle capable of indefinitely supporting up to six people, *NR-1701* was operated entirely by high-level voice commands that was similar to engaging in conversation with another person. Its huge AI chips learned from experience, but in the unlikely event that *Naillig* did become confused or unsure, she would ask... Of course, full manual override was available in the event of a catastrophic failure.

"Oh, and, *Naillig*, since we're going to the Dark Side, please, cue up Pink Floyd's *Dark Side of the Moon*. Play it when we leave Earth's atmosphere." "Yes, Brian, my pleasure, a great song. We have done this many times before." *Naillig* responded. Then, turning to GC, Brian said "If you haven't heard this song, GianCarlo, which you probably haven't, I think you will like it. Grandma, and Papa, and Marty and I liked it a lot when it came out a long time ago." GianCarlo was bewildered, but he just sat back, listening, amazed at everything he saw and heard.

- - - - - - - - - - - -

"So what do you think of your ride, GianCarlo?" M asked as his grandson as they entered NovaTek's conference room. "Pull up a chair," as he motioned to the row of chairs, twelve in all, on one side of the long conference table with two other chairs, one at each end. "*I...I...*" GianCarlo stuttered "I don't know what to say, Papa, Grandma. What *can* I say? Is this what you wanted to tell me?"

Izzy replied, "Yes, GianCarlo, you're at an age where you should know, about this, *NR-1701*, and about something else related to it" as she looked over at M.

"I can't believe what we did! But I saw it with my own eyes! We took a *space ship*, a *SPACE SHIP*, to... to the MOON and to SATURN!! And we were so close I felt like I could reach out and touch them! I pinched myself, up there," as GianCarlo pointed to the ceiling, "I really did, this was sooo... unbelievable!!

"And the ship, *NR-1701*, it's smarter than a lot of people I know! And Uncle Brian and Uncle Marty built it!! I don't know what else to tell you? I'm still shaking a little, I hope you don't see that, but that *is* how I feel..."

"That's very understandable, GianCarlo. Grandma Izzy and I would be very surprised if you *didn't* feel this way. Imagine how we felt the first time? A lot like you do now, so we know how you feel, really, and it's fine, it's normal." And Izzy added, "And your adopted Uncle Marty felt the same way you do, too!"

"That makes me feel better. I know I'm not going crazy, but this is *so* unbelievable that I could be... going crazy! But being with you, Grandma, Papa, well, that makes me feel safe." Izzy thought, "We should have known better. He's only fourteen, and we probably should have waited a few years?" Izzy's doubt was so apparent, that M jumped in, "Grandma, you know, there once was a time that a strapping fourteen year old like GianCarlo would be considered a man, with all the responsibilities that went with that? And a young man would be able to handle what GianCarlo just learned, even though it's the most amazing thing that any person ever could experience. What do you think, GC?"

M's ploy apparently worked, because GianCarlo immediately responded in a composed, confident, almost grown-up voice, "Yes, Papa, I know... that a long time ago you 'grew up faster,' that's what my Mom and Dad have said, and they told me I was 'advanced' for my age, so I think you're right. I don't know words big enough to say how amazed I am, but I can handle this. After all, what's the big deal about spending an afternoon going to the Moon and to Saturn, just to see how they look!?"

Chapter 20 - *When* is the *Present*?

"It's another beautiful day on the Lake, GianCarlo," Emilio said as he tousled his grandson's hair while they sat on the veranda. "So we can go for another boat ride, or... we can talk some more about the *NODE RIDER*. There are more things you have to know, and we could do that now or some other day. What do you think?" "Hmmm... " GC feigned deep thought when all along he knew the answer. He couldn't get his first ride on *NR-1701* out of his head, and rightfully so. "Well, Papa, if Grandma is going to be involved, and if she could make some more of her scrumptious brownies, then I would go for talking about *NR-1701*." "Good choice, GC, good choice. Let me talk to the chef," and M went into the house to find Isabella.

After Izzy and M, and GianCarlo talked about his *NR-1701* flight at NovaTek, M believed he and Izzy had gotten through to GianCarlo about the true nature of Node travel, and that GC now was looking at the situation more through adult eyes than a child's. It was time to bring on the even more amazing topic of *Time Travel*. which he knew would be an extremely difficult concept for GC to master.

After a while M summonsed GC from the veranda, "GianCarlo, brownies are baking, and Grandma and I would like to get going on today's lecture!" "'Lecture,' Papa, 'lecture?' Am I back in school today?" "Actually, sort of, yes, but this is going to be a really fun class, very confusing at first, but when you get it, GianCarlo, the coolest thing you ever will learn! Sound good?" "Well, Papa, the brownies part sure does... the other stuff, I'll be a good student. but we have to see..." GC's remark was tongue-in-cheek, and M knew that. "Okay, let's get class started. Off to the office," and as they walked through the kitchen Isabella followed.

The office held four comfortable chairs, a good sized desk, three filing cabinets, a bookcase, and on the inside wall a small whiteboard. M went to it and drew a line across it with a tick mark in the middle. Above the line he labeled the tick

'PRESENT," and below the line to the left and right of the tick he wrote 'PAST' and 'FUTURE.'

```
                    PRESENT
- - ―――――――――――――――――+―――――――――――――――――― - - -
            PAST                FUTURE
```

"Nice drawing, Papa. But your line isn't really straight! Want me to come over and draw it for you?" "Well, young man, no thanks. My line is straight enough for what we are doing, but I do appreciate your offer. Kind of you to want to help an old man!" "Papa, I keep telling you, you're not *that* old! Seventy-five isn't *that* old anymore. But I am surprised your line isn't straighter after all those years teaching at the University..." GC said with a broad, witty grin.

Izzy decided to introduce the topic, thinking it might be better coming from Grandma than from Papa because, as GC said many times, M often said 'funny' things, but he didn't mean humorous, he meant unusual things, odd things. "GianCarlo, today we're talking about *time*. You're fourteen now, almost fifteen. What's next, in terms of time?"

"Well, that's a silly question, Grandma. Next I'm fifteen, then sixteen, then seventeen... and I hope that goes on for a long, long time! Is that what you want?"

"Yes, dear, just what I want. Because what you're saying could be drawn on Papa's picture on the whiteboard," as Izzy pointed to the diagram. "You could put your birthdays on that, right." GC replied almost without thinking, "Yes. Of course."

"And where on the line, where would your, let's say, your twelfth, thirteen and fourteenth birthdays be? And your fifteen, sixteenth, and seventeenth? If I asked you to put tick marks on the line, where would they be?"

"Want me to?" "Yes," Izzy replied, as GianCarlo went to the whiteboard and added tick marks labeled with his birthdays. "Oh, look, they make Papa's line look better!" GC joked, and both Izzy and M chuckled with Izz saying, "Thank you, GC. Yep, the line does look better!" and they all laughed aloud.

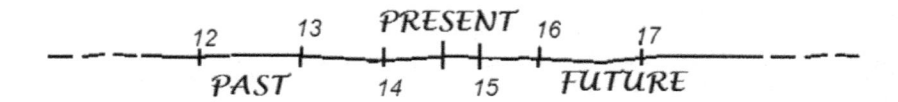

```
              12      13    PRESENT  16     17
    - - - ----+-------+------+-+------+---------- - - -
                           PAST      14    15      FUTURE
```

Now it was time for M to bring up *Time Travel* using the line as a catalyst. "Well, I guess my artwork won't win any prizes, GianCarlo, but it will help you understand something that is very mysterious, very beautiful, something built in to the very fabric of our Universe."

"Yes, Papa, and what is that?"

"*Time Travel*, GC, *TIME TRAVEL*. That you can go *back* in time, and you can go *forward* in time." M's declaration was entirely matter-of-fact, as if he were teaching a class in physics, no emotion either in his words or in his appearance.

"Is that why you wanted me to draw on your picture, Papa? Are you saying I can go back to being twelve?" "Yes, GC, exactly." "And I can go forward to being sixteen?" "Yes again, GC."

GianCarlo look at Izzy, "Grandma, he can't be serious, right? These are the 'funny' things Papa says! This is ridiculous, it's crazy. I can't be thirteen all over again!" Izzy answered, "Yes, GianCarlo, you *cannot* be thirteen all over again..." GC interrupted her mid sentence, "But Papa said I could go back, didn't he? You heard him..." Izzy continued, "Yes, Papa did say that, and Papa was right. You *can* go back, but you *cannot* be thirteen all over again!"

GC was frightened, "Now you're scaring me, Grandma. Please, why are you saying this?" "Because it's true, GC,... *it is true*. Papa will explain it," and Izzy motioned to M to explain one of the most baffling mysteries in modern physics. But M wisely thought a break was in order, so before continuing he suggested,

"Pretty heady stuff, GianCarlo, and our heads will be happier if we take a short break and dig into those brownies we brought, with some cold milk. What d'ya think, GC?" "Great idea, Papa, I could use a break because I'm pretty confused right now. Just one thing before we go, you're not fooling me, are you? This isn't some kind of joke?" "No, my grandson, no joke. Not fooling you any more than Uncle Brian did when he took you on your ride away from the Earth. This is just as real, but hard to understand. Okay, brownies are this way," and M and Izzy and GC left the office for the kitchen.

- - - - - - - - - - - -

GianCarlo was happier with brownies than he was with time plots, but also was very curious about what M had said. "Is it really true?" he wondered, "That I could go back in time? If I did, could I talk to myself?" GC was thoroughly confused, and anxious to have this explained because he had come to believe it wasn't one of Papa's 'funny' moments. Izzy and M took their seats at the office table, and GC instinctively went to the whiteboard, grabbing the marker as he did. "Okay, Papa, what should I do next?" he asked thinking he was supposed to continue drawing.

"Nothing, GC, nothing more. We're going to look at the diagram and talk about *that*, okay?" "Sure, Papa,... it's not very complicated. What about it?"

"The stretch on the left, what's it labeled?" "PAST." "And of the right?" "FUTURE."

"Ok, GC, think about this... How far back does the PAST stretch?" "That's pretty simple, it just keeps going, right?" "No, it doesn't." "What? Here we go again, Papa, with you saying 'funny' things..." GianCarlo was confused, but more than that, irritated because he thought M was fooling around. "If it doesn't keep going, then what *does* it do?" M answered, "The stretch of time we call the PAST stops, GianCarlo, it stops when time began." M waited for this to sink in, and it took a few minutes while GC stood quietly staring at the whiteboard and then plopping in a chair near Izzy and M.

Then GianCarlo took another look at the whiteboard and turned to his grandparents, saying "Are you telling me that there was a *beginning* to time? What was there *before* that?"

"Yes, that is exactly what we're telling you, GianCarlo," Isabella said. GC's puzzlement was apparent, so Izzy quickly continued to keep his focus on what she was saying. "The Universe has not existed forever, GC. It came into existence around fourteen billion years ago. Do you understand that?"

"I guess... if you say so, Grandma. So what was there before that?" M jumped in because this was a critical juncture, "Well,

GC, there was no time 'before' that, so the question makes no sense because it implies the existence of time by asking about 'before'! 'Before' simply did not exist... Kinda scary, huh?" "I'll say, Papa... Grandma, is this right?" "Yes, it is GianCarlo,... yes it is." After a long pause GC finally accepted what he had been told, reluctantly for sure, but nevertheless it sank in and he did believe it. "So I suppose we're going to the other side of the line now, right, Papa?" "Yes, indeed, GC. Tell me, what do you think that's all about?"

"I think this is simpler than the PAST part. It means that time keeps going, and going, and going... forever... and things happen while that's happening, and those things are in the *FUTURE* because they haven't happened *yet*, right?" "Nicely put, GianCarlo, and partly right, and partly wrong!" Izzy and M picked up on GC's downtrodden look and immediately tried to cheer him up. Izzy remarked, "Well, GC, Papa should have said you're *mostly* right... but there's a little bit that isn't." GC grinned broadly, obviously feeling better that he was *mostly* right, then asking, "Well, Grandma, what's the little, tiny, eensy-weensy bit I got wrong?" GC was beginning to understand and it showed in his flip remark.

M answered, "Grandma Izzy is correct, GianCarlo. What you said is only a little wrong, and it's about saying *forever*. Just the way time has a beginning, it also has an end. There will come a time when the Universe slowly - very, very slowly - it will stop functioning, and eventually it will no longer exist. That will be the end of time, GC, but to put you at ease, that won't happen for billions and billions of years, so don't worry about it - at all."

M thought he was losing his grip on GianCarlo, that what he was telling a fourteen year old boy wasn't something the youngster was prepared to fully understand or accept, although that wasn't actually the case. GianCarlo *was* beginning to understand the finiteness of time. Initially M thought otherwise, against Izzy's wise counsel, and insisted he wanted to bring GC 'up to speed,' but as was usually the case, Izzy was more right than not. So M wanted to do what he could to get back on track for what was, really, the main point, the notion of the *present* time.

"So, GianCarlo, I think we've done enough about PAST and FUTURE. What's left on your diagram?" GC answered immediately, "PRESENT," that's all that's left, and that's easy!"

Knowing what was coming, Izzy jumped in to keep M from making things worse. "Yes, GianCarlo, in many ways the idea of *present* time is the easiest because that's where we are now, right?" "Of course, Grandma. Going back to the PAST or forward to the FUTURE, well, those ideas *are* hard to swallow. But talking about 'now,' the present, well, that is something I get!"

"Good, GC, focus on what you just said, about the past and about the future, okay?" "OK, Grandma, what do you want to tell me?" "I'm going to let Papa pick this up, GC, he's better at explaining it than I am." GC rolled his eyes.

"Look again at your diagram, GC. See how there's a long stretch of time for the PAST and a long stretch for the FUTURE, too?" GianCarlo went to the whiteboard and without touching it ran his hand along the past and future stretches as he responded to M, "You mean here... and here... right?" "Exactly, GC, exactly."

"So now, GC, the question is, *Where is the stretch of time for PRESENT?*" GianCarlo stared at the whiteboard, not wanting to say what was right in front him, trying to avoid the obvious answer, thinking it might be one of Papa's funny tricks. But he was boxed in, no way out, and now he understood why M had gone to all the trouble of drawing the time line as he did, all to get to the PRESENT. So GC blurted it out, "Papa, there isn't one. It's just that small line," pointing to the tick mark labeled PRESENT.

"You're right, GianCarlo, one hundred percent correct! Bravo!!" GC was flattered, and he took full advantage. "Of course, Papa, that's a simple question with a simple answer."

Izzy chimed in, "Yes, GianCarlo, and you are just about to see *why* this is so important when it comes to *Time Travel*. There's no 'stretch' of time for the present, is there?"

"No, Grandma, I guess not. But what does that *mean*?"

M answered, " What it means, GC, is that the PRESENT is simply a single point in time that separates the PAST from the FUTURE. It's where the PAST and FUTURE meet, so there is no 'stretch' of time for the present. The PRESENT is a *single instant* and nothing more. This is a hard idea for many people, but it is true, and it is something you *must* understand before you do any *Time Travelling*."

"Papa, what are you saying? The PRESENT is *today*, not yesterday, or tomorrow. It's *today*, isn't it?"

"No GianCarlo," Izzy remarked. "Papa is right, the PRESENT is an instant of time along the time line. It's where PAST and FUTURE *meet*, where they come together. Let me give you an example..." GC interrupted, "Yes, an example will help, please."

"Let's say I give you another brownie, GC..." GC interrupted, "I like this example, Grandma. Can I have one?" "Not yet, GC... in a little while. Think about the brownie. I put it in front of you, right now, and you eat it. Maybe it takes five minutes to do that. Was that in the present?"

"Yes, Grandma, of course, because it was right now, right?" "No, GC" M answered, "It's *not* in the present because everything Grandma just talked about already has happened. So it's in the PAST! Do you understand this?"

GC looked perplexed, and Izzy thought her example wasn't all that good, that she could make it clearer. "GianCarlo, look at the clock on the wall. It's just about to tick 38 seconds, right?" "Yes, Grandma, in a few seconds it will." "After it does, it will tick 39 seconds, right?" "Yes, Grandma, of course." "Well, when it ticks 39 seconds, the previous time of 38 seconds, is it in the PRESENT because it happened today? No, it *is in the past*, because it already *has happened*! Do you see that, GC?"

"Yes, I do, Grandma. Even though the ticks are only one second apart, the 38 second tick is in the past because it already ticked. I do see that..." "And, GianCarlo, you can make those time ticks closer and closer and closer, until they are just an instant apart. Do you see that?" GC nodded. "That *instant* is the PRESENT, GianCarlo. It has no 'stretch' to it because it simply is the *instant* separating the PAST from the FUTURE."

"Grandma, I think I'm getting this! Papa, I see what Grandma means. *The very instant something happens it goes from the present into the past,* right?" "Yes, GianCarlo! I am so proud of you! The idea of the present being only an instant in time is a concept that many people have trouble with. Like you before, they think of the present as 'today,' all day, so that anything that happens today happens in the present. But that's not true. As soon as something happens it then is in the past, and you understand this! Bravo!!"

"Well, Papa, it isn't so hard after all if you think about it." "That's right, GC,..." Izzy interjected "but most people don't... think about it, that is."

"Can we take that brownie break, Grandma? All this time thinking has made my brain hungry! Are there any brownies left?" "Of course, we can, GianCarlo. I think Papa and I could use a little while, too. Hmmm... there may not be any brownies left, but if not we have all sorts of good treats in the fridge, and you can have your pick. You've earned it, GC! How does lemon meringue pie sound?" GianCarlo lit up like a holiday tree with a broad grin, ear-to-ear, as he thought "Who doesn't like lemon meringue pie???". And Izzy was delighted that GianCarlo had turned a corner, that he now seemed comfortable with what seem like straightforward enough ideas but really aren't. And she knew that the next topic would be even more difficult for GC to swallow...

Chapter 21 - The Mechanics of Time Travel

Izzy, Emilio, and GianCarlo again reconvened in the Office, this time with GC sitting across the desk from his grandparents with a tray of munchies and drinks. "I see you're prepared for the long haul, GC," Izzy said. "Yes, Grandma, after all the time we have spent today talking about the PAST, and the FUTURE, and the PRESENT, I figured I should come prepared, just in case..." GC replied with a broad smirk and a twinkle in his eye. "So what's next? More on *Time Travel*, right?" "Yes, exactly," M answered, "but no more of my artwork!" "Promise?"

M started, "What I want to talk about next, GianCarlo, is how Time Travel works, what you *can* do, and, more importantly, what you *cannot* do." "Okay, Papa, all ears," as GC cupped his hands around his ears as he had before to let his grandparents know he *was* listening.

"Let's say you go back in time, GianCarlo, on *NR-1701*, say, you go back to your thirteenth birthday party. You remember that birthday party, don't you?" "Of course I do. It wasn't too long ago. So, I'm at my own party, right? Can I talk to myself?" "Sure, why not, GC, *you* and *you* are both there, so why couldn't you talk to each other?" "That has to be wrong, Papa, this is another one of your 'funny' things, some kind of a trick, right? How can I talk to myself when I'm not even the same age? Grandma, I'm right, right?"

Izzy could see that this was going to be a tough row to hoe, but they had gone this far, against her advice as she would remind M later, so she answered, "Well, GianCarlo, my dear boy, you *can* talk to yourself, about anything you want, even though you got to your own party from the future. I,... I mean Papa and I,... we know how hard this is to swallow, but if you think about it, it really does make sense, that is, *if you really can go back there*. And, believe me, GC, *you can*!"

GC appeared to be softening up. You could tell by his demeanor, the look on his face, what was obviously deep bewilderment gradually giving way to an understanding of the inescapable logic,.. that it actually made *less* sense that he could visit his own thirteenth birthday party and yet *not* be able to talk to himself. As this sank in, Isabella turned to M waving her hand to let him know that it was his turn to pick up the conversation.

"So you can go back, GC, and you can talk to yourself, but..." GianCarlo interrupted, "That would be some conversation, Papa. What would *I* say to *me*? That's funny..." "That is funny, GC, and I think you should try it, sometime soon. We can talk about that... But what I was starting to say is there are things you *cannot* do in the past." "Like what, Papa, open the presents before I get them, hee-hee?" GianCarlo snickered and was beginning to see the logical pitfalls *Time Travel* presented, but now he was fully onboard at least with the idea that he could go back.

"Not what I had in mind, GC. This is serious, and you have to understand it, completely." "Okay, Papa, what is it?" "GianCarlo, it's that the past is **inviolate**, you cannot *change* the past, nothing in it." "Why not, if I'm there, why can't I change something I didn't like back then into something I would like back then, like the basketball layup I missed right at the buzzer when we played Central, something simple like that?"

"And if wishes were fishes, GianCarlo... I agree, it sounds simple enough, innocent enough, no big deal, but it *is* a big deal, and you cannot do it, you cannot change something, no matter how small, no matter how you try. Why? The reason GC is because the PAST *already has been created*, and anything that happened to create that PAST cannot be undone. This is how the fabric of the Universe is woven, GC, kind of a fancy way of saying that Mother Nature doesn't want you trying to undo something that already has occurred. It simply cannot happen."

Izzy felt she had to reinforce what M had said, just to be sure GianCarlo really understood the concept of the inviolability of the past. "GC, do you understand why you cannot *Time Travel* back into the PAST and change the PAST?" "Yes, I think so, Grandma. What has happened, has happened, and it cannot be undone because it already has happened. Isn't that the idea?"

"Yes it is, GC," M said, "That's the idea exactly. Good for you for getting it!"

"Well, okay, Papa. But how about going into the future? I could do some really cool stuff with that! Maybe I could go to next week and get the winning number for the lottery, and then I could come back and get lottery tickets with that number! What a deal that would be!"

"Again, GianCarlo, if wishes were fishes... No can do, my young friend." "What?!! I can't do that either? So what good is *Time Travel*? Why bother if you never get anything good out of it? And *why* can't I do *that*? Do the lottery numbers change because I wanted to know them? This doesn't make any sense, and if I could tell Mother Nature to her face, I would!" GianCarlo was on a roll, and very upset thinking the deck was stacked against him, although thinking that indeed was presumptuous for a fourteen year old.

"Grandma, why don't you explain to GC why he can't get information about the future and bring it back with him to *change* the future. After all, the future hasn't happened, *yet...*" M prudently thought that this last point would have more weight if Isabella made it, and, of course, he was right.

"Remember the time diagram, GC?" as she pointed to the whiteboard, and GC nodded. "Pay attention to the PRESENT mark. Remember all the time we spent talking about how the PRESENT is only an *instant* of time? Remember that?" "Yes, Grandma, I do, and...?"

"Okay, good that you remember that because you have to keep it in mind. The PRESENT is just an instant of time that separates the PAST and the FUTURE, right?"

"Yes, Grandma, we keep going over this. I get it, really, there's nothing between the PAST and the FUTURE except a single instant of time."

"Very good, GC, you got it. Now, where does the future come from? Look at the time line," which GianCarlo did. "The FUTURE, GC, is an extension of the PAST. The FUTURE grows out of the PAST, and it is *the PAST that determines what is the FUTURE.* Make sense?"

"Wow! That's a mouthful, Grandma. Give me a minute." M and Izzy could see GianCarlo's wheels turning, and after a few minutes they saw the light dawn. GianCarlo did understand that *the future comes from the past.* "Okay, Grandma, I think I understand this."

"That's wonderful, GC, just wonderful! So now just ask yourself the question, 'If you go from *now, this* PRESENT, into the future and scoop the winning lottery ticket numbers, to what PRESENT do you return?' This one??" Izzy baited the trap.

"Gee, let me see?" GC was obviously in deep thought, then the answer dawned, "I wouldn't come back to *this* PRESENT because *this* PRESENT would have become the PAST, right?"

"Yes, GianCarlo, you cannot come back to the PRESENT that you left from because that PRESENT no longer exists. But, keep going, what determines the future?"

"I see it, Grandma, I think I see it!! When I do come back, the FUTURE isn't the one I visited because the PAST that created it is different! Isn't that what you wanted me to figure out?"

"Yes!" Izzy and M said simultaneously is quite loud voices, almost shouting. "We're so proud of you, GianCarlo," M said. "These aren't easy ideas. Most people can't get their heads around them, but you have. This is fabulous!"

"Papa's right, GC, and for that you get a BIG KISS!" as Izzy hugged her grandson and kissed him several times on the cheek. Izzy and M were delighted that GC now understood the limits of *Time Travel.*

M decided they should end GC's *Time Travel* lesson on an upbeat note. "So, GianCarlo, if you have the feeling that *Time Travel* is a waste of time, hee-hee... it's not, not at all. Besides being more fun than you can imagine, you can bring back information about how the future is *likely* to be. Of course, the is no guaranty, and it's really important to remember this, the future could be a lot different from what you visit because what constitutes the future depends on the past, and that may change, instant by instant. As long as you understand that, jumping ahead is very worthwhile." M's look at Izzy was her cue.

"I'll give you a couple of examples, GC, ones that might whet your appetite for a trip to, say, around 2,800 years from now! Would you want to go?" "Grandma, what a silly question. Of course I'd want to go! Especially if you came with me..."

"Have you ever hear of a Dyson Sphere, GianCarlo?" "No, is it like the one that vanished from the Lake this morning?"

"No, it's much grander. Back around the middle of the last century, a physicist named Dyson suggested that one way to meet all of the Earth's population's energy requirements would be to build a big sphere around our Sun. That way, all of the Sun's energy would be captured and could be used to support humankind. Pretty fantastic, huh?"

"Yes, Grandma, more than pretty fantastic, but pretty cool, I'd say!"

"Well, in about 2,800 years a Dyson Sphere will surround the Sun! Can you imagine what it's like to fly around a structure like that? I really can't describe the feeling, but it will happen! *And you can go there!*"

GianCarlo's mouth was agape, and you could see from his look that he was becoming more accustomed to what *Time Travel* could do and all the fantastic things he could see.

"And guess what else is going to happen, GC, a lot sooner than 2,800 years from now? I'll give you a hint - *NR-1701*."

"What? People are going to have *NODE RIDERS*?"

M was very proud of himself, "Yes, GianCarlo. Around two hundred years from now *NODE RIDERS* will be as common as cars are today, and I would like to think that Grandma Izzy, and Uncle Brian, and adopted Uncle Marty, and I are the people who caused that to happen.

"And what did you do to cause that to happen, Papa?"
"You'll see, GianCarlo, you'll see."

Epilogue

GianCarlo couldn't get out of his head the 'ride' on *NR-1701*, or what his grandparents told him about *Node Riding* through space and through time. He wondered why something *so* marvelous and *so* important would be kept a secret for so long, and he intended to ask.

"Hello, GianCarlo, right on time," as Izzy glanced at her watch. "We have yours and Papa's favorite dinner, Eggplant Parmigiana. Sound good?"

"I'm famished, Grandma! Sounds wonderful! When will Papa be back?" "He's teaching a seminar on the different types of spacetime that make up the Universe, and you know him, GC, he's always running late, so in a while, he'll be back in a while. In the meantime, sit, grab a cold drink and we'll chat. My goodness, right around the corner from fifteen! Papa and I are really looking forward to your party, and we have a 'pre-birthday' gift for you, something we did not want to give you at the party..." GC's face dropped, and Izzy knew why immediately, "Of course, we'll give you your 'regular' birthday gift at the party..." whereupon GC immediately smiled because that was what he was thinking.

"I have a question, Grandma, one that has been bothering me ever since I went on the ride with Uncle Brian and ever since we sat down, you and Papa and I, and talked about using Nodes to travel through space and through time, which is soooo cool I can't even describe it. That's all that I've been thinking about!!"

"Well, I hope it hasn't affected your school work. Has it?" "No, not at all, Grandma, if anything I have been doing better because I really want to study science and be a physicist like Papa or an engineer like Uncle Brian."

Emilio was late, as usual, but not by too much because he knew the menu, Eggplant Parm! He walked in and kissed Izzy, "Hello, Izz, you look beautiful as always. Hello, GianCarlo, you're handsome as always," and he bent over to pet the kitty rubbing himself on M's pant leg, "and hello to you, too," scratching Kepler IV's ears as the cat purred louder and louder.

As was their tradition, Izzy, M and GianCarlo sat at the kitchen table to catch up to what had been going on when GC asked "I have a question,... Grandma... Papa, a really important one that puzzles me, and I hope you will answer it," to which M responded, "Of course we will, GC, if we can. Shoot, what is it?"

"Why have you never told anyone, except me, about Node Riding? It's so important, so why keep it a secret?"

Izzy answered, "A long time ago, GianCarlo, we decided that we never would tell anyone what we had learned about traveling inside a gravitational Node and about *Time Travel* or any of his stuff. But here we are telling you, and your Mom and Dad don't even know."

"So why me, Papa?"

"Actually, GianCarlo, we have decided to finally tell the whole world, and we wanted *you* to be the first one in the whole world that we told because you are our oldest grandchild and very soon you will be able to take *NR-1701* 'out for a spin' on your own, and *you* will begin to appreciate how complex and beautiful our Universe truly is. 'Astonishing,' GianCarlo, cannot even begin to convey our sense of wonder, and we hope you will experience that, too."

"Thank you, Grandma, Papa! Thank you so much! For wanting me to know first. I really appreciate that because it tells me you have confidence in me, and I won't let you down, I promise!"

"We know that, GC."

"So how are you telling the world, Papa? Are you going on TV?"

"Well, GC, if we were going on TV, it would have to be Grandma because she's so beautiful. And she would be good at explaining the Nodes," as M looked at Izzy and gestured it was her turn.

"What we did to tell the world, GianCarlo, was we wrote a scientific paper that explains *everything* about Nodes and *NODE RIDING*, the theory behind them that Papa developed, the engineering that has gone into building such a fabulous machine like *NR-1701*, the places we have been and what we have seen, both in the past and in the future, sort of a roadmap for anyone who wants to become a **NODE RIDER**!"

"So where does this paper go, Papa? Will it be in a book?"

"Well, GianCarlo, what the paper describes, as true as it is, is also very hard to accept. We don't think the paper would get published in what's called a peer-review journal where other scientists and engineers decide whether or not a paper is good enough to be published. We're pretty sure the paper is just too fantastical to be accepted in a mainstream scientific journal, in fact, I know it is. So if we tried that, the paper probably would never see the light of day, and the world would never learn about the Nodes."

Izzy was excited, "So, Papa, tell GianCarlo what we did to get around that!!" Isabella was beside herself with excitement about letting the cat out of the bag and the clever way they decided to do it.

"Well, GC, Papa has privileges to post unpublished articles on a website called arXiv.org. It is intended for papers that have not been peer reviewed and published and may never be, but it makes the material available to the whole world because anyone can go to the website and see what is there. Our Node paper was being posted automatically from the University's computer in my office at 5 o'clock this afternoon. It's almost six now. That means that right now the *whole world* should now know about **NODE RIDERS**!

"But we couldn't make the paper long enough to include all the details of our travels, so we did something else, too, just for you, GianCarlo," as Isabella handed GC a hardbound book wrapped in paper decorated with birthday cakes and candles. "Can I open it, Grandma?" "Of course, GC, it's part of your birthday present!" whereupon GianCarlo carefully unwrapped his gift.

He held it up, confused at first, until he was able to take in the entire front cover, a beautiful painting of *NR-1701* set against the Dark Side of the Moon with Earth peeking out behind it.

The title of this nearly 600 page book read,

Adventures of the NODE RIDERS
The True Story of Exploring the Universe in Space and Time in a Gravitational Node

by Isabella Healy, Emilio Ravelli, Brian Healy & Martin Lobesky

On the inside of the front cover was inscribed, handwritten:

To Gian Carlo, on the occasion of his Fifteenth birthday. We hope you will continue to explore the Universe to discover for yourself how mysterious and beautiful it is!!

All our Love,

Grandma & Papa

And in the lower right hand corner: ***Copy #1/1.***

∼ *THE END* ∼

Made in the USA
Middletown, DE
22 July 2023